FRONTIER

A NOVEL BY

Michael Ansara

PROTEUS BOOKS
LONDON/NEW YORK

PROTEUS BOOKS
is an imprint of
The Proteus Publishing Group
United States
PROTEUS PUBLISHING COMPANY INC.
733 Third Avenue
New York, NY 10017
distributed by
THE SCRIBNER BOOK COMPANIES INC.
597 Fifth Avenue
New York, NY 10017
United Kingdom
PROTEUS (PUBLISHING) LIMITED
Bremar House
Sale Place
London, W2 1PT

First published in 1981
© 1981 by Bruce Crowther
All Rights reserved
ISBN 0 906071 24 0

Printed in Great Britain by
Anchor Press Limited and bound by
Wm. Brendon & Son Limited, both
of Tiptree, Colchester, Essex

FRONTIER

AUTHOR'S NOTE

This is a novel rooted in our recent history, and several real and noted personalities necessarily feature in minor roles. The government agencies and offices mentioned exist.

But it is a work of fiction, and all the major characters are imaginary and should not be mistaken for anyone actually involved in the American space program. Any apparent similarities ae unintentional and greatly regretted.

The purpose of this book is not to denigrate specific agencies, administrations or individuals. Political pressure is a tide that can run out of check in any country and at any time.

The West was so ready to believe, two decades ago, that near-space was littered with the corpses of Russian cosmonauts who'd failed in secrecy before Gagarin succeeded, that any objective mind has to concede that something like the Frontier Project might have happened.

MA April, 1981

The problems are not all solved and the battles are not all won, and we stand today on the edge of a New Frontier: the frontier of the 1960s – a frontier of unknown opportunities and perils – a frontier of unfulfilled hopes and threats.
John F. Kennedy; July 15, 1960

1960
August 24–September 15

WASHINGTON, D.C.

The President shook his head slowly, 'I don't think NASA can be swayed,' he said. 'Push too hard and they'll dig their heels in.'

His aide didn't answer. Instead he carefully studied a sheet of paper on top of the pile before him, hoping the President would not take his silence for what it was – a silent rebuke. After a moment he looked up. Eisenhower was gazing through the windows of the Oval Office, his expression suggesting mild regret at having to spend such good golfing weather cooped up indoors preparing for a meeting he had already decided would be unproductive.

Clearing his throat the aide plucked nervously at a seam on the sleeve of his tan jacket. 'Magadini will be more.....malleable than either Gilruth or Webb,' he said. The President dragged his eyes and his attention back to the matter at hand . 'Maybe, but there's a limit to what he can do without cooperation from others. We need von Braun as well.'

'Wernher will go along. He has ambition coming out of his ears. As soon as he knows what we want, he'll get the whip out.'

The President leaned forward, resting his elbows on the desk. 'If we persuade Magadini, and if von Braun agrees, can we be sure it will be worth it?'

The aide hesitated. He recognized the negative note in Eisenhower's voice. Already the President was more than half way to talking himself out of the project. 'Maybe we can decide after we've talked to Magadini,' he said eventually.

'When will he be here?'

The aide glanced at his watch. 'They're due in ten minutes.'

'They? Who's coming with him?'

'Colonel Ziegler. He's the Astronaut Liaison Officer.'

'I know that,' Eisenhower said, testily. 'Why is he coming?'

'Magadini is an administrator, von Braun a scientist.'They'll give answers based on everything but the human factor. Knowing that a rocket can be ready in time is one thing – having a man ready to pilot it is another.'

Eisenhower nodded. 'You're right. Too often we forget people, we're so damn busy playing politics.'

The aide stood up. 'I'll go along and meet them,' he said. The President didn't answer and the aide crossed to the door, glancing back fleetingly before he went out. Eisenhower had leaned back in his chair, his eyes closed. He looked very old and desperately tired. The aide shut the door softly, went into his own office and picked up a telephone which was not routed through the White House switchboard.

His call was answered quickly. 'I don't think he's going to push it,' he said. He paused, listening. 'No, not yet. Magadini will be here soon but if he resists, and I think he will, there won't be any pressure from the President. He'll let it slide. That should please our man.' He listened again. 'Very well, tonight, seven-thirty, usual place.' He eased the phone back on its cradle, a satisfied smile on his face. Glancing at his watch again he strode out of his office and along the corridor towards the west wing.

At the West Gate of the White House a guard was peering into a limousine, carefully inspecting the faces of its two passengers. Content that they were who they claimed to be, he stepped back, saluted and let the long black Cadillac enter the grounds.

Jim Magadini grinned. 'I feel like a goddamn hoodlum in this thing,' he said. 'Do you think it's armor-plated?'

Joe Ziegler laughed. 'You've been seeing too many movies.'

'Not recently. My God, I can't remember the last time I saw a movie, or a show, or had a night out with the boys.'

'Or the girls?'

'Are you kidding? You know Sylvia. One whiff of someone else's perfume and she'd be reaching for the hatchet. And it wouldn't be my nails she'd be thinking of trimming!'

Ziegler laughed again. The thought of Jim Magadini chasing women seemed faintly ridiculous. Small, considerably overweight, with thinning, almost completely grey hair, Magadini looked exactly what he was – a harrassed, overworked executive trying to keep control of a project that, like Topsy, had jes' grew and grew.

Magadini glanced at Ziegler. 'How are things with you and Paula?'

Ziegler shrugged. 'Okay.'

'Still not thinking of making it permanent?'

'Permanent? You mean marriage? No, once was enough for both of us.'

The limousine stopped and the President's aide, tall in a tan gaberdine suit opened the door and thrust his crew-cut head inside. 'Gentlemen, follow me please.' He strode briskly into the building, the others several paces behind. Ziegler, upright and immaculate in his Air Force uniform, kept up easily but Magadini, his black suit crumpled and too-tight, scurried along perspiring heavily, a scuffed document case under his arm.

10

Neither man had visited the White House before but they had no time to take in their surroundings. Abruptly, the tan-suited aide stopped and motioned them to seats. He tapped softly on a door, opened it and went inside. Magadini sank gratefully onto a chair but Ziegler remained standing. Beside the door a young Navy officer sat, his posture upright but relaxed. Ziegler looked at him, his eyes taking in the black leather case resting on his knees. He realized the officer was the man who always accompanied the President and the black case held the means of starting another, perhaps the last, holocaust. He caught the officer's eye and smiled. The young man didn't return the smile, but his expression changed sufficiently to indicate he wasn't being churlish. Smiling at strangers simply wasn't part of his duties.

Magadini noticed the exchange and, like Ziegler, recognized the Navy man's role. He felt slightly uneasy but took his cue from Ziegler and tried a smile which had equally little effect. The Navy officer looked ridiculously young, but then, so did Ziegler. The Colonel was tall, straight, obviously fit, and although forty, looked at least ten years younger. At forty-five Magadini knew he looked nearer sixty and, what was worse, usually felt it. He shook his head sadly, regretting that he had spent all of his adult life behind a desk while men like Ziegler had traveled the world, flown aircraft, risked their lives in wars – had *lived.*

Not that Ziegler had everything. At forty he was one year too old and at six feet he was two inches too tall to have qualified for the astronaut training program. The Colonel didn't often think about God, but when he did it was with a feeling that somehow, in his case, the Almighty had screwed up.

The door opened and the tan-suited aide reappeared. He beckoned to Magadini and Ziegler who followed him into the Oval Office.

The President came around the desk as the two men entered. 'Good of you to come at such short notice,' he told them.

Neither man let his expression show he'd had no choice in the matter.

'Sit down,' Eisenhower said as he settled himself in his own chair. 'You have all the information?'

'Yes, Mr. President,' Magadini said, starting to open his case.

'No, hold the details for now. First, give me a summary of the past six months' developments.'

Magadini did so, not needing his notes. Despite his disparaging view of himself and his role in the space program, Jim Magadini was very good at his job. Administration, co-ordination, were his meat and drink. And the events of the past few months had stretched all his skills. NASA had grown with astonishing rapidity, but somehow the many disparate groups had welded together with surprisingly few problems. Even the last major influx, Wernher von Braun's staff from the Army Ballistic Missile Agency, had fitted in even though their presence had, numerically at least, down-graded the previously dominant CalTech staff. The centralization of effort at Huntsville had helped as many of their earlier problems had arisen from having to co-ordinate activities at widely scattered locations. Not that everything was done at Huntsville. Astronaut training was one aspect of the program that still used the facilities of many different places.

When Magadini finished the President nodded. 'Thank you,' he said. He turned to Ziegler. 'And the astronauts, Colonel. How are they?'

'Mentally and physically, they are in fine shape, sir.' Ziegler hesistated. 'Apart from Slayton's problem, of course.'

'Has a final decision been reached on him?'

A year earlier the medical team had discovered a minor irregularity in the condition of Deke Slayton's heart. Everyone had expressed the same general opinion – that it wasn't serious enough to cause any problems, either before, during or after a space flight. That opinion hadn't prevented NASA's top brass from feeling uneasy. Part of their unease lay in the knowledge that someone would have to tell Slayton of any decision to ground him. It was a task no one would welcome.

'No, Mr. President, a decision hasn't been reached.'

'But you have made contingency plans?'

'Yes, sir. We re-opened the files of the original applicants for Project Mercury and made a further selection.'

'Who is he?'

'His name's Herriman. T. Garfield Herriman, Air Force Captain.'

'Herriman?' The President's brow wrinkled. 'Any relation to General Herriman?'

'His son, sir.'

'That should please the General. I don't think he likes sitting behind a desk in the Pentagon. Seeing his son active in something as important as this will give him a boost.'

There was a tinge of regret in the President's voice hinting that his own relative inaction since abandoning his military career gave him something in common with the desk-bound general. With a sudden flash of insight Ziegler guessed that Eisenhower, the soldier, had been a much more contented man than Eisenhower, the politician.

12

Recent attacks on the Executive in the press and on television and radio suggested that, despite his immense popularity with the American public, the President had lost his drive and enthusiasm and was eagerly awaiting the end of his term in office. Ziegler kept away from politics and politicians as much as possible, though he guessed that, to some extent, the press was probably right. But not where the space effort was concerned.

It had been Eisenhower's initiative that had pushed through the National Aeronautics and Space Act, thus ending a costly Army-Navy feud and bringing von Braun's powerful ABMA under NASA's wing.

The President glanced across the room to where his aide had stationed himself. He turned back to the others, something in his manner telling them the preliminaries were over.

'When do you expect to have a man in space?' Eisenhower asked.

'The first of the sub-orbital series is scheduled for early next summer,' Magadini replied.

'No, I said a man in space. A fully orbital flight, not sub-orbital.'

'The schedule is for some time in 1962. No precise date, of course, but the second half of the year seems likely.'

'No earlier than that?'

The question was casually asked but instinctively Magadini knew that the truth, which would be a flat 'No', was not what the President wanted to hear. He decided to hedge until he knew what lay behind the questions. 'I don't see how it can be improved upon, sir. We're doing everything as well and as efficiently as possible.'

The President's face was impassive but his mind was actively searching for an opening. He sensed that, as his aide had suggested, Magadini was prepared to bend. Eisenhower's problem was that he hadn't much enthusiasm left for the political game. And, on top of everything, time was rapidly running out. The idea had come about when, aware that his administration was doomed to go down in history as weak and uninspired, he had invited suggestions for a last, grandstand play. Something that would light up his last days in office bringing back the fire and excitement that had accompanied his triumphant arrival at the White House back in '52. Good as the idea was – there was no doubt that the Chief Executive would gain much reflected glory from the first man in space – it needed a lot of political wheeling and dealing and Eisenhower had already had enough of that to last him to his grave. It also needed time and now that Lyndon Johnson's Senate committee was proposing a moratorium on space spectaculars until after the election, he had too little of that.

He had no illusions about Johnson's motives. The salty-tongued Texan had no love for the young Democratic candidate for the Presidency whose ticket he would share, but he was undoubtedly alert to the fact that if NASA did something big now it could make the Republican administration look good, which would only give a boost to the GOP candidate, and incumbent Vice-President, Richard Nixon.

Eisenhower knew that when the request for a moratorium was formalized he would have to go along with it; so unless NASA could do something very, very quickly the opportunity to capitalize on a space first would be lost.

He decided to probe for an opening in Magadini's apparently pliable defense. 'You haven't any problems down there, have you, Jim?'

'Problems, sir?'

'Staff? Budget? You're not running out of money?'

Magadini swallowed hard, feeling himself break out in more perspiration. He flicked a sideways glance at Ziegler who appeared coolly correct and relaxed. He wouldn't get any help there, he knew. Not because of any antipathy Ziegler might feel towards the idea but simply because the Colonel's concern began and ended with the well-being of the astronauts. This was something else. Magadini made himself form an answer. With millions of dollars being pumped into NASA he dare not suggest they were unable to come up with something to show for it all.

'The budget is appropriate to the program,' he tried. The President raised an eyebrow and Magadini stumbled on, trying not to sound pompous. 'The factors governing the speed of the program are linked to scientific and engineering matters, not those of finance.'

'But more money would be welcome?'

There was only one answer to that. 'Yes, Mr. President.'

'Well, maybe something can be done. In the meantime I want you to give some thought to possible ways in which the program can be speeded up. What you will need – people, equipment, facilities.'

Magadini nodded. 'Yes, sir. I'll get onto it right away.'

The President glanced at Ziegler. 'Bringing forward the first flight won't cause any problems to you and your men, will it, Colonel?'

Ziegler looked at the President, his light blue eyes level and unsmiling. 'We'll be ready if the rockets are ready,' he said. 'But they have to be ready and right.'

Eisenhower smiled with little humor. 'No one would expect them to fly a machine that wasn't perfect.' he said.

Ziegler didn't answer. He was sure the President wasn't consciously avoiding the truth. The man who had commanded the biggest army ever assembled in the history of the world had to know that men were regularly sacrificed on the altar of badly made or ineptly serviced equipment. Like all officers of the high command, Eisenhower had trained himself to overlook some of the less pleasant realities, and this was one of them.

The President glanced at his aide and an unspoken message passed between them. Crossing the room the aide opened the door. Magadini and Ziegler stood up as the President, pushing himself up out of his chair, came around the desk to shake their hands in farewell.

'I do not need add this conversation has been in the very strictest confidence,' he said.

Ziegler nodded and Magadini said, 'Of course, sir.'

'You'll let me have your suggestions on ways we might speed things along?'

'Yes, sir.'

'As soon as possible, Jim. I'd like your report by this time next week.'

Moments later the door of the Oval Office closed behind them and they followed the Presidential aide along the corridor, past the young Navy officer who hadn't moved from his post, out to where the black Cadillac awaited them.

The limousine passed through the West Gate with even less fuss than had been evident when it entered.

'Chief Rogerson would die a thousand deaths if he could see the security system here,' Ziegler remarked.

Magadini didn't answer and after a moment Ziegler looked at him. 'You're not worrying about that business in there, are you?' he asked.

'It's something to worry about.'

'It'll pass. Another few weeks and there'll be another man in that chair.'

'What makes you think either Kennedy or Nixon won't have the same idea?'

'Why should they? There are enough problems for them to face without that. Anyway, they won't need to make a big splash. Not yet.'

'They might. I can think of worse ways to start a Presidency. An opening play like that'd give them a honeymoon with the great American public that would last damn near through to re-election.'

'Maybe you're right, Jim. But if that's what the new man's banking on he won't need to speed up the program. The present schedule will make it happen soon enough.'

Magadini glanced at the back of the driver's head and frowned.

15

Ziegler saw the look and nodded in understanding. For a few moments the two men sat in silence as the Cadillac threaded its way through the traffic along Constitution Avenue.

'How long will you be at Huntsville?' Ziegler asked Magadini.

'Depends on von Braun. I need a couple of hours of his time, but you know what he's like. I expect I'll be there the better part of a day.'

'In that case, after I've dropped you off there I'll go right on back to Langley. Herriman arrives this evening and I've got those Senators to nursemaid tomorrow!'

'Bullshit the bastards,' Magadini said.

Ziegler grinned. 'Don't worry, I'll put on my best Duke Wayne act.'

'Call Sylvia when you get in, will you? Tell her I'm still employed and in one piece.' Magadini clasped a hand to his forehead and groaned. 'Oh, Christ. She gave me orders to look at everything in the White House. Furnishings, drapes, what kind of pictures were on the walls. I can't remember a damn thing.'

'Tell her there was a flag behind the President's desk.'

'What? Was there one..? Oh, right, make a joke about it. If you were married to Sylvia you'd have lost your smart-ass sense of humor by now.'

They talked on idly, watching the traffic as they neared Bolling Air Force Base. Once there they left the Cadillac and boarded their T-39 which had been refueled in their absence. With Ziegler at the controls, they taxied out and, quickly cleared, took off over the Potomac.

The driver of the black Cadillac watched them go, lit a cigarette and waited. After a few minutes a brown Chevrolet, which had come into the same parking area right behind the limousine, started up and crossed the lot. The driver of the Chevy wound down the window and asked the other man for a light. As he took the proffered book of matches and lit up his cigarette the driver of the Chevy asked a couple of quick questions. He received equally terse replies, then handed back the matches and drove off. A short while later the Cadillac left the parking lot and began its return journey to the White House.

In his office the President's aide finished work on a pile of correspondence arising from the day's work, checked his watch and decided he had just enough time to shave before keeping his seven-thirty appointment. All things considered, it hadn't been a bad day. He was certain of two things: one, Magadini would come up with some corner-cutting; two, the President would not exert the pressure needed to put those savings into effect. Which meant that not only would the aide have some inside information on how the space program could be speeded up, he would also be in a position to gift-wrap the entire plan for the man who could make most use of it.

LANGLEY AIR FORCE BASE, Va.

Garfield Herriman eased his cramped leg muscles, letting the car coast for a moment as he did so. 'Almost there,' he said.

Stella opened her eyes and looked at him. 'You're sure you really want this, Gary?' she asked.

He frowned and brushed a hand across his short, fair hair. 'Who wouldn't? It's not the kind of thing every flier gets offered. Out of the entire damn Air Force there are only nine of us.'

Stella said nothing, aware that he hadn't answered her question.

Herriman was also silent, concentrating on his driving, unwilling to let his thoughts go down that particular road again. Along with just about every other Air Force and Navy test pilot who met the age and height requirements, he had volunteered for Project Mercury way back in the spring of '59. He had been rotated back to the States a year earlier, from Germany, and he found Wright, near Dayton, boring to the point where, had it not been for the General, he would have quit the Air Force. What little anyone knew of Project Mercury sounded anything but dull and uninteresting. He had been short-listed, but when the final eight had been announced he had gone back to his duties, resigned to a few more drab years until something else came along.

Then, out of the blue, he had been offered a place on Mercury. At first he assumed he'd be joining a second band of trainees for a later stage of the program, but he discovered that the impossible had happened – he was joining the favored group of eight astronauts who would become America's first line of space men. That was when the doubts began.

His doubts were nothing too serious. He had no qualms at the prospect of being shot into space on top of the giant fuel silo that was a rocket. It couldn't be any worse than being launched from a carrier smack into a gale-force wind in mid-Pacific. He didn't have any worries over his ability to learn what would be needed. If NASA could train the others it could train him. The problem, if problem it was, lay in his ever-present doubt that he was really cut out for the lifestyle he had more or less drifted into. Becoming an astronaut would mean there was no road back. Any hopes of a quiet, withdrawn life would vanish forever. He would become a public figure, people would recognize him on the street, he would have to attend functions, make speeches, give interviews, talk endlessly on the radio and on tv. That kind of thing would hold no fears for a man like the General, but Gary Herriman was under no illusions – he was not from the same mold as his father.

He sensed Stella's awareness of his misgivings but made no attempt to talk to her about them. He wasn't sure why, but over the past couple of years they had grown apart. They talked, they made love, but the talk was inconsequential and their lovemaking had become mechanical. He took a deep breath and let it out slowly. Maybe his assignment to Project Mercury was just what was needed to jolt him and his marriage back into life. That was a distinct possibility, he decided. The new experiences he would undergo might very easily provide the spark that was needed to make things burn again.

He smiled wryly. If it did nothing else it would certainly lift the General's spirits. His father's career had reached a dead end soon after VE Day. As a junior officer Herriman's father had excelled in the heat of battle and had been a trusted and loyal member of Patton's field staff. Patton's fall from favor had dragged several others along behind and since then, despite a slow crawl up to three-star rank, General Herriman had never commanded anything more powerful than a Pentagon desk. He hated it, resented it, and was only now starting to live again, even though vicariously, through the sudden and dramatic turn in Gary's career.

'We're here,' Herriman said, pointing ahead.

Stella stared at the unpromising-looking buildings that would soon provide her limited horizon. Langley looked pretty much the same as every other base they'd lived on. Every house alike and much too close to where Gary would be working. No chance for any life that wasn't surrounded and influenced by the Air Force, except whatever she forcibly carved for herself the way she'd done at Wright. It crossed her mind that doing the same here might not be too easy. Eyes would be on Gary and, inevitably, upon her too. She'd seen the newspaper stories about the astronauts and she'd read the articles in *Life* magazine. It seemed as if none of them had any private lives. Neither the astronauts nor their wives, not even their children. At least that was something she didn't have to put up with. They had no children, she didn't want any and Gary never raised the subject. Not recently, anyway.

At the entrance to the base Stella waited in the car while Gary talked with the guard, then waited some more when he stopped by

18

the administration building. She spent the time repairing her makeup and combing her long, straight, blonde hair. She examined herself critically in a mirror, aware that however hard she tried she was beginning to show traces of the secret life she led.

Her husband came out of the building and walked across the lot towards the car. Stella watched him, conscious that he was still sexually attractive to her. He moved lightly, like a dancer or an athlete. It wasn't really surprising that she tried to let his physical qualities black out her concern about the other side of him. The fact that he had almost no interests outside the Air Force and that he was so self-effacing he could be bullied out of things he wanted or into things he didn't want. Like this Project Mercury business. Stella would have bet her last dime that, given a free choice, he wouldn't be here. But Gary didn't have a free choice. Not with the towering specter of the General calling the shots from behind a Washington desk.

Gary reached the car and climbed in. 'I have to report to Colonel Ziegler as soon as he gets in from Washington. That'll be in about an hour from now. Time for a shower.'

'What do I do?'

'What?'

'What do I do while you're seeing this Colonel Ziegler?'

Herriman frowned as he started the engine. 'Moving in should keep you pretty busy.'

Stella bit back a sharp retort. If he wanted to view her as some glorified housekeeper, it would at least keep him from inquiring too closely into how she spent her days.

Taking Stella's silence as acquiescence, Gary concentrated on what would be happening to him during the coming weeks. Not that he had any clear idea of the training program. True, he'd read newspapers and magazines but they had all seemed ill-informed. The scuttlebutt up at Wright was probably no more accurate, built up as it was out of a combination of speculation and envy. Well, soon he wouldn't be an outsider peering over the wall at Project Mercury, he'd be part of it.

Parking in front of the house they'd been allocated, he led the way inside. 'Not bad,' he said.

Stella didn't answer.

'I'll take that shower,' Gary said and went up the stairs.

Dropping into an armchair, Stella examined her surroundings. Everything, furnishings, carpet, drapes, even the pictures on the wall, looked just like those in the house they'd occupied at Wright. Upstairs the shower started to run. There were some advantages, she allowed. Clothing was all they needed to bring with them, everything else was laid on. No, she amended, there was something else that wasn't provided.

She went out to the car for the smallest of the soft-leather bags stowed in the trunk. In the house she opened it, took out a traveling pint of vodka and drank straight from the bottle.

Screwing the cap back on she re-examined their new home. Already it was looking better. Hearing the shower cut off she went into the kitchen, opened a cupboard and hid the vodka behind a pile of regulation-issue dishes.

She heard Gary moving about upstairs. As soon as he had gone to meet Colonel Ziegler she would take the car downtown and look around. She could check out the possibilities of the area – like the locations of the liquor stores and discreet motels and, most important of all, the availability of men who had things on their mind other than goddamn aircraft and rocket ships.

MOSCOW

Oscar Lennox crouched on the narrow parapet trying not to think about the cold drizzling rain and the forty feet of dark space between him and the ground. It was a hell of place to be, even if CIA operatives were supposed to be accustomed to this kind of thing. Water trickled down the roof of the big house and collected where his left foot strove for a hold. Then his discomfort vanished as he heard voices in the room immediately beneath him. He leaned forward, trying to make out words.

He had stumbled across the two men in a small restaurant where they were dining and conversing quietly. One of the men had seemed vaguely familiar to him, the other he had never seen before. What aroused his interest was one word of their conversation which reached his ear. Baikonur. Like everyone at the Embassy, where he masqueraded as a cultural attach´e, Oscar Lennox was attuned to any mention of Baikonur. High on the list of priority interests of Washington, Baikonur was the Russian space effort's equivalent to Cape Canaveral.

The voices in the room beneath Lennox's feet became clearer and he guessed the two men were now standing close to the window. He listened, the cold and the rain forgotten, and when the two men ended their conversation he knew he had chanced upon something big. Very big.

He had worked his way around to the fire escape at the back of the house, the route by which he had climbed to the roof, when luck deserted him. He was lowering himself towards the topmost handrail of the steel ladder when he slipped and fell awkwardly onto the top deck-plate of the escape. He felt his ankle give and bit back a cry, but he had already made too much noise. A light came on at an adjacent window and he heard a voice call out.

He started down the fire escape, his movements hampered by his twisted ankle. Reaching the ground he hurried painfully towards a gate set in the garden wall. As he reached the gate he heard the door of the house open. A brilliant beam of light shone out. Involuntarily, he turned and for an instant was caught in the beam as if in a spotlight. Then, opening the gate, he ran out into the street.

His pursuers were in the street before he reached the main road. On foot, handicapped as he was by his damaged ankle, he knew he would not get away. Turning onto the main road he saw a line of parked cars. He tried each door handle as he passed. The fourth was unlocked and the keys were in the ignition. He said a small prayer to whichever saint looked after secret agents and moments later he was heading rapidly towards Novaya Square.

After a few minutes he slowed down, aware that the odds were against his pursuers picking up a vehicle so quickly and easily as he had. This was no time to be stopped by an over-zealous Muscovite traffic cop!

A hundred yards past the Metropol Hotel he stopped the car, knowing that was the longest distance his ankle could manage. He straightened his clothing as he walked, hoping the bad weather would be sufficient explanation for his disheveled appearance. Inside the hotel he made a telephone call, then sat, edgy and uncomfortable, until an Embassy car came for him. During his wait he went over and over the conversation between the two men. He couldn't afford to risk forgetting anything.

It was past three o'clock before he finished typing his report. Then he strapped up his ankle before making himself a cup of strong coffee, pouring into it a generous helping of bourbon. He sat for five minutes, sipping the coffee and thinking. Certain he had missed nothing, he went along to the dormitory wing to wake Ross, his nominal superior.

Ross wasn't very pleased. Neither that he had been woken at such an ungodly hour, nor that it was Lennox doing the waking. Ross didn't approve of spies in embassies. An elderly man, with the manners of an English country gentleman, he found the activities of Lennox, and the other CIA operatives with whom he occasionally had to deal, vaguely distasteful. He read the report, then glanced at the man who had written it.

Lennox knew what the look was trying to convey. 'I'm sure it's important,' he said.

'What about the two men? Sure you can't identify them?'

'If I could it would be in there,' Lennox said irritably.

'Put fully detailed descriptions in your report,' the older man said quietly. 'Washington can run them through the files and may come up with an identification.'

Lennox stared at Ross, angry with himself that the excite ment of the evening had made him overlook a fundamental of his calling – more so since a career diplomat who should have been retired years ago was the one to point out his failing.

He took back the report, went out of the room and added descriptions of the two men. One, the man who had seemed faintly familiar, was short, dark-haired, about five feet six, and had large liquid eyes protruding from a thin, almost haggard face. His accent was educated, his clothes expensive and obviously tailored for him. And he carried them well. The other man wore a cheap suit nowhere nearly broad enough for his thick shoulders. He was tall, over six feet, burly and had a lumpish, ruddy face. His straw-colored hair stuck up at the crown and a sprinkling of dandruff covered the collar of his ill-fitting jacket. His accent suggested he came from the south, maybe Khrushchev-country.

For a moment Oscar Lennox hesistated. The big man seemed so unlikely to have anything to do with a space program. Then he shook his head. Missing their descriptions from the report was enough for one night – he wasn't about to compound his error by letting appearances influence him. What mattered was what the two men had talked about.

By the time he was finished Ross had gone back to bed and Lennox took that to mean he should go ahead. He went down to the radio room and stayed until the report was encoded and cabled to Washington.

Later, lying in bed, his ankle throbbing painfully and refusing him sleep, Oscar Lennox wondered how promptly Washington would react. That was always a problem. With the election little more than two months away there was a good chance his report would be pigeon-holed. Well, if it was, that wasn't his problem. He'd done his part and if Washington chose to ignore what the Russians were up to at Baikonur, it wouldn't be his head on the block.

'It doesn't look like a hell of a lot for the money.'

Ziegler held back from responding to the white-haired Senator's remark, guessing it was a deliberate attempt to rile him.

'That's because you can't see any further than the end of your nose, Harry,' the other Senator said, winking at Ziegler as he did so.

The wink told Joe he had managed to break through to one of the two men and that was a relief. Nursemaiding politicians, particularly when they were members of the Senate sub-committee concerned with Project Mercury's financing, was not his line. But the job had been dumped on him and, as with everything he did, he was determined to do it right. Magadini wanted these visitors to have the five-star treatment and a liberal helping of bullshit. Well, that was what they'd get, just so long as nothing interfered with the astronauts' training program.

The target of the white-haired Senator's criticism was the Flight Procedure Trainer. Although Ziegler would never admit it, when looked at in physical terms, there really wasn't much to show for the many thousands of dollars it had cost. He knew there was no point in explaining that the machinery they could see was only the tip of an iceberg of engineering research.

'How often is it used?' the younger Senator asked.

'Probably the most-used piece of equipment we have,' Ziegler told him. 'Each astronaut spends many hours per week on it. In fact it's hardly ever out of use.'

'It's out of use now,' the older man said.

'Someone will be along directly,' Ziegler said, striving to keep irritation from his voice. 'Then you can see it in operation.'

'One of the astronauts?' The Senator was suddenly eager and interested, his critical pose deserting him.

Ziegler didn't miss the change of tone. It wasn't uncommon. He was accustomed to it by now but at first it had surprised him, the way outsiders reacted to the pilots who formed the operational team for Project Mercury. It was as if some deeply buried hero worship had suddenly resurfaced. When it did, finding that Babe Ruth and Tom Mix were long gone, new idols were needed. That was just what these new all-American heroes were fast becoming, idols for the least expected people. Like the older Senator, who had arrived at Langley Base obviously ready for battle. His anger stemmed from the fact that the state he represented had no plants building rockets

23

or electronic components or radio equipment or any damn thing that could be seen to be contributing to the man-in-space program.

'Two of them will be along soon,' Ziegler assured him. 'Maybe you'd like to meet them. I'm sure they'll be happy to meet you.' In a pig's eye they will, he thought. However, the situation was nothing new to the astronauts. Most of them didn't care for the PR side to their duties but they went along, recognizing that pandering to skeptical politicians was as much a facet of the job as weightlessness training, and also aware that sometimes it reaped rewards. Like less trouble from upstairs.

Out of the corner of his eye, Ziegler saw one of Joe Schmidt's space suit technicians approaching. A little man, known as Specs because of his inadequate eyesight and the correcting thick-lensed glasses he wore, he had a mordant sense of humor and couldn't stop telling jokes, most of which seemed to feature pilots who hadn't gotten out of burning aircraft fast enough to avoid losing parts of their anatomy. Ziegler reached a rapid decision – Specs was someone the Senators would be better off not meeting.

'Let's get a cup of coffee while we're waiting,' he told them and started across the floor of the FPT building without waiting for their agreement.

A few minutes later the three men were crowded into a temporarily vacated office behind the FPT, each clutching a Styroform cup of gruesome coffee. There was better coffee around but Ziegler reckoned that any suggestion of taxpayers' money being diverted into such things as top quality provisions might well set the Senator off again.

The younger Senator sipped the coffee, grimaced and then grinned at Ziegler. 'You could use this stuff if you run short of fuel,' he said.

Ziegler returned the smile, the action setting up deep laughter lines at the corners of his light-blue eyes. At least this was one politician who wouldn't give him a hard time. Unlike his colleague, the young Senator came from a state which had a large plant building telemetry equipment for the program.

He took a sip of the coffee and held up the Styroform cup as if considering the suggestion. 'We might have to, especially if there are cut-backs,' he said.

'You expect them?'

Ziegler shrugged, rubbing a hand across his tanned face. 'The program is already getting some attention in the election campaign. Maybe it will become an issue. Who knows?'

The Senators nodded in unison, as if trying to suggest their involvement, when in fact all three men knew that if the program did become a political football it would be at the instigation of the Presidential candidates, not the Senate.

The older Senator seemed to take that as a signal to change the subject. The one he chose couldn't have been better calculated if he wanted to irritate Ziegler. 'Tell me something, Colonel,' he said. 'How come you're Astronaut Liaison Officer and not an astronaut?'

His colleague fixed him with a glare which he either didn't notice or chose to ignore.

Ziegler shrugged. 'Height,' he said.

'Height?'

'There's a height restriction on astronauts, Harry,' the other Senator told him irritably. 'Surely to God you know that!'

'What? Oh, yes, I recall it now. So, too tall. Well, that must be a pretty lousy thing to have happen, eh Colonel?'

Joe Ziegler tried to convince himself the man was being merely tactless and not deliberately trying to open up an old wound he couldn't possibly realize was there.

'Everyone on the space program has a job to do, Senator,' Ziegler said, picking his words carefully. 'It doesn't matter who he is, all the way from a guy out in San Diego punching rivets into an Atlas shell to the man who presses the button that sends the bird up into space. It's all part of the same job and anyone who figures his part is more important or less important than the next guy's is just kidding himself. I know my job's important. I admit I like it better than I would if I was the riveter and I like it less than if I was going up there with Schirra and Grissom and Simons. I'm proud of doing what I do and I don't reckon I'm getting a lousy deal.' He stopped, aware that his answer had been too long, that he had given way to anger. Then he saw the white-haired Senator nodding, his face serious, while his colleague was grinning widely. He guessed that, in spite of himself, he'd managed to convey the right impression.

He swallowed the dregs of the coffee and waited for the others to do the same, taking perverse pleasure in their obvious distaste. 'Okay, gentlemen, let's go see what's happening out there now.'

Back in the FPT building two of the Project Mercury astronauts were already partially suited up. He introduced the Senators to them both. First was Scott Carpenter, good-looking, athletic, and amiable in his attitude towards the politicians. The other was Alan Shepard, small, puckish and, as always when he was at Langley or any of the other training bases except the Cape, correct and without Scott's instant friendliness. The Senators responded with uncharacteristic deference and Ziegler hid a smile, wondering what they would have

25

thought had they been able to see the other Al Shepard, the one who stepped out of his shell at Cocoa Beach and could live it up with the best of them.

'Who's on first?' Ziegler asked.

'I am,' Shepard said.

'Okay, Lieutenant,' Ziegler said, turning to Carpenter. 'Maybe you'd like to give the Senators a commentary on what's happening while Commander Shepard is in the FPT.'

'Right, Colonel,' Carpenter said, sliding a quick grin at Ziegler which the visitors missed.

The formality was part of an unwritten script always used when they were on show to outsiders. From the outset of the program the natural cameraderie of flying men had transcended such artificialities as rank. However, the general public, which included Senators, had instinctively placed the astronauts onto a reverential, almost mystical, plane. The very least they expected was to hear them spoken to with respect. Even by one another.

'What happens in there is this, gentlemen,' Carpenter began as Alan Shepard disappeared from their view. 'Commander Shepard will "fly" the FPT as if it were a spacecraft. The instruments are controlled by the computer and everything is exactly as it will be in flight.' He took the visitors across to the computer banks and let one of the technicians take over and deliver a description containing enough multi-syllabled words to make the Senators think they were being treated as intellectual equals. In fact, the description the technician gave was cursory to the point of being hopelessly inaccurate but it didn't much matter. Jim Magadini's request for bullshit had been passed through channels and everyone, technicians, engineers, and astronauts alike, was prepared to put in his two cents' worth.

Inside the FPT Alan Shepard was lying on a couch in a cockpit precisely duplicating the Mercury capsule. Had the machine been tilted through 90 degrees his position would have been that of a man sitting upright in a high-backed chair, his feet planted firmly on the floor. As it was, his back was parallel with the floor. Any minor discomforts this position brought long since ironed out by regular use of the machine.

On this particular occasion Shepard was flying a simulated sub-orbital mission from start to finish. All launch, in-flight, and splash-down procedures would be followed, something he had already done scores of times. The intention behind frequent use of the FPT was simple enough. When launch-day dawned everything the astronaut was called upon to do would be familiar, reflexive. That way, whatever happened, routine or emergency, there would be no surprises, no fear, above all no panic. The real thing would be just like the FPT only maybe a little less dramatic; it would, hopefully, not be subject to the vagaries thrown in by imagin ative engineers determined that the simulated flights cover every eventuality.

Just as important as familiarity with the hardware was the fact that this extensive training helped weld ground controllers and astronauts into a tight, cohesive unit. By the time launch-date arrived this unit would be expected to act as one man, a man who would carry out his duties in such a manner that perfection would be an inadequate word.

'Okay,' Carpenter said, as the technician ended his part in the charade with a flourish of words which sparkled like the lights on the control panel of his computer. 'By now, Commander Shepard has been launched onto his trajectory.'

'How much control has he?' the younger Senator asked.

Carpenter hesistated imperceptibly before answering. Control of spacecraft was a sore point with the astronauts, one that was the subject of constant battles with the engineers. Initially the spacecraft had been designed to be controlled exclusively from the ground. This stemmed from the thinking of many engineers that putting a man in the ship was a waste of good space that would be better filled with instruments. When that piece of intelligence had seeped through to the astronauts they had been first irritated, then frustrated, finally angry. They were pilots, for chrissake, and pilots flew machines. They were not flown *by* them.

'The astronaut can exercise all necessary control,' Carpenter answered the Senator's question. That was not exactly true in the case of sub-orbital flights. They would be like glorified rifle shots in which the capsule was the bullet. A bullet with a man inside it. Things would be different when the orbital flights began. They had argued and fought and eventually, thanks largely to the efforts of Deke Slayton and Joe Ziegler, they'd won. During the orbital flights, if the need arose, the astronaut would be able to take control of the capsule and really *fly* it.

Inside the FPT Al Shepard began transmitting confirmatory data. To the watching Senators the only signs of activity were the lights which flashed on the control panel of the computer.

'The flight is now nearing its end,' Carpenter announced.

'This soon? For God's sake, he's only just started.'

Carpenter looked at the older Senator for an instant before answering. 'The sub-orbital flight is a testing operation. It lasts about fifteen minutes,' he said evenly.

27

'Fifteen minutes? Millions of dollars for fifteen minutes?'

Carpenter took a deep breath, then let it out slowly, afraid to answer in case he betrayed his contempt. Didn't the damn fool realize the Atlantic Ocean didn't go on forever? At 4,500 miles per hour, much longer than fifteen minutes and the capsule would be making a hole in Europe or Africa instead of splashing down harmlessly in the sea.

He glanced across at the computer. 'The mission is over. Now, if you'll excuse me, it's my turn.'

Ziegler stepped forward and picked up where the astronaut had left off. 'From this point what happens is pretty much a repeat performance, with Lieutenant Carpenter at the controls of the FPT in place of Commander Shepard.'

The Senators took the hint, thanked Scott Carpenter for his time and then, a little reluctantly, followed Ziegler from the building.

It took the Astronaut Liaison Officer another half hour before he'd gotten them out of his hair and on their way back to Washington. Then he headed for his office to change out of uniform into the regulation-issue coverall he usually wore.

He checked the time, saw it was already past six, and swore mildly at the time-wasting exercise he'd just endured. He still had a workload to get through before he could quit for the day. For one thing, there was Gary Herriman's training schedule to finalize. He'd already briefed the new arrival and was impressed both with his record and his relaxed, easy-going manner. Ziegler was sure he would fit in well with the rest of the team, but he had a lot of catching up ahead of him. Whatever else Gary Herri   man expected out of Project Mercury, an easy ride wasn't on the list.

Ziegler suddenly recalled something else the Senators' visit had screwed up. He had a date with Paula Blake but now there was no way he would be able to keep it. He reached for the telephone, dialled and when she answered made his excuses while she listened in silence.

'That makes three in a row,' she said when he was through.

'I'm sorry, you know that.'

'As always, Joe. Trouble is, life around here is pretty damn boring.'

'Tomorrow night, Paula. That's a promise. Even if the President calls and invites me over for a round of golf.'

Paula laughed. 'Okay, Joe. Tomorrow.'

She replaced the telephone and stood for a moment looking across the living room of her apartment. It was untidy as hell and she knew she should spend the evening clearing it up but that wasn't her style. She picked up the telephone, dialled a number, let it ring twice, then pressed down the cradle before dialling again. One of the advantages of dating an unmarried man like Joe Ziegler was the absence of any need for that kind of subterfuge. Sleeping around with married men, particularly those with jealous or suspicious wives, might be fun but it sometimes had its problems.

WASHINGTON, D.C.

The man in the tan suit fiddled with his cuffs, then adjusted his tie for the fourth or fifth time in ten minutes. His companion took note but said nothing.

'How much longer?'

'He'll be here when he's ready,' was the unsatisfactory reply.

The two men were in a bar just off Wisconsin Avenue, two blocks south of Bethesda Naval Hospital. The President was due to check into Bethesda in a few days. Nothing serious, just a routine physical, but it gave his aide an excuse for being in that part of the city.

'Another drink?'

The President's aide shook his head. 'This is taking unnecessary risks,' he said.

'Our man thinks it's important.'

'Dammit, if someone sees us.'

'They won't.'

A shadow fell across them and both men looked up. The newcomer gestured towards the door. 'He's outside.'

Moments later they were in a car parked across the street from the bar with the aide repeating everything he could recall from the meetings between Eisenhower and the men from NASA who had visited the White House during the past week. Ziegler and Magadini had been preceded by Jim Webb and Bob Gilruth who had come up together, and followed by Wernher von Braun who had left Washington less than an hour earlier.

The Vice President listened carefully, interrupting only once to clarify something von Braun had said. His report delivered, the man in the tan suit left the car, hurrying towards his own car, so eager to get back to the White House he didn't see two men watching from a brown Chevy parked a few yards along the street.

The man who had waited in the bar with the aide tried to make himself comfortable in the jumpseat. 'It's clear what the President wants,' he said.

'Will he get it?' Nixon asked.

'Doubtful. Gilruth and Webb are opposed, von Braun is for it, Magadini will go along with whatever is decided.'

'Ziegler?'

'Doesn't rate, so long as he can be shown his astronauts aren't about to get their asses burned.'

'So. Where does that leave us?'

'It means that when you're elected you start up the whole ball game again only this time the President gets what he wants.'

'Why do I get it if Eisenhower can't?'

'Time...and money.'

'Explain.'

'You'll have four, maybe eight years. Gilruth and Webb can stall Eisenhower until November but they can't stall for eight years. They need the appropriations to keep NASA functioning which means they'll bend.'

Nixon nodded. 'Okay. Keep close to this. As soon as the election is over we open things up. Start pressing.'

'What about him?' his companion asked, pointing in the direction taken by the man in the tan suit.

'What do you mean?'

'He's not doing this for love. He expects something out of it. A job like the one he's got now.'

The Vice President was studying the backs of his hands. 'Like hell! Am I about to hire a disloyal sonofabitch like that?' he murmured. 'Like hell.'

The other man stepped out of the car. 'That's nice to hear,' he said. If there was irony in his voice it was lost on the Vice President who snapped an order to the driver. The man stood on the sidewalk, watching the car disappear from sight, before going back into the bar for another drink.

The two men in the brown Chevy relaxed and lit cigarettes.

'Are you sure all this has to do with NASA?' one of them said.

The driver nodded. 'It has to be. All these meetings, now the President's aide talking to Nixon.'

'But surely all Nixon has to do is ask Eisenhower what's going on. He doesn't need to play it this way.'

'Maybe he does. Maybe the President is keeping this one close to his chest. We know there's no love lost between them.'

His companion shook his head. 'Seems a hell of a way to run the White House. The Veep spying on the Man.'

The driver laughed. 'Just wait until *our* man is in there. Poor old Lyndon ain't gonna know what the hell's going on, either.'

'Well, what do we do now?'

The driver glanced at the entrance to the bar. 'We could find out just how much our friend in there knows.'

'How?'

'Check his apartment. You never know, he might have something on paper we can use. Same with the President's aide.'

'Their apartments? You mean burglary?'

'Something like that.'

'That's against the law for chrissake,' the other man said weakly.

The driver wound down his window and flicked a half-smoked cigarette into the street. He started the engine and pulled away from the curb. 'Only if you're caught!' he chuckled.

WRIGHT AIR DEVELOPMENT CENTER, Oh.

'Hey, Gary, how does it feel to be going back to Wright this soon?'

Gary Herriman turned to grin at the speaker. Wally Schirra was the most openly friendly of the astronauts. He was also an inveterate practical joker and constantly gave the outward impression of taking nothing seriously. Herriman already knew differently. Like all the others, Schirra was very serious about Project Mercury but, also like the others, he managed to convey an outward impression that everything they were called upon to do was either easy or boring or both. It was all part of the facade which Air Force and Navy pilots acquired within minutes of getting their wings.

'I hoped I'd never see the place again,' Gary told Schirra.

'Well, this time you'll be trying something new.'

The visit to Wright, where Herriman was based when his assignment to Project Mercury came through, would be his first taste of the training program the others already knew well. In the days since joining the program he had undergone an intensive series of lectures, tests and familiarization procedures, which would allow him to settle in beside the other astronauts without feeling too much the outsider. At Wright they would be flying in the stripped-out belly of a C-131 freighter, which would be taken through a series of carefully calculated parabolic curves. At the top of each curve everyone on board would experience about twenty valuable seconds of weightlessness. For the astronauts, all of whom would be fully suited-up, these brief moments would be their closest pass to the real thing until the time came for them to be shot into space on top of a screaming, burning rocket. No one was kidding himself. These few seconds in the safety of a C-131 would be nearer a quiet doze in a

31

fireside armchair than what they would experience atop a Redstone or Atlas rocket.

Herriman looked around the Sabreliner which was starting its approach into Wright. Apart from himself and the stockily-built Schirra there was Gus Grissom, dour, usually unsmiling but somehow conveying an impression he was a man worth knowing; Bill Simons, intensely competitive to the point where he was the butt of running humor among his colleagues; Gordon Cooper, casual, easy-going, his Oklahoman drawl suggesting simultaneously that everything was a drag but that if the need arose he could act swiftly and decisively. And Joe Ziegler, always around.

Herriman felt a glow of warmth towards the older man. In the past few days he had seen more of Ziegler than anyone, even Stella. Ziegler had already shown Herriman that he hadn't been brought onto Project Mercury as a makeweight. He was a full member of the team and, providing he got through the rigorous schedule needed to catch up with the others, he would be right up there in the reckoning when the flight timetable was prepared.

An hour later they were on board the C-131, beginning the first of the parabolic arcs which would allow them to float free of earth's gravity.

Schirra caught Herriman's eye. 'I hope you took my advice and skipped breakfast this morning.'

'Only ham, eggs, hash browns and three cups of coffee.'

'You'll regret it. Five minutes from now it'll all be floating around in here just like you never ate it.'

Joe Ziegler heard Schirra's comment and grinned at Herriman. 'Don't take this guy seriously, Gary. No one else does.'

'Don't worry, Joe, I'm learning.'

Ziegler hung onto the nearest bulkhead as the freighter entered the part of the curve which made everything that wasn't held down float, wraithlike, through the fuselage. The astronauts, ponderous-looking in their space suits, were suddenly graceful, light, like underwater swimmers. The freighter reached the end of the curve and began to climb into the next one.

Ziegler caught Gus Grissom's eye and the short, compact astronaut came over to him. 'The next couple of days I have a lot on, Gus,' Ziegler said. 'Keep an eye out for Gary, let me know if any problems arise.'

'Sure, Joe. Not expecting trouble, are you?'

'No, he's fitting in well and fast. Just don't want him to hit any avoidable snares, that's all.'

'He seems a solid man. Pretty impressive record.'

'Good family.'

'The General? Yeah. That didn't have anything to do with his selection, did it?'

'You know better than that, Gus.'

'I guessed not but I thought I'd ask. Come to think of it, being the son of a three-star General can't be a barrel of laughs.'

'Not when that general is General Herriman. From what I hear, he can be a regular fire-eater.'

'Gary doesn't take after him, then. He seems a pretty easy-going kind of guy. Not like Wild William over there.'

Ziegler didn't need to look to know Grissom was indicating Bill Simons. 'Still trying too hard, is he?'

'You know he is, Joe. He'll be trying hard until the day he dies.'

'I keep telling him to ease up, but he just doesn't know what the hell I'm talking about.'

The C-131 reached the top of its second arc and Grissom floated away from Ziegler for a few seconds. When the freighter came out of the curve Bill Simons and Gary Herriman were too close to allow Ziegler to continue the conversation he'd started with Gus. He guessed Simons was pursuing some point he'd been making earlier.

'Performance is what counts,' the astronaut was saying, one finger jabbing forcefully into the air. 'Whatever the hell you're doing, do it flat out.'

Grissom grinned at Ziegler, the change of expression lightening his usually somber look. Ziegler returned the grin but mentally decided he would have to try again with Simons. Aggression and ambition were not failings in the true sense but he knew they could cause problems. At least that was what Diana McNair, the team's psychiatrist, was always telling him.

Bill Simons' remark to Gary Herriman had not been intended as encouragement to the newcomer. Simons didn't make a practise of helping others, but he had already made a personal assessment based on Herriman's service record and his own first impressions. It told him that T. Garfield Herriman wasn't about to offer any serious competition. He was much too mild-mannered, too gently polite. Unlike the others, Simons did not see his fellow astronauts as members of a team from which each would be drawn, either by lot or by chance, to take his place on the spaceflight schedule. Simons did not accept repeated statements, from people like Joe Ziegler, that the schedule was a matter of unplanned rotation. He firmly believed that the order of flight would depend on only one thing – ability. Fitness for the task was something to be proved in a competitive spirit among all candidates. Maybe the others didn't think that way – at least they *pretended* not to.

He was determined that no one else on Project Mercury, not even John Glenn, whose dedication to the training program was already taking on elements of legend, would beat him to the hot seat on the first flight. But he was realistic enough to recognize that he was running from behind. He figured three men were ahead of him, but with the first of the sub-orbitals still several months away a lot could happen. He planned on seeing it did.

The C-131 began the final parabola of the day and after it was over, with all the astronauts on board having carried out the exercises they'd been allocated, they returned to Wright.

They would be going up again the next day; the day after that Al Shepard and Scott Carpenter were flying in from San Diego where they'd been giving a boost to workers at the Atlas shell plant. And John Glenn and Deke Slayton would be reporting back from a few days' leave. Not that they would all go up in the same freighter. Accidents did occasionally happen despite the most rigorous safeguards and, if the unthinkable hit, NASA didn't intend losing an entire team in one big bang.

Ziegler wouldn't be with them during the next couple of days' training. He had assessments to prepare and for that he needed to talk to Diana McNair and Jim Magadini back at Langley. It was with a tiny pang of regret that he left the astronauts and bummed a flight back to Virginia. He decided he was starting to feel his age. Watching young guys like Gary Herriman and Bill Simons, Gordo Cooper and Gus Grissom, was like looking at an old home movie of himself. Those few years, five or six, made all the difference.

Even the others, Shepard or Glenn and Slayton, who were only a year or two younger than he, enjoyed that happy accident of being within NASA's age limit. He sighed as he watched Wright fade behind the aircraft taking him back to Langley. Age and height. One arbitrary, the other mechanical. He still couldn't believe that men capable of designing rocketry of fearsome power and spacecraft of staggering technical sophistication couldn't figure a way to get someone who was just two inches over the limit into one of their goddamn machines.

34

HAMPTON, Va.

'This is the first time I've had more than two drinks in a row since Jim Junior was born.'

Linda Simons smiled at Sylvia and tilted her glass. 'Here's to four in a row,' she said.

Sylvia Magadini grinned and sipped at her third dry martini. She wasn't fooled by the make believe hard-boiled tone the younger woman was using. 'I'm not joking,' Sylvia said. 'My parents are down from Ann Arbor. Seemed like a good chance for Jim and me to get away from the kids, you know what they're like.'

Linda laughed, the action shaking her fluffy blonde head. 'I know, I still have bruises from the last time I acted as baby-minder.'

'Then, at the last minute, Jim had to go away. He's back now but tied up at Langley. As usual. Anyway, I couldn't miss the chance to leave Mom and Dad holding the fort, so here I am.'

'I'm glad you are. I was beginning to think I'd be doing my drinking alone.'

'What's got into you? I thought fruit juice was your limit.'

'Usually it is. In fact this is the first time I've had a real drink since Bill and I were married. I got drunk on our wedding night and I never have managed to live it down.'

'So what's the reason for today's martinis?'

Linda shook her head and laughed again, this time looking slightly embarrassed. 'I got some news today and I'm celebrating.'

'Oh, what is it? Or shouldn't I ask?'

'I'm pregnant,' Linda said before adding hastily, 'Bill doesn't know about it yet.'

Sylvia smiled. 'Was the baby made to order?'

'Not exactly but Bill and I are the only ones without children. Not that there are any rules but...'

'Well, congratulations anyway,' Sylvia said. She looked up and smiled as she saw Paula Blake coming across the room. Paula had changed her hairstyle since the last time Sylvia had seen her. Now her reddish tinted dark-brown hair was worn short and loosely curled around her lively, tanned and usually smiling face. It was impossible to see if the smile extended to her eyes because even in the darkened interior of the hotel bar Paula wore sunglasses. She was smiling now as she approached the other two women, pleased to see Sylvia, who she liked more than most of the project wives she met. An attractive divorcee, Paula knew she was included in social gatherings only because of her current affair with Joe Ziegler. Most of the project wives made it obvious she wasn't really one of them, but Sylvia Magadini was the exception.

'Hi, Sylvia, someone leave the lock off the door?' Paula slid into the booth, the movement displaying considerably more of her thighs than was absolutely necessary and was, the other women were sure, an automatic come-on to any male who happened to be looking that way.

'Nice to see you, Paula.'

'Who else is coming?' Paula asked.

'Rene and Betty, if she gets her car fixed in time, and Louise said she might make it later,' Linda said.

The barman came over to take Paula's order, one watchful eye on Linda Simons. Sylvia gave him what she hoped was a reassuring smile. He seemed to accept that as confirmation that he wouldn't have any trouble, although Sylvia wasn't sure he had grounds for such confidence. Her own intake of martinis was beginning to make itself felt.

Paula glanced at Linda, taking in her obviously happy state. 'What's the occasion?' she asked.

Linda flushed slightly, then shrugged. 'I guess everyone will know soon enough. I'm going to have a baby.'

Neither of the other women noticed the tiny pause before Paula smiled. 'Congratulations. What does Bill think about it?' 'He doesn't know yet.'

I'll bet he doesn't, Paula thought. What was more, when he finds out he's going to be a whole lot less than delighted. Her relationship with Bill Simons had begun as a direct result of Joe Ziegler's preoccupation with his work. Not that Bill wasn't over-dedicated, but the astronaut had a work-hard, play-hard philosophy Ziegler lacked. Paula, who took sexual relationships a good deal more casually than most women, had picked up Bill's wandering glances at a party to which Joe had taken her. She hadn't been at all surprised when, while they were dancing, he asked to see her the following night. Since then their meetings had been irregular but frequent. To her, Bill was a substitute when Joe was busy; to Bill, she knew, she was just one of a number of releases he took from the restraints of a marriage he was wearying of.

Bill's behavior wasn't surprising. Linda Simons was pretty but empty-headed. Paula had never asked but would've bet she'd been the girl-next-door to Bill's home in Akron, Ohio. The fact that she was now in the public gaze frightened Linda out of her wits and given half a chance she would have high-tailed it back to obscurity. But she wasn't likely to get the chance; certain ly, Paula knew, Bill had no intention of passing up his shot at celebrity. There was nothing specific in the rulebook about divorce, but the big wigs at NASA had made it pretty clear that they didn't expect the astronauts' images to be tainted by messy domestic situations. Even separation was out, as one of them had already discovered.

The barman brought the new round of drinks across to the booth just as Rene Carpenter and Betty Grissom came in together.

The new arrivals were both surprised and pleased to see Sylvia, and the conversation was soon lively and noisy and devoted almost exclusively to talk of children and their exploits, education, and health. During the next half hour Paula, the only unmarried woman present, took little part in the conversation. From behind the shield of her oversized sunglasses, her expression tried to project polite interest, but she felt completely out of touch.

Sylvia made a couple of attempts to bring the conversation around to something in which Paula could participate, with little success. But gradually it turned to the new member of the team, Gary Herriman. Betty Grissom said she'd met Herriman's wife, Stella, in the town, and that Stella hadn't seemed very happy with the house they would be occupying at the base. The talk drifted onto houses and interior decorating but Sylvia could see that this too was something in which Paula could not participate, as she lived alone in a small apartment in Norfolk to which none of the others had ever been invited.

Linda was the first to make a move to leave the gathering. She looked carefully, and for a long time, at her watch before announcing that she would be in serious trouble if she didn't get home within the hour. As the Simons' lived over in Newport News, the chance that she would make it in time was slim and the effects of the martinis were beginning to show.

Sylvia picked up her bag. 'Leave your car here,' she told Linda. 'I'll drop you off.'

Linda giggled and swayed slightly. 'Okay,' she said. 'If I scratch the car it'll be something else for Bill to shout about.'

Sylvia glanced at the others and saw only smiles, no raised eyebrows. Everyone knew about Bill Simons' abrasiveness.

Sylvia and Linda had started for the door when Paula caught up with them. 'Time I was going too,' she told them. 'Joe said he would get away early tonight and take me to Fitzgerald's for dinner. It's my birthday, although I've stopped counting.'

Sylvia glanced at her. She knew Paula was twenty-four and the imminence of her own fortieth birthday was making her overly sensitive to such things. 'Try not to worry about it,' she said. 'Worry gives you wrinkles.'

Paula's hand moved up quickly to touch the corner of her eye beneath her dark glasses, then laughed, realizing the remark hadn't been a serious comment directed at her. 'Maybe Joe will get to like older women,' she said.

'Maybe he will,' Sylvia said in a deliberate attempt to sound mysterious. She was pleased to see that Paula received the comment with more consideration than it deserved.

Sylvia negotiated her suddenly unsteady companion into the front seat of her battered Buick station wagon, started the engine and in a cloud of blue exhaust drove out onto the roadway. As she accelerated away from the hotel she caught a glimpse of Paula in her rear-view mirror. She had a momentary twinge of affection for the young woman and the fact that she was so out of place in their company.

Paula watched the old Buick disappear up the road. She had been pleased to see Sylvia Magadini again. Of all the women she knew, Sylvia was probably the only one who didn't automatically put up a defensive shield in her presence. Paula smiled to herself, a little unkindly, at the thought that Sylvia no doubt realized her husband wasn't target material.

She unlocked the door of her MG and climbed in, her action displaying her legs to the driver of a Pontiac sedan and distracting him so much he almost clipped the wing of another car as he tried to park. Paula didn't notice, she had been using her body to attract men for so long now it was reflexive. She swung the car into the road and accelerated hard. After her short-lived marriage ended she had bought the MG with part of her share from the sale of the house in Healdsburg. Ownership of a foreign sports car was a gesture of nonconformity, one which gave her spirits a boost at a time when she had been at her weakest and most vulnerable.

Her marriage had been stormy and she was pleased when it was over, though for a time the loneliness of the small, cluttered and not particularly attractive apartment she rented in Norfolk had gotten her down. The lonely nights hadn't lasted long. There had been a steady stream of men until Joe Ziegler. For a time she stayed faithful to him, but it hadn't been easy and she soon allowed herself to be tempted. It was a pity he was so engrossed in his work. Joe was the kind of man she could imagine herself marrying, if she ever decided to chance it again.

She stopped at a red light and glanced incuriously at a car alongside her. The woman in the passenger seat was young, pretty and blonde. The lights changed and as the other car moved off Paula thought she recognized the driver. It looked like Mike Leandros,

Diana McNair's assistant. She felt an unreasonable twinge of jealously. She'd enjoyed a few wild nights with Leandros in her time, though they had meant nothing to either of them. Just sex for the fun of it. She wondered briefly who the blonde was, but then pushed the thought aside and began to look forward with pleasure to the postponed evening out with Joe.

LANGLEY AIR FORCE BASE, Va.

'How are you making out?'

Gary Herriman looked up and smiled wearily at Joe Ziegler. 'I haven't read so many books since high school.'

'Yeah, I know what you mean. You'd think somebody would come up with a way to learn that didn't involve reading.'

'Like an injection?'

'That would do it.' Ziegler glanced at his watch. 'I have to go over and talk to Jim, after that let me buy you a drink.'

Herriman nodded. 'Thanks, where'll I meet you?'

'Come across to Jim's office in about twenty minutes.'

After Ziegler had gone, Gary Herriman pushed the books across the table and stared around the library. He was alone but didn't feel it. To his surprise he was beginning to feel at home in the space program. All his earlier fears and unrest had faded, largely due, he guessed, to the guys who had all gone out of their way to make his induction into their select group as painless as possible. His training was going well, he knew that, and the technical back-up he was getting was faultless. But he still faced a heavy reading load and that was something with which no one could help. He yawned, stretching his arms above his head, thought about reading some more but changed his mind.

He would have an early night. The drink with Ziegler wouldn't take long, then he'd go home and maybe take Stella out to dinner. It hadn't been possible for him to spend much time with her since their arrival at Langley but she seemed happy enough. She was out a lot, so he guessed she had made friends, probably among the wives of the other astronauts. He put his books back on the shelves thinking about the people he was working with. He liked them all, particularly Ziegler who seemed almost like an older brother to him. He wondered fleetingly what Ziegler's meeting with Jim Magadini was about, but pushed the thought aside. If it concerned him he'd know soon enough.

At that moment Joe Ziegler was climbing the stairs to Jim Magadini's top floor office in the main administration building. He seldom used the elevator for any climb of less than six stories, regarding such things as unnecessary for a man who kept himself at the peak of physical fitness. The higher he went in the building the further he felt removed from the astronauts and the nuts and bolts of the space program and he had the uneasy feeling that was how the people who worked up here felt.

None of them seemed able to relate to the men who, one day, would sit on top of that ninety foot candle, waiting patiently for someone to set it alight and boost them into the sky and beyond, along with several thousand gallons of highly inflammable liquid. Liquid that wasn't nearly as stable as the PR wizards made out. Technicians! Give them a re-entry trajectory to calculate, power-weight ratios to compute, any amount of electronic gadgetry to fit into an impossibly small space, and they'd beaver happily away for hours on end. Expect them to imagine themselves into the mind of the man who would sit on top of it all and they went blank.

That was the biggest problem. No one could imagine it, not even the bunch of gung-ho over-sized kids who called themselves astronauts. The non-stop training, the constant psychiatric surveillance, and the determined effort to fill every second of the astronaut's time right up to the moment of lift-off, were as much devices to keep his mind off the potentialy lethal assembly of hardware beneath his ass as essential preparation. Yet for all the training, for all the ground crew seated behind dials at Mission Control, the sucker in the capsule was on his own once the lox ignited.

He reached the top floor and walked along a tiled corridor, knocked on a door at the far end, and went into the office of Jim Magadini's secretary. The girl smiled at him, the smile just a little bit brighter than the one with which she usually favored visitors.

'Is he free?' Ziegler asked.

'Go right in, Colonel.'

Ziegler rapped on Magadini's door, opened it and walked in without waiting for an invitation. Magadini looked up with a start from the file he was studying and hastily closed it. The action didn't fully register for a moment, but when it did Ziegler set aside the thought it generated. There was a whole bundle of secrets around NASA he wasn't party to.

'How was von Braun?' he asked.

Magadini grinned. 'He's starting to let the jokes get to him. Seems all that about Germans having no sense of humor might be true after all.'

The jokes had begun to appear on notice boards around the Huntsville complex where von Braun was Director. They were always anonymous, not very funny, and usually on the same general theme – that, at the end of World War II, the Russians had gotten the best of the German rocket experts; the Americans had had to settle for the ones the Russians deliberately left behind. Sometimes, tacked alongside the jokes were clippings from the *New York Times* speculating on the progress of the Russian space program and hinting very broadly that America was being left behind.

'Anything else getting at him?' Ziegler asked.

Magadini's face closed up. 'Such as?'

'Such as the reason we went up to Washington.'

Magadini hesistated before replying. 'You'll find out soon enough, I expect,' he said eventually. 'He's had the same trip and he's getting the same pressure.'

'And?'

'I'm not sure what kind of answer he gave the President. One thing I am sure of, he wouldn't give him a flat negative.'

'Well, it isn't von Braun's finger on the button. There are plenty of people who come between the President and the launching of a Redstone. People who can resist any pressure he can exert.'

Magadini looked less sure. 'It isn't Eisenhower I'm worried about. Another nine or ten weeks and there'll be a new man in the White House. My guess is, he won't wait for the Inauguration before he starts poking around NASA.'

'Don't they trust us to know what we're doing out here? This ain't no kindergarten.'

'Maybe not,' Magadini muttered dryly.

Ziegler didn't speak for a moment. 'Is there anything we can do to keep them off our backs?' he asked eventually.

'We can do something that will keep Eisenhower happy now and maybe give us ammunition later if his successor comes on strong.'

'What?'

'We can look at ways of speeding the program. Maybe find a way to set an earlier launch date.'

'Jim, you know as well as I do that the only way to get a man up there ahead of the present schedule is to cut corners, take risks.'

'What corners, what risks?'

Ziegler stared at him in disbelief. 'Are you asking me to think that way?'

'Yes. Now, hold onto your temper.' Magadini went on hastily. 'Just think about it. The idea of putting the entire can of peas through a strainer isn't such a bad one. One, you'll be able to keep a careful eye on any areas where dangerous short-cuts might be made, just in case anyone tries something without telling the rest of us. Two, maybe, just maybe, you'll come up with something we can do without taking an unwarranted risk.'

Ziegler shook his head slowly. 'I'll give it some thought, Jim, but I sure as hell hope it doesn't start a fashion around here.'

After Joe Ziegler had left his office Jim Magadini re-opened the file he had been studying. It was the flight schedule for Project Mercury. The documents in the file were not highly confidential, almost everyone around the Research Center either had a copy or had access to one. What made Magadini's copy different was that he had scribbled notes alongside almost every part of the program. Notes which suggested ways of doing the very thing he had just assured Joe Ziegler wouldn't happen. Ways of cutting corners, of taking certain, carefully calculated, risks which would bring forward the date of the first sub-orbital Redstone-powered flight. From that he planned to determine a date for the first manned spaceflight.

Already he had an idea the date could be much more attractive than the present estimate of late 1962. It wouldn't be early enough to please Eisenhower, but it might very well keep his successor in the Oval Office sweet.

He remembered he hadn't asked Joe for his preliminary recommendations for the flight-sequence of the astronauts. It wasn't critical yet, but the sooner he had some names the sooner he could relay a little more information to the White House. He hoped that would help deflect any suggestion he wasn't doing all he could to fulfill the President's hopes.

Magadini felt a momentary pang of conscience at doing so much behind Joe Ziegler's back. Then he brushed the thought aside. Ziegler was Astronaut Liaison Officer and while that postwas important it was well below the level where heads rolled if Washington got angry.

He called his secretary and told her to send a memo down to Ziegler, then changed his mind telling the girl to deliver a verbal message the next morning. Some security had to be observed, after all.

When Joe Ziegler reached the parking lot he remembered he'd told Gary Herriman to meet him at Magadini's office. He turned to head back but saw the astronaut coming across from the library. He called out to him and a few moments later, having discovered that

Stella had Herriman's car, they were in Ziegler's Bel-Air heading into town and the first bar they saw.

For a while they talked desultorily, Ziegler unable to get out of his mind the conversation with Magadini.

'Time I was getting home,' Herriman said when Ziegler was about to call for another round of drinks.

Ziegler checked the time. 'Me too, I have a date I can't miss without giving myself a lot of grief.'

They went outside and Ziegler drove the astronaut back to the base and the Married Officers' Quarters. There were no lights on at Herriman's house and his car wasn't around.

'Stella not home?' Ziegler asked.

Herriman didn't answer for a split-second. 'Guess not.'

Ziegler stopped and let the other man out. 'See you in the morning,' he said. 'Get some rest, we have another big day tomorrow.'

Herriman grinned, looking more youthful than ever. 'That's new?'

'I know what you mean,' Ziegler said with a laugh.

As the car drove away Herriman turned and looked at the darkened house. He had no idea where Stella was but then he'd never given too much thought to what she did when he wasn't around, which was most of the time. He let himself into the house, made a snack and sat watching tv until, two hours later, she came home. She told him she'd been to a movie with one of the other wives and he believed her, refusing to think about the smell of stale tobacco on her clothing and of alcohol on her breath.

NORFOLK, Va.

As Joe Ziegler drove towards Paula's apartment the evening was already darkening. He caught a glimpse of flashing lights from an aircraft coming in low over Chesapeake Bay and felt an immediate pang of nostalgia for the days when it seemed he had spent more time in the air than on the ground.

He missed those high-flying days, especially the time he'd spent out at Muroc, before the base had been renamed for Glenn Edwards. Then there had been a spirit that now seemed absent from the Air Force. There was no longer the easy-going camerad erie of those happy, hectic nights at Pancho Barnes' place. There was none of the tension and excitement generated through trying something no one had done before high in the air above the Mojave Desert. He knew, in retrospect, he was conveniently forgetting the long hours of sitting around doing sweet damn all, about living conditions that made a flophouse seem welcoming, but for all that he missed those days.

Not that Project Mercury wasn't exciting and demanding, but it came to him at a different level now that he piloted a desk. He shook his head sadly then rebuked himself at such unaccustomed self-pity. Come to think of it, the astronauts themselves were not having it all their own way. Training, training, and then more training. Recently, some of the edge had been taken off their growing irritation with the granting of flying facilities. The machines they'd been allocated, two nailed-together F-102s, were not up to the standard they would have liked, but at least they were getting their tails off the tarmac and up into the air where they all firmly believed they belonged.

Ziegler sighed and tried to shake off the mood he felt settling over him like a dark and damp cloud. He parked outside Paula's apartment, switched off the engine and sat for a moment trying to psych himself into a better frame of mind. For reasons he didn't want to begin to explore, he wasn't looking forward to the evening with Paula. A recent run of missed dates was only part of it. Some of the dates they'd made hadn't ended as brightly as had once been the case.

As he let himself into Paula's dimly lit apartment he called out. She answered him from the bathroom, telling him to make drinks for them both. Ziegler poured out scotch for himself and gin for Paula, adding a generous splash of vermouth to her glass. He went into the small kitchen in search of ice. Several plates sat on the shelves of the icebox, each containing oddments of food, most of it looking anything but edible. In the months he and Paula had been regularly in each other's company he had grown accustomed to her sloppy habits and they had stopped irritating him. Now, however, he felt a mild twinge of annoyance but he pushed it aside, he had no business criticizing her life.

Ziegler carried the drinks back into the living room, sipping at his own before finding space for the glass on top of a pile of magazines which littered the tiled coffee table. Then he took Paula's drink into the bathroom, standing in the doorway for a moment, looking at her. She was stretched out in the bathtub, eyes closed, excessively foamy water covering everything except her head and neck and one leg which was draped artistically over the side. She looked for all the world like a supposedly candid camera shot of a Hollywood star from the past generation of movies and he knew that was precisely the effect she was striving for. The attempt was not altogether a success, principally because the state of the bathroom was as chaotic as the rest of the apartment. Discarded clothing lay wherever she had stepped out of it and every available flat surface was covered in bottles of various shapes, sizes and colors, most with stoppers removed and left lying alongside instead of being replaced. Towels lay in tangled heaps on the floor and everything was coated in a fine dusting of talcum powder which floated into the air at any movement in the room.

Paula opened her eyes. 'I thought you might wear your best uniform tonight,' she said.

'And risk spilling soup over it?'

Paula frowned, a tiny crease forming between her eyes. 'You never make an effort for me, anymore. Not even on my birthday.'

Ziegler groped for a change of subject. 'Where did you go today?' he asked after a moment.

'The Coliseum.'

'Alone?'

'No, the girls were there.'

'Which ones?' The question was not just idle politeness. He knew that Paula meant the wives of the men on Project Mercury and anything that impinged on them interested him.

'Oh, Rene Carpenter, Sylvia Magadini, Betty Grissom and Linda Simons. Linda got drunk.'

'Linda?'

'Yes, but it was just the novelty of being on the loose.'

Ziegler nodded. Paula was probably right. Linda Simons seldom went out alone or in the company of anyone other than her husband.

'She get home allright?' he asked.

'Sylvia drove her.'

'That's okay. How was Sylvia?' He hadn't seen her for some time and decided he would make an effort to get over to see her one day soon. He liked Jim's wife and her outspoken manner. The trouble with visits to the Magadini household was that the children behaved towards visitors in much the way he imagined the Apache had acted towards the first waves of the US Cavalry.

'She was fine, I like her.' Paula answered, unconsciously agreeing with Joe's opinion.

'Everyone else okay?' he asked.

'No one else got drunk, if that's what you mean.'

'That's not what I meant,' he said, surprised at her tone which was slightly more aggressive than usual.

'You never rest, do you. Can't you leave the goddamn program behind, just for a few hours?'

'I'm sorry,' he said, meaning it.

Paula stood up in the bathtub, the foam from the surface of the water clinging for a few seconds to her shoulders and breasts before slowly disappearing. She stepped onto the floor and bent to search for a towel that was still serviceable. She found one and handed it to Ziegler. 'Dry me,' she said.

He took the towel from her, simultaneously handing her the martini. 'I have a confession to make,' he said.

'What's that?' she asked, moving closer to him as he began to dab the towel gently on her shoulders.

'I'd forgotten it was your birthday today.'

'I didn't expect you to remember,' Paula said, barely concealing her disappointment.

He moved the towel lower, touching her breasts lightly then moving onto her waist, then her hips. He stopped the movement, drew her closer to him and kissed her gently. She responded, her body pressing hard against his. After a moment she disengaged herself and walked past him into the living room, her naked body arousing him as its dampness glistened in the lamplight. She went over to the drinks tray and topped-up her glass with neat gin. He followed her and poured himself another small scotch.

Paula looked at him over the rim of the her glass. 'Haveyou reserved a table?' she asked.

'No, this time of the week there shouldn't be too many people at Fitzgerald's.'

'Do you want to go now?' She paused. 'Or later.'

'Later,' he said, slipping off his jacket. Out of habit he started to fold it, then remembered the action usually caused a few critical comments. He let it drop to the floor and unbuckled the belt of his trousers.

'I like to do that,' she told him.

A few moments later they were in her bedroom, the already crumpled sheets becoming increasingly tangled beneath their moving bodies. For Paula, already warmly stimulated through her intake of martinis and the heat of the bath, the need for their usual foreplay was almost lost and she forced herself, skin still moist, up against Ziegler's tautly muscled body. Sensing her desire for quick satisfaction he shifted his position, allowing her legs to draw up on either side of him, then eased forward as she raised herself off the bed. She exhaled noisily as he entered her then drew breath in again as he began to move. Slowly at first, then, taking his timing from her, he gradually increased his speed of movement. The girl's legs lifted and tightened around him, her heels digging into his lower back and increasing the already insistent pressure of his forward movement.

46

'Oh, Jesus,' she said, softly, her breath warm against his neck. 'Jesus, Jesus, keep it going, keep it...now. Now.' Her back arched and her upward-thrusting body almost unbalanced Ziegler who, thankful that he did not have to restrain himself any longer, allowed himself to climax.

For several moments Joe lay still until, aware that his weight, fully relaxed as he was, must be uncomfortable for her, he rolled far enough to one side to allow her to move if she wanted to. She didn't stir.

'Another drink?' Ziegler asked.

Paula shook her head without replying. He swung off the bed and went through to the other room. Once there he hesistated. He didn't want another drink for himself, his drinking being relatively temperate. He stood for a moment, unsure why he had chosen to leave Paula in the bedroom.

'What are you doing?'

He turned to see her standing in the doorway. 'Just thinking,' he said.

'About me?' There was no artificial coyness in the question. Paula seemed to want to know.

'In a way.'

She came forward and put her arms around him, her body soft and still moist although now as much from a light filming of perspiration as from her bath. 'We've been together almost a year,' she said.

'Seven months,' Ziegler corrected her.

'It seems longer.'

'I'm not sure if that's a good sign or not.' he said lightly.

She snuggled her head against his chest. 'Very good,' she said. 'I feel as if I'm becoming part of you.'

Ziegler felt himself tensing but the constriction was more emotional than physical as he sensed what was coming next. 'A few minutes ago you were,' he said jokingly, trying to ease what he felt might prove a difficult moment.

'I don't mean just sex. We should be together all the time. We're good for each other.'

Easing himself out of her encircling arms Ziegler walked back to the bedroom with Paula following. Picking up his scattered clothing he started to dress, casually but quickly.

Paula looked disappointed. 'There's no need for that, we have time before we go out.'

'Time's one thing, ability's another.'

'You're the best I...there is.'

Ziegler let the slip go by. He knew Paula's past was far from pure and, come to that, he had his doubts about the present. There was nothing to be gained by talking about it. He didn't own her and he never would. Despite their sexual compatibility they had little in common. Apart from anything else there was a sixteen-year age gap that would become more and more of a problem with the passage of time.

'I'll fix my eyes,' Paula said and went into the bathroom.'Can you take some hours off tomorrow?' she called to him. 'We could drive down to Hatteras.'

'Sorry, I have a lot on. There's a new man on the team.'

'The girls were talking about him. Herriman, is that him?'

'That's right. Gary Herriman, Captain, USAF.'

'What's he like?' Paula's question wasn't entirely casual. To a lot of women, particularly those down at the Cape, astro nauts took on a sexual magnetism out of all proportion to their real physical attraction.

'Young,' Ziegler said.

Paula, still in the bathroom, missed the bitter inflection. 'I'd like to meet him some time,' she said, coming back into the room where Joe was waiting.

'Some time,' Joe agreed.

During dinner their conversation drifted over several topics, most of them forced. Joe wasn't sure why but something was hanging between them. He guessed it was probably Paula's irritation over his preoccupation with the program.

For Paula the evening disappeared in a haze as she continued drinking steadily. The following morning she felt awful and part of her state of mind was due to the knowledge that her affair with Joe was nearing its end. She wondered about Bill Simons but after a while accepted what she had known about him all along. Casual sex was one thing, a permanent relationship was something else. Damn them all. There had to be something wrong with any man who thought more about rockets and a flight into space than he did about real, lasting, earthbound relationships.

MOSCOW

The elevator stopped at the first floor of the department store and a very fat woman, clutching an old canvas shopping bag, wheezed out. The doors closed and the elevator continued upwards. Apart from the operator, a middle-aged man with one arm, there was only one passenger, a small, darkly attractive woman who was probably in her mid-forties but looked younger.

'Maisky was careless,' the man said.

'Perhaps, but at least he recognized the American, Lennox, when he looked back.'

'So what do we do about it?'

'It can be turned to our advantage.'

The one-armed man raised an eyebrow. 'How?'

Before the woman could answer the elevator stopped and the doors opened. A young woman with two small children peered in. 'Down?' she asked hopefully.

The operator shook his head. 'Up'.

The doors closed and the elevator resumed its upward journey.

'There are some problems at Baikonur,' the woman said as if there had been no interruption since her companion's question.

'What sort of problems?'

The woman made a dismissive gesture implying the nature of the problem did not matter.

The man looked at her inquiringly but learned nothing from her face.

The woman wondered for a moment if she should confide her thoughts to him but decided against it. The scheme was complex, far-reaching and dangerous. The fewer who knew about it the better. Still, he was her pipeline to Maisky and there was no one else who could handle an operation like this one promised to become.

'I want to see Maisky,' she said.

'Why?'

The woman's eyes sparked with sudden anger. 'You ask too many questions,' she snapped.

The one-armed man's cheeks flushed but he said nothing. The elevator stopped at the top floor of the store and for a moment there was silence. Then, grudgingly acknowledging his status, the operator pressed the button to open the door. 'Tomorrow,' he said. 'Here. Children's clothing department.'

The woman stepped out of the cage without a word or a backward glance. Only when she heard the doors close and the elevator begin its descent did she permit a tiny smile to touch her lips.

LANGLEY AIR FORCE BASE, Va.

Diana McNair closed the file and sat for a moment, one finger tapping gently against its green cover, her thoughts focused on the man whose life was set out, in sharp detail, in the file's pages.

Mike Leandros, sitting across the desk from her, took the opportunity to study her face. Leandros liked women and, usual ly, women liked him. Diana, it seemed, was an exception. He had sent out all the signals and had gotten none back in return. It irritated him, not because he needed another sexual conquest but because it spoiled an otherwise excellent record and dented his pride.

Diana McNair was slim and attractive. If her long black hair had not been pulled back tightly from her face she would have been even prettier, less austere. She focused her eyes on Leandros, then slid the file across the desk.

'Let's take another look at Captain Simons,' she said.

Standing up, Leandros replaced Gary Herriman's file in the top drawer of the fire-proof cabinet and took out another. He dropped it on the desk in front of her and leaned over, letting his arm brush against her shoulder. She didn't pull away but neither did she respond. In fact she didn't seem to notice his action. Leandros gave up for the moment and resumed his place at the far side of her desk.

'They're very different men,' Diana said, looking up from Simons' file.

'They all are,' Leandros said.

Diana nodded, her eyes dwelling on Leandros for a moment. It was a pity he had such a high opinion of his sexual attractiveness. He was good-looking, had black curly hair, and was tall and well-built but his self-esteem came between them. Not that it came between him and many other women, she knew. Leandros's reputation was no secret around Langley.

She pulled her thoughts back to the file on Bill Simons. Leandros was right. All the astronauts, despite many similarities of a physical nature or in relation to their careers, were different. Yet, a few minor problems apart, they all seemed well-suited for the task which lay before them. If any man could be suited for the extremes of physical and mental stress to which they would soon be subjected.

'He's very ambitious,' she said.

'He isn't the only one.'

'Ambition comes in different forms, with Simons it's combative.'

'Is that bad?'

Diana didn't answer for a moment. She was looking at Simons' file again because Joe Ziegler had asked her to make a reappraisal. She knew why Joe had made the request. A few weeks hence he would have to submit recommendations for the flight schedule – the sequence in which the astronauts would fly. She knew the importance of the schedule, not only to the success of the program but to the individuals concerned.

'It could be,' she said, answering Leandros's question. 'Suppose Bill Simons is faced with a problem. One where internal pressures conflict with the wisest course of action. Maybe at that moment, when he should back off, something drives him on. In any spaceflight there will be several moments like that, when delicate judgments have to be made. I'm not sure he's equipped to make them.'

'There's a cushion,' Leandros said.

'Cushion?'

'Ground Control. The name means what it says: they're in control.'

Diana nodded, still studying the file.

Leandros stared at the top of her head, wondering how she would react if she knew of his encounter with Stella Herriman. He hadn't planned it. Astronauts' wives were off-limits, the risk wasn't worth it but at first he hadn't known who she was. He'd met her in a bar along Ocean View Avenue, bought her a couple of drinks to add to several the barman told him she'd already consumed, then took her across Hampton Roads to a restaurant in Newport News. He'd driven her car because the only drunk driver he trusted was himself, and afterwards he'd been all set for an evening at his apartment when she'd told him her name. He'd gotten her back to a point a mile from Langley Base and left her to drive the rest of the way on her own. It had taken him an hour to return to where his own car was parked but it was worth the inconvenience. He hadn't acted out of any sense of duty or chivalry. He just didn't want to lose his job.

'Okay,' Diana said. 'Let's break for lunch.'

'Great idea, I know just the place.'

Diana glanced at her assistant, wanting to smile but maintaining a cool expression. 'Not together,' she said.

'Oh, come on, Diana. A lunch date won't hurt.'

This time Diana allowed a slight smile to appear. 'With your reputation, even something as innocent as a lunch date would blow up into an affair that would make Sadie Thompson's seem like kid's stuff.'

Leandros shook his head sadly. 'I can't figure you out. Any other...' He broke off and grinned. 'No, that's not the thing to say, is it?'

Diana nodded her head. 'You're learning,' she said.

'But I'm not giving up.'

Diana looked at him, her expression serious again. 'I think you should, Mike. I'm not about to change, certainly not with someone like you.'

He whistled softly. 'Boy, you don't pull your punches, do you?'

This time Diana smiled openly. 'I don't want you wasting all that wonderful talent on a lost cause.'

Leandros matched her smile. 'Okay, you're the boss.' He left to go back to his own office and Diana sat for a few moments thinking about him and the fact that his obvious sexuality did nothing to her. Unexpectedly, her thoughts drifted onto Joe Ziegler, at first not as a man but on his role in the program. It was hard to define. Less important than many of the engineers, less important even than most of the relatively low-level technicians in determining the success or failure of the program, he was nevertheless much closer to the heart of things than anyone else, the astronauts included. He was in tune with the men who would be putting their lives on the line come launch-day and he had the unenviable position of buffer between them and the large, often uncaring, bureaucratic machine NASA had become.

She wondered what made him tick and decided to look up the file on Colonel Joseph A. Ziegler. She realized her interest in him was beginning to take on a non-professional bent and felt her cheeks warm. She made an unconscious movement of her hand, brushing at her hair. It was a gesture Mike Leandros would have recognized.

Diana replaced Simons' file and cleared her desk before leaving the office. She had a lunch date and didn't want to be late as it was one she had arranged herself.

Regular meetings with the wives of the astronauts was a duty she had set herself soon after her appointment and they had become a standard feature of her monthly reports. A few years earlier, while working at CBS on a Rockefeller Foundation grant studying men and women under stress, she had observed the relationships of executives and their families. Those relationships, how decision-makers behaved at home, often played an important part in determining their performance at work. She had introduced her ideas at NASA and no one objected. Certainly the wives hadn't. Diana knew the regular lunch dates were merely tolerated by them, and so long as she kept the thing low-key and informal they would play along. This was one of the few areas in her work where being a woman was an asset. When she had first arrived on the project her sex had created a number of real disadvantages but her complete professionalism had won over almost everyone with whom she worked. In fact she had made an extra effort. At the beginning of her

52

career she had conditioned herself against attempting to prove things just because she was a woman. She bent her own rules at NASA because she didn't want to fail at a job she very much wanted to do well. Within a few months she achieved her aim, finding herself firmly established. Since then she had felt no further need to impress herself upon anyone. The recent enlargement of NASA had brought in several other psychiatrists who hadn't failed to note the prestige of Diana's job, but they didn't cause her any problems.

During lunch with Linda Simons and Jo Schirra, Diana was concerned by the young blonde woman's appearance. She had heard about her little drinking spree and the apparent motive for it. She'd checked; Linda was certainly pregnant but she doubted if the drinking was purely in celebration of the fact. There had been some talk around the base that Bill Simons regularly saw other women, not just down at Cocoa Beach (where "anything goes" was the rule) but here, around Norfolk, where secrets were not so easily kept. It could be that Linda knew, or at least suspected, something.

Diana turned her attention to Wally Schirra's wife, Jo. She was her usual self, cheerful and displaying no sign of the tensions that were undoubtedly building up around them all. More by accident than design the astronauts' wives had turned out to be a remarkably stable bunch. It was not by design, because selection had not followed the tradition of key corporate appointments by including an investigation of applicants' wives. Despite this, the results had been pleasing.

Among the eight there were no drinkers, no sexually undesirables, even the one rocky marriage had been stabilized. Maybe Linda had a hang-up but it seemed likely to be a small one. Diana hoped that the ninth wife, Stella Herriman, would turn out to be similarly free from problems.

Diana realized she had been thinking so much about the two women she was with that she had lost track of their conversation and tuned back onto their wavelength.

The two wives were talking about a party planned as a welcome to the Herrimans. Diana was pleased to note that Linda seemed to be brightening at the idea, almost like a child forgetting a toothache at the promise of a treat.

'Problem is, where do we hold it?' Jo Schirra asked. 'The base isn't the most cheerful place in the world.'

'We could try persuading the men to take us down to Cocoa Beach,' Linda suggested.

'No, the beach is strictly off-limits to wives.'

Linda frowned for a moment and Diana, sensing she might slide into depression again, spoke up with a suggestion. 'You can use my apartment. It's big enough, it's off the base and my neighbors are away until next year.'

'That's an idea. You don't mind?'

'Of course not.'

'Okay. Your place it is. I'll talk to the girls and work out the best date.'

'Who will you invite?'

'Just the nine men in the team and the nine wives.' Jo Schirra broke off. 'There's you of course, Diana. Can't leave you off the guest list if we're using your place.'

'That's okay. If you want to keep it just to astronauts and wives I don't mind.'

'No, of course you must be there. Just promise to leave your notebook locked away.'

'I promise.'

'We'd better have another man along, just to keep the numbers right.'

'I...'

Linda interrupted Diana. 'What about Joe Ziegler? We really shouldn't leave him out.'

'You're forgetting Paula.'

There was a short silence, then Linda laughed. 'Maybe Diana will appeal to Joe's intellectual side.'

Diana glanced from one to the other of her two companions. Apart from Linda's slightly impish grin there was nothing to suggest that the last remark had been anything other than an off-the-cuff joke. Nevertheless she felt her color rising and that, more than the remark, irritated her. 'Invite who you like,' she said. 'I don't mind, just so long as they don't stamp out their cigarettes on the carpet.'

The subject changed again and once more Diana let her mind drift away. Since the road accident which had cost the lives of her husband and their two-year old son she had kept away from as many social functions as was reasonably possible, given the nature of her work. She certainly had never actively involved herself in anything. Now, suddenly, she had offered her apartment for a party. Although the suggestion had come into her mind without forethought she had no doubt that her impulse indicated that at least a part of her was ready for more social contact. She realized that she was psychoanalyzing herself and laughed softly.

Jo Schirra glanced at her, eyebrows raised. 'What's the joke?'

Diana shook her head and stood up to leave. 'Nothing. Let me know what you decide about the party. I'll have to make sure the place is clean and all the empty brandy bottles are well hidden.'

After she had gone the other two women began talking about her, with genuine interest.

'I didn't notice any of the usual searching questions today,' Linda remarked.

'No. Her offer was unexpected too.'

'Maybe the shell is starting to crack.'

'It can't be easy,' Jo said. 'Building your life again after your man has died. Especially so young.'

'No, it can't,' Linda said and for a moment both women were very quiet, aware that their remarks, casual at first, had suddenly come unpleasantly close to home.

JOHNSVILLE, Pa.

For Gary Herriman it was like a dream, a fast-moving kaleidoscopic dream in which many things happened at once. He was fast catching up to the others and with a few more special training stints, like this one on Johnsville's Big Wheel, Joe Ziegler reckoned he would have made up for lost time. He was already beginning to feel like one of the team, no longer an intruder. Everyone treated him that way, from the broadly humorous Wally Schirra to the coolly correct Al Shepard.

He had become friendly with them all, but not yet close to anyone in particular. That was not a result of any wall thrown up against him but because he was still a little unsure of them. He had an impression about them all that they were each two men. On the surface the relaxed, almost jaded, seat-of-the-pants flyer; beneath that surface someone much less easy to know. John Glenn was like that: on top, an open friendly manner which charmed anyone he cared to; beneath, a shrewdly analytical brain which knew precisely why he was there, what he was doing, and where he was going.

Al Shepard, too, affected a withdrawn, distant manner which threatened to freeze out anyone unwary enough to treat him as anything less than a US Navy Commander. But, according to Wally, beneath that crust of ice was another man who came to life in places like Cocoa Beach.

The reason for the trip to Johnsville was an extra workout on the human centrifuge, the piece of machinery known to the astronauts as the Big Wheel. As usual Joe Ziegler was with him, along with Gus

55

Grissom who had joined the party although all nine astronauts were due there for a protracted training spell in October. Now he was being helped into the gondola on the end of the fifty-foot arm of the machine. The seat was plastic, contoured to his body, and he settled himself comfortably into it.

Two technicians, a young Texan, Harry Maxted and the short-sighted Specs, who had traveled up from Langley with the astronauts, were helping him.

His helmet was lifted over his head and carefully secured. Specs leaned over so he could be seen and held up a thumb, a signal which Herriman returned.

'Okay, Gary, we're about ready up here.' It was Grissom's voice coming over the headset from the control room.

'Ready down here. The boys are just closing up.'

The technicians eased the door of the gondola closed and began to snap the catches.

'Okay, Gary. Ready to go?'

'Roger, control.'

'Switch on.'

'Switches on.'

The controls of the Mercury capsule had been duplicated in the gondola down to the last switches and display. Even the sounds were the same, achieved by tapes of a Redstone launch being piped directly into the astronaut's headset.

The movement began, gently at first, then rapidly increasing. Simultaneously there was pressure, pressure against his body forcing his back against the plastic seat. As the gondola's speed increased still further, centrifugal pressure began to force Herriman's torso outwards.

'What is he up to?' Grissom asked the senior engineer in the control room.

'Five g's.'

'That today's limit?'

'No. We're going up to ten, maybe more.'

'Ten?'

'New instructions,' the engineer said noncommittally.

Grissom flicked the switch to speak to Herriman. 'Okay, Gary?'

There was a momentary hesitation before the astronaut could force out his reply. 'Roger, control.'

The pressure against Herriman's chest was fierce but not yet painful.

'Increasing speed.'

'Roger.'

56

The pressure increased and Herriman felt the flesh around his mouth tighten, his lips being forced apart to bare his teeth. He tried to swallow but the action conflicted with his breathing.

He reached a hand up to begin the repeat sequence of switching. A standard procedure, its object was to determine if man could function under multi-gravitational pressure. The rocket's roar echoed in his ears, the vibration and movement of the gondola matching it with such effect that for an instant he thought he really had been launched atop a Redstone.

His pulse began to echo in his ears, the pounding of blood gradually overwhelming the recording of the rocket. He was vaguely aware of a voice straining to make itself heard above all the other sounds. Somehow he knew it was Gus but, try as he did, he could not form words.

Slowly his vision began to deteriorate. Blackness formed all around him as he stared ahead into an endless, curving tunnel.

In the control room Gus Grissom was watching the section of the control panel where dials responded to sensors taped onto, or even inserted into, various parts of Herriman's body.

'I don't like it,' he said.

'He's okay,' the engineer told him.

'Then why isn't he answering?'

'Pressure against his diaphragm.'

Grissom looked at the engineer with frank disbelief. 'Jesus, the guy's in trouble!'

The engineer tapped the dials Grissom had been studying. 'Nothing there to worry about, Gus.'

The astronaut had an inbred mistrust of instruments which contradicted his instincts. 'Slow him down,' he snapped.

'Not yet.'

'Goddamn it, slow him down.'

The engineer glanced at the astronaut's set face, took in the forbidding gleam in his eyes and nodded slowly.

In the gondola Gary Herriman was still trying to force words out. When the speed began to drop he was at first unaware of any change, only that there was a marginal reduction in the tightness in his chest. He forced a word out.

'Say again, Gary.' Grissom said.

There was a muffled sound from the speaker in the control room.

'What did he say?' the engineer asked.

'Cut the rocket tape, I didn't catch it.'

The gondola was visibly slowing down and Herriman's vision improved dramatically. His breathing was almost back to normal and he realized the sound of the rocket was no longer in his ears. He heard Grissom's voice, sharp and clear.

'Okay, Gus. No need to holler.'

'You okay, Gary?'

'Fine. What did we reach?'

'Ten g's.'

'Ten? Must be my lucky day.'

Grissom looked out of the window as the gondola came to a stop. Across on the far side of the circular chamber he saw Joe Ziegler and decided to talk to him about the change in instruct   ions which had allowed Herriman to be pushed well beyond the six or seven g's expected when the Redstones were launched. Grissom thought about the word Gary had been trying to force out. He was pretty sure it had been a woman's name but it certainly hadn't been Stella's. He decided to say nothing about it. He had strict views on fidelity in marriage but he had no intention of either imposing those views on anyone else or getting caught in any cross-fire.

Down in the gondola Gary Herriman could feel his pulse returning to normal as an aide opened up the hood and started to release his straps. He grinned at Specs and Harry, allowing them to help him out and up onto the balcony. As he unstrapped and lifted off his helmet he caught sight of Joe Ziegler across the chamber and waved. Ziegler headed around the balcony and Gary waited for him.

'Okay, Gary?' Ziegler asked.

'Fine, Joe.'

Ziegler looked closely at the astronaut. 'You look pale, sure you're all right?'

'Sure. Just some residual dizziness.'

'Let's grab some coffee.'

Ziegler, Herriman and the technicians went out of the centrifuge chamber and headed for the dining hall. On the way Gus Grissom came out of the control room to join them.

'That was a hell of a run,' Grissom told them. 'Over ten g's during the last few circuits.'

'As much as that?' Specs asked.

Ziegler avoided Grissom's eye. During the past few days there had been small but noticeable changes in the astronaut's training schedule. He had asked Jim Magadini about them but had not received a satisfactory answer. The indication was that the doctors wanted to expand their knowledge of severe stress reactions and although he went along with it, Ziegler was far from happy.

'They're out to get you,' Specs added.

'Could be,' Ziegler said lightly.

'Maybe one of them served under your father,' Gus added. 'Trying to even old scores.'

Herriman grinned. 'I doubt it. The General's been in command of a desk for more years than he cares to remember.'

The chat drifted to the wrench that many bull soldiers experienced when the smoke of war cleared and peacetime entered their lives. Herriman didn't join in, feeling that to do so would be somehow disloyal to the General.

They crowded into an elevator, already jammed with people heading for the dining hall and conversation faded. On the lower level Grissom caught up with Ziegler who was a few paces ahead of the others.

'Someone pushing things, Joe?' he asked.

Ziegler glanced at the astronaut's face, noted the concerned expression but resisted the temptation to reveal his own thoughts. 'You know what the medicos are like, Gus,' he said mildly.

'Gary, all of us, we're supposed to be undergoing training. What happened up there was more like a survival test. I know we're all expendable but not here, not at the hands of our own goddamn people.'

'Okay, Gus, I'll talk to them, tell them to ease up.' Ziegler saw the others catching up and was relieved to change the subject. 'Have you fixed a ride back to Langley?' he asked Gus.

With Gary due to take a couple more test runs on the Big Wheel the next day, Joe was staying over along with Specs. Knowing Gus would want to spend no more time away from Betty than necessary he had suggested the astronaut hitch a ride with some flier going down to Langley.

Gus gestured towards the other technician who had come up with Specs. 'Harry's taking me back with him.'

The technician grinned. 'My brother-in-law had to leave his car up here on a trip last month. He stripped the ring gear and now it's fixed. I offered to take it back for him.'

'Could be expensive,' Specs said. 'Where did he have it fixed?'

'Over in Hatsboro, a repair shop two blocks along from Payne's Motor Lodge.'

'I know it. Good place. They do a fine job and don't charge an arm and a leg.'

As they stood in line for coffee, their conversation drifted from automobiles to the best route back to Langley. Joe didn't take part in the discussion, concentrating instead on what he had to do during the next few days. When he finished his coffee he pushed back his chair and stood up. 'I have a couple of things to do, Gus,' he said. 'I'll see you back at Langley.' He left the table, intent on pursuing the reason for the unexpected changes in the training program, although he had already formed what he was sure was the right answer.

Grissom watched the Astronaut Liaison Officer leave the dining hall aware of a tiny, nagging thought that Ziegler was being evasive. He shrugged the thought aside, not wanting to color his high regard for Joe.

Nevertheless, the thought was still buzzing around his head that evening when he and Harry took a cab down to the repair shop to collect the brother-in-law's Ford sedan.

By mutual consent they pushed on along Interstate 95 for some time before stopping for food and coffee as both wanted to reach Langley by morning. It was past midnight when they stopped and after the break Gus took the wheel while Harry slid down in the passenger seat, closed his eyes and slept. They were heading out of Baltimore, a couple of miles beyond the Laurel Race Track turning, and descending a steep gradient, when Gus felt the steering tremble. He had been driving automatically, his mind running over the thousand-and-one things still to be done on the program, but came alert in a flash. It wasn't fast enough. He felt the steering vibrate again and this time he lost control. He touched the brake pedal, felt no resistance and jabbed harder. Still nothing.

Grissom's movements awoke Harry who straightened in his seat. 'What's wrong, Gus?'

'More than a goddam ring gear,' Grissom ground out.

He leaned forward, peering along the beam from the headlights, and saw the right-hand curve quickening. He tried steering out of trouble but the Ford was hitting sixty, much too fast for the curve. He felt the off-side wheels lift, the tires lose their adhesion, and the sedan begin to roll. 'Hold on,' he snapped out.

Then, before he could say anything more, the Ford rolled further and he felt the seatbelt bite into his groin. Still traveling fast, now on its side and with tarmac just inches from Gus's left ear, the sedan reached the sharpest section of the curve but kept moving straight ahead through a white-painted fence. Gus felt something smash into the side of the car and was jolted sideways. His right foot caught under the gas pedal and he felt a sharp pain. Then he heard the windshield disintegrate and felt pieces of it strike his face along with a sudden inrush of air. Seconds later the car came to a stop, still on its side and Grissom, curiously detached, reached out and turned off the engine.

'I've known better landings,' he said. There was no reply and he eased himself sideways, managed to unfasten the seatbelt and tried to orientate himself. The car was lying on the driver's side which put him at the bottom. He couldn't figure why Harry wasn't lying on top of him. Fumbling in the dark, he gripped the back of the seat to pull himself up towards the passenger-door. Opening it he scrambled out and lowered himself down to the ground. As his weight settled on his right foot he felt the same sharp stab of pain and almost blacked out.

He leaned against the underside of the car, then forced himself to hobble to where the ground was illuminated in the splash of light from the headlights. Something was lying across the hood, partly trailing on the ground. Now he knew why Harry wasn't in the car and what had caused the windshield to smash. Before he went to sleep the young Texan must have released his seat belt so he could relax in comfort. It hadn't been a very smart idea. Grissom heard voices and realized people were coming to their assistance. Kneeling awkwardly he felt for a pulse in the other man's neck. There was nothing.

Moving into a sitting position he began fumbling at his shoelace aware that his foot was beginning to swell and was pressing against the confines of the shoe. His brain seemed to have compart-mentalized. One part was concerned with easing the pain from his foot; another was regretting the death of his companion; still another part was aware that if they hadn't changed roles it would be Harry sitting here with nothing more than an injured foot to worry about while he, Gus Grissom, would be stretched out dead. More practically, a further section of his brain was already calculating the effect this would have on his training schedule. Immediately after a buddy had died wasn't a good time to think things like that but Grissom was honest with himself. He knew that the effect this would have on his role in Project Mercury was a damn sight more important to him right now than anything else in the world.

WASHINGTON, D.C.

Bobby Kennedy looked up from the last of the documents spread across his desk. 'How did you get these?' he asked. One of the two men flushed but the other merely raised an inquiring eyebrow.

Kennedy sighed. 'Okay,' he said. 'Maybe it's best if I don't know.'

He arranged the papers into a neat pile then leaned back in his chair and hoisted his feet onto the corner of the desk. 'Question, what is Eisenhower going to do with this? Question, what will Nixon do with it? Question, what do we do with it?'

The man who had looked embarrassed earlier shuffled his feet, looked at his colleague, then at Kennedy. 'We're not even sure it amounts to anything,' he said. 'It's all speculation, guesswork.'

His colleague fished a pack of cigarettes from his pocket and lit one before entering the discussion. 'Guesswork or not, we know how important it could be to the President, either the one we have now or the one who'll be sitting over there in the Oval Office come January.' He pointed his cigarette at Kennedy. 'The answer to your first question is almost certainly, nothing. Eisenhower hasn't time to do anything whether NASA plays ball or not. Lyndon's moratorium demand will be official in a few weeks and that wraps it up. The answer to your second question is that, like us, Nixon can't do anything right now. All he can do is use this information if he makes it to the White House.'

'He won't.' Kennedy's interruption was forceful but the speaker ignored it.

'If he doesn't make it there's not a damn thing he can do to stop us making use of it. That brings us to your third question, what we can do with it. As of now I think we just sit tight. Later, if our man makes it to the Oval Office...' He paused, observed the gleam in Bobby Kennedy's eye and amended his state ment. ' *When* our man makes it we kick NASA in the ass and get the whole thing rolling.'

'You're forgetting we've been laying into NASA pretty heavily during the campaign.'

'Won't do any harm. The top brass down there will be pissing in their pants in case their appropriations are out. They'll be only too ready to see things our way.'

Kennedy indicated the papers on his desk. 'There's one thing we haven't talked about. Do we really need something like this?'

'Why not? A space spectacular won't do us any harm.'

'But why rush it?'

'We don't. We just push things along a little. Then, if we need to do it, we can.'

Kennedy nodded. 'Okay, I'll talk to Jack, tell him what we have and what the options are.'

'Do you want to talk to any NASA people?'

'Not yet. As soon as the election's over we'll talk, tell them we know what's been going on and make it clear that, big as they are, they dance to our tune.'

After the two men had left Bobby Kennedy stayed where he was, feet on his desk, thinking over the conversation, occasionally referring to the papers. A little while later he had almost convinced himself that Eisenhower had really cottoned onto something. In their enthusiasm to nail the administration for its incompetence and wastefulness with public money, they had very nearly overlooked the fact Eisenhower had spotted. That NASA was sitting on the biggest public relations bonanza ever conceived by the mind of man.

LANGLEY AIR FORCE BASE, Va.

'How's Gus?'

'Mad as a bear,' Ziegler said.

Magadini nodded 'I expect he is. How will this affect the flight schedule?'

'No need to make any changes just yet.'

A few days before Grissom's accident Ziegler had supplied Magadini with his list of recommendations for the sequence in which the astronauts would fly the Project Mercury missions.

Magadini nodded. 'Okay, for now we'll leave things as they are. But keep me informed of his progress.'

A full-scale physical of the astronaut had revealed that several small bones in his right foot had been fractured but, apart from minor bruising and a couple of slight lesions where flying glass had struck his forehead, there was nothing to cause serious concern. Grissom's participation in the training program would be inhibited but he had time to get back into line with the others long before the point he would be expected to fly a mission. There seemed no need to add to Gus' growing frustration by suggesting he might be moved down the list.

'Have Rogerson's people turned up anything?'

Magadini shook his head. 'No, just what anyone who drives a beat-up automobile risks. The goddamn thing wasn't roadworthy and hadn't been for a couple of years.'

Ziegler hid a smile. Magadini's own battered Buick was in the same league as the Ford that had cost Harry Maxted his life and injured Gus Grissom but this didn't seem a good moment to say so. The examination of the wrecked vehicle by NASA security had been routine as had the inquiry into why Ziegler had agreed to the trip. For his part, Joe had been highly self-critical. He should have taken a look at the automobile himself, not just assumed it would be a late model rather than a ten-year old heap barely fit for sacrificing at a Saturday night stock-car meet.

Magadini glanced at a typewritten list of names lying on the desk before him. 'If we do cut the number of Redstone flights to three then it will be Al, Wally and John.'

'Right'.

'John won't like that. If I was him, I'd be hoping for better.'

'Someone has to do it.'

The way the Mercury program had been planned every astronaut would pilot a sub-orbital Redstone-powered flight, then everyone would make an Atlas orbital flight. Recently it had been suggested, and all but finally decided, that there was no need for such elaboration. Three Redstones was now the likely number.

Magadini sighed. 'Okay. Now the Atlas flights. You're sure you don't want to move Gus out of number one slot?'

'No need. We have a year and a half. That's more than enough time for a few bones in his foot to heal.'

Magadini glanced up as if to comment but changed his mind. He resumed his analysis of the flight schedule. 'Bill goes in at number two Atlas?'

'Yes.'

'He's a hard-nosed sonofabitch.'

'All the tests put him up there with the others. He checks out technically, medically, every which way.'

'What does Diana think?'

'She worries about his habit of hanging on when other people might let go.'

'Maybe she's right to worry.'

Ziegler didn't answer for a moment. He had asked the psychiatrist to reappraise Bill Simons and her report had come back with a note that he might be better in a Redstone-powered sub-orbital than in an Atlas fully-orbital flight. During the rifle bullet-like Redstone shots the astronauts would just have to sit there but in the later flights they would have the facility of overriding Mission Control. Ziegler had thought carefully about her comments but eventually overruled them.

'Hanging on when others might let go can be an advantage just as easily as it can be a disadvantage,' he told Magadini.

'That sounds like seat-of-the-pants flying theory, Joe. This is the age of the computer and we should learn to live with it.'

Ziegler grinned. 'Maybe it is but I can't help being a lone voice against the crowd.'

Magadini shrugged. 'Okay, so it's Simons as number two Atlas. Then you're putting Gary in?'

'Yes, he's doing well. By the time we get to him, late 1962, maybe even '63, he'll be at least as good as the others.'

64

Magadini frowned at this second mention of the timing of the flights but again he didn't comment. He knew that to raise the matter of the pressure from Washington would anger the Astronaut Liaison Officer and he needed him on his side. Magadini had been at Huntsville for the dedication ceremony of the already fully functioning George C. Marshall Center where he had tried to get a few moments alone with the President. He hadn't managed it. For one thing von Braun had made sure none of the gentlemen from the press who were present could possibly overlook the fact that he was the man who counted down there. To reinforce that impression he stuck to the President like glue and on the one occasion when von Braun did leave Eisenhower's side Magadini had been neatly sidetracked by the President's aide.

Magadini had settled for what he could get which was to bend the aide's ear, telling him that White House pressure to speed up the program was unreasonable and unwise. He'd gotten a mixed reception. The aide didn't seem worried that the President wouldn't get what he wanted but at the same time he dropped in a very broad hint that after the election Richard Nixon would be making the same request. Magadini had been a lifelong Republican but he found himself hoping the Democratic candidate would win in November. Kennedy's lack of enthusiasm for the space race was well known and it just might be that cut-backs would be a welcome alternative to corner-cutting, risk-taking, publicity-oriented space spectaculars.

He turned his attention back to the flight sequence and together he and Ziegler ran through the rest of the names, spending most time over Deke Slayton's place and the problems that might arise if he had to be grounded. The decision to add Gary Herriman to the team had eased matters; grounding Slayton would not be detrimental to the program. That didn't stop both Magadini and Ziegler from worrying over how such a move might affect the man concerned.

'Thank God the final decision won't be mine,' Magadini said when they were finished. 'Deke's heart, Gus's injuries, Bill's over-aggressiveness, Gary still untried and untested.'

'They're not permanent problems.'

'Maybe not, but they don't help.'

'Look on the bright side, Jim. Think how it would be if we had to act like those big corporations. We'd be taking wives into our calculations and you know how that would complicate the final choice.'

'You're right, but it doesn't make this any easier.' Magadini reached for the telephone and called his secretary into the office. He dictated a memorandum to Bob Gilruth, setting out the proposed schedule with comments where he felt they were needed. Ziegler noted that, as always, Jim was fair and didn't put in anything based only on personal feelings or unsubstantiated impressions.

When the girl had gone Ziegler gathered together all the documents he had brought with him. 'How about coffee?' he asked.

Magadini waved a hand at the littered expanse of his desk top. 'Thanks, but no thanks. If I don't clear this before tonight it'll mean coming in tomorrow and Sylvia's made it clear that the next time I work Saturday she's heading for Ann Arbor. And she won't be back until we put a man on the moon.'

Ziegler grinned. 'Okay, message received and understood. I'll see you Monday.'

He went out of Magadini's office, waved a hand at Jim's secretary, who broke off from a telephone conversation to give him a wide smile, and went down the stairs to his own room. He filed away the papers he'd brought from Jim's office, locked all cabinets, cupboards, and drawers, and headed for the parking lot. He'd promised to take Paula to the beach over the weekend and, following yet another run of broken dates, he knew this was something he dare not cancel. In the car it crossed his mind that he was acting like Jim Magadini, as if he was married. He shook his head, that wasn't the way he had it figured with Paula and he was certain, despite occasional references when she was feeling low, that it wasn't the way she wanted things to go. Even so, he admitted, there had to be something else in his life apart from the program. If he didn't find that something, or maybe someone, soon then he might be in danger, once Project Mercury was over, of ending up like one of those empty rocket shells floating around in space. All used up, as lonely as hell, with no place to go but down.

1960
October 24 – December 22

NEWPORT NEWS, Va.

'Are you ready?' Gary Herriman called out. When there was no reply he crossed to the stairs to call again. As he did so the bedroom door opened and Stella came out to go into the bathroom.

'We should be moving,' he told her.

'Five minutes,' Stella said.

Closing the bathroom door she leaned against it, eyes shut, waiting for the dizziness to pass. It had started a couple of months ago, sudden moments when whirling blackness enveloped her and she could do nothing but hold on hoping it would pass. She hadn't told Gary because she knew his response would be to insist she saw a doctor and that was the last thing she wanted. A full physical would reveal things she didn't want anyone at NASA to know about.

She ran cold water into her cupped hands and splashed it onto her face. Then she brushed her teeth, following that with generous use of Gary's mouthwash. When she was sure the smell of alcohol on her breath was effectively concealed she opened the bathroom door. Gary was standing immediately outside, a look of mild concern on his face.

'We'll be late,' he said.

Stella nodded. 'Two minutes. You get the car, I'll be right down.'

In the bedroom she ran a comb through her long blonde hair, looking at herself in a full-length mirror. Up close the skin around her eyes was slightly puffy but, that apart, she didn't look too bad. She stepped into a pair of extra high-heeled shoes to lift her from her usual five-three to a height that made her feel less defensive. She turned to go down, then hesitated. Quickly, silently, she opened a drawer and lifted out the clothes she kept there. From underneath she took out a flat bottle of gin, half full. She unscrewed the cap and took a hasty swallow from the bottle.

A few moments later, as she slid into the passenger seat, she realized that the extra drink had sabotaged her efforts with the mouthwash so she kept her head averted from Gary as they drove off the base and headed towards Newport News.

The parties at Diana McNair's apartment had quickly become a regular affair. Most of the astronauts and their wives lived on the base where the houses were standard-drab and, externally at least, uninviting. The relative luxury of Diana's home had helped make the

69

gatherings successful and very few of the select group failed to turn up. Each party had a reason, usually contrived. The excuse for this one was that a couple of days before the astronauts had returned from a seventeen-day training stretch at Johnsville and needed loosening up.

When Stella and Gary arrived a few couples were dancing to an Everly Brothers disc. Two of the dancers were Joe and Diana. He was holding her close but hadn't spoken for some minutes. Diana had already learned that idle conversation was something that did not come easily to him but was aware this wasn't one of his usual silences. 'Problems?' she asked quietly.

Ziegler shook his head. 'Nothing that can't be handled.'

It was a stock answer and both of them knew it was really a polite way of saying, "Astronauts' business – keep out". She decided on a change of subject. 'Did you see the big debate, evening before last?'

Ziegler didn't need to ask what she was talking about. The Presidential candidates had been battling with one another on television and the fourth and last of their encounters had just taken place. Ziegler was an uncommitted Democrat but, party loyalties apart, there was no doubt who had been the more impressive of the two men. John Kennedy had conveyed an air of confidence and youthful enthusiasm while Richard Nixon had looked surly and tired. Ziegler had been interested to note that only Nixon made any reference to the space race and that was a hopeful comment hinting that the Americans were well ahead of the Russians. He didn't know where the Vice President had gotten his information but he had an uneasy feeling that not only was it untrue but it indicated the pressure wouldn't ease if Nixon won the race to the White House.

Ziegler had eventually tackled Jim Magadini about altera tions to the astronauts' training program but Jim fielded his questions casually enough, telling him that the changes were at the request of the space-medicine people. Joe had reluctantly decided not to push the matter further because to do so would have suggested he thought Jim was lying. It troubled him that he was beginning to think this just might be the case.

The thought was implanted in his mind with the discovery of signs that small, time-saving operations were being effected in various parts of the program. None of them, taken alone, amounted to very much, and even added together they couldn't have made more than a few weeks difference to the Atlas program and no difference at all to the Redstone schedule. But that didn't stop him worrying that some half-assed idea from Washington could, by the time it had worked its way down through several layers of NASA's administration, be taken by all concerned as official policy.

Ziegler didn't like the way politics was easing into the program but he knew there was no real way to keep it out. NASA needed taxpayers' money and it provided taxpayers with jobs. Then there were matters like national defense and prestige. But it didn't alter the fact that, come launch-time, it would be an astronaut with his neck on the block, not a goddamn politician.

'I didn't know I'd asked such a difficult question,' Diana said.

Ziegler realized he hadn't answered her remark about the tv program. 'I'm sorry,' he said. 'It started me off down a side-road. Yes, I did see the debates.'

'And?'

'I guess I'll stay a Democrat.'

'Me too. Lucky we're not political appointees like some I'd better not name.'

The record changed and Little Richard began belting out something at a tempo faster than Joe's basic dance steps could manage. 'Come on,' he said. 'I know when I'm licked. Let's get a drink.'

They joined Stella Herriman who was standing alone, sipping a ginger ale. Joe got a drink for Diana and for himself.

'Stella, another?'

'No thanks.'

'You won't get the party spirit on that,' he remarked.

'It suits me,' she said lightly.

They talked for a few minutes, Joe half-listening as Diana joined in to ask Stella about her childhood in West Virginia. He looked around the room pleased to see that, whatever the pressures and problems might be, everyone seemed to be having a good time. Then he corrected himself as he caught a glimpse of Linda Simons' face when, for an instant, thinking no one was looking at her, she let the party smile fall away.

Excusing himself from Diana and Stella he went across to her. 'Enjoying yourself?' he asked.

The smile switched on. 'Sure, great party.'

He stared at her intently for a moment then, seeing he was embarrassing her, grinned cheerfully. 'If they get back to my kind of music, how about a dance?'

Linda's smile became genuine. 'Sure Diana won't object?'

'Diana?'

'Oh, come on, Joe. Don't tell me you're immune.'

He frowned for a moment. 'I think I must be missing something.'

71

Linda laughed. 'I think you are.'

He looked across to where Diana was still talking to Stella and shook his head slowly. 'I really never thought about Diana that way.'

'Then you're just as bad as all the rest. All work and no play.' Linda's smile suddenly faded. 'No, not all. Some of them have too much play.'

'You don't begrudge them Cocoa Beach, do you?'

Linda shook her head. 'Of course not. It's just, well, Cocoa Beach is one thing. Right here in Newport News, or across in Norfolk, that's something else.'

'I take it we're talking about Bill,' Joe said.

Linda touched her lips in a childlike gesture, looking suddenly both frightened and unhappy. 'No, Joe, I shouldn't have said anything.'

'But you did.'

Linda glanced nervously across the room and, following her look, Ziegler saw Bill Simons talking to Gary Herriman and Scott Carpenter.

'I'm sorry, Joe,' Linda said. 'Forget I said anything.' She turned and deliberately went across to join Rene Carpenter.

Ziegler stood for a moment, unconscious of the talk and music all around him. He knew about Bill Simons and his liking for women but had assumed he kept it quiet and discreetly well away from his own front porch. It appeared he was wrong about that. He shook his head. It could be awkward. For one thing it really wasn't any of his damn business and to say anything to Bill would probably do more harm than good. But keeping quiet wouldn't help Linda. He decided he'd have to compromise. Say nothing to Bill but have a word with Diana, asking her to take any steps she could to alleviate some of Linda's obvious distress.

'When does the world end?'

He turned to see Diana McNair had left Stella to join him. 'Maybe tomorrow, maybe never.'

'Is that supposed to be a happy thought?'

'For happy thoughts you have to apply in writing.'

'How's Linda?'

He hesitated. 'I think she might have a problem.'

'What?'

'Not here, we'll talk about it tomorrow.'

'Tomorrow's Saturday.'

'So it is. All days are starting to look alike to me.' He remembered Linda Simons' remarks about Diana and looked intently at the psychiatrist for a moment. To his surprise she flushed. On impulse he said, 'Saturday or not, meet me tomorrow. We'll have lunch, talk a little shop, then find some way to spend the afternoon that has nothing to do with NASA, rockets, astronauts, politics, or any damn thing connected with our penny-ante space project.'

'That sounds a tall order.'

'We can only try.'

Diana smiled. 'Okay,' she said. She hesitated, wondering whether she should ask if his affair with Paula Blake was over. Then she decided not to mention her. One invitation to lunch, and an afternoon together, didn't give her any rights to inquire into his private life.

'About Stella,' she said, looking for a change in subject.

'What about her?'

Abruptly Diana shook her head. 'That can wait too,' she said. 'In case we run out of subjects to talk about tomorrow.'

Joe grinned. 'I don't think that's likely,' he said lightly.

Diana wasn't sure if she wanted to raise it tomorrow or any other time. She had noticed, despite the impression Stella liked to convey that she either didn't drink or drank only sparingly, that there was a strong smell of alcohol on her breath. Apart from the smell there were other things which could have been signs of a dozen complaints including simple tiredness but it would be as well to check them out. Provided she could find some discreet way to do it.

Raised voices over in one corner of the room drew their attention and Diana was happy to let Stella drop from her thoughts for the moment.

The argument turned out to be on the relative merits of foreign sports cars and home-produced varieties. Bill Simons, as argumentative as ever, was condemning American sports cars in general and Shelby Cobras in particular. The fact that Scott Carpenter had recently acquired a Cobra and clearly regarded it with pride and joy served only to give Simons more enthusiasm for his criticism of its road-holding, acceleration, and everything else he could think of.

'Tell me something better,' Carpenter said, some of his amiability deserting him in the face of Simons' unnecessarily vigorous denunciation.

'Anything made in Italy, for a start. Maserati, Ferrari, you name it, they make 'em better.'

'Fiat?' Gus Grissom asked, with a wink at Carpenter.

'I'm talking about sports cars, damn it.'

'How about the British?' Gus asked, not at all put out by Simons' irritability. 'Wally's Austin-Healy's a hell of a fine car.'

'Pretty but no guts,' Simons said dismissively. He glanced up at

Ziegler who had drifted over with Diana. 'Like that MG of Paula's, Joe. Doesn't hold the road worth a damn, does it?'

'It's okay,' Ziegler said, conscious of not wanting to talk about Paula in Diana's presence, a feeling which puzzled him a little.

'What did you drive in your Edwards' days?' Gus asked Joe.

'Me? I had a beat-up Buick, even worse than Jim Magadini's, with a bored-out engine, raised suspension and tuned like an F-86.'

The conversation shifted slightly to contrast fast car driving with flying and an artificial dividing line appeared between the astronauts who had flown combat missions over Korea and those who were too young to have served in that, or any other, war. Ziegler avoided getting involved. His own record in Korea was exemplary but he didn't want anyone thinking he was pushing himself and his achievements.

He saw Gary Herriman wasn't participating and joined the younger man. 'Fast car driving not one of your relaxations?' he asked.

Gary grinned. 'Never saw a point to it. All that happens is, you get some place you probably don't want to be that much faster.'

'Glad to hear it. That's the way I think now and it's beginning to worry me. I figured it as a sign I was getting old.'

Ziegler glanced at the others, pleased to see none of them showed any symptoms of tension and stress. Even Gus appeared to be cheering up despite the fact that his foot was in plaster and still giving him some pain. His gentle delight in baiting Bill Simons showed that, so far, he wasn't taking the break in his training routine to heart. In fact, he'd put it to good advantage and was beavering away in the library, expanding his already formidable grasp of the principles of navigation.

'How long is it to the next test-launch?' Gary asked Ziegler.

'Three weeks from Monday.'

'Should be interesting.'

'Of course, you haven't seen one yet, have you?' Ziegler said. 'Well, we'll all be down there. It's a full-scale dress rehearsal this one. Everything except the astronaut. Him apart, it will be exactly the same as a Redstone sub-orbital.'

'Can't wait. It'll be good to see what we'll look like from below when all the tests and rehearsals are over.'

Ziegler grinned at the enthusiasm even though it was pitched at an almost boyish level. Then he pulled himself up. He had to stop thinking this way. There was no reason to put an artificial age barrier between himself and any of the astronauts. As far as Gary was concerned they had more things in common than not. He began to run through the procedures they'd be following down at the Cape with Herriman listening eagerly.

For the young astronaut the spectacle of the launch was something he eagerly wanted to witness first hand. He'd watched a few on tv and he'd seen a couple of movies during training but the full sound and smell and sight of the real thing would tell him much more about his own probable reaction when his turn came.

The party broke up around one and everyone left together in a barrage of slamming car doors and over-revved engines. Alone, Diana tidied the apartment although not much was needed as the wives, grateful for the use of the place, saw to it their hostess was never left with a real mess to clean up. Her thoughts were centered on the following day and the time she would be spending with Joe Ziegler. She was annoyed to find she was looking forward to it like a teenager approaching her first date.

On their way back to Langley, Stella and Gary Herriman said very little. He was still thinking about the test-launch from the Cape and she was preoccupied with trying to figure how to get away for a full weekend without arousing Gary's suspicions. She had finally persuaded Mike Leandros that his reluctance to sleep with an astronaut's wife was pointless, especially as she wasn't about to put up any struggle. She had no special feelings for him and he certainly wasn't the only man around but he was convenient and he was attractive. Neither quality was essential, but they helped.

Joe Ziegler was almost home when his thoughts fastened onto Bill Simons' comments about the road-holding qualities of Paula Blake's sports car. It could have been merely a generalization, but what if it wasn't?

Linda Simons had noticed the same thing as Joe, only she had picked it up right away. And, unlike Joe, she had no doubts about the origin of the remark. Bill must have been making it with Paula and that was really getting too close to home. The Simons lived just a few blocks from Diana and they reached the house before Linda had found a way to bring up the subject without provoking what she feared most, an out and out confrontation with her husband.

In the house Bill showed no signs of wanting to go to bed, instead he dropped into an armchair and picked up a magazine.

'Aren't you tired?' Linda asked.

'No, you go on up. There's something in here I want to read.'

'I'll wait, there are a couple of things I need to do.'

He shrugged and turned his attention to the magazine leaving her to find some excuse for staying in the room. It hadn't always been like this but, she had recently forced herself to admit, the happy days had been a long time ago. Certainly things had deteriorated since Bill's assignment to Project Mercury but even before then there had been warning signs, if only she had been able to read them.

She had always known he would go far. That was apparent from the aggressiveness he'd shown when they were in high school together. But she hadn't expected, in those early days, that he would choose a career in the armed services. That had been difficult to accept because it meant leaving Akron, something she had never imagined doing. The enforced separation from home town, parents, and friends had not been easy but she accepted it uncomplainingly. She loved Bill and if it was what he wanted, that was what she had to do. But now she could see that that was when the problems began. He took to the new life, the frequent changes of home, the irregular working hours, no constant circle of friends, but she didn't. She had wanted a home in which they could live for the rest of their lives, a fixed social circle, her parents close at hand. In fact, almost everything she wanted was the opposite of what Bill's career gave her. She didn't complain, didn't even build up a quiet resentment. But recently she had sensed the gulf widening between them. On one or two occasions she had even noticed him looking at her with an expression in his eyes suggesting both mild irritation and dissatisfaction.

'Joe and Diana seem to be hitting it off,' she said, eventually deciding to try raising what was troubling her.

Bill looked up from his reading. 'Seems like it.'

'I guess the thing with Paula is over.'

He shrugged. 'I guess so.'

'I haven't seen her around much recently,' she said. 'Have you?'

Bill lowered the magazine and looked at her levelly. 'Why should I?'

Linda swallowed hard, then looked away. 'No reason.'

For a moment there was an awkward silence before he turned his attention back to the magazine. Linda stood, looking down at him, uncertain what to say or do next. She felt tears forming in her eyes and quickly went out of the room and up the stairs.

Bill let the magazine drop to the floor and sat for several moments staring unseeingly at the wall. After a few minutes he went into the kitchen to make coffee and it was almost an hour before he followed Linda to bed. She was lying with her back to him and he slid between the sheets trying not to disturb her, more through a desire to avoid any contact, either verbal or physical, than out of regard for her rest.

In fact Linda was not sleeping and she remained wide awake until long after Bill's breathing told her he was asleep. Perhaps the baby would make a difference, she told herself. With a child their life would take on a new dimension and they would be drawn much closer together. Later, as she began to drift into much-needed sleep, the thought came into her mind that she was placing too much hope upon the restorative powers a new-born baby would bring to their strained marriage. Fortunately for her peace of mind, that thought had vanished by morning leaving her with the hope that a child might yet be their salvation.

HICKORY HILL, Va.

The children considerably outnumbered the adults and their voices, raised and occasionally shrill, filled the crisp, cold air. It was just one of a string of family gatherings the Kennedys had been having since Jack's election victory. Not that these gatherings were purely family or social affairs. None of the adults who attended, family or not, were outside the American political mainstream. They couldn't be outside it. The Kennedys were a political family, always had been and always would be. That was why now, as the youngest children played some complicated game on the sloping lawn and the older children were busily arranging a party and dance for the following evening, the two oldest Kennedy brothers were shut away in Bobby's study at the back of the house.

For the moment their conversation was desultory, almost idle. They hadn't had many opportunities to talk about the election without others being present. Then, gradually, inevitably because they were Kennedys, the talk came around to plans for the beginning of Jack's first term.

Jack's wish to appoint Bobby to the post of Attorney General was currently causing a few problems, not least among them his brother's unenthusiastic response. On the desk, opened at its editorial, was the *New York Times*, but both men were avoiding direct reference to the lead writer's blast against the hint Jack had given reporter Bill Lawrence. Despite the flinty view the editorial had taken of the younger Kennedy, Jack was still set on his proposal and was now deliberately pushing their conversation into one area where he felt Bobby might come up with some much-needed reorganization. This was among the secret services and Bobby soon showed he had strong views.

'There have to be wholesale changes,' he said, pacing the floor. 'The FBI and the CIA act like enemies. You'd never believe they're both on our side.' He shook his head in despair. 'As for Hoover, he'll have to go.'

'Edgar won't be easy to pry loose. He's been clinging to the rock for so many years he's almost a part of it.'

'Clinging to the rock? Under it, more like.'

'Maybe, maybe. It doesn't alter the fact that he'll be a difficult man to dislodge.'

'He's had too many years of Presidents going to him. From here on he's going to be coming to the President.'

'I'm not sure that's a battle I want to fight right away.'

'You don't need to fight it, Jack. I'll fight it for you.'

John Kennedy grinned at his brother whose pacing increased in speed as his enthusiasm for the hunt quickened.

'The CIA needs a shake-up, too,' Bobby went on. He crossed to the large desk in front of the window to pick up a sheet of paper. 'I got this from a friend.' He paused, looked at his brother, then grinned. 'At least he's a friend now. I don't know how long he's known about this but he waited until the election results were in before he brought it to me.'

'What is it?'

'An intelligence report from a CIA operative in Moscow.' He glaced at the paper to refresh his memory. 'A man by the name of Oscar Lennox. He picked up some information on the timing of the Russian spaceflight program.'

'When?'

'That's the whole point. He filed this report on August 25 and as far as I can see nothing, not a damn thing, has been done about it.'

The President-elect shook his head. 'No, I mean when are the Soviets planning to make their first manned spaceflight?'

Bobby handed the paper to his brother. 'May next year. April if things go well.' He resumed his pacing of the room and his remarks about the government's intelligence agencies, seemingly unaware that he no longer had his brother's attention.

For John Kennedy the space program was a problem area. During the election campaign he had been openly critical of the colossal drain the program caused to the nation's financial resources. Although the matter had never been a significant issue between himself and Nixon there were moments when he was tempted to let it become one. In the end he had settled for letting his views permeate NASA and various areas of government interested in the program, particularly the military. He knew that his lack of enthusiasm for the space program in general, and Project Mercury in particular, would set up a few effective echoes in certain quarters and that could be no bad thing. But now that the election was won, he was beginning to think about the potential for building international esteem.

'I told this new friend of the administration to let the Moscow office know we're watching them,' Bobby was saying. 'I've also told them that this subject is now top priority. Nothing else about the Russian space effort gets filed at the back of the shelf.'

John Kennedy nodded his head, only half listening. 'There could be some mileage in the space program,' he said.

'Go on.'

'Prestige, national and international. A lot of it, if we can show we're beating, even matching the Soviets.'

'Right now we're behind. We've known that for some time but if this report from Moscow is correct then we're even further back than we thought.'

'But what if we caught up with them? Took the lead. Looking further ahead than what NASA's trying to do now, looking ahead to the Moon. That could mean a great deal to us.'

Bobby sat in a wing-backed armchair his heels resting on the edge of the seat, knees thrust high under his chin. 'I think I might be ahead of you,' he said.

Briefly he outlined to his brother the result of the surveillance on Eisenhower's aide and the people he'd been dealing with.

'I hate to admit it,' Jack said, 'but I think Ike was on to something. We've done a lot of talking about the new frontier we're facing. A frontier that can give something to every man, woman and child in this country. Maybe not directly but certainly indirectly everyone can benefit. I haven't given it all the thought I should have but my guess is that we'd have to search pretty damn hard to find anything more symbolic of that frontier than a man in space.'

'A man on the moon would be better.'

'A man on Mars would be better still but that isn't the point. Mars is unattainable during my administration. It will be touch and go for a man to be on the moon inside the next eight years. No, the only thing we can be sure of achieving, inside the time we have, is a man in space.'

'Only the Soviets look like they're getting there first.'

'Which brings us back to Ike trying to boost NASA into getting things done faster.' The President-elect reached over and picked up Oscar Lennox's report. 'We need to move quickly if we're going to beat them.'

'We can lean on the same people Eisenhower talked to. Webb, Gilruth, von Braun, Magadini.'

Jack Kennedy thought for a moment. 'Let's talk to Magadini first.'

'He can't do much unless the others go along. They have more clout.'

'You're right but if we start with him we can discover how feasible the project is before we talk to the big boys.'

'Okay, I'll get him up to Washington next week.'

'No, do it faster than that. Tomorrow's Sunday, get him over here.'

'What do we want from him?'

'First, we want a full survey of the program, what can be done, where we can speed things up, where we can save time. The same things Eisenhower asked for but now working to a specific timetable. If the Soviets are planning on a launch late in April then we want a target date no later than mid-April.'

'Okay but he's going to holler. He'll claim it isn't possible.'

'So, before he comes back with the result of his survey, talk to a few people who won't have the same restricted vision. Put it up as a theoretical exercise and see what answers you get. The Chiefs of Staff can give you the military's angle; talk to MIT and, so long as you're careful, there's no reason why you shouldn't talk to a few people at CalTech.'

'But completely under wraps.'

'For now, yes.'

'No public statements?'

Jack Kennedy hesitated. 'We have a couple of months before the Inauguration. We could work something into the address. Tell the nation what we expect from NASA. That way we can shift failure to deliver onto their heads.'

Bobby's mouth widened in a grin. 'That's devious enough to have come out of Tricky Dick's mind.'

'My bet is he had something like this lined up anyway.'

'Okay, I'll call Magadini and tell him to come over here tomorrow,' Bobby said. He paused for a moment. 'You know there's always the possibility of getting someone else to do this for us. Magadini's an appointee of the last administration. We can put a new man in.'

'No, not yet. It might come to that but for now it could prove counterproductive. Magadini, Webb, Gilruth, all the senior administration people down there, have their fingers on the pulse. It could take weeks, months, for a new man to break himself in. No, for the moment we stick with who we've got. Anyway, we can't move anyone out until January.'

There was a tentative knock on the study door and Bobby went across to open it. Two of his children stood there. 'You promised you'd play football with us,' the smallest one said.

Bobby glanced at his brother. 'Have we finished?'

'Just the call to Magadini.'

'Okay,' Bobby said to the children. 'Two minutes.'

He dialled a number, spoke softly, then scribbled down a telephone number. As he dialled Magadini's home he glanced through the window into the garden where the voices of the children could be heard.

'Maybe we should both play,' he said to Jack. 'There won't be many opportunities for playing touch football once we get to Washington.'

Jack grinned. 'Not with real footballs.'

MOSCOW

Oscar Lennox did not like ballet. Come to that, he wasn't particularly interested in any art form. Music, painting, theater, all left him unmoved. The fact that whatever else Moscow lacked it more than made up in the arts meant nothing to him. Although many of his colleagues at the Embassy filled their time happily enough, for him the Russian winter was proving an unalleviated desert of boredom. When he was obliged to put in an appearance at a cultural event to help maintain his cover, it was an agonizing experience. Tonight he was entertaining a West German newspaperman who had done a couple of favors for the Ambassador. The newsman, Helmut Groetchen, seemed grateful and if he was aware that the cultural attaché was really a secret ser   vice agent he was too circumspect to say so.

In reality, Lennox knew his cover was something of a joke. None of his opposite numbers in the Russian secret service seemed to have any doubts about the dual roles he and his colleagues played. That was something Lennox had learned very soon after his arrival in Moscow at the beginning of the year. It was almost as if it was a game between the two sides. Complex, costly, sometimes dangerous, but a game nevertheless. Occasional moments, like the scramble over the roof that had led him to valuable information about the Russian spaceflight program, came under the heading of dangerous. The entire setup through which information was gathered and distributed, however, was merely bureaucratic and correspondingly costly.

Overriding everything was the feeling of acute, mind-bending tedium. Like the never-ending performance of Swan Lake he was watching now. The Bolshoi Theater was packed, the audience

81

watching and listening with rapt attention. Lennox had sat through the first act with a simulation of interest but now, as the evening dragged on and on, he let his mind and his eyes wander idly.

It was then that he noticed a man three rows in front of him and a few seats in from the center aisle. From his seat, well to the right of the auditorium, Lennox had a good view of the man's profile and he was certain it was one of the two men he had overheard talking about Baikonur. It was the small man with dark, intense eyes and the smart suit. He checked the people in the seats to the man's immediate right and left but the big, burly, untidy individual was not with him this time.

Lennox knew their names now. The big man was Ivan Stepanovich Kropotkin who, despite his rough appearance, was assistant to Sergei Korolev, chief architect of the Russian space program. The small man, now avidly watching the dancers on the stage, was Mikhail Aleksandrovich Maisky who was almost precisely what Lennox was, a spy. Much higher up in the Russian secret service than Lennox ever would be in the CIA, Maisky had spent twenty of the past twenty-five years in a dozen countries, mostly in the West. His recent, six-month long sojourn in Russia had puzzled a lot of people but, until Lennox's chance encounter, no one had any idea what he was working on.

After Lennox's report had gone to Washington there had been a long period of silence. Then, a week ago, a message had arrived at the Embassy giving the first hints that changes were in the wind following the election of John Kennedy as President. An unofficial warning, stemming from the same individual who had leaked Lennox's report to Bobby Kennedy, had reached Moscow. The warning urged all CIA operatives to shape up and insure that future reports were marked in such a way that they wouldn't disappear from sight at the Agency's Langley headquarters. There was also a strong hint that any further developments on the Lennox report should be regarded as top priority. As a result, Oscar Lennox had suddenly found himself in line for promotion. It pleased him greatly but it hadn't quite made up for the Moscow winter.

Although there had been moments when he thought it would go on forever, Swan Lake eventually came to an end and Lennox eased out of his seat, taking care to keep his face turned away from Maisky. Despite his recent upgrading in the eyes of his superiors Lennox occupied a lowly place in the CIA's Moscow detachment but he knew that Russian thoroughness meant every Embassy face, CIA or not, would be known to every Russian agent.

In the side aisle he made a hasty and, he was sure, unconvincing

82

excuse to his companion, claiming a sudden return attack of some old and unspecified ailment. Groetchen seemed not to mind, saying he wanted to go backstage and try for an interview with one of the leading dancers.

Lennox collected his topcoat from the crowded cloakroom and as he left caught a glimpse of Maisky putting on his own street clothes. He wasn't alone, a woman was with him. A few minutes later, as Maisky and the woman stood patiently waiting in line for taxicabs, Lennox was able to get a good look at her. She was small and dark but not in the same intense way of her companion. She smiled a lot, her manner alert and vital. Lennox guessed her age at forty-plus but she could have been younger. Lennox had come to the theater by car but he stayed where he was until he was sure the couple would not change their minds about waiting. When they were close to the head of the line he slipped away, returning in his car just as Maisky and the woman climbed into a cab.

Twenty minutes later he was watching as Maisky paid off the driver before following the woman into what appeared to be a large apartment building.

When Lennox entered the building he found two elevators, one with its door open, the other stopped on the eighth floor. He took the waiting elevator up to the tenth floor, walked down two flights of stairs, leaned against the wall, lit a cigarette and assessed the layout. There were twelve apartments and after he had walked slowly along the corridor and back again he reckoned he could eliminate more than half of them. Five of the twelve had a television set switched on to a soccer match, from one came the sounds of a party, in another a baby was crying. Of the remaining five, two were silent and in darkness. That left three possibles, one of which was silent but with lights on, the other two with music playing from either a radio or a record player. He checked those three again and this time from the one that had been silent came the sound of orchestral music. Lennox might have been tone deaf, but after three hours he knew Swan Lake when he heard it.

One of the dark and silent apartments adjoined the one from which Tschaikovsky's music was drifting and he decided to take a chance. The worst that could happen to him was a speedy deportation, something to which he wouldn't object strongly, anyway. Fumbling for a credit card, which had lain unused in his wallet since his arrival in Moscow, he slid it into the space between the door and the jamb. It took him longer, and he was far noisier, than his instructor back at headquarters would have liked, but eventually he had the door open at the cost of a piece of twisted plastic money. Inside the apartment he made a hasty reconnaissance to satisfy himself he was alone, although only the deaf could have slept through his fumbled entry.

The layout of the two apartments was such that the living rooms adjoined. He put his ear to the wall but the music was so faint he knew he would never make out voices. Drawing back the drapes he peered through the window into the darkness. Each apartment had a small balcony and opening the window he stepped out into the cold night air. Only inches separated the balconies of the two apartments and by leaning over the rails he was able to position himself so that he could listen against the other window. This time he could clearly distinguish voices, a man's and a woman's.

He stayed where he was, leaning awkwardly across the two sets of rails for two or three minutes growing steadily more uncomfortable in the biting cold. Then, to his relief, the music stopped and he could hear the voices distinctly. There was no doubt that he had the right place. He recognized Maisky's voice from his previous clandestine surveillance of the Russian.

'......a matter of tempo,' Maisky was saying. 'Scherchen takes it too slowly, Hollreiser too quickly. Mravinsky was exactly right. That shcwed in the way the dancers responded to him.'

'A good conductor should always take his tempo from the dancers, not the other way around, that is the secret.'

'Perhaps, perhaps. Still, you enjoyed it?'

'Of course, it was delightful and even more so because you were there with me. It is a long time since we went to the ballet together, Mikhail.'

'Twenty years. We were both very young. It was Nutcracker, remember?'

Lennox didn't hear a reply and guessed the woman had nodded or silently indicated her recollection of that past event.

'How are things with you now?' the woman asked.

'Better,' Maisky answered.

'It must be difficult after so long in other countries. Have you adjusted?'

'Almost. You know what it is like when those whose experience is limited only to what they have learned behind a desk are brought face to face with men, or women, who have spent years in the field. Theory against practice. It's an age-old conflict. I don't suppose it will ever be satisfactorily resolved.'

'But your relationship with Kropotkin and Korolev must have helped.'

'Certainly but only since the pressure started to build up in Kazakhskaya.'

'All going well there?'

There was a short silence and in it Lennox could hear his own pulse. The names of the two men, Korolev and Kropotkin, and mention of the region in which Baikonur Cosmodrome was situated meant he might be onto something important. Then, to his disappointment, he heard music start again in the room and guessed that the Russian was taking an elementary precaution. Fortunately, when Maisky began to speak again he was standing much closer to the window.

'They are so far ahead of their original program that May and April have already been discounted. March certainly, even February is a possibility but Korolev is digging his heels in. He wants more tests and, I have to admit, his reasoning is sound. Khrushchev doesn't agree with him so there is little doubt a compromise date will be the result.'

'What is Kropotkin's estimate?'

'Somewhere between March 10 and 20. Any earlier than that and Korolev would make difficulties, sick as he is.'

'How bad is he?'

'Deteriorating but he's receiving the very best treatment.'

'So, March it is.'

'Yes.'

'I'll prepare our publicity for March 10. Will the Chairman want to see it?'

'Of course. That's one of his failings. Too interested in imposing his personality on matters that are the result of the work, the effort, of others.'

'Careful, Mikhail.'

There was silence from the room for a moment before Maisky spoke again. When he did Lennox guessed he had gotten everything of value he was going to get because the Russian had begun to talk in general terms about the Kremlin's bureaucracy. No names were mentioned and with every other word indistinct Lennox decided to get out while his luck held. He eased back over the balcony's railing, went into the apartment and silently closed the window. Leaving the apartment he closed the door as quietly as his damaged credit card would allow. He went down the stairs to the seventh floor, then called the elevator and rode the rest of the way to street level. Within minutes he was on his way back to the Embassy, pleased, excited, the boredom of Swan Lake and even the cold and discomfort of the past half hour forgotten.

In the apartment Lennox had forcibly entered the lights were on and Maisky was carefully checking the room. When he had looked everywhere, including the little balcony, he went back into the other apartment where the woman was lying on a soft-cushioned couch, listening to a recording of the Nutcracker Suite, her eyes closed.

'Well?' she asked, without opening her eyes.

'He did as we expected.'

'No imagination.'

'The CIA isn't noted for the imagination of its agents. Lennox's use of the fire escape at Kropotkin's house suggested he would not be averse to doing something similar here.'

'It was fortunate you recognized him at the house.'

Maisky shrugged. 'I was lucky. It compensated for my carelessness.'

'You assume he heard everything that night?'

'I have to,' Maisky said tersely. There was an uncomfortable silence for a moment before he went on, his tone suggesting he did not want to spoil the mood of elation he was experiencing. 'In any event, what happened at Kropotkin's, unfortunate though it could have been, provided the lever we need.'

'It is dangerous, Mikhail.'

'Everything I do is dangerous.'

'But this is complicated, extremely so, and you know as well as I that complexity breeds failure.'

'Perhaps. We shall see. After all, we cannot guarantee that the Americans will react as we want them to.'

'But we proceed on the assumption they will,' the woman said.

Maisky nodded. 'Yes. Then we can take good advantage of all your efforts in Villingen.'

The woman smiled. 'So long ago. What was it? Five, almost six years. I never really thought anything would come of it, certainly nothing as big as this.'

Maisky poured himself a drink, then carried the bottle to the couch and refilled the woman's glass. 'Luck, other people's mistakes, and weaknesses. That's what our world is built upon.' There was more than a touch of bitterness in his voice.

'It's the way things are, Mikhail. Look on the brighter side. After this is over you, all of us, will be held in very high regard. The Chairman...'

'We don't know how the Chairman will react when he learns what we are doing.' Maisky interrupted.

The woman swung her legs off the couch and sat up, looking at him, her face serious for the first time that evening. 'We cannot go on forever without letting him know,' she said.

'I know that. But you know what he's like. He'll want to control, direct, meddle. This is something too complex for amateurs.'

'Mikhail. Calling Khrushchev an amateur is not the way to keep your job. Or your head.'

Maisky gave her a smile that did not reach his eyes. 'The truth isn't supposed to hurt.' He topped up his drink and sat beside her on the couch. 'We will tell him when everything is set up, when we know the Americans are hooked and that the plan is proceeding.'

'And until then?'

'Until then, we keep our little secret.'

The woman shrugged and drained her glass. 'Very well. You're the expert.'

'Another drink?'

'When do you go to America?' she asked, holding out her glass.

'When there is nothing left to do here and our people over there need my help.'

'Do you want me to come with you?'

Maisky shook his head definitely. 'No. The risk that you would be recognized is small but it is unwarranted. Anyway, you'll be more useful here.'

'I have my uses then?'

'Of course,' Maisky said before he realized she was laughing at him. 'Am I taking things too seriously again?' he asked.

'It is serious but I think we have talked enough for one night.' She reached out to turn off the lamp by the couch.

Maisky didn't need further encouragement and moments later they were naked, their bodies responding to physical urges which had no foundation in love or even affection. There was no room in their lives for either but the need for occasional sexual release had to be accommodated. Maisky had little need to do anything. The woman took the lead, as she always did. It never failed to surprise him that someone as slight, as girlishly attractive as she remained, could be so dominant when it came to sex. Still, he reminded himself, her talents had their uses, especially when she turned them to the service of their country.

He let her pull him down to the floor and straddle his body, her still taut stomach muscles drawing him up into her. Later, when he had climaxed and the woman was using her hands and mouth to raise his interest once again, Maisky found his mind could not quite leave Oscar Lennox. The American would be back at the Embassy by now, perhaps he was already encoding his report for transmission to Washington.

Within days, hours maybe, moves would be made that would precipitate the action he had planned. When it did, word would come back from his eyes and ears in NASA. Then he could set up the final stages, head for America and prepare for the greatest coup of his career. He remembered the woman's comments about Khrushchev and fleetingly felt a slight chill. Among the Chairman's least desirable traits was his unpredictability. What would happen if he didn't respond the way Maisky hoped?

'Mikhail.'

He looked up to see the woman regarding him with angry eyes. 'What?'

'Am I wasting my time?'

Pushing thoughts of the plan and the Chairman from his mind, he reached up for her. 'No,' he said. 'You're not wasting your time.'

CAPE CANAVERAL, Fla.

Glancing across the runway Scott Carpenter nudged Wally Schirra. 'At least Gary's enjoying all this. If I have to stand here much longer I won't be able to get this smile off my face for a week.'

Aircraft had been flying in for two days, some big, some small, every one disgorging pressmen, Senators, Representatives, top military brass, anyone who could be termed a VIP even by fairly loose standards. And most of them were greeted by astronauts all ready with a smile and a handshake.

The occasion was the latest rocket test – only this was to be no ordinary test. This was the first time a Mercury capsule would be launched on top of a Redstone rocket, just the way the real thing would happen come the first sub-orbital manned flight – all except for the astronaut.

Gary Herriman heard Carpenter's remark and grinned. 'I am enjoying it, this is the first time I've been this close to a real live rocket launch.'

'Well, let's all just hope, and maybe pray, that it's an improvement on the last time we had the brass down here,' Wally said.

'Amen', said Joe Ziegler who came up just in time to catch the last few words.

He glanced across the flat sand and scrubland surrounding the landing strip. The scene was far from the Florida landscape the real estate and holiday home brochures proclaimed to potential residents. Almost no trees grew between where they stood and the dull gleam of Banana River separating Merritt Island and the Cape from the mainland. The few buildings rose, plain and forbidding, anonymous in pre-stressed concrete. The scene evoked in Ziegler's mind the events Wally had referred to. Back at the end of July the same deal had been set up. VIP's shipped in by the planeload, flags flying, speeches, hurrahs, excitement. Every damn thing except a team of cheerleaders. Which was just as well, because there hadn't been anything much to cheer about. It had been a lousy day, rain and low cloud – not at all the kind of thing visitors expected of Florida in July. The gloom of the day was lit when the button was pressed and the rocket's motors ignited. It was an Atlas rocket that time, complete with a Mercury capsule, the very thing that would be used on the first fully orbital flight. Everyone stood there, eyes glued to the rocket as it lifted up and turned its nose to begin its fast flight towards the distant horizon. Everyone had their mouths open ready for the big cheer. But before they could get a peep out there was a bang you could have heard all the way to Washington. The goddamn thing had exploded.

The disaster had caused a lot of head-scratching, manylong and sleepless nights, and it had caused more than its fair share of red faces. Since then everyone had just about convinced himself that it couldn't happen again, but no one was prepared to risk antagonizing the fates by suggesting it might.

So, once again, the big build-up, the whole deal, grandstands for the VIPs, astronauts greeting them on the runway, flags waving in the breeze. Like before, everything but a team of teenage lovelies high-stepping it across the tarmac.

'Okay,' Ziegler said. 'Time we were on our way. Let's get in the bus.'

Gary Herriman didn't object to the gentle ribbing his enthusiasm for the occasion had generated. He *was* enjoying himself and he didn't care who knew it. The bus carrying the astronauts bumped gently across an uneven patch of sand as it moved up onto the road which ran, arrow-straight, to the Cape. 'Any of you guys feel like a wager on this one?' the driver asked.

No one answered and the busdriver turned his head to find himself on the receiving end of a glacial stare from Al Shepard. He became suddenly very concerned with his driving and after a few moments the air warmed and the astronauts began conversing again. The incident, fleeting though it was, told Gary Herriman something he was only just beginning to learn about his fellow-astronauts. Among themselves they could, and often did, speak disrespectfully about the capsules that would house them; the rockets that would boost them; the engineers who would insure nothing went wrong; the doctors who drove them insane with their needles and probes and damn fool questions. But when an outsider stuck his nose in and made a crack about Project Mercury, they closed ranks.

A half hour before launch time the astronauts joined the other spectators on the rapidly filling grandstands, their appearance triggering off an appreciative ripple of applause and more than a handful of sidelong glances from the females among the VIPs and newspaper reporters. The mysterious cachet was working, just the way it worked among the well-proportioned, eagerly available, young women who had appeared out of nowhere one day and now could be found all along Cocoa Beach ready for anything and anyone. Especially those who wore the magic, invisible, badge – astronaut.

The countdown for the first Redstone-Mercury launch was well under way and soon all eyes were dragged around to focus on the tall, sleek, distant shape of the rocket, white against the sky.

Someone, probably buried deep in one of the faceless concrete buildings, was wired up to the public address system and the countdown echoed across the grandstand where all conversation had ceased.

'....seven..six..five..four..three..two..one..we have ignit-ion.'

They did have ignition and there was noise and flame and vibration to prove it. Only the rocket didn't lift off the launch pad.

The Mercury capsule sitting up there, tiny and frail, seventy feet or more above the ground, quivered but that was all. The capsule, identical in every respect to the one which would house the astronauts, differed from previous launch-test payloads in one important respect – it was heavier. The difference wasn't great but it was enough to retard lift-off so that the two umbilicals, instead of separating simultaneously did so an immeasurable moment of time apart. That fleeting instant wasn't much but it was enough to tell the abort sensors in the rocket that something was wrong. The rocket's engines were snuffed out automatically but, bad as that was, worse was to come. The countdown procedure had progressed far enough for the capsule's own automatic systems to come into operation.

The capsule's system was time-controlled, not altitude-controlled. According to time-lapse it should have been more than fifty kilometers above ground. That was where it was supposed to jettison the escape tower. So it did so.

In the sudden stillness that had fallen over the Cape, more than five hundred pairs of eyes stared skywards as the pencil-slim, fragile escape tower rose through the air. Someone at the back of one of the stands, apparently thinking this was what was supposed to happen, started to applaud. The patter of hands echoed for a few seconds before tapering off into embarrassed silence.

The fiasco wasn't quite over. The launch tower's electronic gadgetry realized it was much closer to the ground than it was supposed to be and it instigated normal recovery procedures. A beacon light began to flash and a parachute broke out.

As the escape tower drifted gently earthwards there was a sudden rattle of feet on the grandstand as first one, then another, then a mad rush of engineers, administrators, even astronauts began. Someone would have to talk to the press, explain to the assembled VIPs. Someone would have to do it but there was no point in hanging around to volunteer for the job.

After all the hours spent smiling at VIPs none of the astronauts would have thought it possible ever to reshape their faces into gloomily despondent contours. But, three days later, and the inquest over, they had achieved the impossible.

'There's one good thing about it,' Gus Grissom said.

'What's that?,' Gary Herriman asked.

'One of us could have been up there. Just think about it. Having 78,000 pounds of thrust kicking you in the ass might not be the best feeling in the world but I'd trade that any day for having to come down and try explaining what happened out there wasn't any of my damn fault.'

Gary nodded slowly. For the first time since he had joined Project Mercury the full extent of the responsibility of the tasks before them registered in his mind. There were a hundred thousand people who could make an error and there were, correspondingly, a hundred thousand things that could go wrong. But let any one of those things happen during a manned flight and it wasn't the engineers who'd be blamed, it wouldn't be the technicians, or the doctors, it wouldn't be the designers or the administrators. It would be the man who would be sitting up there, who would get all the credit if it went right, and all the flak if it went wrong.

NORFOLK, Va.

Joe Ziegler switched off the tv set and swore angrily. The debacle at the Cape had provided the media with more ammunition than they'd had for a long time. Coming when it did, within a few days of

John Kennedy's election victory, he had an uneasy feeling that press and tv reporters would not be alone in seizing the opportunity to attack NASA.

He had planned on staying down at the Cape for a few days, feeling the need for some relaxation, but a telephone call from Paula had brought him back on a flying visit. On the telephone Paula had sounded drunk and Joe's first inclination was to stick to his original plans and deal with the problem, whatever it was, when he got back. Then, deciding he was being unfair, he changed his mind and flew up to Langley.

He'd called Paula from his apartment and she told him she would come over. She had sounded much calmer, not drunk and he began to think he had changed his plans unnecessarily.

He heard her arrive in the small parking lot which served the building, the squeal of tires and brakes indicating that her driving technique hadn't altered. He opened the door of the apartment, reflecting that it seemed to have been quite some time since he had seen her. Her first words, when she reached him, suggested she'd been thinking along similar lines.

'You still live here, then,' she said, unmistakable aggression in her voice and manner.

'Of course.'

'Of course,' she mimicked. 'Christ, Joe, why do you have to be so calm about everything?'

He hesitated, not sure for the moment how to respond. Then he grinned at her. 'Okay, Paula, if it's fight time let's get at it but first, how about some coffee?'

She didn't return his smile but some of the aggression left her and she dropped heavily into a chair. 'I know you're busy, Joe but these past few weeks I've seen even less of you than usual. Is it deliberate?'

Ziegler looked at her for a moment before replying. He didn't believe he had consciously avoided making contact with her but equally he had felt no compulsion to do so. He'd managed to find a few hours free time during recent weeks and had spent most of them with Diana McNair. Their meetings had all been in public places, he wasn't sure if that was accident or design on her part, but he hadn't pushed things. He was conscious, all the time he was with Diana, that if a relationship was to develop between them it would be very different from that with Paula, or any other woman he'd known since his marriage had broken up during the Korean War.

'Well?' Paula asked.

He decided there was no point in being evasive. 'I don't feel the same way about you, Paula,' he said.

'Why, Joe? We had fun, we're good in bed. Why?'
'I can't argue with that. We did have fun and the physical side of things was always good. It's just that I don't think I want the relationship to become permanent. I get the feeling that's the way it was drifting.'
'Would it be so bad if it did become permanent?'
'I don't think it would work.'
'Is it me or would the same thing apply to any woman?'

He suddenly thought of Diana and realized that his statement didn't necessarily apply to all women but now wasn't the time to say so. 'The same would apply to anyone,' he said quietly. 'It certainly isn't you.'

Paula looked at him steadily, then smiled. 'Ah, well, never would've worked. You're married to those damn rockets. You all are. A girl can't beat that kind of competition.' There was very little hint of bitterness in her tone and he recalled the telephone conversation which had brought him back from the Cape. Whatever had been behind the call, it seemed to have faded.

'Why did you call me?' he asked. 'It sounded as if the world was about to end.'

She laughed without much humor. 'I was pretty low, things suddenly looked black.'

'And now they don't?'

Paula hesitated. She had been feeling unwell for a few days and was over two weeks late with her period. She couldn't really believe that she was pregnant but couldn't rule out the possibility. With Joe away she had called Bill Simons, the only other possibility if she was going to have a baby, and for once their telephone call routine hadn't worked. Linda had come on the line, had recognized Paula's voice, and became hysterical before Paula managed to convince her that she really wanted to talk to her, not Bill.

Later, Bill had called and told her, angrily, not to try to get in touch with him again. He would call her. She could hear the finality in his voice and knew that, anyway, she couldn't push him. She knew the adulation the public bestowed on the astronauts. If it became known that one of their heroes had gotten two women pregnant at the same time, one his wife, the other a casual girl friend, it would make bad trouble for him. So, she had backed off, had a few drinks, become really depressed, and called Joe.

Now, as Joe had sensed, things didn't look quite so grim because when she woke up that morning one of her problems had vanished. She wasn't pregnant.

'No,' she said. 'I'm feeling better.' She paused for a moment, looking up at him. 'It's over, isn't it?'

He nodded. 'I think it is.'

Standing up, she moved close to him. 'Unless you have anything else planned for today we could say good-bye in style. After all, like I said, we are good in bed.'

He kissed her gently. 'I'm tempted but maybe it would be best for us both if we just say good-bye in the usual way and leave it at that.'

She nodded, a look of mild resignation on her face. 'I always knew you were too much of a gentleman for me,' she said.

She turned to leave then hesitated, looking at him uncertainly.

'What is it?'

'I don't know if I should tell you this but...' She broke off, then started again. 'I know a few things about your astronauts that maybe you should know.' She held up her hand as if to stop him speaking. 'No, I don't mean just gossip, things that could hurt them.'

For a moment Ziegler didn't answer, unwilling to encourage her but at the same time concerned in case she did have something important to say. 'You'd best tell me,' he said.

'Bill...Bill Simons, is unfaithful to Linda. Maybe that isn't troubling him any but I'm not so sure about her.'

'Anyone else?'

'Gary Herriman'

'Gary?' Now don't tell me he's tom-catting around.'

'No, of course not.' Paula smiled. 'He seems a nice guy, the sort every girl should have for a brother, if nothing else. No, I think he might have trouble with Stella. I've seen her around a lot. She drinks heavily and she's man-crazy. I know I'm no angel but she seems to be making a career out of it.'

'Any man in particular?'

'I've seen her with several but mostly with Mike Leandros.'

'Leandros? Diana's assistant?'

'The same. You know what he's like. Well, maybe you don't, but he has quite a reputation around Langley as some kind of superstud. As far as I know he's always steered clear of astronauts' wives but he seems to be making an exception in Stella's case.'

'Anyone else?' Ziegler asked, unhappily aware that he was being disloyal to the nine men for whom he had such high regard.

Paula shook her head. 'Nothing too serious. You know what goes on down at Cocoa Beach better than I do.' She smiled. 'After all, that was where we met.'

He nodded. 'Okay, Paula, thanks. I'll take care of it, you needn't...Well, don't...'

'Come on, Joe, there's no need to spell it out. I won't talk to anyone else if that's what's on your mind.'

He nodded. 'Thanks.'

She turned and went out of the apartment, leaving the door open behind her. Crossing to the door he stood for a moment, listening to her steps fade down the stairs, then the MG start up and take off in a screech of tires even louder than she usually managed to create. Slowly, he closed the door, the latch engaging with a sharp, final, click.

For some minutes he wandered around the apartment, thinking about Paula and the small but rapidly filling hole her departure had made in his life. Then his mind turned to her comments about Bill Simons and Stella Herriman. He wasn't too worried over Bill. No one expected the astronauts to be pure as snow but he would check into it, just in case a bad rift was developing between Bill and Linda. He knew something like that could create a storm, if allowed to get out of hand.

Stella Herriman was a different matter. He hadn't detected anything in Gary's behavior which suggested he was aware that his wife was either a drinker or was playing around. Maybe Paula was exaggerating but he had to be sure. And if Mike Leandros was involved he'd need to do something about that, too. If a psychiatrist was taking advantage of his professional standing it could have serious consequences.

He decided to talk to Diana McNair about her assistant. As he reached for the telephone he recalled the thought he'd had earlier. The idea of a permanent relationship with Diana didn't alarm him at all. He wondered how she would feel about it.

Moments later, when she answered his call and he experienced a sudden uplift in his spirits, he was left with no doubts about what his feelings would be.

NEWPORT NEWS, Va.

'Are you sure?' Diana asked.

Ziegler shook his head. 'No, I'm not. But I think we have to check it out. If Leandros is playing around with Stella Herriman it could cause us a few problems.'

'Us?'

'The program.'

'Is that the way you see it, Joe? A problem for the program. Isn't it a problem for Stella and Gary, too?'

'Of course it is,' Ziegler said, feeling defensive and irritated that he should.

When he had called, Diana suggested he come over to her apartment. He'd agreed, pleased at the opportunity to see her alone there, something that hadn't happened before. Now the chances of their having a pleasant evening together seemed to be diminishing and he wasn't sure why.

In fact, Diana was angry at the suggestion that her assistant was breaking the rules, written and unwritten, by seeing Stella Herriman for reasons which were apparently anything but professional. She wasn't questioning the accuracy of what Ziegler had said, even though he wouldn't tell her the source of his information. She knew Mike Leandros well enough to accept there was a good chance it was true. Her mood stemmed from a combination of anger at Leandros, annoyance with herself for failing to do anything about her suspicions about Stella and irritation with Joe for putting Project Mercury ahead of people. Or more accurately, she corrected herself, his habit of putting the Mercury astronauts ahead of other people. She didn't like his casual assumption that astronauts were extra-special human beings. It wasn't good for anyone, she felt, least of all the astronauts themselves. They were human, had human failings, and to pretend otherwise could have far-reaching consequences.

'Okay,' she said. 'I'll see what I can find out. I won't talk to Leandros right away. First I'll see Stella and try to get some indications about her sex life and her drinking. What about Gary? Will you talk to him?'

Ziegler hesitated. 'I'll keep this in mind when I'm with him but for the moment I don't think I'll say anything.' He saw Diana's expression change and went on hastily. 'No, I'm not evading the issue. I can't go to the guy and say, I hear your wife's sleeping around and hitting the bottle, can I?'

Shaking her head Diana managed a tiny smile. 'No, I suppose not. But if it turns out your information is right, or even partly right, you'll have to tell him.'

'Maybe,'

'Not maybe, Joe. Look, I know that all this is hypothetical but if Stella does have these problems then Gary ought to know.'

'I said, maybe, Diana. At this stage, I'm not prepared to go further than that.'

'Damn it, Joe, he isn't a god. None of them are. There's nothing to be gained by treating them that way.'

'Avoiding telling a man about to undergo hazardous duty that his wife is a drunk, or is laying one of his medical advisers, can't be classed as treating him like a god.'

They stared at one another for a few moments before Ziegler grinned. 'Anyway, like you said, this all might be a crazy hypothesis based on nothing more than idle gossip.'

For a moment Diana was tempted to observe that he was the one who had brought up the subject but then recognized the olive branch and smiled. 'Maybe we should have a drink.' As she poured out drinks she asked him how he saw the state of readiness of the astronauts.

'Physically, you mean?'

'Mentally too.'

'I thought that was your department.'

'No, I meant as far as knowing what they need to know. I'll tell you when one of them goes crazy under that workload.'

'Don't worry, we have no problems. Sometimes they frighten me, the amount they've squeezed into their minds. They all have specialist areas where you'd expect them to know a lot, but every last one of them seems to have become obsessed with a desire to know everything.'

'Is that good? I mean, aren't there some dark and secret corners about which the less they know the better?'

'You mean, if they don't know what can go wrong with a rocket they won't worry about it. It doesn't work that way, Diana,' Ziegler said, taking a sip from his drink. 'When I flew combat missions over Korea I knew every nut and bolt in those F-86s. I knew what every change in temperature would do to the thermals in the hills above Huichon, and I could have navigated my way back home blindfolded in zero visibility fog. The way I had it figured was, the more I knew – the better my chances. I guess they see things the same way, only...' He stopped, thoughtful.

Diana looked at him curiously. Involuntarily she found she was making a comparison between Joe and her husband, Lew. To her surprise the comparison neither hurt Joe nor did it evoke the pain that usually came when she recalled the tragedy that had taken the lives of Lew and their infant son.

'Only, what?' she prompted.

'Only, maybe I would have stood more chance, coming down north of the 38th Parallel, than they will if someone, somewhere, hasn't done his job right.' He looked at her, his expression serious. 'That includes you and me, Diana. We have our part to play. If we get something wrong, send a man up there who isn't one hundred percent then it could be our fault. It may be his head on the block, but it'll have been our fuck-up.'

'I have a feeling this is getting too serious,' she said lightly. 'I think a little relaxation is called for.'

Joe smiled. 'Is that a medical opinion?'

'Partly that.'

'What's the other part?'

She felt herself coloring slightly. 'Partly a woman's view of what is in danger of becoming a world where "men only" signs are too much in evidence.'

'I'm not too sure what that means.'

'It means there's room in all your lives for women. Maybe some of you should remember that.'

'They all have women in their lives,' he said, uncomfortably aware that he had avoided telling Diana the other part of Paula's comments, about Bill Simons. That was because he'd begun to suspect Paula was involved with Bill and anyway he didn't want his own relationship with her to come into any conversation between himself and Diana.

'Does that include you?' Diana asked.

He hesitated.

'I know about you and Paula,' she went on. 'But you haven't seen very much of her recently, have you?'

'No.'

'I know that because you've been seeing a lot of me. Even if we have been studiously careful not to let emotions get in the way of a good working relationship.'

'What does that mean, for chrissake?'

Diana's color heightened even more. 'Do I have to spell it out? Or have I just put a foot into my mouth all the way up to the knee? Is what I'm starting to feel about you entirely one-sided?'

Joe shook his head. 'No, it isn't.'

'I'm not embarrassing you, am I? Not rushing you.'

'I have a feeling you are but I don't think I mind. In fact, maybe that's just what I need. Someone to take charge.'

'That is something I do not believe. You have control of everything you do. Maybe too much.'

Crossing the room Joe took her in his arms. 'In that case, let's stop all this talking, analyzing, soul-searching, and worrying about other people.'

'Why don't we,' she said.

She led him into her bedroom and very slowly, and very gently, almost dispassionately, they undressed one another.

It was the first time Diana had made love to another man since her husband's death. More than that, it was the first time anyone had so much as kissed her, but there was no strangeness, no awkwardness, no shyness. Everything Joe Ziegler did to her, his warmly gentle kisses, the touch of his hands and lips on her breasts and thighs, his slow and tender entering of her body, all seemed as natural, and as right, as if they had been together countless times before.

For Joe, making love to Diana was a revelation. The affair with Paula had become a series of automated responses bringing with them little more than physical release. What was happening to him now was different. Different even to the way things had been with his wife back in the days when their marriage had seemed as if it would last forever.

Afterwards, lying together on Diana's bed, their bodies touching but, for now at least, satisfied, it crossed his mind that, unless he was reading the signs all wrong, he was in love. He turned, raising himself sufficiently to look down at her.

'I have a feeling I should say something very serious about now,' he said.

'So do I,' Diana said. 'But, maybe you should wait.'

'Why?'

'We both have a lot to do. You said so yourself. We have responsibilities to a lot of people.'

'What about our responsibility to ourselves?'

'Careful, talk like that in front of Jim Magadini, or any of the astronauts, and I'll be accused of subverting you.'

He grinned. 'Maybe you have but if so, I'm not complaining.'

She looked up at him, her expression serious. 'I think, maybe, we should let a little time go by. I know we've been seeing a lot of each other recently, but not this way. Let's be sure, Joe.'

'Okay. I have to go back to the Cape tonight. See the guys don't get into any scrapes down at Cocoa Beach. Then we have a session up at Lewis, then some more work at the Cape. Altogether I'll be away a couple of weeks, maybe three. That gets us pretty close to Christmas. Unless you have anything better planned we could spend the vacation together.'

'I'd like to. Where? Here or your place?'

'How about Madisonville?'

'Where on earth is that?'

'Kentucky. Home town. I have one relative left up there, an aunt. She's probably a hundred years old but she cooks like a dream and I haven't seen her for too long.'

'Will she mind? The two of us descending on her like that?'

'She'll love it.'

'Then that's what we'll do.'

A little while later they began to make love again and, good as the first time had been, this was even better.

Several hours afterwards, as he went quietly out of Diana's apartment to start the journey back to Florida, Joe felt happier than he had for a long, long time. Oddly enough, the happiness brought with it a touch of remorse that he could feel that way when the marriages of two of the men he thought of as his charges, and for whom he felt responsible, were in trouble. He was pleased a spell at Cocoa Beach was imminent. The opportunity to relax and have a good time would help them all.

COCOA BEACH, Fla.

Some of the gloom of the Redstone-Mercury debacle had lifted and everyone was determined that the whole thing should be forgotten. Cocoa Beach was for enjoyment. Fast cars, women to match, booze, the chance to unload weeks of pent-up frustration and nervous energy. Above all, no one looking over shoulders counting the drinks, checking the speedos or preaching on the subject of domestic bliss. Not that everyone went completely bananas at Cocoa Beach. Most of the crew were fairly circumspect even in their abandon, making careful, considered choices from among the available attractions. Some aimless hot-rodding, rat-racing along narrow, dirt-topped roads; a few more drinks than were customary; desultory glances at the hip-swinging, tight-sweatered, young women that hung around. Though glancing wasn't all that went on the way the girls told it, twittering with competitive zeal in the bars that lined the beach, but always when there were no astronauts around to question their more extravagant boasts.

The girls were not hookers, their services were free of charge, at least in plain monetary terms. They gathered there because that was where the action was and there were plenty of high-rolling, famous men to be seen with. Hollywood, in an earlier age, knew women like these; so too did most football and baseball teams; the fight game knew them; and the newly emergent rock 'n' roll bands knew them. They were seekers after glamor. Not that there was very much that could be termed glamorous about the shack-lined strip of sand and dirt that was a world apart from the shining white buildings and carefully raked beaches of Miami, a few miles down the road.

The bars were wood and corrugated-iron with peeling paint or no paint at all. At night they looked marginally better because the lighting was subdued inside with garish-green and blood-red neon outside. The living accommodation suited the residents, mostly transients, who had drifted in on the tails of the space program and would very probably drift out again when they got bored with it all. They didn't want neatly manicured lawns and hedges or homes that needed maintaining. They wanted something they could fall into late at night and get out of fast when the sun rose the following day. Whatever else Cocoa Beach might have had, permanency wasn't one of its features.

The bar where Gary Herriman had begun the evening was neither better nor worse than any other, its only decor courtesy of Schlitz. It did have one minor advantage, it was farthest along the strip from the one bright spot of luxury, the Holiday Inn. That meant it was less regularly frequented by the girls who knew that the astronauts generally started off at the Inn where a decent steak could be had. Gary didn't want to be pestered by any girls, though as the newest addition to the team, he still enjoyed relative anonymity.

He had nothing against being stared at or approached by bold-eyed, attractively nubile, young women and part of the time he enjoyed their attention. It was just that he was feeling low. The failure of the Redstone had been a great disappointment and, although he knew the others felt bad about it, he regarded it as a personal setback. Everything had been going well. He was ahead with his studying. His intensive training schedule had let him make up ground on the others, he'd even passed Gus Grissom who was fuming impotently over the refusal of his broken bones to heal as fast as everyone had expected. Now it all looked suddenly gloomy. However ready the astronauts might be, scientists and engineers were failing to respond with the hardware that was both ready and right.

The door of the bar banged noisily open, the fly-screen almost coming off its worn hinges. Gary glanced up and sighed. His plans for a quiet evening were over. Bill Simons saw him first and waved, pointing him out to his companions. Gus Grissom, gamely striding out with the aid of a cane, Scott Carpenter and Joe Ziegler came over to Gary's table, leaving Bill to buy a round of drinks.

'What kind of car do you drive?' Gus asked Gary, apparently tying the question to something they'd been discussing.

'I have a '58 Ford.'

'A Ford?'

'A Ford!'

Gary looked at everyone, saw a mildly amused grin on Joe Ziegler's face and appealed to him. 'What's wrong with Fords?'

'Don't worry about it, Gary. Tonight's sermon is on cars. Cars not for getting from a to b but cars for showing off your stuff in.'

'I never thought about them that way. Sorry.'

Bill Simons joined them, hands clasping too many glasses, some of the contents spilling over and intermingling with other drinks. 'Anyone who thinks a car is just for transport should take the bus or the train,' he said.

'Why?' Gary asked, a slight upturn at the corner of his mouth telling Ziegler he wasn't as innocent as he sounded of Bill's notorious delight in racing cars to the limit of their design capability, and then some.

'Why?' Bill demanded. 'If you're gonna lay out a couple of thousand bucks for a set of wheels then you have to do something special with it, otherwise what's the point?'

'I haven't seen you racing your new Corvette,' Gus put in. 'Well, neither have you,' Simons snapped back.

'Dammit, with this foot, what do you expect?'

'Okay, okay. Well, I haven't had time.'

'There's time now,' Carpenter put in.

'Is that a challenge?' Simons demanded.

'Why not,' Carpenter said.

The two men stood up and started for the door. Ziegler finished his drink in one swallow. 'Come on you guys, we can ride shotgun.'

'Not me,' Grissom said. 'I'll stay here, nurse this lousy foot of mine and feel sorry for myself.'

'Gary?'

Herriman shrugged his shoulders and stood up. 'Okay,' he said.

Outside Simons and Carpenter were arguing fiercely over the rules for the competition, eventually, and reluctantly, agreeing to a timetrial over the same run, the time to be checked by Gary riding with Scott and by Joe with Bill.

Carpenter's Shelby Cobra was the first off and rumbled away into the darkness its engine sounding more like a World War II piston-engined fighter than a motor car.

Bill Simons' Corvette was brand new, recently acquired from the local Chevy dealer. Bill waited until Ziegler had fastened his seat belt, before starting the engine. Joe was going along because this might prove a good moment to see first-hand some of the excessive zeal that was causing doubts about Bill Simons. He also hoped for an opportunity to inquire cautiously into the astronaut's private life to see if Paula's comments had been true, and how any problems between Bill and Linda were affecting the astronaut.

Ziegler checked his watch. 'Go,' he said.

The Corvette took off in a hail of grit thrown up by its spinning wheels and headed after Carpenter's Cobra.

Twenty minutes later Ziegler knew several things. One was that when Bill Simons let himself go he was a wild driver, capable of showing even Gus Grissom a thing or two. He brought to his driving the same determined dedication he brought to everything. It seemed as if pushing the cream and green Corvette to crazy speeds along narrow, dirt-topped roads was just another way to impress himself on the man who would help select the flying order of the astronauts.

That was when Ziegler realized he had overlooked an important aspect of Simons' character. Just so long as Ziegler was present he would not behave naturally, he would *perform*. That was what he was doing now. He wasn't driving the car the way he would drive with Gus or Gordo or even alone against Scott's Cobra. He was driving like an Indianapolis 500 favorite – driving to win. They turned into a long straight and Simons accelerated hard, the action producing a miniature g-force. Ziegler grinned, Simons would have to try hard to frighten him.

Almost as if he had heard the unspoken thought Simons swung the Corvette around the bend at the end of the straight, the passenger wheels bouncing against the shoulder and jolting Ziegler despite the restraint of the seat belt.

'Try a soft landing next time,' he said casually.

Simons grunted a reply and spent the next ten minutes trying to impress Ziegler that he could drive hard, fast and well. He very nearly succeeded but Joe had no intention of letting him know it.

'With practise you might be safe to let onto a race track,' he remarked. 'As it is, I'm not even sure you should be out on public roads.'

Simons slammed his foot on the brake pedal, brought the car to a sliding, dust-shrouded, halt and opened his door to climb out. 'Do better,' he snapped over his shoulder.

Ziegler scrambled across into the driving seat without hesitation and almost before Simons was properly in the car he was accelerating hard along the road. He spotted a wider section and braked hard, spinning the wheel as he did so to send the car around in a one hundred and eighty degrees turn. Moments later he was heading back the way they had come, making sure he covered every straight faster than Simons and taking every bend closer to the shoulder.

Somewhere along the way they passed Scott and Gary who were also returning to the bar having completed their timed run. When the bar came in view Ziegler didn't slow down but took the Corvette up onto the black-top and really burned up the stretch the local hell-raisers used when the county sheriff was looking the other way. At the end of the stretch he slowed, turned off the road and parked the car with almost exaggerated care, contrasting with the wild but controlled driving he had just demonstrated. He turned off the engine and tossed the keys to Simons.

The astronaut caught them and reached out to turn on the courtesy light. 'Okay,' he said. 'So you're a regular Junior Johnson. What are you trying to prove?'

Ziegler looked at him for a moment before replying. 'All it takes is skill, which you have plenty of, guts, which none of you lack...'

'And?'

'And just a touch of relaxation.'

'We don't get much time for that.'

'The others manage it. Make a point of it in fact. You should do the same, Bill.'

'Is that what all this has been about. Teaching me to relax?'

'Partly that.'

'What else?'

'Just getting to know each of you a little better.'

Simons' expression became suddenly knowing. 'You're preparing the flight schedule. That's it, isn't it?'

'Maybe it's already prepared.'

Simons shook his head. 'No, I don't think so. Or if it is, there's still time for changes.'

'Look, Bill. Let's not make a big thing out of this. You're good at everything you do. Your as fit as anyone, you know the procedures backwards, forwards and sideways. You check out in every way there is...'

'Except?'

'Except...'

'I don't know how to relax. Is that all you can find wrong with me?' Simons asked with a touch of bitterness.

'That isn't how I look at it.'

'There's more to flying a spacecraft than being able to relax.'

'Maybe, but a lot of what you have to do calls for a man who can relax some of the time.'

'Are the others getting this treatment, or is it just me?'

'Answer that yourself, Bill. Look at Gordo. Can you imagine me having to tell him how to relax? He could give lessons to Perry Como.'

Simons laughed, the noise sudden and unexpected. 'Okay, okay. I guess there might be something in what you say.' He reached out to switch off the courtesy light and opened the door. 'Come on, let's get a drink.'

They changed seats and Simons drove back to the bar, the journey almost stately after the way they had been driving. When they reached the parking lot Carpenter's car was already there.

Simons pointed at it. 'Care to bet who won?'

Ziegler opened his mouth to reply, then realized Simons was laughing at him. 'Okay, Bill. No bets. I reckon you beat him, and if you didn't...'

'Then you did,' Simons said as he switched off the engine and opened the door.

'Hold it, Bill,' Ziegler said.

'Now what?'

'I don't want you going off half-cocked again but, is everything okay between you and Linda?'

'Linda? What are you driving at?'

'I've been hearing things, maybe rumor, but I have to check them out.'

'So?'

'Don't get defensive on me, Bill. I'm not making rules and I'm not about to impose any moral standards on you. I just have be sure that nothing you do reflects on the program or on the other guys on the team.'

'I don't see how anything between Linda and I can do that but, okay, there are a few problems. For God's sake, Joe, here we are, about to shoot a man into space for the first time. A few years from now maybe we'll be putting a guy up there on the moon, and all she can talk about is what color drapes to put in the dining room and whether we should invite her folks over at Thanksgiving or mine.'

'Linda's a home town girl, Bill. The publicity, all the big-time excitement you take for granted, it can be pretty frightening for someone who isn't cut out for that kind of life.'

'I know, I know. She'd be better off married to some jerk who sells insurance or repairs cars. Maybe I'd be better off too, if she was.' Simons shook his head. 'But we're stuck. At least, we are for now. I can't take the risk of separation, and divorce is right out.'

'That's not very fair on Linda, or you, deciding something as important as your life together on the basis of what it might do to your career.'

Simons turned to look at Ziegler in the glow from the bar's neon sign. 'What I'm doing down here, what we're all doing down here, *is* our life. If our wives, our families, don't go along with that then they're not going along with the rest of it either.'

Ziegler shook his head slowly. 'Okay, Bill, okay. Just take it easy, will you? I don't want to add marriage counselor to my list of duties, but try to see some of it from her viewpoint. Maybe ease back on the, well, the playing around. If you must have other women, then do it down here. Up at Langley, keep it all pure and publishable.'

Simons nodded. 'Okay, I get you.' Climbing out of the car he headed for the entrance to the bar. At the door he paused and waited for Ziegler, the green neon turning his face into a living Halloween mask. 'I think I should make a confession,' he said.

'Oh?'

'About Paula and me.'

'No need,' Ziegler said. 'That's a closed book for me, and I hope for you as well.'

Simons nodded, pushed open the door and went into the bar, with Ziegler, after a moment's pause, following him.

In the bar the contingent from the base had increased. There had been a recent duplication at the Cape of many of the facilities at Langley, the object being to eliminate much of the time-consuming commuting that took place. Among the duplicated facilities was a Flight Procedures Trainer now being built in Hangar S. With each of the astronauts spending many hours daily in the FPT having machines in two places would allow greater flexibility in the training schedule. Some of the engineers concerned with the FPT were in the bar, along with a handful of STG technicians including the ever-joking Specs who was holding the floor with a steady stream of wisecracks that would have done credit to Milton Berle, from whom he'd probably stolen the cleaner ones.

Scott Carpenter glanced up and waved a hand at Bill and Joe. 'I thought the timed run was going out,' he said.

'It was,' Bill replied.

'Then what was that green and cream machine that went past me on the way back? A low-flying Cessna, maybe.' Scott turned and grinned at Gary Herriman. 'Scared the hell out of us, didn't it?'

'Right. That was a really fancy piece of driving, Bill.'

Simons glanced at Ziegler who grinned and said, 'It sure scared the hell out of me.'

Simons nodded slowly, accepting Ziegler's gesture. 'Right,' he said. 'My turn to buy.' He waved an arm at the barman, ordered drinks for them all, then leaned across the table, commanding attention. 'I think it's time we had a little...er, relaxation around here. Now, what we need is some serious racing. Not one of these half-assed rat-races you guys have been playing with. Something that needs brains.' He began to outline a scheme involving fast driving, navigation by compass and map, together with a complicated system of penalty points for anyone arriving late at a series of check points. Points that were to be paid out, by the losers, in whisky.

Ziegler sat back in his chair and saw Gus Grissom eyeing him quizzically. He shrugged his shoulders. It was, he decided, too much to hope that Bill would take to relaxation in a relaxing way. Not when he could turn it into a competition. Still, at least he had tried and, more to the point, it might just have the effect of making Simons relate a little more closely to his colleagues.

Gus Grissom could guess what was going through the Astronaut Liaison Officer's mind. Bill Simons' attitude towards the project and to his fellow astronauts was already on the borderline between being something to joke about and a cause for concern. Gus had begun to think it was time to have a quiet word about it to Joe. He and Ziegler went a long way back, to Korea in fact which was where they first met. Grissom had flown even more missions than Ziegler but with less success when measured in terms of enemy aircraft put down. Not that Gus hadn't tried hard enough, it was simply that the breaks hadn't come his way. Ziegler, on the other hand, had been lucky. Not once, but twice he had found himself alone with a small formation of North Korean MiG-15s. Maybe lucky wasn't the word a civilian would have used but to hard-flying young Air Force pilots such things were the stuff of dreams.

Gus caught Joe's eye and moments later the two men were standing at the bar which, although crowded, was somewhere they could talk without appearing to make a big deal out of confidentiality.

'What's on your mind, Gus?'

'What was all that about?'

'Trying to get Bill to take things easy.'

'It doesn't look like you've succeeded.'

'I guess not. Still, I tried.'

Grissom looked across the room at the other astronauts. 'Have you settled on a flight sequence for us?' he asked.

Ziegler started to shake his head, then changed his mind. 'It isn't my decision, you know that, Gus, but I've submitted recommendations.'

'What about me?' Grissom gestured at his foot. 'This isn't helping, is it?'

'No, it isn't. Look, Gus keep this quiet but if the top brass follow my suggestion you're number four on the list.'

'Four.' Grissom frowned. Then, after a moment his face brightened. 'Are we going for three Redstones?'

'That's not decided yet.'

'If we do, that makes me number one Atlas.'

Ziegler nodded. 'Yes.'

'Well, well. That's pretty good. So long as this damn foot of mine heals.'

Ziegler shrugged. 'There's time. We're still on a schedule that will put the first Atlas flight into the middle of 1962. Even your foot can't take that long.'

'How soon will there be an official announcement of the flight sequence?'

'As soon as it comes down from Gilruth.'

'When will that be?'

'I don't know, but, until it does, keep this to yourself. Right?'

'No need to ask me, Joe.'

Ziegler grinned. 'Tell me something I don't already know.'

As the two men started back to rejoin the others Gary Herriman came up towards the bar. Ziegler hesitated for an instant. He wanted to talk to Gary. Having already responded to some of Paula's remarks by talking to Bill Simons about his tom-catting, and his behavior towards Linda, he thought he might as well complete the evening by talking to Gary about Stella. Then he changed his mind. Diana had said she would try to find out more from Stella herself and he wouldn't gain anything by jumping the gun with Gary if there ended up being nothing to Paula's story.

LANGLEY AIR FORCE BASE, Va.

The telephone rang four times then stopped. Diana McNair, eyes still closed, had reached for it but fell back against the pillow. She opened her eyes, stared at the ceiling, realized it was still dark and stretched her arm again, this time to turn on the light. By her bedside clock it was just past three. She decided it must have been a wrong number, no one she knew was likely to call her at that time in the morning.

She was reaching out to turn off the light when the telephone rang again. For some seconds she could neither understand the words nor recognize the voice. When she did she tried to interrupt but it was some moments before the other woman would let her speak.

'Stella. It is you, isn't it?'

'Yes.'

'Take it slowly now, what's troubling you?'

'I want to talk...to...Oh, hell, I'm sorry, I shouldn't have called.'

'No. No, it's okay, Stella I don't mind. Where are you, at home?'

'Yes.'

Diana thought for a moment. The astronauts were at Lewis and she guessed that Stella was alone and, from her voice, had been drinking heavily. She had tried several times to get close to Stella but had failed all along the line. Now, out of the blue, it seemed that the opportunity she'd been looking for had arrived.

'Stella?'

'Yes.'

'Give me an hour to dress and drive over there.'

'There's no need.'

'There's every need.'

'No, I don't...'

Diana spoke firmly but quietly. 'I'm on my way, Stella. Why not put on some coffee. I think I'm going to need it. Any hour before seven and I'm not exactly at my best.'

It took Diana a little over forty-five minutes to reach the Herriman house. Like all the houses at Langley it was boxlike and uninviting from the outside. Inside, when Diana opened the unlocked door and looked in, it wasn't much better. She called out, heard a muffled answer, and went on through to the kitchen where Stella was sitting at the table, her posture straight and rigid as if she was forcing herself into a position very different to that her body demanded. The kitchen was a mess. Glancing through the open door into the living room Diana could see that care of her home was pretty well down on Stella Herriman's list of priorities. At least all the other homes she had visited, even though the basic material with which the wives had to work wasn't very much, were bright, cheerful, and clean. This one was the exception to end all exceptions. The contrast between the house and Gary Herriman, who was always neat, tidy, and shining clean, was startling. Diana looked at Stella, noting the fact that her hair, and the dress she wore, looked in need of washing.

She glanced around the kitchen for a percolator, didn't see one, then saw a jar of instant coffee. She touched the kettle which was cold, filled it, switched it on, then sat at the table across from Stella. 'Do you want to talk, or shall I?' she asked.

Stella didn't reply but, after a moment, shook her head slowly.

Diana guessed which part of her twin-barrelled question the gesture answered. 'I haven't been here before,' she said. 'But I feel as if I have. All the houses on the base look alike, don't they? You'd think some preferential treatment wouldn't hurt the Air Force. After all, the astronauts are special, aren't they?'

Stella made a sound that could have been a laugh.

'They are special, you know,' Diana went on quietly. 'They have pressures ordinary fliers don't have, not even in wartime. Sometimes those pressures spill over and affect others, without anyone meaning it to happen that way.'

'It can't all be blamed on the project,' Stella said, her voice muffled.

'What can't?'

'Gary, the way he treats me.'

'What happens?'

Stella shrugged and turned away.

'Tell me, Stella. Is he violent?'

This time there was no doubt that Stella was amused, her laughter genuine although heavily tinged with tears. 'Gary violent? I don't think he could be, even if he tried.' She shook her head and for a moment Diana thought she wouldn't continue. When she began again her voice was low and hesitant. She was clearly unhappy at confiding in Diana, a woman she scarcely knew. 'He doesn't care about me anymore. Once it was different.'

Diana waited for Stella to continue but then, when it became obvious that if she was to learn anything more she had to do a little prompting, she asked a question. 'When did all this begin?'

Stella shook her head. 'I don't know the moment. Just a steady slide downhill.' She looked at Diana, her gaze suddenly direct. 'There's nothing to be gained by pretending it's one-sided, is there? I can't blame it all on Gary. He doesn't care about me, that's true enough, but maybe he has a cause. I...I drink a little more than is good for me. And there are...well, I like men. I need to have...' She broke off again and this time Diana sensed she wouldn't continue unless the way was cleared for her.

'Some people need others,' Diana began. 'Maybe they just need someone to talk to, or to listen. Often there's a need for more than that, for a physical relationship. It isn't anything unusual for a women to need a man, or a man to need a woman. It's as old as life. If two people are married and one needs the other and doesn't get a matching response it can be difficult. One solution is to seek a physical relationship outside the marriage. It doesn't mean the marriage has to fail.'

'That sounds like you're recommending sleeping around as a solution.'

Diana smiled fleetingly. 'Don't quote me.'

'Then you think Gary and I might be able to get back together again?'

'You still live together.'

'We both occupy this house, that's not the same thing.'

Diana stood up to make coffee for them both, then sat down again. 'Is that why you drink?' she asked.

Stella looked at her for a moment. 'You mean, which came first? Is Gary's indifference a result of my drinking or is it my drinking that has made him look elsewhere.'

Diana frowned. 'You mean, Gary is having an affair?'

Stella looked down at the table. 'Perhaps not,' she said. 'Maybe I tell myself he has another woman because it makes the fact that he doesn't touch me anymore easier to bear.'

Diana laughed softly. 'Careful,' she said lightly. 'You're doing my job for me.'

Stella looked up again, a tiny smile trying to force its way onto her face. 'Sorry,' she said. 'And I'm sorry I dragged you out here at this time of the night. It wasn't really worth the effort, was it?'

Diana shrugged her shoulders. 'I'm not paid just to look after astronauts,' she said. 'I leave the mother-hen routine to Joe Ziegler. I'm here to help anyone who needs me.' She hesitated, unsure whether to say what had come into her mind. Then she decided to continue, aware that the opportunity might not present itself again. 'That's what the psychiatric staff are for. Not just me, all of us. Mike Leandros too. You've met him, haven't you?'

Stella looked at the table top again, her eyes invisible to Diana. 'Did he tell you that?'

'No. But you haven't been trying too hard to keep it secret, have you?'

Stella shook her head. 'Mike gives me what I want, what I need.'

'I think you could have made a better choice, Stella.'

Stella looked up, eyes suddenly angry, her color heightening. 'You're not jealous, are you?'

'Jealous? Of you and Mike? Of course not.'

'He's told me about you. The way you won't let...' Stella's voice trailed off and her eyes fell again.

'What has he told you?' Diana asked, her voice tight.

Stella shook her head.

For a few silent moments the two women remained motionless,

one angry, the other not feeling any particular emotion, but both defensive.

After a while Diana knew that nothing more was to be gained by staying and after saying good-bye, to which Stella made no response, she went out of the house and began the drive back to her home in Newport News. Along the way she decided she would have to insist that some time soon Joe Ziegler talked to Gary about Stella. It was necessary, if Stella wasn't to deteriorate still further. She recalled the other woman's half-spoken comments about Leandros and could guess what her assistant had been saying. Her rejection of his occasional advances must have burned at his self-esteem and it was natural for him to think about her that way. But talking about her to Stella Herriman was going too far.

Back in the kitchen of the house at Langley, Stella hadn't moved after Diana's departure. She had made a mess of it. When she had called Diana it was because she needed to tell someone, anyone, what lay at the back of her drinking. The opportunity had been there but she hadn't taken it. Now, she knew, there might never be another chance. Which meant she was trapped in a meaningless, loveless, life in which her only companions would be men like Mike Leandros, and from which her only escape would be through alcohol.

She began to cry, silently at first, then deep, racking sobs. After a time she stopped and went through into the other room for a bottle of vodka. It took what remained of the hours of darkness, and most of the contents of the bottle, before she could sleep.

LEWIS RESEARCH CENTER, Oh.

Way back when Gary Herriman had first joined Project Mercury, Wally Schirra had made several pointed remarks about the designers of the MASTIF. Since then, Gary had undergone several sessions on that particular piece of training equipment and whole-heartedly agreed with every one of Schirra's bitter comments. He had no doubts at all that the MASTIF had been conceived by minds which, in other times, could well have been employed in designing memory-jogging devices for the Spanish Inquisition.

The MASTIF looked simple and harmless enough, almost like a child's tinker-toy. A replica of the Mercury capsule was hung on three sets of gimbals mounted inside a fragile-looking framework. The mounting was such that the capsule was free to twist and turn and tumble simultaneously along all three axes. Movement along one axis was an acceptable, everyday experience; movement along two wasn't too grim, provided it didn't last more than a few minutes. Movement in three axes was impossible to tolerate. Minutes were exceptional, most men couldn't last long enough to start counting in anything but seconds.

The astronaut's job, in theory, was to keep the capsule on-target despite simultaneous rolling, pitching, and yawing. They rarely succeeded because those who did manage to stay in the thing for more than a few awful seconds were too busy concentrating on not throwing up to actually try to steer the monster. Of all the instruments on board the MASTIF, the one most used was the only one which had any effect upon the virulent sickness and massive disorientation which hit the astronauts. That was the instrument which stopped it dead in its tracks.

It wouldn't have been quite so bad if the astronauts were convinced that the MASTIF had any relevance to their training. They couldn't persuade themselves it had, because they knew damn well that if conditions such as those created artificially hit them during a mission then they would have bought a one-way ticket to nowhere. In those circumstances, prayer was all that was left and few of them believed that even the staying hand of the Almighty would be a match for an out of control spacecraft.

Gary Herriman's latest session on the machine had ended with the predictable hitting of the cut-off switch in no more than the average number of seconds and he was sitting, pale and unsteady, facing the machine with an expression on his face suggesting he was ready to blow the goddamn thing into a thousand pieces.

Joe Ziegler watched him, conscious that he wasn't about to endear himself to the young astronaut. He had been pressured by Diana into talking to Gary about Stella and the prospect wasn't something he relished. Now, studying the other man's face, Ziegler was suffering a pang of conscience that he had chosen this moment but it would serve another purpose. Confronting a man with the fact that his wife had a drinking problem was bad enough at any time. To do it when he was at a low physical ebb as a result of a session on the MASTIF approached sadism, but physical, mental, and emotional stress were all things the astronauts had to be able to handle. There was no time, no place, for anyone who couldn't cut it whenever, and from wherever, the pressure came.

Fifteen minutes later Ziegler was beginning to wonder why he had worried so much over the moment. Gary had listened in silence, the only change in his expression being a gradual return to his normal coloring, which would have returned about then anyway, as the effects of the sickness wore off.

'I knew she was drinking,' he said after they had sat without speaking for a few moments. 'I saw the bottles around the house, the bills from the liquor stores, but I hadn't figured it to be a real problem. I mean, I didn't think she was an alcoholic.'

'Hold on,' Joe interrupted. 'We don't know that it's gone that far. It's just that it seems as though it might be heading that way.' He paused for a moment, deciding whether to go the whole way and tell Gary about Mike Leandros. Then he pressed on. Coming back for another crack at the man's equilibrium later wouldn't prove anything about his stability he couldn't discover now. 'I think there might be another problem,' he went on carefully. 'Stella's drinking isn't always done alone. She sometimes does it with a companion. A man.'

To his astonishment Gary nodded his head. 'That doesn't surprise me,' he said. 'Things, you know, sexually, haven't been very good between us for some time. Stella is, well, she's the kind of woman who needs more than I am able to give her.'

'How long has it been like this?' Ziegler asked, unhappily accepting that he had to dig deeper. 'The drinking and the other men.'

'Two, maybe three years.'

'And before that?'

Gary's forehead creased in thought. 'Pretty good, I think. I was never a great lover, but we seemed to do ok.'

'What caused the change?'

'I don't know. Maybe it was coming back to the States. Stella liked it over in Germany. So did I.'

Ziegler stood up and rested a hand on the astronaut's shoulder. 'I'm sorry I had to lay all this on you,' he said.

He felt Herriman's slight shrug. 'I guess you had to, Joe.'

'Okay, well, let's talk about it some more later.'

Gary stood up. 'What do you want me to do? I can ask Stella to see a doctor for the drinking but I'm not sure what I can do about...about the other.'

'Well, the drinking will be a start. I'll get Diana to talk to her as well. Maybe she can find what started it all off.' He tried a not very convincing grin. 'That's what psychiatrists are for, getting to the root of problems.'

Gary nodded and walked away leaving Ziegler feeling resentful that he had been obliged to invade his private life in that way. It wasn't the kind of thing he thought of as part of his work but, like it or not, he would sooner do it himself than let an outsider take over the shit work.

For Gary Herriman the past few minutes had been almost like a dream faintly recalled on waking. Everything Joe Ziegler had said had been news to him and yet, at the same time, there was a strange feeling of *deja-vu*. It was as if he had known of it all along but had somehow repressed the knowledge, keeping it deliberately beneath the surface of his mind. It was an uncomfortable feeling, that he might have been very unfair to Stella. If it was so, he would have to find some way to make up for any unhappiness she might have suffered.

In the locker room he changed his clothes, then walked through to the office they used on their visits to Lewis, intending to call Stella. Bill Simons was in the room, talking on the telephone. The other astronaut looked up guiltily as the door opened, then relaxed when he saw it was Gary. He said a couple of hasty, quiet, words into the telephone before replacing the instrument.

'Hi, Gary. Seen Joe?'

'I left him about five, ten minutes ago. Do you want him?'

Simons shook his head. 'No, that's okay. How did the session go?'

'As usual.' Herriman managed a grin. 'I didn't throw up this time, so maybe I'm getting used to it.'

'Goddamn crazy machine.'

'Finished with the telephone?'

'Sure. I was just leaving anyway. See you later.'

As Herriman started to dial Bill Simons went out, closing the door behind him. In the corridor Simons checked that Joe Ziegler wasn't around. The telephone call he's just taken had surprised him. Both from the fact that it was Paula Blake, who didn't usually make calls to any of the training centers least of all this one in Lewis, and because she was right here, a couple of miles down the road, at a motel.

He reached the motel in ten minutes, taking in a liquor store for a bottle of Jack Daniels he expected would see them through the rest of the evening.

Paula was in the room, the door unlocked, lying on the bed wearing stretch-pants and a sweater which left very little to Simons' imagination. She didn't speak when he came in, didn't even smile. He poured drinks, deciding to let her play things her own way for the moment. At least until he knew why she was there.

She took the glass he proffered and raised it up. 'Luck,' she said.

He acknowledged the toast but didn't return it.

'You haven't called recently,' Paula said.

'You know how it is. We're kept pretty busy.'

'Is that the only reason?'

'What else?'

Paula sat up and held out her glass for a refill. 'I thought maybe you'd found someone else.'

'Nobody but you, Paula,' he said with a grin.

'Don't make fun, Bill.' She looked at him for a second or two over the top of the glass. Then she finished off the drink in one swallow.

'Hey, that's best sour mash. Made to be savored.'

'Maybe it's that kind of night.'

'Come on now, Paula, what's all this about?'

She took a deep breath, then let it out slowly. 'I'm going home. So I thought, instead of letting you get back to Langley and find me gone, I'd come this way through and say good-bye properly.'

'Home? Good-bye? What is all this?'

'Like I said. I've decided it's time I called it a day. It'll be interesting to see if good ol' Healdsburg's changed any in the past few years.'

'What's brought this on?'

She shrugged. 'Things. People.'

'Me?'

'Among others.'

'Joe?'

Paula looked away, shaking her head. 'Don't worry, I haven't told him.' She glanced back and was relieved to see Bill appeared to have taken her statement at face value.

'Well,' Bill said. 'I'm pleased you called. Are we going to celebrate, or what?'

Paula began to regret the impulse which had made her drive to Lewis. Her decision to return to California had been similarly impulsive, but it was one she was happy she'd made. With Joe out of her life, and Bill Simons an unreliable companion, she knew she would have to start building friendships again. She didn't anticipate any difficulty in that area, attracting men had always been easy for her. But if she was going to start over, there was no reason why she shouldn't do it back on the West Coast. And if Healdsburg proved too quiet she could always try LA or Vegas.It wasn't until she was packing her bags into the MG that it occurred to her Bill Simons might be more responsive to suggestions of a celebratory good-bye than Joe had been. Now, looking at him, she realized something she had known all along but had kept to the back of her mind. Bill was interested only in an easy lay.

'No,' she said. 'No celebrations, just good-bye.'

He frowned. 'Is that it?'

She nodded.

He came over and reached for her but she drew back from his touch. His face darkened with the beginning of anger.

'No, Bill. I think you'd better go. This wasn't a very good idea.'

He pressed both hands on her breasts and kissed her hard on the mouth. She struggled from his grasp but he changed position and pushed her down onto the bed. With one hand he held her there while the other pulled at her sweater. She managed to twist her body away and he released her. For an instant she thought he had given up but then she felt his hands fumbling at the top of her pants. She rolled back to her earlier position and saw a grin break onto his face as he assumed she had decided the game had gone on long enough. Abruptly she brought up her knee, driving it hard into his groin.

His yell of pain was so loud she thought everyone in the adjoining motel rooms would hear it, but if they did no one responded.

Simons straightened up, his face red. 'You bitch,' he said, his voice hard and low.

'Please go, Bill.'

'Too damn right I'm going. I've never had to fight for it before and I'm not aiming to start now.' He went towards the door, his movements awkward. Then he turned and came back into the middle of the room. Paula flinched away from him, expecting he was about to retaliate, but he merely picked up the bottle of Jack Daniels, then left without another word.

She lay back on the bed listening until the sound of his car faded from her hearing. After a few minutes she stood up, packed the few clothes she had taken from one of her bags, and left the motel. There was nothing to be gained by staying. California was a long drive and the sooner she got there the sooner she could start the process of forgetting all about NASA, the fucking space program, and the astronauts and all their problems, their hang-ups, their worries, and their fears.

1961
January 15 – January 30

WASHINGTON, D.C.

Bobby Kennedy was pleased with the way it was building. It was two months since they had brought Jim Magadini up to Hickory Hill for an urgent conference. In that time he had talked to everyone with an interest, however peripheral, in the space program. He'd had the military in, some scientific eggheads from MIT, he'd talked with von Braun and even the CIA. Now he had a military strategist from the Pentagon with whom he was putting together all the various answers he'd assembled.

'So, there's no doubt about it. We can do it if we want to and if NASA says no, it's not because they can't, it's because they won't.'

The military strategist looked carefully at the tousle-haired young man sitting across the desk from him, then slowly removed his spectacles and began polishing them. He wasn't happy with their discussion but he didn't want to say so, certainly not bluntly.

Kennedy had laid out for him the same hypothesis he'd put before everyone he'd talked with. If the nation's security was threatened, whether from conventional or nuclear attack, could they respond with a manned, nuclear-armed spaceflight? The strategist thought the scenario wildly fanciful and he suspected everyone else had thought the same. Apart from anything else there didn't seem to be very much point to it. Sending one small nuclear weapon up into space was not likely to deter the Soviets. Although he couldn't figure out what was behind Kennedy's questions, the man from the Pentagon was rapidly coming to the conclusion that it had nothing to do with nuclear retaliation.

After insuring there wasn't the tiniest speck of dust on his spectacles, the military strategist replaced them and smiled gently at the young man. 'You realize of course that faced with a hypothetical question most people will give a hypothetical answer.'

Kennedy glowered at him. 'What does that mean?'

'It means they will not necessarily have spoken the absolute truth but rather the truth within the confines of your hypothesis.' Or, the man from the Pentagon thought, putting it bluntly, which I dare not do, they've told you what they think you want to hear.

There was more than a touch of truth in the strategist's thoughts. The military had resented the implication that they couldn't retaliate against attack without help from NASA but had sufficient interest in the space program not to say so; von Braun, uncomfortably aware of the amount of government money pouring into NASA, wasn't about to admit to anything that might lead to awkward questions; the CIA were playing along until they found out just how much harm the President's brother would be able to do them; the superbrains from MIT spent so much of their time dealing in hypotheses that they postulated anything with gusto, however obscure or absurd: the lactic content of the green cheese from which the moon was made, for instance.

The only thing out of line in the strategist's thinking was his assumption that Bobby Kennedy believed what he'd been told. He didn't. He knew he was being snowed and didn't give a damn. What he wanted was ammunition for a plan he intended laying out before Jim Magadini, who was due to arrive at his office shortly after the Pentagon strategist left. The plan had nothing to do with military retaliation and everything to do with politics, and that was an area where very few people could teach the young man, who was about to become the new Attorney General, anything at all.

'Okay,' Kennedy said. 'We'll talk again.' He swung his chair around leaving the military strategist to devise a tactical withdrawal from the office without appearing too much like a junior clerk being dismissed from the presence of the chairman of the board.

Less than five minutes later the telephone buzzed and Kennedy's secretary announced the arrival of his next two visitors.

Neither Jim Magadini nor Joe Ziegler thought the meeting to which they'd been called would be for anything trivial but Joe, at least, was unprepared for Kennedy's demand.

'Impossible,' he said.

Kennedy glared at him. 'That word doesn't exist in my book.'

'It should,' Ziegler said, curtly.

'Hold it, Joe,' Magadini put in. He turned to Kennedy. 'You told me to keep what I was doing secret. I did as you asked and that includes Colonel Ziegler here. He doesn't know about the time-saving moves.'

'Tell him now,' Kennedy said.

'Okay, Joe. I'm sorry about this but there were reasons. What we've been doing is putting into operation some time-saving operations right across the program, even stepping up some of the training procedures, intensifying them. Now, wait,' he said as Ziegler began framing what would obviously be an angry response. 'There were no short-cuts, nothing was done which would endanger life.'

Ziegler stared at Magadini in anger and disbelief. 'And what did all this accomplish?'

'I was able to come up with a projected launch date for April,'

'April?'

Kennedy nodded. 'That was the date we wanted.'

'That's right, Joe,' Magadini said. He turned to Kennedy. 'Like I said, we were getting there. Then we had the Redstone launch failure on November 21. Last month we had the Atlas-Able explosion. Either one of those would have thrown us back. Taken together they've destroyed any chance of a sub-orbital flight in April.'

'Are you telling me that you can't improve on April?'

Magadini frowned. 'Improve on it? I'm telling you we can't even make that date.'

Kennedy sprang to his feet, anger showing in his face and his voice. 'Wrong. We do it because we have to.'

'No.'

'Dammit, yes.'

For a moment there was silence as the two men glared at one another. Then Kennedy forced a grin to his lips as if aware that he would get nowhere with a frontal attack. 'So far you haven't been kept fully aware of certain other developments,' he said, almost apologetically.

Ziegler looked at him doubtfully. 'What developments?' he asked.

'First, the Soviets are much further ahead of us than we imagined possible. They're planning an early spaceflight, one that will be much more than a simple straight up and down jaunt.'

Ziegler glanced at Magadini, as if asking, "How can anyone, particularly the new President's brother, think of any kind of spaceflight as a simple matter?" To Kennedy he said, 'We've known for a long time they would probably beat us to it. We've learned to live with it.'

The implication was obvious but Kennedy showed that he for one was not prepared to learn the same lesson. He chose his words carefully, aware that in Ziegler he had met someone who was neither prepared to accept what he was told at face value, nor could be prompted into action by political propaganda. 'We have received information indicating that the Soviets plan to use their flight for military purposes and not for merely political advantage. We don't yet know what this means. It could be nothing that will physically endanger this nation. It could, however, indicate that they plan to use the spaceflight as a means of overt military action.'

Ziegler looked at the younger man, his expression showing Kennedy that he had misjudged his man. When he spoke, the Colonel's disbelief was barely hidden. 'I've no reason to speak out for those people. I spent two years of my life fighting communists in the air over Korea but I don't believe they'd send a spaceship up there just to drop a bomb on us.'

Kennedy's voice was cold. 'What you believe, Colonel Ziegler, is your affair. What we believe is based upon carefully assembled intelligence data. It might be wrong, I grant you, but the President of the United States cannot take a chance that affects thousands, perhaps millions of American lives.'

Ziegler didn't answer. Aware that his foremost impression was that he was being conned, he didn't want to risk that belief spilling out into words.

After waiting to see if Ziegler intended arguing further, Kennedy turned to Magadini and set out the opinions he had gathered from all the people he had talked to in recent weeks. When he was through he leaned back in his chair and waited.

'It's all theory, speculation,' Magadini protested.

'Von Braun doesn't think so,'

'Von Braun.' The disgust in Ziegler's voice was clear.

'Easy, Joe,' Magadini said.

'Why?'

'Von Braun's no fool.'

'He's ambitious.'

'What has that to do with anything?' Kennedy asked.

'It can color a man's judgment.'

'He hasn't said anything half a dozen others haven't agreed with.'

'Generals, college professors, what the hell do they know about it?'

'As much as you, Colonel.'

Ziegler bit back an angry retort. 'Okay,' he said trying to keep his voice calm. 'How about Bob Gilruth and Jim Webb, what do they think?'

'They haven't been consulted.'

'Haven't been..? you're joking! How can you base all this on opinions of people who aren't involved and ignore those who know more than anyone else in the entire country?'

'Because that's the way we're doing it,' Kennedy said with finality.

There was silence for several moments before Jim Magadini spoke up. 'What do you want?' he asked.

'We want a flight preparing for launch as soon as possible and in any event no later than March. No, wait,' he said as Ziegler tried to interrupt. 'There will be reference to this in the Inaugural Address. No precise date will be stated but it will be clearly indicated that we're talking about sometime soon, not next year.'

Ziegler frowned. 'Next year? The first Redstone sub-orbital is scheduled for late this year.'

'I'm not talking about sub-orbital flights. This will be a fully orbital flight. Right, Jim?'

Magadini nodded uncomfortably. 'That's where we've been looking for savings,' he told Ziegler.

'An Atlas flight this year is out of the question,' Joe said.

'Not according to the information I have,' Kennedy said.

'Oh, for God's sake!'

'We might be able to swing it, Joe. It will take a lot of hard work but we can do it,' Magadini said.

'It's impossible.'

'I've already told you, Colonel, that word doesn't exist,' Kennedy said.

'Okay, okay. So what do you expect us to do?'

'Set up a special flight planning team which will report only to you, Jim. Von Braun will establish a similar group at Huntsville reporting only to him. Von Braun and you, Jim, will report directly to me. For now, no one else need know anything.'

'Which team am I supposed to be on?' Ziegler asked.

Kennedy ignored the sarcasm in his voice. 'You're on your own team. You will be responsible for the man who will fly the capsule. Just as you are now, only brought forward a few months.'

'And who else is on my team, as you call it?'

'Whoever you need but keep the number down to the absolute minimum.'

'All in the interest of security? How do you propose keeping anything like this a secret?'

'It shouldn't be too difficult,' Magadini said. 'We have an Atlas-Mercury test flight scheduled, right? So, we introduce an artificial payload into all pre-flight calculations. This payload will be exactly the same as the weight of the selected astronaut. That way, when we make the announcement that the flight will be manned, nothing will need changing or even re-calculating.'

Ziegler shook his head. 'It will leak out.'

'Why should it?'

Ziegler indicated Kennedy with a nod of his head. 'You heard the man. If there's mention, in the new President's Inaugural Address, that a manned spaceflight is imminent, everything we do will be interpreted as part of that program.'

Kennedy nodded thoughtfully. 'You're right. Okay, maybe we'd better drop reference to the flight from the speech.'

'I still think we'll have trouble keeping it quiet.'

'Then you'll have to work at it,' Kennedy said tersely. He grinned suddenly. 'Why not do it this way. You have a program aiming for a sub-orbital flight in the summer. Keep that under way but set up the orbital flight as a test procedure, following the routine step by step. You can say you're insuring there'll be no snags when you come to the big one in '62.'

'That would work, Joe,' Magadini said.

'Maybe.'

Kennedy stood up. 'Okay, that's enough for today. Work out the details and get back to me as soon as you can. In any case not later than next week.'

Half an hour later Ziegler and Magadini were on their way to Bolling and their flight back to Langley. Neither man had spoken since leaving Bobby Kennedy's office.

Ziegler was the first to break the silence. 'I don't like it, Jim.'

'What don't you like?'

'I don't like any damn part of it. Having to keep secrets from Gilruth and Webb, all this footsy-footsy with von Braun, and I sure as hell don't like keeping secrets from the team.'

'From the astronauts?'

'That's who I'm talking about.'

'I suppose you could bend Kennedy's rules. Tell the entire team.'

Ziegler shook his head. 'No. That would be even worse than keeping eight of them in the dark. They're a team, Jim. And as soon as I tell the guy who'll be sitting in the hot seat he steps outside that team.'

'Who will it be?'

'Has Gilruth approved my suggested schedule?'

'Pretty much but with the qualification we wait and see how Deke checks out.'

'In that case we take the top man off the list.'

'Al?'

'No, Al is slated as first Redstone. A fully orbital flight will use an Atlas so we take the top man from the Atlas list.'

'That's Gus, what about his foot?'

'Shaping up but I don't think we can risk his being ready. No, we'll have to go one down, that's Bill.'

'I'm not sure I go with that,' Magadini said. 'I told you before the top brass have some doubts about Bill.'

'You heard what Kennedy said. The top brass won't know anything about this until it's too late for them to put in their two-cents' worth.' Ziegler stopped and shook his head. 'My God. Ten

126

minutes ago I was shooting my mouth off, telling Kennedy it couldn't be done. Now here I am, working out who'll fly the damn mission.'

'Well, let's stay with it on that basis, Joe. Go along until we're given a hard and fast date. Then we can talk to Kennedy again. If what he wants is impossible, that's all there is to it.'

Ziegler didn't answer. He was much less certain than Jim appeared to be. It wouldn't be easy, telling, and convincing, Bobby Kennedy that an early Atlas launch was impossible. He'd made it very clear that particular word wasn't in his vocabulary. Ziegler turned his thoughts to the choice of Bill Simons. He'd had several discussions with Diana in recent weeks. They'd even argued about Bill's suitability as astronaut material during the Christmas vacation they'd spent with Joe's aunt in Madisonville. Eventually they'd called a truce when both had been forced to admit that Bill hadn't done anything recently to give rise to any concern. Now, sitting in the limousine with Jim Magadini, Joe was conscious that all the doubts he'd heard expressed seemed much more significant.

The flight back to Langley was fast and, as always when he flew, Joe ended the journey happier and more relaxed than when he'd left Washington. When his thoughts returned to the subject of the space shot it all seemed a whole lot less worrying. Bobby Kennedy had said they were planning the spaceflight as some sort of comeback against Russian action in space. He had no reason to expect such action was imminent. Maybe the whole damn thing would just quietly fizzle and die.

LANGLEY AIR FORCE BASE, Va.

Gary Herriman looked across the darkened living room at Stella who was sitting in front of the tv, apparently engrossed in a re-run of "I Married Joan". He suspected she was not really interested but was using the show as a reason for not talking to him. Since Joe Ziegler had talked to him about Stella's drinking he had tried to be more attentive, more observant. His attentiveness hadn't paid off, Stella seemed almost resentful at the restrictions it placed on her freedom of movement. His careful observation of her habits had almost convinced him that Ziegler was wrong. Sure, Stella drank but there was a world of difference between taking a drink and being unable to stop. As for Ziegler's hint that Stella might be seeing another man, he'd seen no sign of that at all.

Gary frowned in the darkness. When Ziegler had spoken to him it was as if he was seeing again an old movie he'd first watched long ago and had all but forgotten. He hadn't wanted to argue, had accepted the statement at face value. Now he was beginning to doubt it. Ziegler had to be wrong.

Stella watched the tv screen intently but her brain was not recording the images on the screen. She desperately wanted a drink but dared not take the risk of leaving the house, or even the room. Gary had been watching her every move, had been doing so for weeks. She didn't know why, couldn't believe that after years of disregard he was now reverting to the behavior that had once been so natural.

In those long-past days they had enjoyed every moment of their life together and could not bear to be parted. Stella shook her head slowly. Now, she knew, there was no way back to those days, even if Gary genuinely wanted it that way. She pressed her legs together, thinking of Mike Leandros. She needed him at this moment almost as much as she needed a drink. And what she wanted from him was something Gary couldn't give her, had never been able to give her, certainly not in the past few years.

'Stella.'

She looked at Gary, her eyes vacant for an instant. 'Yes?'

'Can I get you something?'

'Such as?'

'Well, a dr...' He stopped. 'Anything,' he added.

Stella shook her head.

'We could go out.'

'I'm watching this.'

'Oh.' They sat in silence for a moment before Gary tried again. 'I have a few days leave coming up. Would you like to go away?'

'Where?'

Gary shook his head. 'I don't know. Anywhere. Fairmont, maybe. You haven't been home for quite a while.'

'No.' The word was snapped out. The last thing she wanted was to see her parents. She loved them, liked their company, but knew she would not be able to conceal from them the ravages of her recent activities.

Gary was silent, trying to find something to say that would jolt Stella from her apathy without pushing them into a quarrel. He considered suggesting a trip up to Washington to see the General but decided against it. Stella had never been comfortable in his father's presence, although for the life of him he couldn't imagine why. The General had always been polite towards his son's wife, had made no demands on her. He decided to call his father, suggest a visit, then tell Stella what he'd arranged.

At that moment, as if acting on some secret signal from his thoughts, the telephone rang. Stella moved almost convulsively but Gary was nearest and answered it.

After a moment he replaced the instrument, saw his wife watching him, and shrugged his shoulders. 'Wrong number, I guess. Some guy spouting off about remembering things.'

Stella turned back to the tv; maybe it had been Mike Leandros trying to reach her. The hell with all this, she thought. She would call Leandros tomorrow and arrange to see him. Gary was out of the house most days from early morning until late evening. If she couldn't take the chance of going to Leandros, then he would have to take the risk of coming to her.

Gary sat down again, his thoughts drifting. The telephone call had disturbed him. It could have been a wrong number, as he'd said to Stella. But what if it wasn't. What if Ziegler was right? Maybe the man on the other end of the telephone line, rambling on about remembering and forgetting things, had been hoping to speak to Stella. What if she really did have a lover? It wasn't a happy sequence of thoughts and after a while he forced himself into thinking about the training schedule for the next day.

It seemed to work and he began to relax again, so much so that he even dozed off for a few moments finding himself in a pleasant dream of happier times. He would have been less relaxed if he had known that during these moments when he slept Stella had seized the opportunity to slip from the room to take a drink from a bottle of vodka she kept hidden on a shelf in the kitchen.

The following morning, from his desk in the office he shared with the other astronauts, Gary called the General in Washington. He spent some minutes talking to the old man about those areas of his work which could be confided over an open telephone line, then raised the subject of a visit.

'I'd be happy to see you, that's for sure,' General Herriman said. 'Are you certain Stella would like it up here? Not much of a place for a young woman.'

'I think a break from the routine would do her good. It gets pretty monotonous for her, sitting around here while I'm working.'

'Then sitting around an old man's apartment while we talk military-business won't be much of an improvement, will it?'

Gary sighed. 'I guess not.'

'Take her out to the beach, or some place where you can have some fun. That's what a woman needs.'

'Maybe.'

'Not that I don't want to see you, but, if it's Stella you're thinking of, then that might be the best thing to do.'

'I guess you're right.'

'I'm sure I am. Good-bye, Thomas.'

Gary winced at the use of his first name. 'Good-bye, sir,' he said.

'And remember, Thomas, I'm very proud of your achievements, very proud.'

'Thank you, sir,' Gary said and waited until he heard his father break the connexion, then let the telephone fall onto its rest.

That hadn't helped one damn bit, he thought. Then he brightened a little. He'd suggest to Stella that they spend his few days' leave down in Charleston. They could see the sights, eat at some of those fancy restaurants, maybe go dancing. Then he shook his head slowly. Somehow he didn't think that would be what Stella would want, anymore than she would have wanted to visit Washington to see his father. Come to think of it, he no longer really knew what Stella wanted or what she was seeking in her life. It was becoming depressingly futile just trying to figure her ut. After a moment he left the room to join the other astronauts who were assembling for a lecture on astrophysics, but it was some time before he was able to concentrate fully on what was being said. Even when he did bring his attention to bear on the lecturer's words they seemed merely abstractions, nothing whatever to do with the real world and its problems.

BAIKONUR COSMODROME, KAZAKHSKAYA.

'No.'

The two men glared at one another. Korolev, who had snapped out a negative answer to his assistant's suggestion, was angry and tired. He was a man in a hurry but his haste was based not upon desire to see his years of work reach fruition for their own sake, but rather to enable a conclusion to be reached while he was still there to enjoy the accolades which would be his. Not an old man, he was ill and knew that his time could well run out before he had accomplished all he had set for himself.

His assistant, Ivan Kropotkin, ran a hand over his hair, dislodging still more dandruff which drifted down onto the collar of his shapeless jacket. He was worried, very worried. He had hoped that Korolev would play along. Apart from any other reason, his

130

superior's cooperation could have removed the need for using Maisky and his far-reaching, costly, and dangerous plan.

Gathering up the papers strewn over the table he stuffed them into an attach´e case. 'I will continue as originally planned, then,' he said.

'There is no other way,' Korolev said and turned dismissively to a blackboard on which were chalked complex calculations.

From the door Kropotkin glanced back. It was a pity the chief designer was so damned obstinate, he thought. With a little cooperation none of it would have been necessary.

He reached his own office, closed the door, then turned the key, taking care to do it silently. He didn't want interruptions but at the same time he didn't want anyone to know he was being secretive. He spent several minutes thinking carefully over the program, then began to write after insuring the sheet of paper rested on the hard surface of his desk. Maisky had been most particular about such incidental matters as leaving traces of their correspondence on blotters or other sheets of paper. It all seemed a trifle ridiculous to Kropotkin but he knew he couldn't take the chance of ignoring anything Maisky said. He tried to remember just when it was he had first decided to bring the woman into it. A long time ago it seemed. Certainly long enough for her and Maisky to have taken charge of the operation. All because they had run into seemingly insoluble problems at Baikonur.

The problems had been manifold. The guidance system was the first to cause trouble. Then they ran into difficulties with the liquid fuel transfer. Next, the re-entry heat shield. After that, the booster stage. Then another fault, and another, and another. At first they had dutifully reported every single one of their problems but then, someone, somewhere in the hierarchy, had begun to make noises indicating grave displeasure. So they stopped talking about the foul-ups and, almost as if blessed by some ancient god, they began to clear up. Eventually they were back on schedule and everything looked good.

Unfortunately, the difficult period through which they had passed had started people thinking about what would happen if they failed. These people were not scientists, they were politicians. And therefore they were concerned not with scientific matters but with political consequences. The Russian space effort had to succeed. The potential for proving to the world that their system was not merely idealogically right but also efficient, effective and capable of achieving anything the capitalists could do, was enormous.

That was when Maisky had been brought in. His brief was simple enough but extremely difficult to accomplish. Kropotkin shook his head sadly and finished the notes he was writing, sealed them into an envelope, put them in his pocket and strode out of the room. He had a meeting to attend, one which would set, finally, the date for the first manned flight. Then he would be attending a second meeting of even greater importance. At this one the notes he had made would be discussed by all the other leading scientists, Korolev apart, with the political emissaries from Moscow and with Maisky.

This second meeting was the one that really mattered. It would settle the final details of Maisky's plan and when it would be put into operation. It was a scheme that would insure that the Americans would not merely fail to be first into space but would also be massively discredited in the eyes of the rest of the world.

As to how Maisky's plan would work, that was something Kropotkin neither knew nor cared to know. Despite the fact that what they were doing was politically motivated, he was still a scientist. And in that role he sometimes found himself more in sympathy with fellow-scientists in other countries, even America, than he ever could be with politicians. Even those here in Russia.

EDWARDS AIR FORCE BASE, Ca.

Joe Ziegler was feeling mildly pleased with himself. For one thing Bill Simons had responded in an entirely unexpected manner to the news that he was now number one Atlas and that there might, just might, be a chance he would fly before anyone else. The news seemed to have given him new maturity: he was less aggressive towards the other astronauts, even keener to learn all he could about his mission and the machinery that would make it possible. Also pleasing to Ziegler was the fact that he had managed to get all the astronauts something they desperately wanted. More flying time. And not in the usual nailed-together F-102s. He had pulled strings and rank, had begged and cajoled and eventually he had liberated a couple of F-104Bs from their jealous guardians who were not sure the Air Force owed any favors to the already favored nine.

They had come out to Edwards for some additional weightlessness training and, as that was where the F-104Bs were based, they hadn't failed to seize the opportunity for a few hours flying. Six of the astronauts had left that morning, some going back to Langley, others off on good-will tours of factories manufacturing components. The three left at Edwards with Ziegler were Bill, Gary and Gus.

Grissom's foot had at last begun to make real progress but, as Ziegler had told Jim Magadini, it was too late to reinstate him as number one Atlas. The covert flight, if it took place, would be too soon for Gus to get back to full readiness. Joe had kept Gary along with Bill as often as he could, knowing that the latest astronaut couldn't fail to benefit from the experience although it had been decided there would be no back-up pilot for the covert flight. That had been Magadini's decision, one with which Joe had been pleased to agree. There was, after all, a limit to making plans for things that might never happen which, privately, Joe still thought of as a manifestation of some illogical political thinking.

Now, out in the sharp, clear, morning air at Edwards, the scene reminded Ziegler so much of the time he had spent out there with Yeager and White and the other high-fliers that he could almost imagine NASA and the space program were part of a dream. Glancing at Grissom and Herriman he grinned. 'Just like the old days,' he said.

Grissom laughed. 'Wishing them back, Joe?'

'Maybe, maybe.'

Herriman pointed out towards the western horizon. 'Here he comes,' he said.

The F-104B came in fast and low, raising dust from the desert and sending it swirling across the landing-strip where Ziegler, Herriman and Grissom stood. 'Still trying hard,' Gus remarked.

Ziegler nodded. For a moment, as he watched Simons pull the nose of the F-104B up into a steep climb, he felt the old doubts return. Then he shrugged them off. It was too late to revive old worries, old debates with himself. Apart from anything else he would stay happier if he kept in his mind the thought that the whole exercise might never get beyond the planning stage.

'I'll see you guys later,' he told the others and started towards the cluster of buildings which housed the administration offices and the control tower. When he had flown from here, back in the old days, the offices, living quarters, and the hangers had been battered, peeling, Quonsets and tarpaper-covered wooden shacks. Much of the accommodation had even been under canvas. Anywhere else such buildings would have housed spare parts for obsolete aircraft and other unwanted Air Force junk. At Edwards, a decrepit building was just one of many signs which showed that here, if nowhere else, flying came first and the best anything else could hope for was a poor second.

Now, Ziegler gloomily observed, even Edwards was showing signs of conforming. It was sad but inevitable. In those good old days the base had been just about as inhospitable as any place on earth could be. Nothing but sun, sand, scrub, and flying. All the flying a man could want. He felt a pang of regret that he hadn't stayed on here with Yeager, and Crossfield, and White, and the other Bell fliers. Then he felt a contrary twinge of conscience at this implied disloyalty to the astronauts.

The rivalry between the Bell X-series pilots and the new breed of spacemen was well known within the Air Force and occasionally hinted at by some of the more perceptive journalists. The public at large, the politicians, even the top military brass, were not aware of the rivalry or, if they were, pretended it didn't exist. Such rivalry, even if it wasn't in the best interests of the Air Force, was entirely understandable. The Edwards-based men firmly believed their way into space was the best, the most practical, the most economic, and, what was far more to the point, came closest to real flying. They did things that only men could do, they couldn't be replaced by machines the way the astronauts could. Machines or monkeys. Monkeys for God's sake! the cry went up at every conceivable opportunity.

While the astronauts were here, putting in some much wanted flying time, the host base's fliers kept their comments to themselves. After all, they knew that the ballyhoo, the decision to push ahead with Redstone and Atlas rockets was a decision over which the astronauts had no control. Here at Edwards they were all flying men and the only thing that mattered was how a man performed in the seat of a jet fighter.

For Bill Simons the outing was exactly what he needed. He had been eagerly anticipating the trip to Edwards for no better reason than as an outlet for the rebelliousness they all periodically experienced after endless bouts of training on machines that were well and truly bolted to the ground. The news he had been given by Joe Ziegler had really lifted him. He had felt, still felt, a warm glow of delight that all of his efforts had not proved in vain. The drag was that he couldn't tell anyone, Ziegler had really laid that on the line. No one had to know, not even Linda. Not that he would have told her, not yet. Telling Linda there was a good chance of his being literally on top of the world when their first child was being born didn't seem like a hot idea.

He leveled out, then banked the aircraft, and glanced down to the desert floor now far beneath him. Over to his left he could make out a white shimmer he knew was Bakersfield. He began a gentle turn to right and as he did so felt an almost imperceptible tremor. It was unexpected and he couldn't account for it but neither was it anything to heat up over. He glanced at his instruments and saw at once the altimeter was out. He frowned slightly but shrugged it off. Although careful, he couldn't have sworn on a stack of bibles that he'd checked the thing before takeoff. He glanced at the fuel gauges, they didn't look right either. He raked a swift glance across the instrument panel and realized that more than half the dials were either not functioning or were telling him things he didn't believe. He completed the turn to bring him on course for Edwards, noting as he did so that even the compass appeared to be out. He punched the button and called in.

'Field clear for you,' the answer came. 'Didn't expect you back this soon.' Everyone at Edwards knew how the astronauts hung onto every last second of air-time.

'Might have a little problem up here,' Bill said, his voice steady, and as casual, as a cabdriver reporting a flat tire.

'Serious?'

'Nothing I can't handle.'

That seemed to satisfy the control tower but a couple of minutes later he heard a different voice and realized that, whatever he might think about the situation, someone had sent for Joe Ziegler.

'What's this problem?' Joe asked.

Simons told him his instruments were acting up, adding, 'Seemed to have a little shake just before I noticed them. Maybe a connexion, maybe not.'

'Okay, Bill, come on in. The field's clear. We'll keep the phone off the hook in case you need anything.'

'Roger.'

For the next few minutes Simons concentrated hard, ready for any hint that things were deteriorating. He guessed he was at about ten thousand feet which put him at not much more than five thousand feet above the high desert around Edwards. He put the nose down and searched ahead for a sight of the base. He didn't see anything.

Ziegler's voice cut in suddenly. 'We've got you on radar, Bill. Got a date in Vegas?'

'No, why?'

'That's the way you're heading.'

Simons took a quick look at the sun and swore angrily to himself. Not even a greenhorn pilot should have made a mistake like that. What was the matter with him? All the excitement about flying a top secret, Presidentially-authorized trip into space must have gotten to him. He was letting slip the veneer of calm just about every pilot who'd ever lived put on every time he wore his uniform.

'Okay, things are worse than I guessed. I'll make a left then a right so you can be sure it's me you're looking at. Then you'd best give me a visual heading.'

135

'Okay,' Ziegler responded.

Simons made the first turn then, as he brought the F-104B to the right, he felt a tremor again.

'Got that shake again, Joe,' he advised.

'Okay. Continue with the right turn for about 120 degrees.'

'Roger.'

In the control tower at Edwards, Ziegler watched the radar screen trying not to display his tension as the tiny blob of light made the turn he had asked for. He realized he was holding his breath and slowly exhaled. With luck Bill would be in view inside ten minutes. Stepping back he turned to leave the room intent on going up onto the roof of the control tower.

'Colonel.'

'Yes.'

'He's turned again.'

Ziegler reached for the microphone. 'Bill, what's happening out there?'

In the cockpit of the F-104B Bill Simons heard Joe Ziegler's question but made no attempt to reply. Right at this moment he had his hands full. The aircraft had pitched forward into a steep dive and had simultaneously rolled sharply to the left. Not only was he going off course but the ground was rushing up at him faster than he cared to think about. Holding an idle conversation with someone who was in no position to help was low in his order of priorities.

With an effort he brought the nose up fractionally and felt the g-force pressing him down into his seat. By now he was low, much too low for comfort, and try as he did he couldn't get the nose up again. Somehow he had to put the F-104B down before he lost all control of what was rapidly turning out to be a tin tube full of problems.

Ahead he saw a patch of desert that looked pretty level. He considered whether he should put the wheels down or not. At the speed he would be traveling when he touched down wheels would be more hazard than help. As for his speed, with the controls having found a mind of their own, there didn't seem to be much he could do to correct it. He guessed he was still hitting well over 300 mph and that was no speed at which to land an airplane.

That left the eject button – but it didn't hold much promise of a solution. At his present altitude to use it would be suicidal. Staying where he was would probably kill him anyway, but at least he would have the satisfaction of knowing he'd be going out like every flying man hoped to die. Controlling his aircraft. Even if "controlling" was not the most appropriate word just at the moment.

136

Then he turned his full attention to handling the aircraft as it swept towards ground which began to look less and less suitable for landing the closer he came to it. As the underbody of the F-104B scraped along the arid surface of the desert it was, for a moment, almost as if he was landing on the strip at Edwards and he felt a surge of hope. Then he saw an outcrop less than two hundred yards ahead and, in those final milli-seconds before the aircraft hit rock and began its lethal cartwheel, one clear and distinct thought formed in Bill Simons' mind. It was not about his wife; it was not about the unborn child he would never see; it was not even about death. In the last moments of his life he was thinking that someone else would have the glory that had so nearly been his.

Just before the F-104B, now upside-down, smashed to the ground crushing the cockpit and its pilot into one tangled, bloodstained package of metal and flesh, Bill Simons was grinning tightly and murmuring to himself: 'The lucky sonofabitch.'

EDWARDS AIR FORCE BASE, Ca.

Gary Herriman shielded his face from the sand whipped up by the blast from the helicopter's rotor. Turning his back fully to the machine he found himself staring straight at the twisted mass of metal that was the remains of Bill Simons' F-104B. The sight hadn't improved since the previous day. He and Joe Ziegler had been in one of the two rescue choppers sent out after the F-104B's blip had vanished from the radar screen. They had found the wreckage easily enough and they had landed although that had been unnecessary. Even from an altitude of five hundred feet there was no doubt what had happened to Bill.

But they'd gone down and they'd looked, then climbed back into the helicopter and returned to Edwards. All in silence.

Now they were back, this time with the security chief from Langley who was there to investigate the crash. Gary hadn't met him before but Omar Rogerson and Joe Ziegler were old friends.

Rogerson made a preliminary inspection of the site and the aircraft, not speaking, not making notes, just looking. Once he glanced across at Joe and Gary but if he had any thoughts on what he saw they were not apparent in his impassive, dry-skinned face.

After walking slowly along the scar left in the surface of the desert by Simons' aircraft he rejoined the others. 'At least he didn't feel any pain,' he said.

Ziegler nodded. 'I know what you mean, Rog, but it doesn't make it any easier to take.'

Rogerson didn't answer. Death seldom moved him anymore. He had seen too much of it and so too had Joe Ziegler but he knew there was a difference here. For Joe this wasn't just another pilot for whom the everyday risks hadn't paid off – this was one of a small, tight-knit team of very special men.

Rogerson nodded, left Joe and Gary and walked across to his own team who were laying out the equipment they would need.

'Okay,' he said. 'Let's make a start.'

Slowly and methodically the investigators began a comprehensive survey of the scene of the crash. Everything was photographed and its position located on a large-scale plan of the area. Only then was anything moved or even touched.

Joe Ziegler watched for a few minutes, angrily helpless but knowing he would only get in the way if he tried to assist. He looked up into the cloudless blue of the sky above the Mojave Desert. Whatever it was that had caused this crash it was unlikely to be pilot error – some lousy little piece of engineering had failed. The one thing no pilot, good or bad, could protect himself against.

He glanced at Gary Herriman, not missing the unnatural paleness and the taut skin around the eyes and mouth. With sudden concern he realized he was looking at the new number one Atlas pilot. He shook his head angrily. Not anymore, not now. Now, Bobby Kennedy, the President, to say nothing of von Braun and Jim Magadini, and whoever else might be in on the secret, would have to change their tune.

'Come on, Gary,' he said. 'There's nothing we can do out here.'

They took one of the jeeps that had driven out, complete with unnecessary medical equipment, and drove back to Edwards.

Gus Grissom was waiting for them. 'Jim's been trying to reach you,' he said to Ziegler. 'He wants you to call him before you talk to the press.'

'The press?'

'Dozens of them, and more arriving every minute.'

'Where are they?'

'The base commander's fenced them into the mess hall but they'll bust out if they don't get something soon.'

'Okay, I'll see them as soon as I've talked with Jim. Are there any direct lines on this place?'

'No idea, do you want me to find out?'

'No, maybe not. I don't want to make a big deal out of it. Look, just wander over to the switchboard, and see that nobody listens when I talk to Jim.'

'Okay, Joe.' Grissom hesitated. 'Are you just being careful, or is something going on?'

Joe managed a smile. 'I just want to talk to Jim about something I don't think the Bell-X guys should hear.'

Grissom nodded disbelievingly but didn't argue. If Joe wanted to play games that was his affair. Nevertheless, he sensed something was in the wind.

Ziegler watched the astronaut walk away, still favoring his troublesome foot, angry that he couldn't be completely honest with Gus.

When he got through to Magadini he answered the rush of concerned questions which sought to fill the gaps in the bare news that had been passed through during the night.

'How is this going to affect us?' Magadini asked when Ziegler had finished.

'Totally,' Joe said. 'You'll have to call our young friend in Washington and tell him all his plans are off.'

'He won't like that.'

'That's tough.'

'He'll still expect a flight.'

'There'll still be one. The only difference is, it won't be when he wants it.'

'He won't agree to a delay,' Magadini said positively.

'There's no choice.'

'Why? What difference does Bill's...does this make?'

'For God's sake, Jim!'

'Listen, Joe. When did you tell Bill? A couple of days ago. So there has been no time for anything to happen that can't accommodate a different name in the slot.'

Ziegler didn't answer. He stood for a moment looking out through the dust-smeared windows towards the landing-strip.

Magadini was right. All Washington wanted was a rush into space. It didn't matter who was in the hot seat. As far as they were concerned, one astronaut was just as good as any other.

'Gary's next in line,' he said quietly.

'I know. Does that give us any problems?'

'No more than with John, or Wally, or Scott, or any of them.'

'You'd better tell him, then get back here.'

Ziegler was silent for a moment. 'Jim. I want to talk to the...' He broke off, concerned at being overheard. 'I want to talk to the Man,' he said.

'The..! Are you kidding?'

'No, I'm not.'

'What about?'

'You know damn well what about.'

'We've talked to Bobby, what else do you need?'

'Look, I don't care if he is the Man's brother. He's still just a politician. I want to hear, with my own ears, the President himself tell me this is necessary.'

'Joe, you're not indispensible. None of us is.'

'What does that mean? Are you saying you'll fire me.'

'Of course not. But he might.'

Ziegler laughed shortly. 'What makes you think that frightens me? Call him, Jim.'

'How do you expect me to reach him? I can't pick up the telephone and call direct. Bobby will hear, he'll want to know why. He can block me.'

'Then find another way.'

'How, for God's sake?'

'Jim. Go into my office, open the cupboard, and take out my dress uniform. Look at the medal ribbons on it. There are three rows of them. Now, I've never traded on those colored ribbons before but there's a time for everything. This is it.'

'Okay, Joe, I'll try.'

'Right. One other thing, Jim.'

'What?'

'How's Linda taken it?'

'I haven't heard.'

'Who told her?'

'I don't know.'

Ziegler felt his face reddening with suppressed anger. 'For God's sake, this wasn't just any poor dumb flier like me, this was an astronaut. They're supposed to be America's finest, they're the new heroes, the new frontiersmen. Is it too much to ask that, before everybody forgets Bill ever existed, someone looks after his wife?'

'Joe, someone will be taking care of her.'

'Someone? Anyone? It won't do, Jim.'

'Okay, okay. I'll find out what's happening. Anyway, damn it, you know as well as I do that the other wives will have rallied round.'

'Maybe they have but that isn't necessarily what she wants right now.'

'Any suggestions?' If there was sarcasm in Magadini's question it was lost somewhere along the thousands of miles separating the two men.

140

'Where's Diana?' Joe asked.

'I haven't seen her for a couple of days.'

'Does she know about Bill?'

'She must. It's been on tv and we've got a mob of newspapermen besieging the administration building.'

'Same here. Look, call Diana, she'll know what's being done for Linda.'

'Okay. Get back here as soon as you can, Joe. Gary too.'

'Right.'

'And Joe.'

'Yes?'

'No one likes this any better than you do.'

'If that's so, why don't we just tell Little Brother to shove it?'

'We don't because we're paid to do as we're told. Right now we've been told to get a man up there. That might not be the only thing NASA exists for, but it comes pretty damn high on the list.'

'Okay, okay. What do I tell the press?'

'Just the bare facts. Bill was on a routine training flight and crashed. Don't give any details.'

'I don't have any details!'

Ziegler replaced the telephone and stood for a moment before going out into the bright sunshine to look for Gary Herriman.

They could be on their way back to Langley within the hour, the sooner the better. Despite his earlier pangs of regret for having passed up the chance to stay on here after the Korean War was over, Joe Ziegler was finding Edwards a less attractive place than it had once been.

He saw Gary Herriman coming towards him, his color now back to normal. Joe knew he wouldn't enjoy telling Gary the news that he would be replacing Bill Simons. He decided to postpone telling him for as long as possible, preferably not until after he had seen the President.

'Come on, Gary,' he said. 'Let's go and talk to the gentlemen of the press.'

NEWPORT NEWS, Va.

Diana dropped down into an armchair, closed her eyes and sighed deeply. 'I'm glad that's over,' she said.

She had been with Linda Simons for most of the night until finally the carefully prescribed tranquilizers had taken effect. Linda's parents had flown in from Akron and, once she had assured herself they could cope, Diana left them to it.

Joe Ziegler went into the kitchen and made coffee for them both. 'It's scenes like that our politicians should see,' he said when he came back into the room to sit on the arm of Diana's chair.

She frowned. 'Any particular reason?'

'It just might make them think twice before using people.'

'What people?'

'Bill, me, Jim. Now Gary. We're all being used by people who play games with lives. Just so they can catch a few more votes next election, grab an extra line in the history books.'

'You've lost me, Joe.'

Ziegler hesitated then sat back and forced a grin onto his face. 'Sorry. I'm sounding off and you haven't the slightest idea what the hell it is I'm talking about.' He shook his head. 'What's more I don't think I can tell you.'

'Why not?'

'Security.'

'I wouldn't be here if I didn't have top security clearance. You know that.'

'This is something else. Not even NASA's top brass know about it.'

Diana frowned showing her bewilderment. 'If it's so secret then how...' Her voice trailed away.

Ziegler grinned widely, showing the first real signs of relaxation since he had returned from Edwards. 'How does a lowly Air Force Colonel qualify?'

'Something like that,' Diana admitted wryly.

There was a long pause before Ziegler spoke again. 'I'm not sure what the penalty is for going against a directive from the next President's brother but I think I'll chance it. After all, you are the senior psychiatrist on the project and know as much about the astronauts as any of us.'

He quietly outlined the plan for a covert manned flight, using an Atlas rocket, well ahead of the planned Redstone schedule.

'Are you ready for an Atlas flight?' Diana asked when he finished.

'I think we're taking a serious risk with an Atlas flight at this stage. We need more tests with unmanned Atlas rockets and we need the scheduled sub-orbital Redstones. There's still too much we're not sure about.'

'But, technically, it is all possible?'

'Technically, yes, I guess it is.'

'And that's the argument Washington is using?'

142

'Right in one.'

'Have you told them you have doubts?'

'Them? Him. I've told RFK. Now I'm going to tell his brother the same thing.'

'The President?'

'Either someone gives me a better reason or someone calls it off. In both cases, the President seems to be the one to do it.'

'When are you seeing him?'

Ziegler laughed without humor. 'The new frontier hasn't reached the gates of the White House yet. Jim's tried and has gotten nowhere. Now I'm using the back door.'

'What does that mean?'

'I seem to have some pull with Eisenhower. I've made a formal request that he gets me into see Kennedy.'

'Will he?'

'I gave a pretty big hint what it was about and he said he'd try. The Kennedys maybe haven't much in common with the last administration but they're great ones for tradition. I don't think they'll turn Ike down flat.'

'And in the meantime?'

'We keep on planning for an Atlas-Mercury launch ahead of schedule.'

'With Gary in the hot seat.'

'That's right.'

'Is he that far advanced in his training? He's been here less than six months.'

'He's done well, better then anyone could've hoped. He's as ready as any of them.'

'What do the others think about it?'

'The others? My God, they don't know. Bill knew, I told him a couple of days before the accident. I haven't even told Gary he's next in line. As for the others, they stay in sweet ignorance. They have to. Not just because it might cause friction but because its the way the whole deal is set up. All-around secrecy.' He laughed. 'Listen to me. I'm telling you, which is probably enough to have me thrown into Leavenworth for ever.'

'How can you keep it secret, Joe? Surely everyone will find out.'

'If it happens, and I keep telling myself it won't, there'll be no need for anyone to know until the last minute. We proceed as if for a normal unmanned test-flight. Assuming we go ahead, assuming there's no last-minute stay of execution, about half an hour before liftoff we withdraw all personnel from the launch-tower vicinity.

Then we take the astronaut in and place him in the capsule. Once he's installed we continue with the countdown.'

'What about communication, sensors?'

'Mission Control lacks the facility for that at their end; after all, as far as they know there's nobody in the capsule. All communications and medical sensors will be linked into a special control unit we're setting up.'

'And when do you break the news?'

That was something which irked Ziegler. He was certain now that if he hadn't been critical of Bobby Kennedy's intentions they would have gone ahead and included reference to the flight in the Inaugural Address. If they had there might have been a build up of pressure against the flight. Certainly it would then have been possible to harness the press, and public opinion, against taking risks with an astronaut's life. Now, with the public, the press, government, just about everybody but a tiny handful of them, in ignorance there was nowhere to turn for support.

When Joe had gotten back from Edwards Jim Magadini had told him the way Bobby Kennedy intended playing the flight. The rocket would be launched, the capsule put into orbit. Then, when everything was running smoothly, the President would go on tv and tell the world. The security blanket would be lifted and, in Ziegler's view, all hell would break loose.

'Why?' Diana asked.

'There'll be some very angry people around. Gilruth and Webb for two. And the rest of the astronauts. Damn it, they'll all think we've treated them badly over this and they'll be right.'

'So what happens now?'

'Until I've seen the President, we press ahead.'

'And Gary?'

'I'll tell him when I can't delay any further.'

'We never did sort out the problem between him and Stella, you know.'

'How is she?'

Diana frowned. 'I'm not sure. Subdued. She spends most of her time at home, doesn't see anyone much.'

'What about Leandros?'

'I don't think so.'

'Did you speak to him?'

'I bawled him out. I didn't name Stella of course but I think he got the message.'

'Good.'

144

'One thing I got from Stella, the last time I talked to her. She and Gary still sleep together although their sex life is non-existent.

'So?'

'Gary seems to sleep badly, has restless nights, dreams a lot, talks in his sleep.'

'I haven't noticed anything to suggest he's suffering from lack of sleep. Whatever fills his dreams, it hasn't affected his work.'

Diana nodded her head, not in agreement so much as an indication she wasn't interested in pursuing the matter. Dreams and their meanings came into her work but only peripherally. Unlike some of her older colleagues, she hadn't much faith in their value as signposts to the state of mind of patients.

'Can I be there when you tell Gary about the flight? His reaction could be interesting.'

'At the moment you're not in on the act. I'll try to get that cleared officially. No, the hell with it. Kennedy said I could pick my own team. Well, you're on it. Yes, you can be there.'

'I'm pleased you're learning to trust me,' Diana said with a smile.

He grinned. 'I'd better. I forgot to tell you, I heard from Madisonville a couple of days ago.'

'Your aunt?'

'Yes. She just called to ask how you were.'

'She's nice.'

'Maybe we Kentuckians are easily impressed.'

Diana laughed. 'Maybe you are.'

They looked at one another, suddenly serious.

'Come to bed, Joe.' Diana said quietly.

They went into the bedroom and for the first time in their relationship it was Diana who led. Although there hadn't been many opportunities during the past few weeks they had made love frequently since that first time and there had been a deeply satisfying similarity in each experience. Their bodies had seemed perfectly attuned, one to the other, and every time their mutual satisfaction had been complete.

Now, however, there was a different urgency in Diana's body and, although at first he was unsure how to respond, Joe soon found his desire overcoming any remaining inhibitions he might have held. Their coupling was long and demanding and showed little of the tenderness of previous occasions. After what seemed to be an hour Joe felt Diana's body arch beneath his, her legs tightening about him as her breath forced its way between her teeth.

'My God,' she said after a moment. 'That was really something.'

145

'It was certainly different,' Joe said. 'Am I allowed to ask what came over you?'

'I think I wanted to prove something to myself and maybe to you as well.'

'Prove what?'

'The way we made love before, it was beautiful, better than I've ever known, better even than with Lew.' She laughed softly. 'I didn't put that very well, did I?'

'I understand.'

'Yes, I think you do. But there was still some holding back with both of us. Tonight I wanted to let everything go, see what happened. That way we won't enter marriage with any hang-ups about our sex life. Other things, maybe, but not that.'

'You forgot one thing,' Joe said.

'What?'

'You might have let everything go, I didn't.'

Diana sat up, concern on her face. 'What do you mean?'

He laughed and took her hand, guiding it down his body. 'That's what I mean,' he said.

'Well, in that case, maybe we'd better try a little harder next time.'

They began to make love again, just as wildly and Joe was unable to hold back for more than a few moments. They lay in silence, then, as Joe rolled over onto his back taking Diana with him so that she lay close to his side, the telephone rang.

Diana looked at him. 'Well?'

Joe smiled. 'Better answer it. Maybe a patient of yours is standing on a ledge, threatening to jump.'

'I don't have that kind of patient but if I did, right at this moment, I'd be tempted to yell, "jump!"/'. Diana reached out for the telephone, spoke her name, frowned, then handed the instrument to Joe. 'It's for you,' she said. 'Jim Magadini.'

Ziegler took the telephone. 'Yes, Jim.'

He listened intently for a few moments, said a quick good-bye, then hung up. He swung off the bed, reaching for his clothes.

'What is it?' Diana asked.

'Eisenhower pulled it off. I've got an appointment on Pennsylvania Avenue, tonight.'

'Joe, it's only seven in the morning.'

'I have to be in Washington by noon.' He finished dressing, leaned over and kissed her. 'Don't misunderstand, but this is important.'

Diana smiled. 'Hurry back.' After Joe had gone she lay for a while, thinking over what he had told her. Unwillingly, she found herself doubting that he would be able to sway the President. Her

146

experience with corporations reminded her how a decision so readily turned into a runaway truck. Getting it rolling wasn't easy, but once on the move the damn thing was almost unstoppable.

WASHINGTON, D.C.

'Let both sides seek to invoke the wonders of science instead of its terrors. Together let us explore the stars, conquer the deserts, eradicate disease, tap the ocean depths and encourage the arts and commerce. Let both sides unite to heed in all...'

The telephone rang and Joe Ziegler reached out to turn down the sound on the tv before answering the call.

The caller was a secretary at the White House, someone pretty junior, Ziegler guessed, otherwise he would have been at the Capitol where the new President was delivering his Inaugural Address. The secretary told Ziegler what time to be there and hung up, as if angry at missing all the celebrations. For a moment Ziegler watched the tv screen, taking in the scene of the wind-tousled bare headed young man in whom so many had placed their hopes for the future. Then he turned up the sound before stretching out again on the bed.

'And so my fellow Americans: ask not what your country can do for you – ask what you can do for your country. My fellow citizens of the world: ask not what America will do for you, but what together we can do for the freedom of man.'

That was the problem, Ziegler thought; it didn't matter a damn what you wanted to do. In the end it always came down to the other guy. If he helped, you just might get there; if he didn't, all the wishing and hoping in the world would have no effect. No effect at all.

He turned off the tv and tried to sleep but couldn't and when the time came to keep his appointment he was impatient to get down to some hard talking with the new President.

The White House was a brilliant, almost incandescent blaze of light. The building, the grounds, the roads and avenues surrounding it were all illuminated with what must have been a million lights. It was almost as if there was an attempt to show that the new administration would not only be dynamic but would also be open.

Joe Ziegler had been escorted to a small room in the East Wing where he waited, a little edgy, unsure how the new President would respond to someone who had used back-door methods to get in to see him.

The door of the room opened and a young woman looked in. 'I'm sorry you've been kept waiting, Colonel. Can I get you anything? A cup of coffee, or something stronger than that?'

'No, thank you,' Ziegler told her. 'Have you any idea how long the President will be?'

'No, I haven't. Oh.' The sudden note of surprise came as the young woman realized someone was behind her. She turned, letting the door open wider and Ziegler found himself face to face with the new President of the United States.

Kennedy reached out and firmly clasped Ziegler's hand. 'Colonel Ziegler, I'm sorry I was delayed.'

'It's good of you to see me, Mr. President. I know this is a busy time.'

As the door closed behind the young woman the President sat down, motioning Ziegler to do the same. Ziegler did so looking intently into the other man's face. Close up, the family resemblence with his brother Bobby was less evident than in photographs. The face was squarer, more relaxed although the same intensity of purpose glowed from the eyes.

Ziegler had no illusions. This man wouldn't be any easier to sway than his younger brother. The only hope he had was that Jack Kennedy might be prepared to apply more discretion to his ambition.

'President Eisenhower thinks highly of you, Colonel,' Kennedy said. 'I took a look at your record after he called me. Impressive. You're not a man who wastes time, either his own or that of others.'

'I don't think I'm doing that, sir.'

'Good. Okay, Colonel, fire away.'

'You know we have set in motion a full-scale countdown for a manned Atlas-Mercury launch on February 20.'

'Of course.'

'And do you also know how we've been pressured into making that date? We're cutting corners, taking chances. All along Project Mercury has operated on the principle that the progress of our work, both on the equipment and with the men, determines the date of any launch, even a test-launch. Now we're throwing that system away and operating one that is its complete reverse. This time equipment and men are at the mercy of an arbitrary date.'

'Arbitrary?'

'That's the word I used, Mr. President.'

'What gives you the idea the date is arbitrary?'

'Your brother gave me the idea. He has some crazy notion that a Russian spacecraft is going up sooner than we thought. So, because we have an unmanned Atlas-Mercury test slated for February 20,

148

we're going to send a man up in the damn thing, ready or not.' Ziegler stopped, aware that he had allowed his irritation to get the better of him and his voice had risen.

'What you've said isn't an entirely fair assessment of the situation, Colonel,' the President said. 'First, the inform ation that the Soviets are planning an early launch, March 10 to 20, we believe, isn't a crazy notion. Our intelligence appears sound and we have no reason to doubt its accuracy. As for using the unmanned test-flight you have scheduled for February 20, yes, I'll agree that seems like opportunism but if we're going on any date between now and March 10, that date is as good as any.'

'Or as bad.'

'You expect the test to be a failure?'

'Of course not.'

'Then where is the problem?'

'We're putting a man in the damn thing, that's the problem.'

'Why is that a problem?'

Ziegler was silent for a moment. He was boxed-in and he knew it. The countdown for the scheduled Atlas-Mercury test was as near perfection as it could be. Whether a man went with it or not it couldn't be improved. He took a deep breath and started again.

'Mr. President. We have had some poor results from the last few launches.'

'I know that, Colonel. The whole world knows it.'

'It was our intention to have a series of Atlas-Mercury launches and some more Redstone-Mercurys before a man went up. Successful launches, I'm talking about.'

'I'll give you that,' the President said. 'A string of successes would make everyone feel better about the chances of any succeeding launch but there isn't very much logic in it, is there?'

Ziegler shook his head, feeling that already he was losing the battle. 'Tell me something, sir. What's so damned important about being first? First doesn't mean best. Let's get it right, put the capsule up when and where we want it, get it down the same way, and prove that we can do it again and again, as often as we choose.'

The President shook his head, stood up and went to the window to look out at the brightly lit gardens. 'The Soviet launch will be aimed at one of two things. Either to give them a military advantage or a propaganda advantage. Either way, I believe that the American people will be best served if we do it first.'

It had come into the open slowly and for a moment Ziegler didn't speak. His conversations with Bobby Kennedy and Jim Magadini

149

had hinted this was the way the politicians' minds were working. Now it was clear the hints had been pointing the right way.

'It's a hell of an expensive publicity stunt,' he said bitterly.

Kennedy turned and looked at him. 'I think I'll make out I didn't hear that, Colonel.'

There was a long, awkward silence before Ziegler spoke again. 'What do you want us to do?'

'Continue with your preparations. We are intensifying our inquiries in Moscow. If we learn anything which suggests they are falling back, then we'll postpone. I give you my word.'

'And if they look as if they're going ahead?'

'Then we do too. On February 20.'

'Ready or not?'

'No, damn it.' The President's voice rose slightly. 'If we're not ready, for any genuine reason, then of course we put a hold on the countdown until it's cleared up.'

'And if we don't clear it up?'

Kennedy smiled. 'That doesn't seem very likely, does it, Joe? Not with all the brains, the expertise, and the money, down at NASA.'

Ziegler nodded slowly. He hadn't missed the change to the informal use of his first name. The President knew he had won this particular round. The trouble was, it looked like it was the last one.

He suddenly recalled the President's Inaugural Address and particularly the part where Kennedy had called upon Americans to ask, not what their country could do for them, but what they could do for their country.

Now, suddenly, a small group of Americans, including himself and especially Gary Herriman, were about to discover not what they could do for their country but what their country expected of them.

EDWARDS AIR FORCE BASE, Ca.

Omar Rogerson sat back on his heels, wiped sweat from his face and chest, and tried to make himself comfortable against a chunk of rock like the one that had removed any hope Bill Simons might have had of getting his aircraft down safely.

The heat and discomfort didn't bother Rogerson. He had served in North Africa during World War II, and in Korea, which was where he had first met Joe Ziegler, and neither of those places had been strong on comfort. Although, he had to admit, he wouldn't like to be

150

on this patch of the Mojave Desert in mid-summer.

He glanced over to where the main pieces of wreckage lay, some still containing parts of the pilot's body the medics had been unable to separate from the twisted metal. That sight didn't trouble him either. He'd seen too many wrecked aircraft, some with a personal involvement like when his brother had landed a Liberator upside-down outside El Adem. He barely knew Bill Simons. Come to that, he didn't know any of the astronauts very well. His duties kept him on the move, never letting him establish close friendships with anyone.

Maybe that was it. Maybe, at last, he was getting too old for all this activity. Pushing sixty, and nowhere nearly as fit as he'd once been, Rogerson was starting to think about retirement. He even had a place picked out. A little house in Clearwater, close to the sea, and warm all the year round. Not cold, like some of the places his duties took him, nor as damn hot as others.

One of his assistants came into view, heading towards him, and Rogerson sighed as he levered himself upright. This was the kind of thing he was up against now. Bright young guys, with fire in their bellies, believing all things were possible and that even the job of security officer could lead onto great things. Trouble was, they were right. Being Chief of Security at one of NASA's biggest plants could open many doors, always assuming you were the kind of man who could take advantage of such opportunities. Rogerson shook his head sadly. Now he wasn't just feeling old, and looking old, he was starting to think old.

His assistant reached his side and held up a hunk of metal. 'I think we might have a little curiosity here, Chief.'

'What is it, Jerry?'

'The altimeter. Or, maybe I should say, what's left of it.'

'So?'

'So, I'd like you to take a look.'

Rogerson stared at the other man trying to read something in his eyes, then gave up with a sigh. He knew the principle involved, damn it. The young man was only following his own instructions. When in doubt, have your work checked by someone else but don't compare notes beforehand. He took the damaged altimeter and went across to the panel-truck they were using as a mobile laboratory. Slowly and methodically he took the instrument apart, trying to keep his mind on what he was doing and away from what the fishing would be like out in Tampa Bay. When he was through he called the assistant over.

'What did you get?' he asked.

Jerry flipped open a notebook. 'Scratches along the back of the instrument, particularly around the terminals.'

'The whole goddamn thing is scratched,' Rogerson said.

'Not like that.'

Rogerson sighed. 'Okay. Let Pete have a look at it.'

His assistant called over another of the team and while Pete worked on the altimeter Rogerson and his assistant sat in the sun trying not to get too excited about what could be the result of a mechanic's carelessness with a screwdriver.

When the third set of notes were ready for comparison the three men went over everything with care and deliberation.

'Looks bad,' Pete said, the first to put into words what the others were thinking.

'Let's not get hot over this,' Rogerson cautioned. 'Maybe the altimeter was faulty, but even if it was damaged deliberately, that wouldn't have caused the crash.'

The others looked at him in silence for some moments until Rogerson shook his head slowly. 'Okay, okay,' he said. 'Let's go back to the beginning and run through everything again.'

'Those tremors the pilot reported.'

'What about them?'

Jerry grinned suddenly. 'Maybe nothing, just an idea.' He wandered off, trying to appear casual but Rogerson could sense the excitement the young man was feeling. He didn't blame him for wanting to play it his own way, it was the kind of thing he would have done. No, he corrected himself, it was the kind of thing he had done in the past.

'Okay, Pete,' he told the other investigator. 'Let's you and me see how much of the engine we can put back together.'

They toiled away in the sun for a couple of hours before Rogerson called a rest-period. In that time they had gone a long way towards piecing together the engine of the F-104B. The main part was still in one piece and too damn big to handle without the special lifting equipment they would be bringing in later. They compromised by moving all the smaller pieces to the main section and comparing breaks and burns as adequately as they could without a microscope. After the break they restarted but already Rogerson was pretty certain the engine had not been damaged by an explosion and neither had there been a flame-out. He wasn't prepared to put his opinion into writing but he would have wagered the downpayment on the house in Clearwater on it.

'Chief.'

Rogerson looked up to see Jerry standing beside him, an

expression on his face that combined delight with something else he couldn't quite put a word to. 'What?'

'You got a minute?'

Rogerson followed Jerry across to the starboard wing of the wrecked aircraft. The younger man lifted up a strip of aluminum with a jagged edge. 'Careful you don't cut yourself, Chief,' he said.

Rogerson grunted at the unwelcome solicitude, refraining from telling the young man that he had survived this far in his life without such helpful suggestions.

'There,' Jerry said, pointing.

Rogerson followed the direction of the other man's finger. On the inside of the skin, just by the inboard end of the aileron was a patch of what looked like black paint. Some of it had been scraped off, he guessed by Jerry. He rubbed at the black stain with his forefinger, then sniffed at it.

'There's more,' Jerry said, reaching inside the wing. He pulled a section of the aileron control free and showed it to Rogerson. The same black stain was present only this time tiny slivers of something which reflected the sunlight were lodged in the blackness.

'Glass?'

'That's right, Chief.'

'And the black stain?'

'Some kind of acid. From the speed it all happened, something fast acting. The vial that contained it was probably exploded by a small device, maybe a tiny piece of plastic explosive just big enough to smash the glass. The acid did the rest. If the aircraft had caught fire we wouldn't have found a damn thing. That black stain would've blended right in with any charring.'

Rogerson nodded his head slowly. He knew now what Jerry's expression had been conveying earlier. His delight, in finding something that might easily have been overlooked, had been tempered with the cold realization Rogerson now felt. Bill Simons' death had not been a result of accident, or pilot error, or even just plain old-fashioned bad luck. The F-104B had been sabotaged.

LANGLEY AIR FORCE BASE, Va.

After parking his car, Gary Herriman went into the administration building. He was tired, having slept badly, but Joe Ziegler's call had sounded urgent. He rubbed at his eyes and stifled a yawn. The previous night Stella had suddenly snapped out of the torpor she'd been in for weeks. She had told him she wanted a vacation, not with him but alone. The statement had surprised him, chiefly because it was spoken so positively, in direct contrast to the apathetic manner she had displayed recently. He hesitated for a few minutes then agreed. Since she could do so without his permission there wasn't much point in arguing.

A half hour later, while he was in the bathroom, he heard her making a telephone call and when he came downstairs Stella was watching tv again. Before he spoke he sensed that her apathy had returned. He asked about the proposed vacation but she merely shrugged, telling him she would go later in the year.

By the time they went to bed the silence had deepened into one that lay between them like a medieval sword. He didn't sleep well and, on the few occasions he dozed off, was jolted awake by dreams which wouldn't stick in his mind. Altogether he felt lousy and, despite efforts to the contrary, couldn't help but blame Stella. He'd tried improving things between them but she'd made no comparable move towards him. It wasn't simply a matter of meeting half-way, she hadn't even moved off the baseline.

Joe had told him the meeting would be in Jim Magadini's office and Gary was the first to arrive. He spent a couple of minutes talking to Magadini's secretary who gave him some black coffee which helped brighten the day a little. By the time Joe arrived, along with Omar Rogerson, Gary was beginning to feel much better. His feeling of well-being didn't last long.

Rogerson made his report, detailing the results of the investigation of Bill Simons' crash. From their lack of reaction to the news that the aircraft had been sabotaged, it was clear the basic facts had already been communicated to Ziegler and Magadini. For Gary the news was more than the shock of a colleague's death. This was an admission that their tight, closely-guarded, world was not impregnable and that they were not everybody's heroes.

'I was slow,' Rogerson wound up. 'I did something a crash investigator should never do. I formed advance opinions, even to the point of ignoring the information you gave me, Joe, about the tremors Bill reported. I assumed either a pilot error or a simple

154

mechanical or electrical malfunction. Since Bill was a good pilot I was more than halfway to believing the crash was a result of a malfunction.'

'So what exactly happened?'

'Several instruments had been tampered with, the altimeter and the compass among them. That caused him problems but the real damage was done by two small explosive devices. Nothing big. You could stand them on this desk, fire them off and none of us would be hurt, wouldn't even blow the papers off the desk. But placed where they were, and discharging concentrated acid, the first severed all controls to the tailplane. Once that happened Bill was in bad shape. When the second cork was popped in the starboard wing, he hadn't a hope unless he could glide in onto a nice flat runway. All he had was a patch of not very level desert and a hunk of rock that couldn't have been in a worse place.'

'Any ideas on who or why?' Ziegler asked.

Rogerson shook his head. 'Too early. I can theorize, but that's all.'

'Let's hear the theories,' Magadini said.

'Simple act of sabotage against the Air Force. The why of that could be anything from a dissatisfied employee all the way to a nut who doesn't like his sleep being disturbed by low-flying aircraft.'

'Not many people are disturbed by what goes on at Edwards,' Ziegler said. 'Boron's the nearest town of any size and I don't reckon they'd object too much. Anyway, they would have neither the opportunity nor ability to do anything like this. Some ground-crewman with a grudge, well, I suppose that's a possibility. He would have opportunity and maybe expertise, but surely nothing as drastic as this? Setting fire to the mess hall maybe, not blowing an aircraft out of the sky.'

'Anyway,' Magadini said. 'How many cases of sabotage, really serious incidents like this, have there been in the last five years?'

Rogerson nodded his head. 'I don't know the statistics but I guess not many.'

'What about sabotage specifically against NASA?'

'That's more like it, I suppose. Someone who wanted to slow down the space effort. Cause delays.'

'The Russians?'

'Who else?'

'Why should they bother?' Rogerson asked.

Ziegler looked at Magadini who nodded his head. 'There's something you don't know, Rog,' he said. 'You too, Gary, which is why you're here this morning.' He went on to outline the circumstances surrounding the plans for a secret flight which would beat the Russians into space.

'And Bill was the man who would be flying the mission?' Rogerson asked.

'That's right.'

'So now what happens?'

Ziegler turned to Herriman. 'You're next Atlas,' he said.

For a moment Herriman didn't answer. 'Well,' he said quietly. 'I guess that's what I'm here for. Whether I fly next year or next month doesn't make a hell of a lot of difference.'

'I still hope it will be next year, not next month.'

'What do I need to do?'

'We continue as before, intensify your training schedule, push you even harder than you've been pushed so far.'

'I didn't think that was possible.'

Ziegler grinned. 'Neither did I but now I'm starting to think like the powers that be, nothing's impossible.'

'What about the others?' Gary asked. 'Do they stay in the dark?'

'Yes.'

'They won't like it, the secrecy part.'

'I know, Gary. Believe me, we've thought hard about it but it's best for everyone if they know nothing. Later, well, as soon as we have the all-clear from Washington, they'll be the first to know.'

'When will that be When will Washington allow you to release the news that I've gone up with the rocket?'

Ziegler hesitated. 'There's no hard policy but I get the impression that we'll be releasing the information as soon as we know everything is going well.'

Herriman thought for a moment, his face serious. Then he laughed softly. 'So if we have another affair like the Atlas-Mercury snafu, you sneak me out and say nothing?'

'That's about it.'

For a moment none of the four men in the room spoke. At least two of them, Joe Ziegler and Gary Herriman, were thinking that if the launch turned out like the Atlas-Able disaster there would be nothing of the astronaut left to sneak out. Just an insignificant addition to a massive heap of ashes on the launch pad.

Looking at Gary's untroubled face Joe remembered he had promised Diana she could be present when Gary was told he would be flying in place of Bill Simons. Well, it didn't seem to matter much, his reaction had been practically nil.

'Who knows about it?' Gary asked.

156

'I'll brief you,' Joe said, 'Until then, tell no one without clearing it with me.'

'What about Stella?'

Ziegler hesitated. It was an awkward one. He didn't see how it could be kept from her indefinitely but so long as Stella's personal life needed some attention she seemed less than a good security risk.

Gary seemed to read Ziegler's thoughts. 'Maybe we keep it from her, for now. Until we know it's certain to go ahead.'

Ziegler agreed with relief showing in his face. 'Now,' he went on. 'The inquiries into the sabotage on Bill's aircraft will need more attention than Rog and his boys can give it without outside help. The problem is, we've decided to keep that under wraps as well.' He laughed shortly. 'All these secrets will catch up with us if we don't watch out. I've offered to help prepare a program to run through NASA's personnel computer. We're looking for anyone who has the technical ability to sabotage Bill's aircraft and who would also have access.'

'That's right,' Rogerson said. 'I've arranged for an outside man to come in and run the program but a lot of advance work can be done for him. In any event, he won't know the background.' He glanced at Joe. 'Another secret.'

'Anyway,' Ziegler said. 'I can use help, Gary. When you've finished your stint with the rest of the team, can you come over to the personnel department? You know where it is, two floors below this one.'

'Right. It will be late this evening.'

'That's okay. I reckon I'll be there until the small hours.'

The meeting broke up but as Ziegler and Herriman made for the door, Jim Magadini caught Omar Rogerson's eye and indicated he wanted him to stay behind.

When the door closed Magadini hesitated for a moment. He didn't like what he was about to ask Rogerson to do. 'Joe won't like this,' he said. 'Come to that, I don't much like it myself, but we have to put a guard on the astronauts. We can't ignore the possibility that whoever killed Bill might plan on going after the others. They'll object to bodyguards, and Joe will side with them, so we have to do it quietly. Put a man on each astronaut. Disreet surveillance, just as a precaution.'

'It will stretch us,' Rogerson said. 'Like Joe said, we need outside help for all this extra work on the sabotage investigation.'

'I'll get you the men,' Magadini told him. 'Both Bobby Kennedy and the President said we can call for any help we need. So, I'll tell them and they can deliver.'

Rogerson nodded but made no move to leave.

'What is it, Rog?' Magadini asked.

'That business out in the Mojave. I went at it all the wrong, Jim. I formed conclusions before examining the evidence and I just sat there in the sun dreaming about going fishing. If it hadn't been for Jerry I would have missed out on the explosive devices.'

'That's what he's paid for,' Magadini said.

'No, no. That's what I'm paid for. I think, maybe it's time I admitted I'm too old for this game.'

Magadini leaned back in his chair. 'Look, Rog, I'm not about to start a battle with you. You make your own decisions and I'll go along with it. If you decide to quit I won't argue even though I won't like it. The only thing I ask is, don't make any moves until this thing is over. Okay?'

Rogerson nodded slowly. 'Okay,' he said. 'I'll keep at it, but as soon as this baby's behind us I'm heading for the ocean where my biggest headache'll be which bait to use on the end of the line.'

After Rogerson had gone, Jim Magadini began working on the papers on his desk. He hadn't gotten very far when the telephone rang. It was Sylvia, and she was steaming. It took several interruptions before Jim managed to calm her down enough to learn that one of their two children, the one most likely to become a terrorist, had been arrested.

'Arrested?' he exploded. 'For chrissake, he's ten years old!'

'Now tell me something I don't know,' Sylvia snapped.

'And it's only nine o'clock in the morning.'

'Jim.' There was an edge to his wife's voice he hadn't heard in a long time.

'Okay,' he said. 'What do you want me to do?'

'Get down here and act like a father.'

'I have a space program to run.'

'I'll expect you in half an hour,' Sylvia said and hung up.

'Goddamn!' Jim spat and slammed the receiver back onto its cradle.

His secretary opened the door and peeped in nervously. 'Problems?'

'You can say that again. Look, I have to go out for a while. Family problems. I'll be back as soon as I can.'

After Magadini had gone his secretary sat at his desk sorting through the papers he'd been working on, filing some, making notes on others. When she came to his scribbled notes of that morning's meeting she studied them for some time, struggling with his scrawl. After two years in the job she still found his writing largely

158

indecipherable. Those parts of the notes she could manage to read seemed to be very interesting. Later she made a guarded telephone call and the reaction of the man she spoke to told her that the notes were even more valuable than she'd imagined.

NEWPORT NEWS, Va.

'Is that everything?'

Linda looked around the room. 'I think so,' she said.

Her mother smiled tentatively. 'I'll call your father, let him put all this into the car.'

Linda nodded. She didn't want a discussion on every little point of the packing that had been going on for the past two days. Her mother seemed to think it was necessary, however, and so far Linda hadn't felt like arguing about it.

The room looked cold and impersonal and she wondered how she had ever managed to think of it as home. She could hear her mother speaking to her father in the kitchen, the voices muted, funereal. Linda wanted to scream. Not in sadness, or in anger, but in a desire to let out some of the pent-up emotions of the last few days. Since Bill's death everyone had been so kind and attentive that she had begun to feel engulfed by the pity of others. They all meant well, she knew. At first it hadn't been so bad, with Jo Schirra and Louise Grissom managing to find exactly the right things to say. Diana McNair had been good too, not a shadow of a suggestion that she was merely performing an irksome duty.

Some others had been less helpful. The few friends she had among her neighbors seemed not to have any understanding of what it was like to have woken up to discover the vague threat under which she had lived for the six years of her marriage had finally become reality. It wasn't the same as having a husband killed in a car smash or collapse with a coronary at his desk. Sure, you expected cars to crash and you expected heart attacks but not in the same way that you expected an aircraft to fall out of the sky one day. She knew, the way the wives of all flying men knew, that there were such things as statistics, odds. And the odds shortened every day the feared accident didn't happen.

Eventually, if they kept at it, luck ran out. For some it happened sooner, others later. In Bill's case it had been much too soon.

She'd seen most of the other astronauts but they hadn't stayed long and she knew why. When they looked into her eyes they caught

159

a glimpse of what might well be their own futures. Her father came into the room to pick up the last case and carry it out to the car. He didn't speak, in fact he'd barely spoken since his arrival. He'd never liked Bill and was afraid it would show in his voice. Linda knew it but no longer cared who had liked her husband and who hadn't. She was aware he had been less popular than any of the others and knew why. She wasn't too sure just how much she had liked him towards the end, when his betrayals had become less cautious.

Her mother came back into the room. 'We're all ready, Linda,' she said.

Linda nodded her head slowly then turned to follow her mother from the room. She sat in the back seat of her father's car, her eyes fixed on the road ahead, not looking at the familiar streets as he headed for the Interstate highway. She didn't want to carry any memories back to Akron with her. A chapter was over, a chapter representing almost a quarter of her life but one she knew she could forget.

She rested her hands on her stomach. The baby would help her do that. She knew she could not tell her mother or father. They wouldn't understand. For that matter she wasn't at all sure she understood herself. The baby should be a link with the past, with Bill. But she wouldn't let the child make that bridge, instead she would seize the opportunity she had wished for every time she had been forced to face tv and press cameras. Those moments had been terrible for her, even worse had been fatuous questions about her thoughts and actions, about what she wore, what she cooked, what she and Bill did in their free time together.

Now, she could escape from all that, she could use the fact that she had a child to escape into obscurity. Slowly, as the miles stretched out separating her from Langley, Linda Simons began to experience a strange sensation. It took quite a long time to decide just what it was and when she did, she felt guilty. The sensation was one of sheer, glorious, relief.

LANGLEY AIR FORCE BASE, Va.

Mike Leandros came back from the bathroom and leaned against the bedroom door looking at the woman lying on the bed. Her arms and legs were stretched wide in a position that made her simultaneously defenseless and wanton.

Leandros was taking a chance, really pushing his luck to the limit.

160

He had tried to slide out of the relationship with Stella Herriman but she had come to him, demanding attention and he was weak-willed enough to go along with her needs. But coming here, to her house slap bang in the middle of the base, that was dangerous. Somehow the thought of the risk he was taking stirred him again, which was, considering what he had done in the past few hours, something of a minor physical miracle.

Moving into the room he closed the door behind him. On the bed Stella opened her eyes and looked at him. His outline was hazy and the dark hair on his chest and stomach made his dark form difficult to see. She shook her head but that only made the haziness worse. She closed her eyes again but even the darkness seemed to move.

In the past few days her drinking had exceeded anything she had managed before. For a few weeks she had tried controlling it just as she had tried to keep at bay her desire for Leandros. No, her desire was not specifically for him, almost any man would have done. But the effort hadn't been any use. Gary had made ineffectual attempts to restore some of the old pleasures their life together had known but without any real hope of success. The efforts, a few weeks back, had been slightly pathetic. She had tried, half-heartedly, but her responses had been mechanical and despite her sexual urges nothing Gary tried to do was any stimulus.

His inability to satisfy her in bed had become worse and they spent most nights, until sleep came, lying rigidly side by side as if afraid that letting their bodies touch would start off something neither was prepared to risk.

The evenings were just as bad. After the first feeble tries at entertaining her he drifted back to his books and technical papers, things she couldn't, and didn't want to, share. The tension that hung between them was almost tangible. Even sleeping didn't provide relief from it. Without a drink she slept badly anyway and lying awake for long stretches of the night just made her craving worse. Gary slept equally badly and although come morning he usually awoke as if he had slept the night through, he talked in his sleep, destroying any hope she had of real rest. She had stuck it out for a few weeks and then gave in to the craving for liquor and sexual satisfaction. She called Mike Leandros and their meetings began again.

She felt the bed move as Leandros knelt beside her, then the weight and heat of his body on top of hers. She tried to coordinate her movements to his but she had drunk far too much. Just how much she had consumed since morning she couldn't remember, but it had certainly been a binge to end 'em all.

For Leandros, this particular coupling was providing little pleasure. He had reached the stage of engaging in a disinterested exercise out of an almost academic desire to determine just how good his sexual prowess really was. He had already subjected Stella to every sexual variation he had ever tried in the past and had even experimented with a couple of things he had previously only fantasized over. She had gone along with every suggestion with no hint that she found any of them distasteful or strange. For the hundredth time he wondered what kind of life she led to give her such an appetite for the bizarre and just what kind of a man her husband was to be so blind to her nature.

Stella was only vaguely aware of what Leandros was doing to her. From the start of their relationship she had seen him only as a male hooker. Good-looking, young and arrogant, but a hooker for all that. She rolled away from him and reached out to try to make him enter her in yet another way.

'For God's sake, Stella,' he said. 'Damn near everything we've done today has been illegal in one state or another. If I do that to you I reckon it's a federal offense.'

'Just do it,' she said.

'I need a drink first.' He sat up and searched for the bottle. 'Now this one's empty,' he said.

'Try the shelf in the kitchen. Behind the cook books.' Stella laughed sourly. 'Never use those any more. No one comes here.'

Leandros didn't hear the end of the sentence. He was going unsteadily down the stairs into the kitchen. He found the bottle where Stella had said it would be and carried it towards the stairs. He had just reached the bottom step when the front door to the house opened and Gary Herriman walked in.

Gary had completed his training stint for the day earlier than expected and had decided that, instead of going directly to join Joe Ziegler, he would stop home to shower and change his clothes. It hadn't occurred to him to call Stella and tell her he was on his way. There was no reason, that he was aware of, why he should.

For several long, breathless, seconds the two men stared at one another. Leandros, naked, clutching the vodka bottle as if undecided whether to use it to protect his nakedness or to defend himself against Herriman. He had no doubt that the astronaut would attack him even though he could see no expression since Herriman's face was in shadow.

The astronaut stood motionless, his thoughts whirling, disconnected, somehow seeing the bottle the other man held as a greater

162

threat to Stella than the fact that Leandros wasn't wearing any clothes.

He let the door swing closed behind him and stepped forward. Leandros backed away but as Herriman moved into the light he could see that his visage seemed calm, unmoved. Herriman turned his head slightly, looking upwards, then moved slowly towards the stairs.

In the bedroom Stella lay where Leandros had left her. The effect of the alcohol she had consumed steadily throughout the day had reached a point where she was emerging on the other side of drunkenness into an uneasy kind of sobriety. For the first time she was aware of pain in several parts of her body, and a slight feeling of disgust at what she had allowed Leandros to do welled up inside her.

When she heard a sound in the doorway she began to sit up, ready to tell him the party was over. She saw the uniform and, before her eyes had dragged up to his face, knew that Gary had found out all the things she had never taken too much trouble to conceal. The self-disgust faded, being replaced by a strangely perverse delight that he had found her like this. Now he would know what she was really like, what she needed, what he had been unwilling or unable to provide.

Leandros came up the stairs behind Herriman and edged into the room where he began to pull on his clothes.

Stella was the first to speak, her voice unnecessarily loud. 'Well, isn't anyone going to say anything?'

Gary stared at his wife, a slight frown on his face, as if uncertain who she was. For a moment it seemed to him that he had come into the wrong house and that neither of these people had anything to do with him.

Leandros finished dressing and stood for a moment, wanting to leave before the astronaut snapped out of the strangely placid state he appeared to be in, but aware that whether he stayed or went there would be trouble for him later.

Gary turned and looked at the other man. 'Get out,' he said quietly. Leandros looked inquiringly at Stella but she was staring hard at her husband, a slightly puzzled expression coming onto her face as she realized he wasn't reacting the way she expected. Leandros went quickly down the stairs, paused for a moment, then left the house and headed for his car without looking back. He had some leave coming and he was already planning on calling Diana as soon as he reached home. She wouldn't like his going off without warning, but that would be her problem, not his.

In the bedroom, Stella stood up and was trying to put on a dress, a gesture towards making her feel not quite so defenseless in the event that Gary became violent.

In fact nothing was further from his mind. The scene in the bedroom had seemed unreal, almost like a movie. It couldn't be happening to him because things like this didn't happen in real life. Apart from anything else the people involved, the actors in the scene, were not real to him. He knew Leandros only slightly, having seen him on a couple of occasions when he had been interviewed by Diana McNair. As for the woman now dressing, the woman who had been lying there, naked and wanton, it couldn't be his wife. It wasn't possible for his wife to behave in that way.

Abruptly he turned and went down the stairs. He wandered through the rooms feeling as if he was in a stranger's house. Nothing seemed right. The furniture didn't even look like his. He suddenly remembered he was supposed to be helping Joe Ziegler in the personnel department's offices. He would have to call him, explain why he was late, maybe make some excuse for not going. He needed time to try to sort out just what was happening, why he seemed unable to relate to the people and things surrounding him.

He reached out for the telephone to call Ziegler but as he did so it rang, the sudden noise startling him. He picked up the instrument. He didn't recognize the voice at the other end of the line. After a few moments he interrupted. 'You must have a wrong number,' he told the caller and replaced the telephone. 'Who was that?'

Herriman turned at Stella's voice. 'A wrong number,' he said.

'Maybe another of my lovers,' she said. Her defiance was coming back, aware now that Gary wasn't going to do anything out of character. He'd always been quiet and easy-going and he wasn't about to change.

Gary looked at her and although this time she was no longer the stranger she had seemed when he had been in the bedroom, there was still an enormous gulf between them. A gulf he knew he couldn't bridge, even if he had wanted to.

Without speaking he went out of the house, leaving Stella more uncertain than ever but now with an overlay of anger at his indifference. If he didn't care then why should she? The hell, with him, with all of them. She went back up the stairs intending to get some sleep. Then, tomorrow, she would call Mike Leandros and, unless he was too scared, tell him she was ready to move in with him. It would cause a stir, she knew, an astronaut's wife separated from her husband and living with another man. That would make them all sit up and take notice.

164

LANGLEY AIR FORCE BASE, Va.

In the deserted personnel department Joe Ziegler glanced at his watch. It looked as if something had delayed Gary Herriman but in any event he had done pretty much all that could be done. He had compiled a list of names, several hundreds long, by eliminating certain departments in blocks. It was not the best way to do the job, he knew, but it would make the first computer run a little simpler.

He yawned, stacked the papers he'd been working on and stood up, stretching his arms to ease the cramp in his shoulders. Turning out the desk light he crossed to the door in darkness. He had opened the door and was fumbling for the light switch in the outer office when he heard a sudden sound. He tried to recall the name of the security man in that section of the building but couldn't bring it to mind.

'This is Ziegler,' he called out.

There was only silence. He found the light switch and flicked it up. The room was filled with desks, filing cabinets, and chairs but no security man. He grinned and shook his head. 'Must be getting old.'

He left the outer office and walked along the corridor towards the stairs. He had reached the last half-landing before ground level when all the lights went out. He stood for a moment, then some sixth sense told him he was in danger. Guessing that if someone was at the master-switch any danger would be coming at him from the basement area, he turned and went back up the stairs two at a time. He hadn't made the next story before something snarled past his ear and smacked into the wall. He kept moving, knowing that whatever type of gun was being used he had no defense. A fast departure from the vicinity was his only sensible course of action.

He reached the next landing and decided against going on up the stairs to the higher levels. The stairwell was narrow and afforded no cover. He went through swing doors which opened onto a long corridor. There were more than a dozen offices along the corridor any of which would serve as a temporary refuge where he would find a telephone he could use to call security.

He was halfway along the corridor when he again heard a snarl as a bullet sliced past him. He hadn't moved fast enough, the gunman was in the passage and had the advantage. There was only one reliable way to get an enemy off his trail, so he turned and went back along the corridor, moving fast. In the near-blackness he could just make out a shadowy figure a few yards inside the swinging doors. Without breaking stride he hurled himself forward in a shallow dive

165

and made contact. The man crashed backwards, struck the doors and rolled through onto the landing at the head of the stairs. Following him, Ziegler managed to get grip on the man's arm then brought a knee up hard into his attacker's groin.

He shifted his grip, trying to determine which hand held the gun, and as he did so his assailant retaliated with a blow from his knee. Fortunately he was off-target and connected with Ziegler's hip. Ziegler slammed the heel of his hand against the man's diaphragm and grabbed for the gun. He felt his fingers close around it, forced himself up onto his knees, snapped back the hand holding the weapon and heard the gun fall to the floor.

He hit his attacker in the stomach, then released his grip and reached down for the gun. It was the wrong move. As he bent low the other man swung a powerful kick. His foot struck Ziegler's shoulder and riccocheted against the side of his head. Much of the steam was taken out of the kick by contact with the shoulder but it still held enough power to send Ziegler rolling sideways, momentarily dazed. Before he could gather himself up again his attacker launched another, better-directed kick. This time Ziegler's defensive reaction was less successful and the blow struck glancingly along the side of his jaw. He began to slide into unconsciousness. The last thing he felt was the gun beneath his body and he had a final fading thought that with luck it would remain there.

When consciousness returned he was lying face downwards, a dull ache spreading through much of his face and body. As he pushed himself up into a kneeling position his hand caught against something. He closed his fingers over it, recognized the feel of a gun, and everything came flooding back.

He heard his name being called and moments later the lights came on. He saw a dark figure against the doors at the far end of the corridor. He tightened his grip on the weapon but then identified Gary Herriman.

'Joe, for God's sake, what's happened?'

Herriman reached Ziegler's side and helped him to his feet. 'Someone took a couple of shots at me. When that didn't work out he tried using his feet. Did you see anyone?'

Herriman shook his head. 'No.'

Ziegler shrugged, then winced at the discomfort the movement brought. 'Too bad.' He glanced around. 'Come on, let's see what happened to the security man on this section.'

Ten minutes later they found the man, just recovering from a blow to the head, and Ziegler called the central security office for medical assistance. The duty officer told him he would immediately instigate a search, but Ziegler suspected they'd just be going through the motions. The intruder would be well away from the base by now.

While security set the futile wheels in gear, Ziegler took Gary down to his office and opened a bottle of scotch he kept there for special occasions. He rarely had recourse to it but this seemed to be the kind of special occasion for which it was intended.

They drank in silence and Ziegler refilled their glasses before calling Omar Rogerson.

'I just heard,' Rogerson told him. 'I was on my way.'

'Your boys are making all the right moves, Rog.'

'If they'd been making the right moves it wouldn't have happened.'

'Maybe. Look, Rog, I don't think this was just a chance meet with a burglar.'

'Tell me about it.'

'Whoever it was in here tonight, he was after me. If he'd been just an intruder, whatever he wanted, all he had to do was wait. Another two minutes and I would have been out of the building.'

'Could be our crazy with a grudge against NASA.'

'You don't believe that?'

'Okay, Joe. Give me a description.'

'No can do. But I have his gun.'

'Hand it to the senior officer down there and we'll check it for prints.'

'Sorry but I handled it.'

'We can still try. Maybe he left a print on a cartridge case. Worth checking, anyway.'

'Okay, I'll hand it over. Maybe we should talk tomorrow.'

'Sure. And, Joe, be careful. I'll assign a man to keep an eye on you.'

'That isn't necessary.'

'It isn't your decision, Joe.'

'Rog, I'm a big boy now. I can take care of myself.'

There was silence for a moment. 'Look, Joe, there's something you don't know about. We can't talk over the phone, let's just say if we give you a tail it won't be for the first time.'

Ziegler frowned. 'What the hell does...okay, you'd better tell me tomorrow.'

After he had hung up he thought about another drink but decided against it. 'Gary?' he asked, proffering the bottle.

'What? Oh, no thanks, Joe.'

Ziegler looked at the astronaut carefully, seeing for the first time the lines of tension around his mouth and the pale drawn face. 'Anything wrong?' he asked. 'Apart from what happened tonight, I mean.'

Herriman laughed without humor. 'What happened tonight was enough for any man,' he said.

Ziegler frowned. There was nothing to be gained by playing the heavy. In any event he wanted to get home and take a hot bath before he began to stiffen up.

He capped the bottle and put it away. 'Come on,' he said. 'A night's sleep is something we can both use.'

Gary Herriman nodded, then followed Ziegler from the office and out of the building. He didn't agree with the last statement but he couldn't argue without revealing his own problems and the fact that they wouldn't have vanished come the dawn.

When he got back home he sat downstairs for a long time, not wanting to go up to Stella. Eventually he did but it brought no rest. For one thing he found himself working hard to lie motionless in bed to avoid touching his wife's sleeping body. And every time he dozed he entered a dream world. A world peopled by a naked blonde woman, a similarly naked man who ran, laughing and shouting, around him. There was a man in a general officer's uniform who kept commanding him to salute the flag in front of which stood a youthful man whose face continually switched from being Jack Kennedy's to Joe Ziegler's. Everyone, it seemed, wanted him to do what they wanted for themselves, or mocked him for not being the man they wanted him to be. No one in his dream seemed to want him to be himself or to do the things he wanted to do.

Towards morning he finally slept deeply for a little while but even then he dreamed. Only this time the dream was different, restful. A world where all was serene and peaceful, where he could walk and think, where he had time. In the dream he was alone but all the while he felt that someone was close to him. He kept turning his head to see who it was, but the figure managed to keep in the shadow, just out of his line of vision. What mattered was that this figure was not threatening but caring and protective. Two things he had scarcely known before.

1961
February 3–February 17

LANGLEY AIR FORCE BASE, Va.

'I'm sorry, Joe,' Magadini said. 'I asked Rogerson to do it and I told him to keep it from the astronauts and from you.'

Ziegler shrugged. There didn't seem much point in pursuing the matter. He had been annoyed to discover that the astronauts had been placed under surveillance by the security division but accepted it had been done with good intentions.

Rogerson had told Ziegler about it because of a report from the man assigned to watch over Gary Herriman. He had followed the astronaut back to his house after the training session and had seen Mike Leandros come out looking like a man who had been caught with his hand in the cookie jar. Worried that something had happened which would adversely affect the astronaut, Rogerson had decided to talk about it.

'Gary did seem a bit on edge last night,' Joe said. 'I put it down to finding me laid out on the floor but if something had happened between him, Stella and Leandros that could account for it.'

'What do we do?'

'Maybe the best person to handle it is Diana. She hasn't been able to get very close to Stella but she's closer than anyone else here. And Mike Leandros is her assistant so she has some responsibility.'

'Okay, you'd better arrange something, you're pally with Diana.'

Ziegler looked at him inquisitively. 'I've been meaning to ask you, that time you called to tell me Eisenhower had fixed it for me to see Kennedy, how did you know I was with Diana?'

Magadini grinned. 'I'm not usually blind and when I am, Sylvia isn't.'

'That obvious, huh?'

'How serious is it between you? Or shouldn't I ask?'

'At the moment it's good. I think we both might choose to make it permanent.' He laughed. 'Maybe that's through being around people like you and Sylvia.'

Magadini shook his head. 'Don't be too sure. We're having a running battle at the moment. Those damn kids of ours. One of them has started stealing from stores, a fully-fledged baby Dillinger. The cops have had him in but he doesn't seem to have learned a lesson from it.' Magadini sighed and began to gather papers together. 'I have a few things to do before the meeting, Joe.'

171

'Okay, time I went down to see what the computer's able to tell us.'

Ziegler dropped down to the personnel department where the man brought in to carry out the survey of possible suspects was working. He didn't stay long before heading for Diana's office. The result of the first computer run had been unsatisfactory. Not because it hadn't produced any results, rather because it had produced too many. Several hundred names had been fed in and almost half had remained after the first run. It appeared that more people than he expected had the ability to sabotage an F-104B.

'I knew we had a whole crowd of experts in NASA,' Ziegler complained to Diana when he reached her office. 'I never thought we had so many people capable of wrecking aircraft, maybe even wrecking the space program.'

'No one can accuse us of hiring amateurs.' She smiled lightly. 'Have you figured out why you were mugged?'

'Like I told Rog, my guess is it wasn't by chance but I have to admit I'm hard pressed to figure a motive.'

'It wouldn't be anyone with a personal grudge?'

'I don't think so, Diana. Nobody's perfect but I don't think I've ever been good enough at being bad to make someone come after me with a gun.' He grinned suddenly. 'Not unless someone's jealous of my success with you.'

'Success? Is that what you call it, when you're shooting off in the canteen?'

'No, of course not, for heaven's sake...' He broke off when he saw that she was laughing at him.

'So what could be the reason for the attack?'

He shook his head. 'I don't see it as a grudge against NASA, unless the guy is a psycho.'

'You're important to the program, Joe.'

'Maybe, but not so important that it wouldn't go on without me.'

Diana hesitated for a moment before speaking. 'Could there be a connexion between this and what happened to Bill?'

'What connexion could there be?'

'What were you working on in the personnel department?'

'I was preparing for a computer run to...' Ziegler's voice trailed off.

'Exactly,' Diana said. 'You're working on something that may track down a saboteur.'

Ziegler frowned. 'I don't buy that. It doesn't make any kind of sense.'

'Maybe it would if we could figure a motive for Bill's death.'

'I've thought of all the angles but I still haven't come up with anything that hangs together.'

'How about someone trying to ruin the program by taking out all the astronauts? They just happened to start with Bill.'

'That's ridiculous.'

'Why is it? Look, we started with nine. Bill's out permanently, Deke has a heart problem, Gus nearly died in an automobile accident and is way back in his training schedule as a result. That's three down, six to go.'

Ziegler shook his head slowly. 'No, I can't buy it. If someone wanted to screw up the program there are better ways than killing off the astronauts.'

' *Better* ways?'

Ziegler laughed. 'Bad choice of words. Easier routes that would have a more devastating effect.'

'Well, maybe you'd best keep them to yourself.' Diana glanced at her watch. 'Time for the meeting, we should be going.'

The meeting was being held in the main conference room, the only room in the complex capable of seating everyone who was needed to iron out the final details of the Atlas-Mercury launch.

First on the agenda was settling a long-running argument over the time for lift-off.

'We must have maximum exposure to sunlight,' one of the engineers stated.

Magadini glanced at Ziegler, then argued against the engineer. The need for in-sun orbits was to permit re-charging of the capsule's batteries and they all knew it.

'We need the sunlight to maintain the batteries and we need the batteries to maintain temperature equilibrium,' the engineer explained patiently. 'I mean, this is supposed to be an exact rehearsal for a manned flight, isn't it?'

Ziegler avoided Magadini's eye. The problem was that they needed to get Gary Herriman into the capsule without the knowledge of anyone outside their small group. This would be done when the launch tower crew was withdrawn, ostensibly to enable Ziegler's men to carry out a special safety procedure. But there was still the danger of someone seeing them as they left the medical block where the astronaut would be suiting-up. If they could do that in darkness, or near-darkness, their task would be much easier. They were hoping for a lift-off time of 0400 hours but it didn't look like they would get it.

'If we lift off after 1000 hours, we get 75 per cent in-sun orbits,' the engineer insisted.

The argument continued and eventually a compromise was reached. 0600 hours wasn't quite good enough to be certain they would get Gary out without anyone seeing them but they had reached a point where, had they persisted, they would have aroused the curiosity of the rest of the people at the meeting.

'Okay, let's move on,' Magadini said. 'Any problems with the tracking stations?'

'We have some trouble at Coolidge Field,' one of the communications men said.

'What kind of trouble?'

'Nothing serious. It would be if the flight was manned because it's in the receiving equipment. We'll be able to pick up everything on the telemetry circuits except voice transmission. As there won't be any, there's no need for a hold.'

Ziegler felt himself tensing but the moment passed without any untoward reaction from those in the know.

'If you're worried about it we can always use the Smithsonian Optical Tracking Station at Curacao,' someone chipped in just as Ziegler was relaxing.

'We'll wait and see,' Magadini put in quickly. 'If we need it we'll call on Curacao.' He turned the page of his agenda. 'Right, weather next.'

They moved on to the next topic. Florida winters were never severe but the exposed position of Cape Canaveral meant that wind speeds could be high at times. Worse, they were often unpredictable and too many launch delays in the past had been caused by high winds. There was nothing anyone could do about it, but once they had Gary in the capsule they didn't want a hold if it could be avoided. The longer he sat up there, the greater the risk of discovery.

Ziegler and Magadini listened intently to the long-range weather forecast in the hope it would prove to be on their side. It seemed it was, and again Ziegler felt himself relaxing. Looking across the table at Gary, Ziegler realized that now the launch was less than three weeks away he was already starting to build up for it. He was forgetting all his disapproval of the flight and the motives of the politicians who were pushing for it. It was almost as if the momentum of the project had overcome all the scruples he'd felt in the early stages. But, looking at Gary Herriman, he could very easily convince himself that it was all a crazy dream. The astronaut looked calm, almost detached.

In fact, half-way through the senior meteorologist's report Gary's attention had wandered. Despite the relevance to him of what was being said, there was something about the whole project that seemed to border on fantasy. He didn't really believe the flight they were discussing would be anything other than a test flight. He fully expected the plan, that he was to board the spaceship at the last

174

moment, would be cancelled and he could go back to being number five or six or wherever he was on the official flight list.

But, if the flight did go ahead, it held no worries for him, other than the simple everyday worry felt by all the astronauts. That when the day dawned, and with it the ice-cold knowledge that they really were about to light the big candle and shoot him into space, there would be no crack-up. No panic. He hoped, prayed even, that he would measure up. Just as he knew the others were praying they would measure up when their turn came.

He glanced across the table to where Diana McNair was sitting. He liked her and wished he could talk to her about Stella and Mike Leandros. His reluctance to confide in her stemmed chiefly from the fact that he still hoped to keep his personal problems under wraps. But there was another reason for not confiding in Diana the strangely unreal feeling which had swept over him when he found Stella and her lover together and which still remained.

He had tried to seize hold of the feeling, make it become real, tangible, but he'd failed. It was something to do with the dream he'd had that night. The dream where everyone mocked or goaded him, everyone but one person who had faith, who encouraged him. He'd decided it must have been some long-buried image of his mother, who had died when he was a very small boy, but he couldn't be sure. Maybe it would have helped to talk to Diana about it but there was a lingering antipathy towards psychiatrists after finding Leandros there, in his home.

Stella had not been shocked into sobriety by what had happened. She had continued drinking during the last few days and had been out most evenings, sometimes not coming home until the small hours. Gary didn't know if she was seeing Leandros and could no longer bring himself to care.

He realized voices were being raised and tuned back into the discussion.

'That's 140 pounds of dead weight,' someone was protesting.

Gary knew what that was about. The scientists wanted to put into the spacecraft extra equipment which would advance their knowlege of space travel. It was a reasonable argument. The problem was that Jim Magadini and Joe had to insist that dead weight was placed in the capsule, dead weight which would be replaced by Gary when the moment came. His weight was 132 pounds and he would fly with an eight-pound weight strapped to the underside of his couch. The extra eight pounds would be useless, but it had been decided that if the total dead weight was precisely what he and his space-suit weighed, it might lead some smart-aleck to add two and two together and come up with the right answer.

Ziegler stated the counter-argument, letting Jim take a rest from playing the heavy. 'We want this flight to be as close as possible to the real thing,' he said. 'If we put in more equipment, then we need more instrumentation down here on the ground to record what's being transmitted.'

'I go along with Joe.'

Ziegler looked up, surprised to get support from the engineer who had argued against the early launch time.

The engineer glanced along the table at Magadini. 'With a six o'clock launch we don't get all the re-charging time we need. Put any more equipment in the capsule and we exacerbate the situation.'

Magadini recognized the danger of dwelling too long on that point and hastily pressed on. The meeting was only half-way through but they had passed all the contentious points and there were no further arguments on areas where the true nature of the flight was in danger of being revealed.

As the meeting broke up Ziegler caught up with Herriman. 'See anything in all that to cause problems?'

'No, everything seems okay. It should be a good test flight.'

Ziegler glanced at the astronaut sharply. The remark had been made with no inflection, no hint that he was thinking of the flight as anything other than a test. Well, Ziegler decided, if that was the way he was thinking about it there was no reason to try changing his mind.

Jim Magadini joined them, glancing around to insure no one was within earshot. 'I had a call from the top, just before the meeting began. Couldn't reach either of you before.'

'What do they want this time?'

'We're going ahead. No question about it.'

Ziegler looked at Herriman whose expression didn't change. 'Okay, Gary?'

Herriman shrugged. 'I'm as ready as I'll ever be.' He suddenly grinned widely, surprising the others. 'About time we had a little excitement around here.'

Ziegler matched the smile, feeling a sense of relief the astronaut was taking it so well. 'Okay, we have eighteen days. Let's not waste them.' He turned to Magadini. 'We need cover for the extra time I'll be putting in with Gary during the next few days. I think we'd better make it appear we're doing it because he's falling behind the others.'

'What's the first thing you want to do?'

'A few days down at the Cape. We need a little more time on the

FPT and if we use the one here too many people will want to know why. Down there I can drop in a hint that Gary needs extra work on the machine and no one will question it.'

Magadini nodded. 'Okay, I'll cover you from this end if anyone asks awkward questions.'

'Right, Gary,' Ziegler said. 'Have you anything you need to do before we head for Florida?'

'No. Nothing that can't wait.'

The two men walked away leaving Magadini alone. He watched them go, an unaccountable tension creeping over him. All these years of planning, preparation. All the money directed and redirected, spent and occasionally wasted, had been to put a man into space and now it was about to happen. He couldn't quite believe it. He shook his head slowly and turned to see Diana McNair watching him.

'It's really going to happen,' she said.

'Taking up mind-reading, Diana?'

'Just expressing my own thoughts. Not surprising if we're both thinking the same way, is it?'

'I hope nothing goes wrong.'

'Why should it? Everyone has done their work well.'

Magadini nodded slowly. She was right, but that didn't alter the fact that less than three weeks from now they would be placing Gary Herriman in a capsule and shooting him into the unknown. However careful the planning, no one really knew how the mission would work out. To go ahead, recognizing how little was understood, no longer seemed fair to the young man whose life would be strapped into the capsule just before dawn.

LANGLEY AIR FORCE BASE, Va.

'I'll be away about a week,' Gary said to Stella.

She looked at him indifferently. She didn't care where he was going or why. The fact that he would be away was enough.

She hadn't seen Mike Leandros since his sudden departure on leave and Gary's absence, however temporary, would give her freedom to try finding a replacement for him. Not that there was much need for the freedom her husband's absence would give her. She hadn't let his presence inhibit her in recent weeks and he had done nothing to suggest he would change. That was the trouble, he did nothing. His preoccupation with his work was becoming steadily more infuriating with every day that passed.

'I might go away,' she said. 'Maybe for a few weeks.'

Surprisingly Gary reacted to this. 'No, don't stay away too long,' he said.

'Why? Don't tell me you'll miss me.'

'It isn't that...' He broke off. 'Yes, it *is* that as well, but I'd like you to be around on the 20th of the month.'

'Why, what happens then?'

He hesitated. Ziegler and Magadini hadn't told him that Stella could now be brought into the small group who knew about the manned flight.

'There's a test-flight on that date,' he said.

'Another one? What's going to happen this time? Another big bang? Another popped-cork?'

Gary shook his head. It seemed less than a good idea to tell her. She probably wouldn't believe it and even if she did there was no guarantee she would behave any differently towards him. 'I just thought you might want to be around,' he said quietly.

He went upstairs and began to pack for the trip to Florida. For a few moments he stood looking at the bed, thinking. It was odd, the way he could bring the image of Stella, naked on the bed, into his mind without bitterness. Maybe something in his subconscious had built a defensive wall around the memory. Protecting him. Like the shadowy figure in his dreams seemed to protect him.

He finished packing, went down to where Stella was sitting watching tv and stood behind her, waiting for her to turn round. She didn't and after a moment he put his bag on the floor and leaned over to touch her.

She looked up, her eyes expressionless. 'I'll see you when you get back,' she said.

He nodded and straightened up again, wondering at his sudden impulse to kiss her and the equally speedy change of mind. He picked up his bag and went to the door. 'See you,' he said.

Stella didn't reply and he went out closing the door softly behind him. He walked across to the administration building, where he had arranged to meet Joe Ziegler, thinking about Stella. It was strange the way she had changed. Once she had been a happy, always smiling, pretty young girl. Now, there was a permanently sour, bitter, expression on her face. He decided that when he came back he would make another effort, this time more determined than the last. He would take some leave, no one could argue against that, and they would go away somewhere. Like the place where they had spent so many happy hours together when he was based in Germany. The walks they had taken through the woods where Stella had painted and he had just watched her, enjoying her soft beauty. Yes, that was what they could do, go to Germany and look up old places and any old friends who might still be there, providing they hadn't all been brought back to the States.

In the house, Stella stood up and switched off the tv. She went upstairs and changed her clothes. She would give Gary a half hour start and then head for the bright lights of town. It was time to start living again. Time for a few drinks, time for some real male company. Above all, time for that.

CAPE CANAVERAL, Fla.

The capsule gleamed in the arc-lights suspended immediately above it. Joe Ziegler and Gary Herriman were watching the white-suited technicians who were moving silently around it, their footsteps muffled by the non-conductive soles of their shoes.

'Small, isn't it.' Herriman remarked.

'Too damned small,' Ziegler said.

Herriman grinned. 'If you want to change places, I reckon we could persuade someone to cut a couple of holes in the bulkhead big enough to let your feet hang through.'

'I'm tempted, Gary, I'm tempted.'

'Do any of these people know?' Herriman asked.

'No. We'll have to let a couple of technicians in on things but we'll take that step later.'

The power supply to the capsule was turned on and a test run on the primary electrical system began. Every switch, control, gauge, was etched clearly in the astronaut's mind. He knew which components were responding at that moment, what readings were appearing. The hours spent on the FPT, both at Langley and here at the Cape, had made their mark on his memory. He doubted if it would ever be possible for him to erase them completely.

He saw Specs, the space suit technician, come into the building. 'What about suiting up?' he asked Ziegler. 'Will we need Specs or one of the other technicians?'

'Probably. I guess Specs will be the one for the job.'

'At least we'll get a couple of laughs out of the occasion.'

Ziegler nodded, not wanting to pursue the thought that had come into his head. The short-sighted technician's sense of humor was rooted firmly in disaster and catastrophe. If he was on the team Joe hoped he wouldn't find anything to joke about.

Across the building Specs peered through his thick-lensed glasses. He thought Ziegler and Herriman were looking his way but wasn't too sure. What the Astronaut Liaison Officer and the young astronaut were talking about probably wasn't any business of his and in any event he was feeling considerably less than his usually cheerful self today. Last night he had fallen in with a crowd of locals whose means of livelihood remained obscure but whose capacity for any form of alcohol was formidable. He removed his glasses and rubbed his eyes. A damn sight better capacity than his own, he'd discovered to his cost. As hangovers went, this was a peach.

He replaced his glasses and crossed to the capsule as the electrical test ended. He had to check the connexions which would be used during the flight to relay data back to Mission Control. In the real thing, when the first spaceman to fly the capsule was strapped inside, the connexions would link up with his life-support systems. One of the technicians brushed against him, apologized bruquely, as if it had been Specs' fault, and reached in to make an adjustment to a fitting inside the capsule.

Specs didn't recognize the man which was unusual. He thought he knew everyone. 'New here?' he asked.

The technician glanced at him, irritation clear on his face. 'Yes.'

'I'm Specs, space suit technician.'

The other man put his head back inside the capsule. 'Gray. Communications.'

Despite the muffled reply Specs could register the tone of voice a man used when he wasn't in a mood for conversation. He took off his glasses and rubbed at his eyes again. The man stepped out of the capsule and walked past him, heading for the door. For a moment Specs' face was level with the man's chest. Specs replaced his glasses but by that time the white-suited figure was moving down the aluminum ladder to the next level. Specs' eyesight wasn't good, but just for a split-second the man's name-tag had been within inches of his face. Even at that range he couldn't read the name on the tag but it appeared to be a long word of maybe nine of ten letters. Certainly a hell of a lot more letters than in the name Gray. Might be nothing, might be just an imagination fired by all that booze he'd put away the night before. Even so, Specs decided he would check. It always paid to be careful, especially when so much depended on everything going exactly according to plan.

180

MOSCOW

Helmut Groetchen was bored. Like most newspapermen based in a foreign country he usually mixed with other foreign newsmen but in his case it was out of habit not from choice. The opportunity to attend a Russian wedding had seemed like a good chance to meet some of the natives on their own ground without the restrictions and reservations inevitable at any official function. It hadn't worked out quite as he had hoped because the bride's father, a staff reporter with *Pravda* , had not been content with inviting only Groetchen to demonstrate his international connexions to the rest of his family. He had also invited half a dozen other foreign journalists most of whom were now quite drunk and noisily arguing with one another in a garbled mix of French, English and one or another of the Scandinavian languages.

Groetchen caught the eye of the bride's father and, hopeful of getting away from his immediate companions, threaded his way across the room towards him, doing his best to avoid energetically dancing couples.

The bride's father watched Groetchen coming, his smile widening with delight. 'My dear old friend,' he said cheerfully. 'Come and meet some of my family.' Groetchen happily ignored the inaccuracy of the man's greeting. Their relationship was that of bare acquaintance but the German newsman was happy to let the mild deception continue. It wouldn't do any harm and it might make the Russian feel slightly indebted to him.

His host went through a long series of introductions almost none of which registered in the German's mind. One of the men being introduced leaned forward, breathed alcohol fumes into Groetchen's face and repeated the introduction, confirming his own identity as the bride's uncle.

'Weddings are a bore,' the man roared with drunken geniality. 'Funerals are better. There at least you have no need to pretend to be jolly. Look at the poor devil,' he went on, indicating the bridegroom. 'He doesn't know what he's letting himself in for. My niece is like her mother and you know what she's done to my dear brother.'

Groetchen smiled noncommittally. 'She seems a pretty girl.'

'All women are alike, especially when the lights are out.'

The bride's uncle laughed coarsely and the men in his immediate hearing laughed along with him. Groetchen risked a slight smirk, not wanting to offend either the bride or her uncle.

The Russian swallowed the dregs from his glass and grimaced at the taste. 'Wine. It's a drink for women and invalids. Come on, let's get something a man can drink without having to pretend to enjoy it.'

A few minutes later Groetchen was in another room in the house, carried along with the group who followed the bride's uncle from the main room. Along the way he learned the man's name was Ivan Kropotkin and that he was from somewhere in the east. Half a dozen vodkas later the German newspaperman was beginning to wish Kropotkin had stayed in the east, and that he had stayed on wine. This was degenerating into a session which was likely to end only when no one was left standing.

'Here, your glass is empty.'

Groetchen held out his glass automatically, letting his new host slosh drink into it and over his hand.

'I don't like Moscow,' Kropotkin said. 'Give me air and space all around me, particularly space.' He went off into a roaring hearty laugh for no apparent reason.

Groetchen nodded agreement. 'I prefer Berlin,' he said.

'All cities are alike.'

'Not Berlin.'

'Mmmm? No, maybe not. It must be strange, two cities in one.' Kropotkin swallowed another drink and replenished his glass. 'Tell me, do you ever get into the other half?'

'Sometimes.'

'What's it really like? I don't believe half what they tell us here.'

Groetchen tried to work that out. After a moment he realized the other man was assuming he came from East Berlin. 'No, no,' he said. 'Not that at all.'

'I didn't think so,' Kropotkin said, misunderstanding the German's denial. He leaned forward. 'Never believe anything they put in newspapers, eh?' He roared with laughter again and tried pouring more vodka into Groetchen's still full glass.

Swallowing some of his drink, the newspaperman decided that the effort of explaining which side of the Berlin Wall he lived was more than he was able to make.

The others in the room were getting noisier as they got drunker. What bits of their conversation Groetchen picked up suggested they had reached the stage of vying with one another for who could tell the coarsest honeymoon anecdote.

Kropotkin leaned over and wrapped an arm around the German's shoulder. 'You know, a lot of my colleagues can't forget the war. Even now, more than fifteen years on, they still talk about you

Germans as if you should be lined up against a wall and shot.' His loud laughter boomed out again.

Groetchen grinned weakly. He liked Russia and he liked the Russians. The trouble was they were very difficult people to understand. Their jokes for instance. Despite Kropotkin's loud and infectious laughter there was more than a hint that beneath the show of good humor lay a considerable grain of truth.

'I know better,' Kropotkin went on. 'We have some Germans in our section. Good men. Clever.' He lowered his voice. 'You know, we really did get the best ones. The Americans, they got the second-raters. No wonder they're trying so damned hard. Too damned hard if you want the truth.'

Groetchen nodded wisely, trying to look as if he knew what the Russian was talking about. He sipped at his drink, unhappily aware the action would probably result in a refill. It did. He shook his head and was surprised how clear it felt. He must be developing a tolerance for the stuff. 'The Americans are good at many things,' he said. 'Never underestimate them.'

Kropotkin nodded. 'We haven't. That's why we've taken steps. You'll see. Clever stuff. We've pushed them, made them dance to our tune. Then, when they're in the middle of the dance, they'll find we've outthought them all along the line. All along the line.' He laughed again, throwing back his head and almost tumbling over with the effort. When he recovered he continued talking but on a different subject. It was some seconds before Groetchen realized the subject had changed back to Kropotkin's dislike of Moscow.

'I hate it. Too much official clap-trap, too many little men with little minds holding down jobs with too much power. The bigger the city the more of these petty fools appear. Must be something in the air. Give me Kazakhskaya every time.'

One of the other guests, picking up the last remark, joined the conversation. 'The trouble with you people is that you don't know when you're well off. Look at me, I have more and more papers to complete every day. You scientists have no idea of the problems we have here. Forms. You'd never believe how many forms I have to fill in.'

The two men began a genial argument, neither one listening to what the other was saying.

Groetchen only half-listened, part of his brain still fastening onto oddments from Kropotkin's remarks. It hadn't made a lot of sense but his newspaperman's instinct was aroused. When he saw a chance to slide out of the room he did so and went back to where the main wedding party was reaching a peak of noisy drunkenness which almost equalled that of the breakaway group.

He saw his chance when the bride was momentarily left alone as her new husband was dragged into a bad imitation of a cossack dance which was threatening to maim those onlookers closest to the center of the floor.

He wished the girl much happiness and she brightened a little at this small example of attention in a room which was becoming alarmingly alien to her. Groetchen guessed that she was a rather pleasant if not very bright girl and he felt sorry for her.

'I have met your uncle,' he said. 'A big man who laughs a lot.'

'Ah, Uncle Ivan.'

'He has traveled a long way to be here?'

'Yes, all the way from Kazakhskaya.'

'He was telling me how he likes it there. Have you ever visited him?'

'Oh, no. It is too far. Anyway, visitors are not permitted. Baikonur is a very secret place.'

Groetchen nodded agreement, concealing a sudden thrill of excitement. He continued the conversation but the girl clearly knew nothing more about her uncle. When her husband returned to her side, out of breath and looking as if he would be sick at any moment, Groetchen took the opportunity to excuse himself. He managed to avoid being pulled into another drinking session, this time with the bride's father, and left.

Back at the small apartment his newspaper kept for their Moscow correspondent he dosed himself with several cups of black coffee, took a shower, and changed his clothes. By the time he was finished his head was beginning to clear and he had decided what to do with the random oddments of information he had acquired. He would call Oscar Lennox at the American Embassy.

Lennox would be saddened to learn that the West German had not been fooled by his thin disguise as a cultural attaché but he might well decide the information he was getting in return would be worth admitting his true role to the newspaperman.

Groetchen underestimated Lennox's interest. His reaction to the fragment of information Groetchen risked over the telephone was so intense he was at the German's apartment within twenty minutes.

Less than an hour after that Lennox was back at the Embassy encoding a preliminary report for transmission to Washington.

That done Lennox sat back feeling well-satisfied with the way things were going. His satisfaction didn't last very long.

'We need more information,' Ross, his superior, told him.

'How?'

Ross looked pained. 'For heaven's sake, Oscar. I don't like you people being here but if you're going to play at espionage then get out there and spy.'

Lennox peered into the other man's face hoping to see a glimmer of a smile, any indication that it was a joke. He saw nothing to give that impression.

The older man leaned forward, taking pity on Lennox. 'Look, Oscar, we haven't a hope of getting anyone into Baikonur. No one, not you, not me, not even the best man our masters can produce. Even if they could manufacture a James Bond for us he wouldn't get in there. It's spy-proof. Well, if we can't get in the next best thing is to get close to one of their people when they come out. Kropotkin is out, for how long we don't know, so we have to move fast. Find him, talk to him if you can. See if he's bribable, see if he's stealable.'

Lennox nodded his head unhappily. 'Okay, I'll try.'

'Where will you start?'

'The place where the wedding was held. If they've gone home I'll try the bride's father's home. Failing that, I'll try Kropotkin's house.' He smiled. 'Only this time I'll stay off the roof.'

'Good man.' Ross nodded benignly at Lennox. 'Look after yourself, Oscar. Don't take any risks. No unnecessary ones, at any rate.'

Lennox didn't answer. Ross's qualifying comment seemed to call for a snappy rejoinder, but he couldn't be bothered.

As it turned out the wedding party was still going on but had been transferred to the apartment of the bride's father. From the lights and noise it sounded as if the drinking Helmut Groetchen had so graphically described was far from over. Lennox sat in his car, trying to decide what to do. It was all very well being told to behave like a spy. Intelligence work was the gathering of information, sifting through files, reading reports, newspapers and letters, and tapping in on other people's telephone conversations. Not sitting in parked cars on cold streets listening to other people having a good time.

It was more than two hours, and already dark, before the door opened and the revelers began to disperse. By then Lennox was shivering with cold and angrily cursing himself and Ross. He was cursing Ross because the man had no real authority over the CIA and Lennox had let himself be pushed into chasing Kropotkin without having convinced himself there was any real value in the exercise. Washington hadn't said anything about making an overt approach to discover if anyone from Baikonur was open to bribery and certainly they hadn't even hinted that Ross's other suggestion – kidnaping pure and simple – was in their minds. He also cursed

185

himself for having failed to observe a basic rule of in-car surveillance – visit the head first.

He watched the guests leaving the house and recognized the burly figure of Kropotkin without difficulty. So far, so good. It would have been just his luck for Groetchen to have made a mistake and for him to have patiently allowed his nuts to freeze waiting out the wrong man.

Minutes later the scientist was in his own car which he started up and drove off noisily. Lennox followed, keeping a safe distance and hoping his target was headed somewhere it would be possible to establish more comfortable surveillance. He was so intent on keeping Kropotkin's car in view, without being seen himself, that they had traveled more than ten miles before he suspected another car was following him.

At first he couldn't be certain, so he tried a couple of basic ruses, slowing and speeding. He couldn't risk turning off for fear of losing Kropotkin. The trailing car followed his actions. He decided to take a chance and stay on the scientist's trail for another ten minutes, then make a decision.

Before the ten minutes were up they were in a part of the city with which he was unfamiliar. From what he could see in the car's headlights, it was an industrial zone. He checked his rear-view mirror. The other car was still there. He made up his mind. It was time to get out. He waited for the next inter-section, made a left, and headed south. The trailing car followed and began to close on him.

Lennox accelerated hard trying to get into his mind a clear map of the city. He reckoned that if he continued for another mile, then made a right he could reach the center where, even if he couldn't shake off his pursuer, he would be within sight and hearing of people. It might not matter much but it was better than being caught in the open where there were no witnesses.

He made the right turn and immediately knew it was an error. The road was narrow, running between blank walls of high warehouses. Worse still, about one hundred yards ahead was a high chain-link fence. He dabbed at the brakes, then accelerated, then braked again. This time he brought the car to a halt, jumped out and started to run, looking for somewhere to hide. There was no refuge. He turned and saw the other car had stopped and the occupant, a slightly built man, was coming towards him, strolling casually as if out for an evening constitutional. For an instant Lennox felt a spark of hope that he'd guessed wrong. Maybe this goon was harmless, just a cop out to collar him for some obscure traffic infraction. Then, as the man came closer, he recognized him. Maisky. Lennox knew he had been right all along.

He started to run again, this time back towards the main road. He reached the Russian and thrust out his hands to ward off any attack. Surprisingly, Maisky stepped aside and let him pass. Lennox ran on, his footsteps clattering noisily in the silence of the narrow street.

He didn't hear the shot but felt its blow as the bullet slammed into his shoulders, pitching him forward onto his face. He lay there, feeling no pain, listening to the sharp clear sound of Maisky's approaching footsteps.

Suddenly, he felt something warm around his thighs. The last conscious thought Oscar Lennox had before he died was that he really should have remembered that golden rule and visited the john before setting out on his mission.

CAPE CANAVERAL, Fla.

'How was it?' Gary Herriman asked.

Ziegler drew the astronaut away from the hearing of the technicians who were preparing the FPT computer for a second run. 'Pretty good. In fact it was your best yet.'

'I wasn't happy about the final stages. I thought, maybe I was rushing things.'

'No, everything looked fine from here.'

This latest session on the FPT had been an exact replica of the Atlas-Mercury flight, now only ten days away. Flight duration had been set at three full orbits and, as Ziegler had just assured the astronaut, there hadn't been a moment when his response to the demands placed upon him had been anything less than perfect.

'We're ready,' one of the technicians called out.

Ziegler glanced over to where Gus Grissom was suiting-up and waved a hand to indicate it was time for him to enter the FPT. Ziegler had decided that someone with an astronaut's special abilities and know-how would be an asset in the special Mission Control unit he would be establishing for the flight. During the last planning session they'd had, before coming down to the Cape, he had carefully observed everyone present. Afterwards, he had made a provisional list of those he thought would be suitable for the unit. Now, his short-list of names was being double-checked by Jim Magadini to insure that final selection took into account the secrecy of the project. Most important team-members would be a doctor, qualified in space medicine, whose principal duties would be to monitor the life-support systems, and a communications expert, who would maintain radio links and who also had to be capable of assembling the necessary transmitting and receiving equipment in a few days with a minimum of outside help.

The decision to include an astronaut on the team was primarily for the benefit of Herriman. If a problem arose the astronaut would be happier knowing that a man with similar qualifications, comparable background and ability, and, most importantly, a realistic grasp of the dangers, was around to offer help and support. Ziegler had settled on Gus, partly because he was well-equipped for the job and partly because he had only just gotten back into full training after his injuries. That made it possible to have him along on extra training sessions, such as this one, without drawing curious comments from any quarter.

After Gus had climbed into the FPT and the training run began, Ziegler told Gary what he had in mind.

'That would be good. No disrespect, Joe, but it will help, knowing someone like Gus is down here.'

Ziegler hesitated for a moment before speaking again. He didn't want any of the lingering doubts he felt to be transferred to the other man. 'You know this is a voluntary mission, Gary. You can back out, if you feel you need to. Any reason will do, or no reason at all.'

'Back out? Hell, this is what I'm here for, Joe.'

Ziegler nodded slowly. Then he pushed his doubts far back into his mind. It was too close to launch-day to start questioning again.

As Gary watched the computer read-outs of Gus's run his thoughts were elsewhere. Over the past few days he had made several calls to Langley, hoping to talk to Stella. So far, he had been unable to reach her. He had considered calling Diana McNair to ask if she could find out where his wife had gone but didn't because that would have revealed the rift. At this late stage he doubted he would be replaced on the flight, especially over something as trivial as an errant wife, but he wasn't prepared to take the chance. The flight was precious, too precious to risk losing, even if he lost Stella instead. He found the thought confusing; his career had never seemed all that important before. He smiled to himself. The General would be both pleased and surprised to learn that, at long last, the son was starting to think like the father.

The idea prompted him to turn to Ziegler. 'As soon as the flight is made public will you call my father in Washington?' he asked.

'Sure, I'll be happy to.'

'I'd like him to know before he sees it on tv or someone tells him.

He's a proud kind of guy and if he hears it from you he can make believe he knew all along and was part of the plan.'

'Do you want me to ask the President for permission to tell him now?'

'No, so long as there's a chance the flight might be called off it's better that he doesn't know. If we told him and then it was cancelled he'd be very cut up. It'd seem like another failure to him.'

'Another failure?'

'He'd never admit it but I think he figures his own career as a pocketful of disappointments.'

'He's a three-star General, that's not my definition of failure.'

'It's not the rank, it's the job. For a man of action, commanding a desk comes hard. That's why he steered me towards the Air Force. I guess he figured he'd be able to experience some more action, through me. When I was brought onto Project Mercury it almost made up for all the years he's been decaying at the Pentagon.'

'What did he do to earn a job he doesn't like or want?'

'He was on Patton's staff. When the trouble blew up a lot of people found some of the mud sticking to them.'

'I thought Patton came out of it pretty well in the end.'

'For public consumption, maybe, but he had a lot of enemies among the Chiefs of Staff. They saw Eisenhower's criticism as an excuse for getting even. My father was in the firing line. Just tough luck.'

The FPT run ended a few minutes later and when Gus had changed his clothes, the three men went across to the mess hall for lunch. Gary Herriman didn't pursue the conversation about his father and Ziegler didn't raise the subject again. Nevertheless, Joe was curious about the remark which implied that General Herriman had been instrumental in deciding his son's career. Most of the fliers he knew had never had any desire to be anything else. Yet here was a man who would, perhaps, have chosen another path had it not been for a vicariously ambitious father. And now, as a result of that parental ambition, he had an opportunity for which almost every other flying man in the country would have happily traded twenty years of his life.

WASHINGTON, D.C.

Jim Magadini got through to the President with surprising ease and, carefully choosing his words, complained that the demands for extra security checks on everything from people to machines were likely to cause delays in the timing of the Atlas-Mercury launch.

The President responded politely, assuring Magadini there was a good reason for everything and that he would see what he could do to ameliorate the position.

When he had broken the connexion the President sent for his brother and sat angrily staring out of the Oval Office window until Bobby arrived.

'Why wasn't I told?' he asked after he had repeated the gist of Magadini's call. 'What are these checks and why have they been requested?'

Bobby spread his hands deprecatingly. 'The Firm sent a report from Moscow. The information was vague and it was second-hand. A West German newspaperman picked up something that suggested the Soviets might be trying to damage our program. That, linked to the fact that an astronaut died as a result of sabotage, made us think we should look more closely at everything we're doing in NASA.'

'Without telling me?'

'I'm sorry.'

Standing up Jack Kennedy paced across the room before turning to grin at his brother. 'Okay, I'm starting to sound like a man who doesn't know how to delegate. Magadini caught me on the hop and I didn't enjoy it.'

Bobby returned the smile and made a mental note to insure that Magadini wouldn't find it so easy to reach the President another time. He rapidly summarized the contents of Oscar Lennox's preliminary report before going on to brief the President about the man the CIA operative had been watching.

'Kropotkin is one of their best people. He's a senior assistant to Korolev and in his own right he's an expert on guidance systems. We're guessing, but it seems likely that if something is being planned it could be in that area.'

'Magadini says they've found nothing.'

Bobby nodded. 'I know.'

'Anything more from Lennox?'

Bobby hesitated. 'Lennox has disappeared.'

The President frowned. 'Try to get some hard facts, Bobby. Then talk to Magadini. Tell him we expect the launch to take place as scheduled. No arguments, no discussions.'

'There is something we should consider. Even if there hasn't been an attempt to spike the project so far, the Soviets might be planning something for a later date. I think they should know we won't take any such action lying down.'

190

'I don't think we should risk a formal protest. That would show them we're moving faster than they believe.'

'Maybe, but it could be worth that risk. We don't want them thinking they can take actions which will jeopardize the flight. Maybe you should talk to Khrushchev direct. Tell him that attempts to endanger any future spaceflight, either before or after launch, will be construed as military action. Action against which we will retaliate.'

The President nodded thoughtfully. 'You could be right. Draft a note and we'll talk about it later today. Do it yourself, don't put anyone else on it. Use only general terms, don't mention Project Mercury by name.'

'Right.' Bobby Kennedy turned to leave, then looked back. 'You know there might be a useful side-effect to this. The Premier won't like the thought that we have a road into their intelligence service. Maybe we should drop a hint that this particular channel involves a top scientist at Baikonur. Maybe even point a finger at Kropotkin.'

'That would make Kropotkin's future uncertain.'

'Right, and as he's one of their best people it could cause a convenient hiccup in their own space program.'

The President grinned at his brother. 'I think you're enjoying this.'

'It's nice to be able to make use of all that experience we got outmaneuvering Hubert for the nomination and outflanking Nixon in November.'

'Okay, Bobby, but remember, Khrushchev's in a different class. Play it carefully. Let's not push him into retaliating by doing something before we do. We want this manned flight to have maximum impact for us, not for the Soviets.'

'It's too late for him to do anything.'

'Maybe.' The President was silent for a moment and his brother turned to leave. 'Bobby, about the astronaut picked for the flight.'

'Gary Herriman.'

'Yes. I think I should talk to him before the launch. Just an informal conversation. Bring him here, if it can be done without drawing attention to what we're planning. Otherwise, make arrangements for me to talk to him on the telephone.'

'I will. He'll appreciate hearing from you, I'm sure of that.'

After his brother had left the President sat thinking over the projected manned-spaceflight. Played well, the potential for advancing American prestige throughout the world could be immense. It would simultaneously reassure aligned nations of the power and ability of America and direct the thoughts of uncommitted nations towards the west rather than the Communist bloc. All things considered, the space program, which he had so often derided in the past, was rapidly becoming a major part of his political thinking. The forthcoming manned Atlas-Mercury shot would be, on its own, the most important event of his first term as President and could well become a key issue in determining his re-election in '64.

BAIKONUR COSMODROME, KAZAKHSKAYA

'God, I could do with a drink,' Kropotkin said.

Maisky glanced across the table, taking in the mottled complexion and the blueish tinge to the nose And lips. Kropotkin didn't look very well at all. A pity about his drinking because he was a competent, if not brilliant, scientist who was prepared to think and act beyond the confines of his own sphere if the need arose.

'That's two dangerous comments in one sentence,' Maisky said mildly.

Kropotkin frowned, then his face cleared and he laughed heartily. 'God and booze. Yes, you're right. We must be thankful sex isn't on the list as well.'

'We will soon be finished,' Maisky said, gently nudging the conversation back onto more profitable lines.

Kropotkin took the hint. 'As far as I'm concerned, that's everything. You now know as much as I do. We might make it for April, we might not.'

'It won't matter whether you do or don't. The Americans will try to beat you and they will fail.'

'You're sure?'

'Yes.'

'What do you plan to do? You never did tell me the details.'

Maisky smiled pleasantly. 'The less you know, the less you can tell.'

Kropotkin was indignant. 'I haven't a loose mouth.'

'I know you haven't,' Maisky said, permitting himself a small lie. He knew that Kropotkin's drinking occasionally led to indiscretions. 'But word has come from Moscow that the Chairman has been making noises about our activities here.'

Kropotkin's high color faded perceptibly. 'Khrushchev knows?'

'Of course he cannot know everything. He knows something, a little scrap, and is trying to find out more.'

'He'll send people here?'

'I expect so.'

'Oh, my God.'

192

Maisky leaned forward and gently rested his hand on Kropotkin's. 'There is no need to be alarmed. What do you know? Nothing.'

'I know that you have plans to prevent America beating us into space.'

'Yes, but you don't know how it will be done and you don't know anyone who is involved. Apart from me,' he added enigmatically.

Kropotkin swallowed, his throat suddenly dry. 'I will not betray you,' he protested.

Maisky smiled. 'I know that, my friend.' He turned to stare out of the window. 'I don't know how you stand this place.'

'It's not bad. And we have many privileges. As for Moscow, it gets worse. A man can't have a good time any more. The place is a morgue.' Kropotkin stopped speaking. His choice of words had been unfortunately apt. He watched Maisky for any reaction but the agent's impassive features showed none. He cleared his throat. 'Was it necessary? The American, I mean.'

Maisky raised an eyebrow. 'Lennox? Oh, yes, quite necessary. The Americans have to believe and there is nothing like a death to underline the truth of a message.' He smiled at the big man. 'Don't worry yourself about it, Ivan. Lennox felt no pain and, after all, people like him spend their lives expecting death.'

Kropotkin nodded, unconvinced. 'Do you? Do you expect death?'

'Of course.'

Kropotkin shifted uneasily in his seat. He didn't like this morbidity. Thinking of death made him think again that Khrushchev was sniffing at the edges of their scheme. 'Isn't it time we told the Chairman what we are doing, and why? We have nothing to fear, it is all in the interests of our country?'

Maisky smiled. 'But is what the Chairman does in the interests of the country'

Kropotkin shook his head. 'I'm no politician, Mikhail, you know that but surely we would be better, safer, with his blessing.'

This time Maisky laughed openly. 'Blessing? An inappropriate word, I think.' He leaned forward and spoke softly. 'All of you agreed, the members of the Praesidium, you people out here, that we have to beat the Americans into space and at the same time we have to discredit them in the eyes of the rest of the world. Now, Brezhnev tried to persuade Khrushchev this was so, as did Malinovsky. They both failed. There are only two kinds of idea Khrushchev approves. Those he thinks of himself and those that are presented to him as a *fait accompli.* That's what this will be. Once it has happened and he knows our part in it, he will rant and rave for an hour or two and then he will smile and make believe he thought of it in the first place.'

Maisky stopped speaking and studied the doubt in Kropotkin's face. It was astonishing how naive clever men could be. He wondered what kind of mess they would have made of this operation if he and the woman hadn't been there to work out all the details for them. A disaster would have been the best they could have hoped for.

He smiled at Kropotkin who was still looking much less than happy. 'Don't worry, Ivan. Everything will work out well.' He gestured towards the window. 'After all, there is too much at stake for us to turn back now.' He stood up, ready to leave.

Kropotkin nodded gloomily but stood up to escort his visitor to the door. 'I will see you again, before it happens?'

'Perhaps, perhaps not.' Maisky said before striding away along a narrow corridor leading towards the administration block. There he looked into three offices, spoke briefly to the occupants of those rooms and moved on. The effect of his few words was dramatic. Within minutes papers were being shredded and files amended to deny the papers had ever existed. Let Khrushchev make all the noise he wanted. When his thugs reached Baikonur they would find nothing of any consequence. Except Ivan Stopanovitch Kropotkin, of course, but he could tell them very little. He knew that someone was planning to sabotage the American effort but he didn't know who or how, all he knew was why. That piece of intelligence wouldn't please Khrushchev at all, but neither would it help him.

Two hours later Maisky was on board an aircraft bound for Moscow, pleased to be leaving Kazakhskaya for what was probably the last time. He occupied his mind during the flight reviewing the operation from start to finish. As far as he could see nothing had been left undone and the remainder of the plan was very well prepared. In fact, it bordered on perfection. The Americans were bound to discover some things but, faced with the information fed to Lennox, they would be unable to distinguish what was true from what was false. Given a choice, they would never doubt the central lie because it was something they wanted to believe.

Maisky had learned from his Kremlin contacts that Kennedy had written to Khrushchev and, while the timing of that had been unexpectedly quick, it pleased him. It showed the American President was buying everything. The only danger was that Khrushchev had been brought into it sooner than anticipated, but that shouldn't matter. Kropotkin apart, the organization at Baikonur was sound. His use of the cell system had insured that. As for the Kremlin end, that should prove impregnable. In any event, there wasn't enough time for anything to be done that would interfere with the plan.

When he left the aircraft at Moscow he joined a line of fellow passengers waiting for taxicabs, still thinking about the organization out in Kazakhskaya. It seemed probable that Khrushchev's men would find Kropotkin. If they did, it was reasonably certain he would talk, but there was no satisfactory way of preventing that. He had considered eliminating Kropotkin but if the Chairman's thugs found no one to occupy them they might dig harder and deeper and someone more important might be endangered. If they did find Kropotkin, he would keep them busy while the operation entered its final stages.

Of course, Kropotkin would be able to name him but that wouldn't matter. Maisky didn't plan on being around for very much longer and when he returned to Russia it would be as a hero; even Khrushchev knew the value of being on the same side as heroes.

When he finally reached the head of the line he gave the cabdriver an address in the northern suburbs of the city. He had a little task to carry out before he could go to see the woman, an unpleasant task but one he couldn't leave to anyone else.

Hiding a body was no easier in Moscow than in any other city but there were a few natural advantages, especially in winter. Decomposition of corpses took very much longer in sub-zero temperatures and after he had killed Oscar Lennox he had taken the body to a small garage. Apart from somewhere to keep his car, the garage served as an all-purpose workshop where weapons could be prepared, articles concealed, even men and women hidden when the need arose. It had no heating and its thin wooden walls served only to keep out snow and rain, affording no protection against cold. It was an ideal place in which to hide a corpse.

Now he was ready to let Lennox be discovered. He had taken care to leave the body in the fetal position so he could get it into the trunk of his car without too much effort. He dumped Lennox where casual passersby were few, then drove towards the woman's apartment stopping along the way to call the American Embassy and tell them where they could find their missing agent.

Thinking of the Embassy brought a smile to Maisky's face. A few days earlier, a colleague had obtained a visa for him from the American Embassy in Oslo. The visa would allow him to enter America freely and the ease with which it had been done said much for his organizational ability and little for the American intelligence services.

Much later, after he had left the woman's apartment, he went back to the hotel room he called home to pack a few essentials into an old leather case.

By late evening he was in Oslo where he collected his visa. It was now only a matter of hours before he would be in America ready to take personal charge of the final stages of the operation.

Sitting in the departure lounge at Oslo airport he let his thoughts dwell on the people who had initiated the scheme. Scientists were strange creatures. Full of self-importance on so many matters, yet prone to devastating self-doubts when face-to-face with the bitter reality of the Soviet political system. Their association in this enterprise with politicians was unusual and suggested they were at last making some attempt to grasp reality. Even so, with or without political allies, they would have stood little chance of success without his special talents. And those of the woman, of course.

He smiled as he recalled the hour he had spent at her apartment after dumping Lennox's body. He had briefed her, then made love to her. A hasty, if not particularly tender or satisfying, coupling, it had served a purpose. It meant that both of them could wait through the weeks until it would be safe either for them to meet again, or to take another partner into their beds. Both of them, particularly the woman, knew that sexual liaisons could not be entered into casually in their profession.

LANGLEY AIR FORCE BASE, Va.

Omar Rogerson was feeling angrily impotent. He had nothing to show for weeks of work on the sabotaging of Bill Simons' aircraft, nothing to show for his inquiries into the attack on Joe Ziegler. Well, he consoled himself, maybe nothing was an exaggeration. They had found enough evidence on the wrecked F-104B to show they were after a man, or men, who had considerable technical skill. Which narrowed the field of suspects down to just a few millions.

Arising out of the attack on Joe Ziegler they had a gun they'd been able to trace as far as a gunshop in upstate New York and a partial fingerprint on a cartridge case which they hadn't been able to match even with the reluctant help of the FBI.

Rogerson knew that trying to draw consolation from such fragments came under the heading of self-delusion but it kept him from getting too damn desperate.

He decided to clear his head by looking at something else for a while. He chose the surveillance reports on the astronauts, knowing in advance that they were trivial. Minor-league private-eye stuff and something none of them was proud of doing, especially as the astronauts knew nothing about it. He sided with Joe Ziegler's opinion about that but accepted Magadini's insistence that the astronauts needed the protection his men were giving them.

He was halfway through the pile when he noticed something that sounded a tiny warning bell. He couldn't pull the thought out of the recesses of his mind and continued reading. When he had finished he turned up the file on the attack on Joe Ziegler. He made a couple of notes, the warning bell rang a little more insistently. Probably nothing in it, just some half-assed notion born of creeping desperation, but he decided to talk to the men who had made the reports.

The telephone rang. The caller was the FBI agent in Tampa.

'I've got something that might interest you.'

'What?' Rogerson asked.

'The Titusville police were checking on a complaint. Some guy beefing about a neighbor going out at strange hours and making a heap of noise. There was nothing to it, just a shift-worker who slammed his car door and upset the complainant's old lady.'

Rogerson ground his teeth impatiently. 'So?'

'Well, before the Titusville police had gotten it sorted they'd started to run a check on this neighbor; found the guy had been over here to Tampa and asked the local PD to nose around. Seems our door-slammer's been buying electronic equipment suitable for advanced telecommunications work. He's also been buying small quantities of explosive. Planning to blow a tree-stump out of his garden is his story.'

'What's the connexion?' Rogerson asked.

'Well, like I said, he lives in Titusville so we were curious why he came all the way over here to Tampa to buy stuff he could just as easily have bought in Orlando or Daytona. We made a couple of inquiries, talked to the Titusville police. Something they missed out of their report. The man works shifts all night. He works 'em for you people. He's a technician at Cape Canaveral.'

Rogerson sat for a moment then realized he was holding his breath. Maybe this was the break he'd been waiting for. 'I'll drive over this morning,' he told the FBI agent.

'Make it after lunch,' the agent said. 'Yours isn't the only case renting space on my desk.'

ATLANTA, Ga.

Maisky stepped off the aircraft he had boarded in New York and followed the other passengers into the terminal building. He rented a car at the airport and drove slowly and carefully along unfamiliar roads until he joined Interstate 75 heading south towards Macon. Near Forsyth he pulled into a motel, booked in for the night and made two telephone calls. Then he slept for six hours, waking to a raging hunger. He had never acquired a taste for American fast-food but he didn't want to risk being remembered if he searched out a high quality restaurant. He settled for a diner two blocks along from the motel, ate hungrily, then went back to await his visitor.

When he came they talked for two hours before the man returned to his car to start the long journey back to Florida.

Maisky was well pleased with the report he'd had. Everything was going perfectly. An astonishing stroke of luck had been capitalized upon to the full. It hadn't needed much maneuvering to give them the ace they now held. He could see no danger that the game could not now be followed through to an entirely satisfactory conclusion.

He went back to sleep and later, fully rested, continued his journey towards Zephyr Springs where he planned to stay until the end, confident his plans were about to be fulfilled.

LANGLEY AIR FORCE BASE, Va.

It wasn't working. Gary Herriman had come back from the Cape determined to have another shot at injecting some verve into their marriage. He had pushed the thought that his career came before his marriage into the deepest recess of his mind but it was slowly resurfacing. He wanted to ask where she had been the nights he'd called from Florida but at the same time suspected he didn't want to know. It was strange, the ambivalence. Even his recollection of the time he had found her with Leandros was no longer clear. It wasn't like something that had happened to him, more like some tattle he'd heard about someone else.

As for this evening, already it was more than halfway to being a total disaster. The restaurant was crowded and they'd had to wait for a table. By the time they were seated both had lost any appetite they might have started out with. Cautious about buying drinks, Gary had hopefully found a middle course. He had brought a bottle of expensive wine but Stella had drunk more than half of it before the main course arrived.

'I'm sorry I've had to be away so much,' Gary said, after a long and uneasy silence.

Stella shrugged disinterestedly. 'It's the job.'

'That's right and it is important.'

She looked at him for a moment, then her eyes wandered across the restaurant. She didn't know why she had agreed to this farce. More than that she didn't know why she was still hanging around. There were better places to be, better things to do there, better people to do them with. Here she was, stuck in a town she didn't like, doing nothing but finding ways to make the days pass until she could escape to a bar, keeping company with men who had nothing to offer but their bodies. And even that was seldom enough for her any more.

They finished their meal and Gary asked her if she wanted to go on somewhere.

'Where?'

'I don't know, isn't there any place where we can...' He broke off.

'Where we can do what?' Stella asked, taking a perverse delight in goading him into suggesting they went somewhere they could have a real drink. His disapproval of the way she had drunk the wine at dinner hadn't escaped her.

'Maybe we should have called someone, invited them to have dinner with us.'

'Well we didn't.' Who was there, she thought to herself as they waited for the car-hop to bring the Ford to the restaurant door. Other astronauts and their wives were the only people they knew. With them the talk would have been the usual incomprehensible and boring jumble of things she neither understood nor cared about.

They were almost back in Langley before the silence was broken. Then it was just Gary, repeating his earlier remark. 'The job *is* important, you know.'

Stella didn't bother answering.

In the house she waited until he went to the bathroom before taking a drink from a bottle she kept at the back of a cupboard filled with some of the junk accumulated on their travels. As she pushed the bottle back into the cupboard a packet fell out onto the floor. Picking it up she glanced inside. It contained some color transparencies of their stay in Germany. She fingered them, thinking. That had been good, at first. Then it had all gone wrong.

'What's that?'

She hadn't heard him come back into the room. 'Nothing.'

He came across to her, took the transparencies and held one up to the light. 'Oh,' he said and handed them back.

From somewhere anger flooded into her.

'Is that all you can say?' she demanded.

He frowned. 'What is there to say? They're just pictures.'

'We were...' She broke off, then started again. 'Things were different then.'

He turned away, not wanting to meet her eyes.

'Goddamn it, Gary,' she exploded. 'Don't you feel anything? About me, about our life here. Aren't you interested in any damn thing at all? Apart from those fucking rockets.'

He didn't look at her. 'You said it was my job. Well baby, you're right. It *is* my job and it's all I want to do.'

'That isn't you talking, it's the fucking General. You're thirty-two years old, dammit. That's old enough to do as you want to do, live the way you want to live. It's time you got that old bastard off your back.'

'All my father ever wanted for me was a good career.'

'All he wanted was for you to be a big-shot so he could thumb his nose at the Chiefs of Staff. You're his way of showing them they were wrong to poke a Herriman in the eye.'

Gary shrugged. 'You're wrong...wrong...but there's no point having a shouting match over it.'

'Why not? Afraid that if you shout you'll surprise everyone by showing you're still alive?'

'What the hell's that supposed to mean?' Gary was beginning to feel irritated by her sniping.

'At least in an argument you remind me there's blood in your veins.'

'Oh, for God's sake, Stella!'

'Oh, for God's sake, Stella,' she mimicked. 'Go on, Gary, why not get angry. It could do wonders for the monotony around here.'

He stared at her, took a deep breath, then shook his head and forced a smiled onto his lips. He reached out and took her hand. 'You're tired, let's go to bed.'

She snatched her hand away. 'Tired? Bed?' She laughed, the sound loud and shrill. 'No, I am not tired and no, I dont want to go to bed. Certainly not with you.'

The inflection in her voice made the meaning of her last sentence unmistakable. Gary's face flushed. 'That's enough.'

'Is it? Is it really enough? Well, our sex life might be enough for you but it sure as hell isn't enough for me. I need a man. Men. I need some action, not when you feel like making a feeble attempt at it but just a little more often. You might be hot stuff in the air but when it comes to something earthbound, you just don't make it.'

She stopped, her breasts rising and falling with her breathing which had deepened as she let her anger break out. Gary stood looking at her, his face set and almost as angry as hers. Then he relaxed and to her astonishment managed to smile. 'Well,' he said. 'I'm going to bed, even if you're not. Maybe we'll both feel better by morning.'

Stella stood for a moment, then turned and went back to the cupboard grabbing for the bottle. Staring at him defiantly she unscrewed the cap, then tilted back her head and took a long pull. When she lowered her head he had gone. She listened to his footsteps going up the stairs, then turned on the tv and sat watching the screen, oblivious to the program, until eventually she fell asleep.

In the bedroom Gary Herriman lay staring up at the ceiling, not thinking about Stella, not thinking about the launch, not really thinking about anything in particular. After a while he made himself go over what had been said downstairs. There didn't seem very much point in pretending otherwise, this marriage was finished. All that was left was the hope that any moves that were made didn't impact on his career. Certainly nothing could affect the launch. That was too close. He was going up and if anyone found out about him and Stella when he came down that would be too bad. Too bad, and too late.

He turned onto his side and tried to sleep but the faint sounds of the tv set disturbed him. He remembered the photo Stella had handed him. The tiny images of the place in Germany had stirred memories of happier times and he let his mind drift along paths undisturbed for years. After a while he felt a burning sensation in his eyes and opened them. It was dark in the bedroom the only light coming from the stairs. He moved his head and looked towards the light and instead of a sharp image it was blurred and softened. He realized then what the feeling of burning had been. He was crying.

MOSCOW

'Dead?'

The Colonel didn't answer. Instead he drew himself even more rigidly upright, his eyes riveted to the wall behind the Chairman's head.

Khrushchev glared at the officer, considered throwing a violent rage, then changed his mind. A full-scale performance would be wasted on an audience of one officer. 'Get out,' he said, his voice quiet and filled with venom. He didn't know it but for the Colonel, who had prepared himself mentally for an onslaught, the quiet dismissal sounded like a death sentence. The uniformed officer saluted turned and marched out of the office, his own footfalls sounding in his ears like the fusillade of a firing squad.

Alone in his office the Chairman stood up and walked to the window to look out into a courtyard, his eyes unseeing, the Colonel no longer in his thoughts. Somewhere there had to be an overlooked trifle he could fasten on to turn this whole sorry mess to his advantage.

The note from Kennedy had come as an unpleasant surprise. It was bad enough discovering that in the very heart of the top secret establishment in Baikonur an insidious network of subversion was at work trying to sabotage the American space program. Much worse than that was the discovery, through the Colonel's abortive interrogation of their only lead, that the scientists at the Cosmodrome were not alone. They were hand-in-glove with men right here in the Kremlin. Brezhnev had been named, and Malinovsky. True, there was no first-hand evidence but it was worrying. He wouldn't put something like this past Brezhnev. Ambitious men were always dangerous.

He felt anger bubbling up inside him. Damn all scientists, all his so-called comrades in the Praesidium. All of them meddling in things beyond their own limited range of vision.

He controlled his anger. There was a lot to do and he had to think calmly. First there was the matter of placating Kennedy. That had to take precedence, taking care of Brezhnev and his cronies would have to wait. It was unfortunate that Kropotkin had died. Khrushchev reflected that the Colonel, who had conducted the interrogation and had brought the news that their prime suspect had succumbed to a heart attack in the middle of his statement, had shown courage. He could have sent a junior officer with the news. Khrushchev didn't doubt that the heart attack was anything other than the genuine cause of death. No one would be so foolish as to try to cover up a death by beating or worse.

So, what did he have? The American President had hinted at a plot to damage Project Mercury, the implication being that Khrushchev knew about it, was responsible for it. What was worse, the President had suggested the sabotage attempt originated at Baikonur and he had even identified the post held by a possible suspect. A rapid descent on the installation in Kazakhskaya had soon turned up Kropotkin, a known Stalinist. The scientist had tried bluffing it out

202

but had soon accepted the inevitable. He agreed to make a statement, had begun to do so, and then collapsed. Within hours he was dead, despite determined efforts by the medical team at the Cosmodrome. An unpleasant thought crossed the Chairman's mind, that perhaps the doctors hadn't tried as hard as they might. Then he pushed the thought away. Paranoia was for others less secure than himself.

Khrushchev returned to his desk and fingered the tape recording of Kropotkin's incomplete confession. It was unfortunate the interrogation had taken the course it had. If the questions had been asked in a different sequence they might have had much more. As it was the Colonel had started with questions to determine why, not how, the sabotage was planned.

The Chairman slipped the tape onto the machine on his desk, pressed the key and watched the slowly revolving drum, listening intently as if hoping something that hadn't been noticed before might emerge.

'We had to be sure,' Kropotkin's voice said.

'What about?'

'That we would win the race.'

'What did you think would happen if you lost?'

'Who knows? Siberia is a big place, there's room there for all of us.'

'So what did you decide to do?'

'We tried harder, believe me we tried. We worked day and night, never rested, never...'

'Not that. What did you do about the American program?'

'We thought, if we could insure the Americans were delayed in some way, any way, it would give us more time.'

'What made you think the Americans were ahead of you?'

'Everyone said so. Moscow, your people, everyone. Always telling us to work harder because the Americans were ahead of us. Well, we believed you. The only way we could make certain of winning the race was to damage Project Mercury.'

'We. You keep saying, "we". Who are the others?'

'I don't know any names. We used the cell system. Safer that way. It's hot in here. Can we have the window opened?'

'How did you get your instructions?'

'From a man who came out to Baikonur once every two weeks.'

'From where?'

'Moscow. Can I have a drink? Water will do.'

'What was his name?'

'Maisky.'

'Describe him.'

Khrushchev stopped the machine and ran the tape on past the passage where Kropotkin described the man the Chairman had already discovered to be one of the KGB's top agents. He needed Maisky. Needed him because Kropotkin had never met Brezhnev and Malinovsky and could only offer unsupported evidence of their involvement. If he was to dislodge those two he would gain more support from others within the hierarchy if he had hard evidence.

He started the tape again. The Colonel had reached the technical part, this was where he had to listen carefully as it would be from here that he would draw the central part of his reply to Kennedy.

'Did you prepare the means of sabotaging the American effort?'

'Maisky asked me to make recommendations and I did so. That was months ago.'

'Did he implement your ideas?'

'I don't know.'

'What were they?'

Kropotkin described a component necessary in the guidance system of all spacecraft. The component, used to extend the notoriously short-term instability of the radio-frequency oscillator, had been altered. Externally it looked almost the same. Internally, the unit had been miniaturized to occupy only half the available volume. The rest of the space, no bigger than a man's little finger-end, was filled with explosive. The detonating mechanism was designed to operate under certain pressure conditions. Those conditions existed equally during launch and re-entry but as the internal guidance system would not normally be active until the capsule was returning to earth that was when disaster was expected to strike.

'But you don't know if that is what they planned to do?'

'No, I don't know. I would like to stop now. I feel ill.'

'Did Maisky ever indicate that others were being asked to suggest ways of sabotaging the American spacecraft?'

'No. Oh, perhaps. He did say my work, and the work of everyone else, was invaluable. I don't know if that meant anything.'

'What else did he say to you?'

'When?'

'Whenever he came?'

'He came once every two weeks.'

'You have told me that.'

'So I cannot remember everything he said to me.'

'You will have to try.'

'That's impossible. Look, I must have a rest. I haven't slept for over twenty hours.'

'What did Maisky say to you on his last visit?'

'He said the plan would go into effect as soon as he got back to Moscow.'

'The plan being your electrical equipment?'

'I don't know. Yes, maybe. I don't know. Please, let me have a drink of water.'

'How was the plan to be put into effect?'

'For God's sake.'

'How?'

'I don't know, I think...'

'Yes?'

'Perhaps someone was going...'

'Get him a glass of water.'

'Hold his head up.'

The Chairman stopped the recording. Kropotkin did not speak again on the tape.

Somehow, out of those few answers to what were just preliminary questions Khrushchev had to fashion a response which would both placate Kennedy and reassure the American government that he did not have any evil intent. The wording would have to be careful if he was to prevent the President from recognizing that dissident elements in Russia were prepared to act without the knowledge, or consent, of the Chairman. Neither did he want to risk letting slip a hint that the original motivation behind the plan appeared to have been nothing more than fear of the consequences of being beaten by the Americans.

He reached for a sheet of paper and began to draft a carefully worded reply to Kennedy's note. It took him several attempts before he got exactly what he wanted. He took special care over the passage which hinted that the Americans should thoroughly check all electrical circuits, particularly those connected with the internal guidance system. He could be no surer than Kropotkin if that was where Project Mercury was to be sabotaged but it wouldn't matter much. Once Washington relayed his message on to NASA they would take the spacecraft and the rocket apart, nothing would miss the most searching inspection.

After the message had been transmitted the Chairman noted wryly that it would probably create precisely the effect towards which Kropotkin and Maisky appeared to be working. It would delay the Americans.

For a few moments he sat brooding over Maisky. There seemed

little doubt that the man was not a traitor, at least not in the conventional sense. He was a first-class agent, perhaps the best the KGB had, but in this case he seemed to have walked a finer than usual tightrope. If Maisky's motives were solely to insure Russian superiority he should have brought his ideas to the Chairman, not courted people like Brezhnev and Malinovsky.

He turned his mind to these men, two of his closest colleagues. It was yet to be proved that they were involved but if they were it left an interesting question. Why? What did they hope to gain from it all? There was no obvious attempt to dislodge him from power. Perhaps, just perhaps, there was something more to it. What if Brezhnev really thought Russia would benefit from their actions? If he did, and if he was right, he could gain some advantage over the Chairman within the Praesidium. It needed very careful thought. Now that the immediate problem of an angry President Kennedy was eased he would have to find out a little more. He needed to stay one jump ahead. Especially where there was a danger of antagonizing the Americans. Unlike many of his countrymen, the Chairman had a very healthy regard for the way the Americans might respond to provocation. If his colleagues saw his attitude as softness that was their misfortune. He knew it was just plain, old-fashioned, good sense.

NORFOLK, Va.

The bar was so badly lit it was impossible to recognize any of the customers except from within inches of their faces. Mike Leandros took his time going around the room, trying to quell the feeling that this was a bad place to be.

The call from Stella had come soon after his return from leave. He suspected she had probably been calling the number regularly since his sudden departure. Her voice was slurred and almost swamped by background noise, as though a party was in full swing. She had given him the name of the bar, and its address and then hung up. He had thought very seriously about ignoring the call but eventually decided to chance it. He knew that part of town. He was unlikely to run into anyone he knew down there.

The party sounds turned out to be from a juke box, which was bouncing Bill Haley and his Comets off the walls, and a heaving mob who appeared to be either deaf or drunk. Maybe both. Normal conversation being impossible, everybody was shouting. He found

Stella at last, jammed upright against the wall in a booth on the back wall of the bar. Two young men wearing leather jackets emblazoned with miscellaneous hunks of metal were also in the booth and they seemed to have developed a proprietary interest in Stella. Recognizing Leandros, Stella told them she wanted a few minutes alone. Reluctantly, and only after directing threatening glances at Leandros, they crossed the room to lean against the bar-rail.

Stella seemed even drunker than Leandros had thought from the few words she had spoken on the telephone. 'Where've you been?' she asked.

'I took some leave,' Leandros said as he slid onto the seat beside her.

'Why the hurry?'

'You know why.'

'Not nice, Mike, not nice.'

He shrugged. 'Why did you call?'

'I wanted to know where you were. I wanted...' She broke off.

'What?'

'I was about to say I wanted some company, but I guess I've made other arrangements.' She laughed shrilly and he looked around nervously. No one seemed to notice, or even hear, but the two young men were watching carefully from their station across the room.

'Okay, Stella, so, if you don't need me for that, why *did* you call?'

For a moment she stared at him in silence. Then, suddenly, her face crumpled and she began to weep. One of the two young men eased away from the bar, pushing his way through the crowd.

'For God's sake, Stella, why did you call?'

'I want a drink,' she said.

He turned his head, saw the youth, now in the middle of the crush, and decided against going up to the bar for a drink. 'I'll take you home,' he said. 'There's more privacy and the booze is free.'

Standing up he took her arm to help her out of the booth. As he did so a hand grasped his shoulder and he turned to face one of the leather-jacketed youths.

'Where do you think you're going, Pal?'

'We're leaving,' Leandros said.

'Oh, sure! We buy the drinks, help the lady get happy, you step in and the two of you disappear into the sunset. That the way you got it figured?'

'I'm not looking for trouble.'

'Then bye bye.'

'Stella...'

'Let go her arm.'

207

Leandros released Stella and started to turn. Whether the youth thought his movement was a sign of belligerence, or simply wanted an excuse, Leandros didn't know. A fist came out of the darkness, caught him a glancing blow on the cheekbone; instinctively he struck back. Afterwards, he kidded himself that he was nobly defending a lady but the reality was that his actions were motivated by blind fear. His first blow was lucky, his fist splitting the young man's nose wide open and breaking bone. The youth went down screaming with pain and in panic Leandros swung at his companion who was lunging towards him. This time Leandros wasn't so lucky but his fist caught the second youth's shoulder, overbalancing him so that he stumbled over the legs of a man in an adjoining booth. Suddenly the bar erupted into a scene out of the last reel of a B-Western and, with Stella dazedly stumbling after him, Leandros left in a hurry.

He had parked his car around the corner and he got her to it just as the first police car came howling along the street towards the bar where the clamor of fighting was gradually overcoming the noise from the juke box.

He drove steadily towards his apartment, trying to decide on his safest course of action. He hadn't come up with a good answer before he reached home where, although he doubted he was doing the best thing, he half-carried Stella through the apartment and into the bedroom. Back in the living room he poured himself a long drink and spent half an hour in entirely unproductive thought before deciding that the only really safe way to deal with the situation was to call Diana McNair. It would take a whole lot of explaining, but it was better than the risk entailed in taking Stella home. There, for all Leandros knew, Gary Herriman might be waiting in a very different mood to the last time their paths had crossed. It was also better than keeping her in his bedroom because he didn't know in what con dition she'd wake. She had seemed more stoned than ever and it was certainly the first time he'd known her to pass out. He dialled Diana's number and carefully told her only just enough to make sure she came down without delay.

Back in the bedroom he stood for a moment looking down at the once-attractive woman lying on the bed. Her hair was matted and obviously filthy, her clothes looked stained and creased, and her face was puffed and swollen as if she had been slapped across the cheeks. As he looked at her she stirred in her sleep and began to mumble. At first the words were indistinguishable but gradually they became clearer.

'I'll kill her if she comes here,' she said.

Leandros moved closer, his professional interest aroused for the first time in the case of Stella Herriman.

'He's mine. I love him, I always did. Why do you want him? Leave him alone.'

Intrigued, Leandros waited but Stella rolled over onto her side and fell into deeper sleep. When Diana McNair arrived he told her what had happened that evening, avoiding saying why, of all people, Stella had called him. When he repeated the words Stella had spoken in her sleep, Diana forgot the third degree she had planned for her assistant. They continued discussing Stella, occasionally looking into the bedroom to see how she was. By dawn, when Stella awoke, obviously ashamed to see Diana there, and very ill from the quantity of liquor she had consumed the night before, they had reached no useful conclusion.

Only one thing was certain, the image of a happy, trouble-free team that the Administration cherished was cracking too fast to paper over.

WASHINGTON, D.C.

'It would account for Lennox's death.'

Bobby Kennedy didn't answer. He was decidedly unhappy about the whole damn thing. Not at the death of the agent itself, but at the motive for the murder.

'He was small time,' the CIA Director went on. 'The only reason the Soviets could have for eliminating a man like Lennox was if he'd stumbled on something big. We know he was watching Kropotkin, therefore we have to assume that was why they took him out. They must have figured, or maybe just hoped, he hadn't already made a report.'

'Maybe.'

'It fits.'

'Anything will fit if you push it hard enough.'

The CIA Director bit back an angry retort. It wasn't important enough to heat up over. He had wars and revolutions piling up on his desk back at headquarters, a two-bit caper like an attempt to sabotage a goddamn rocketship came pretty low on his list of priorities.

'Okay,' Kennedy said. 'I'll take care of it. I'll talk to Langley this afternoon, see how they're getting along.'

The CIA Director raised an eyebrow, then realized Kennedy was talking about Langley Air Force Base near Norfolk, not the other Langley where the CIA's headquarters were located. 'You need me for anything else?' he asked.

Kennedy shook his head, put his feet on the desk and stared at the wall until the Director had left the room. He knew his behavior had irritated the other man and was entirely unconcerned that it did so. He would call Magadini that afternoon but he already knew that the most thorough checks and rechecks were taking place and would continue throughout the build-up to the launch. Magadini wouldn't move faster through any prodding and would probably use the opportunity to whine about needing more time. Still, he would make the call if only to reassure himself there would be no last-minute hitches now that there were only four days left to lift-off.

He debated calling his brother, then decided against it. First, he wanted to sound out a new idea. What if all this activity in Russia, the information about Kropotkin, the death of Lennox, the whole deal in fact, was some kind of plot to make them jumpy. Maybe the Soviets were trying to conceal the fact that they were about to pull off a really big space-spectacular. He couldn't prove anything, it was just a hunch. But it would be just like those devious bastards. Always prepared to turn anything, even something as costly and as dangerous as a space shot, into a political football.

CAPE CANAVERAL, Fla.

Specs hadn't cracked a joke for almost two hours which felt like some kind of record. The space suit technician hadn't timed it but he could have identified the moment when he felt that joking about things was no solution. It had been right after orders came down to start yet another check of the life-support systems. He had lost count of the number of times he'd been through the routine in the course of the last couple of weeks. What were they up to? Was it some kind of endurance test? He stretched his arms and sighed. It was time for a coffee break but the way he felt right now he doubted even that would improve his depression.

He went down the steps from the storeroom where the space suits were kept and had almost reached the floor of the building when he noticed a man a few yards away, his back turned as he discussed something with another technician. Something about the man struck a chord and Specs hesitated. Then it registered and he continued his descent. The man was the electrical technician who had called himself Gray. On that earlier occasion Specs had checked the shift rosters, found there was a man of that name on duty, and had let things slide. He had enough to worry about. Nevertheless, he drifted casually across to where the two men were standing and this time got close enough to where the two men were standing and this time got close enough to see the name on the tag on the white coveralls. It was Patterson. Thoughtfully, Specs turned and continued on his way to the technicians' lounge. He drank his coffee slowly. There seemed no reason to doubt it, the man was a phony. The question was, what should he do about it?

By the time his coffee was finished he had decided what he should do. He went out of the building and across to one of the payphones by the parking lot. He made a call, spoke for several minutes to the man on the other end of the line, listened to his comments, then hung up.

He came out of the booth and stood for a moment, thinking. It seemed a hell of a complicated way to do things but who was he to argue? He went into the main administration building and along to the office of Omar Rogerson where he made his report, feeling slightly uneasy as he did so.

An hour later he was back at his task of checking space suits when the door opened and Gary Herriman came in.

'Hi.'

'Hi, Captain.' Specs acknowledged the greeting with the right blend of amiability and respect. He liked this man, admired him, the way he liked and admired all the astronauts.

'Suit all okay?'

'Sure.'

'I'll need it tomorrow. I have a date with the FP Trainer in the morning.'

'You're not going to California?'

'No, not me. Neither is Gus. We have to spend some more time on the Trainer. We're following the others out to Edwards in a few days.'

'I would've thought you all knew that machine backwards by now.'

Herriman grinned. 'Maybe that's the trouble. It's time we learned it the right way around.'

'Hey, hey. I'm the one who tells the jokes around here, remember. Remember it always, never forget.'

Herriman looked at him curiously for a moment, then nodded. 'I'll remember.'

'Private party, or can anyone join?' The voice came from the door and the two men looked around to see Walter Schirra had come into the storeroom.

'Always welcome, Commander, you know that,' Specs said.

'Joe's looking for you, Gary,' Schirra said.

'Okay,' Herriman said shortly and went out.

'What's eating him?' Schirra asked.

'Doesn't like to think he'll miss the fun you guys'll be having out at Edwards.'

Schirra shook his head. 'Wasn't all that much fun the last time anyone went out there.'

Specs' expression sobered as he remembered what had happened to Bill Simons. 'No, I guess not.'

'Okay, let's take a look at the alterations you've been making to the shoulder-webbing.'

Specs reached up for the astronaut's space suit and the two men became engrossed in that small but important matter unaware that Gary Herriman had gone no further than just outside the door. He was standing at the head of the steps which led down to the main floor, oblivious to the activity and noise, thinking about Stella and the mission, the past and the future. Day-dreaming wasn't his style and he started down the steps trying to shake off the uneasy feeling that something threatening was clawing at the back of his mind.

TITUSVILLE, Fla.

The tipoff from Specs had been a lifesaver for Omar Rogerson. The information from the FBI agent in Tampa and the police in Titusville hadn't given him anything hard to go on. He hadn't wanted to risk pulling in a man who, according to his record, was a long-serving, reliable and competent technician on nothing stronger than a few trips to Tampa to buy electronic components and explosives. The man's name was Gray, the same name given to Specs, and it was a simple matter to confirm that it was the same man. Gray's security clearance was limited, which accounted for him using different name-tags when Specs had seen him in highly-classified zones at the plant.

Deciding he now had enough to move against the man Rogerson called Joe Ziegler and told him what he'd gotten so far.

'What are you planning?' Joe asked.

'First, a search of his home.'

'Okay, but I think you should take along an electronics expert, someone who'll know if the stuff this guy has been buying is anything to worry about. And what to do if one of your men drops some nitro on his shirtfront.'

'Will do.'

'Let me fix it,' Joe said. 'I'll be along, too.'

Ziegler had already decided on his special Mission Control team. The electronics man he'd noted from the launch-meeting, Eddie Danvers, had been checked out for security and had jumped at the chance of working on the secret project. Now, he was hard at work building communications and telemetry equipment into two rooms set aside in back of the medical center, ostensibly for some top-secret experiments.

Rogerson picked up the two men and they covered most of the journey to Titusville in silence. Rogerson parked his car around the corner from the small house where the man lived. The house, built of timber, was badly in need of repair. At some time in the past it had been converted into two apartments, one on each story. A rickety staircase ran up the outside of the house to the upper apartment, the one occupied by Gray.

'How long has he been employed at the Cape?' Joe asked.

Rogerson shifted uncomfortably. 'Two years, goddamn it.'

'How did he get away with it for so long?'

'We don't know he's been doing it all along,' Rogerson said, then shrugged away the excuse. 'Come to it, we don't know that he hasn't. Seems like he goes on shift using his real name, that's if Gray *is* his real name, then, when he wants to go somewhere his security doesn't permit, he just hangs on a different name-tag and brazens it out.'

'As easily as that?'

'We checked on the name he was wearing the second time Specs saw him. Patterson should've been on shift that night but had called in sick.'

'And Gray just happened to have a tag with Patterson's name on it?'

Rogerson shook his head. 'Seems like it.'

'Why did he give Specs his real name?'

'I guess he was just confused, had forgotten who he was supposed to be.'

'And tonight?'

'Gray has a shift starting in a couple of hours. I've put a man onto it so he'll be tailed from the moment he leaves here until he reaches the plant. He'll be watched all the time he's there and then tailed right back here again.' Rogerson straightened up in his seat. 'That looks like him, now.'

A man had appeared at the head of the rickety stairs and moments later he clattered noisily down, climbed into an Italian sports car with a crumpled rear fender, and roared off down the quiet street. A dark-blue panel truck started up and followed, the driver inclining his head towards Rogerson as he passed.

They waited ten minutes before entering the apartment. Inside, Rogerson carried out a swift but careful search with Ziegler and Danvers replacing everything as soon as he was finished with it. In a drawer they found a box containing about two dozen name-tags and passes.

'I guess that's how he did it,' Rogerson said. 'Sooner or later he'd get lucky and be able to use one or another of these to get around the top-security sections.' He carefully noted the names before replacing the box in the drawer.

Half an hour after they'd entered the apartment Rogerson dragged a large trunk from the back of a walk-in closet. The trunk was filled with electrical components. This was why they had brought Danvers along and Joe and Rogerson let the electronics expert get on with checking everything, item by item. At first it all seemed to be radio or hi-fi equipment and Ziegler was beginning to wonder if they'd been too ready to leap to some half-baked conclusions. Then Danvers stiffened and whistled noisily.

'What is it?' Ziegler asked.

'Unless I miss my guess, this is what we're looking for.' Danvers sat back on his heels, indicating a small cylindrical object.

'Well?'

'I'm pretty sure it's from the Mercury capsule's internal guidance system. It looks like a stabilizer from the oscillator circuit. I can't be sure without testing it, but I'd guess this will fit into the circuit just like the real thing.'

'Except?'

'Except something's been added.'

'What?'

'Can't tell for sure, not without taking it apart.'

'Can you do that here?'

'I'd prefer to strip it down in the lab.'

'But you could do it here?'

Danvers was reluctant. 'Sure.'

'How long have we got, Chief?'

'His shift ends in seven hours.'

Ziegler looked at the other man. 'Long enough?'

Danvers shrugged. 'It'll have to be. I'll need a flat surface. I'll use the coffee table. Find something to cover it so I don't make any marks.'

'I'll call in,' the Chief said. 'As soon as the guy leaves, someone will telephone us here. That'll give us an hour to wrap things up.'

It took three hours of painstaking, delicate, work before the technician sat back and looked at Ziegler and the Chief.

'Well?' Ziegler asked.

'Nasty. There's a small explosive device in there. Not big. Wouldn't blow a hole in a can of coffee.'

'But?'

'But in the middle of the guidance system it would pretty much write the death warrant of the poor mother strapped into the capsule.'

'Okay,' the Chief said. 'That's good enough for me. Any reason why we shouldn't take him in now?'

Ziegler shook his head slowly. 'Might be better to leave him a while longer.' He turned to the technician. 'Can you put that thing back together again?'

'Sure.'

'Then do it.'

As Danvers began to reassemble the unit Ziegler drew the security man to one side. 'I say leave this here and step up the watch on Gray. There's only one place he can fit the component so we have a man watching the capsule. As soon as Gray makes the switch we move in, take out the bomb, and replace the correct component.'

Rogerson nodded his head. 'Then wait and see where he leads us.'

'Right.'

Now that he knew what he was dealing with Danvers was able to work much faster and a couple of hours later the three men were on their way back to the Cape, prepared to wait out the saboteur as long as necessary.

In the end their wait was a short one. Less than twenty-four hours elapsed before Gray made the switch that turned the capsule into a coffin. As soon as Gray left the area the guidance system was made safe and surveillance intensified. Later, Joe Ziegler found his mind dwelling on the ease with which they had found the man. Everything had slotted neatly together. The information from Moscow via Washington, identification of the intruder at the Cape, finding the explosive device. It had been so easy it made him jumpy.

'How do you feel?' Diana asked.

Stella Herriman tried a smile that didn't quite work. 'I've felt better.'

'Are you up to seeing Gary?'

'No.' The answer came out sharp and definite.

Diana studied the other woman carefully. Stella looked much better than when she had been brought to the apartment. That seemingly simple task had turned into quite a chore. Having helped get Stella into Diana's car Leandros had volunteered to come along with them. Diana refused the offer, thinking she could handle Stella alone. She very nearly didn't because halfway home Stella had been convulsed with violent nausea and, had the attack lasted any longer, Diana would have turned around and driven to the hospital.

Stella had slept for hours, immobile, her breathing shallow, and when eventually she had awakened, Diana managed to clean her up but failed to persuade her to take any food. Then Stella slept again, this time a more natural sleep. When she awoke the second time she ate some toast and managed to hold down a cup of coffee.

'I had to let Gary know you were here,' Diana said. 'He's been calling home. He was worried.'

'Was he?' There was a curious touch of disbelief in Stella's voice.

'Of course.'

Stella looked hard at Diana but didn't answer.

'Do you want to talk about it?' Diana asked after a moment of uneasy silence.

'About what?'

'About why you drink, and what's wrong between you and Gary.'

'What has he told you?'

'He hasn't told me anything.'

'I thought that's what you did. Probed into their minds, made them tell you everything.'

Diana laughed. 'No, I'm not that kind of psychiatrist. I study attitudes, estimate likely behavior under certain stressful conditions.'

'And what's your estimate of Gary?'

'He seems very stable.'

'Too damn stable. Nothing moves him. He knows how I am but he doesn't care.'

'What do you mean, he knows how you are?'

'He knows I drink too much...and he knows I see other men.'

'You're sure he knows?'

Stella laughed bitterly. 'Of course he knows. He found us together, me and...' She trailed off looking away from Diana.

'You and Mike Leandros.'

Stella nodded slowly without speaking.

'And you think he doesn't care?'

'If he did he would have said something, done something. Not just accepted it, walked away from it.'

'He does have a lot of pressures, Stella.'

'We all have.'

Diana was unsure whether to press on with that line. It appeared that Gary hadn't told Stella about the flight and she wasn't certain if it was right or wrong for her to raise the subject. She knew how great an emphasis was being placed on secrecy and quite clearly, in her present frame of mind, Stella couldn't be trusted to keep quiet. She decided to try another tack.

'How long have things been bad between you?'

'How long? Oh, about two years since they got really bad but I think it all started about the time we came back to the States. We both were happy when Gary was based in Germany. It was the first time either of us had been to Europe. First time we'd traveled anywhere really, apart from Hawaii. We went there when we were married.'

'When was that? When did you come back from Europe, I mean?'

'Almost six years.'

'What happened at first?'

'Just little things, he began forgetting my birthday, anniversaries, he would be thoughtless where he'd once been so kind. He would never go out with my friends, and he never made any friends of his own.'

'And that was different to how things were before?'

Stella hesitated. 'He was always quiet but we were happy.'

'How much time did you spend together, before all this began?'

'We had to be apart quite a lot, but that only made the time we were together seem better.'

'Why did you have to spend time apart?'

'His work. While we were in Europe he was ferrying aircraft between Germany and England.'

'And when you came back here?'

'We were together much more. Oh, are you saying that it all happened because we were together too much?'

Diana shook her head. 'I'm not saying anything like that, Stella. I don't know enough to make judgments, form opinions. I'm just trying to find out what differences there were between your lives when you were happy and your lives after things started going wrong.'

Standing up, Stella walked across the room to study herself in a mirror. 'I look a mess, don't I?'

There didn't seem much point in denying a very obvious truth. 'You look better than you did last night but even now you don't look the way you did when you arrived at Langley.'

Stella stared at her reflection. 'I looked really good when we were in Germany, when we first came back to the States too. There was no reason for him to look elsewhere.'

Diana frowned. 'Are you saying there's another woman?'

Stella shook her head. 'I don't know. I've never seen him with anyone but...'

'Go on, Stella.'

'Why else would he ignore me, never want to make love to me unless I made all the moves.'

Diana didn't answer. There were several reasons she could think of, none of which involved another woman.

'He dreams about her,' Stella said suddenly.

'How do you know?'

'I can tell. He talks to her in his sleep and the things he says are different to the way he talks to me.' Slowly tears started to form in Stella's eyes. They were not tears of self-pity but of genuine unhappiness that a life that had once seemed to hold so much now held nothing.

'Have you asked him about another woman?' Diana asked.

Stella shook her head. 'No. If I did that it would all come out in the open, wouldn't it?'

'That might be the best thing.'

'No. He might decide to go away with her, whoever she is. I don't want that.'

'Is what you've got worth keeping?'

'Separation? Divorce? That would finish him wouldn't it. The public wants their astronauts whiter than white. If that happened he'd have to go back to being an ordinary pilot. A nothing man.'

'Being an Air Force pilot isn't being nothing.'

'It is in Gary's eyes. That's the way the General brought him up.'

'General Herriman?'

'Yes. The mechanical man. Have you met him?'

Diana shook her head.

'He's never shown an ounce of affection for anyone in his life. God knows how he ever persuaded Gary's mother to marry him. She must have led a miserable life, as long as it lasted. Do you know, the

218

first time I met the General, Gary was in uniform and he had to salute the old man and call him Sir. I've never heard him refer to his father as anything other than the General. Maybe that's what is happening to Gary, maybe he's becoming like his old man. That would account for how he acts towards me. The General doesn't know what it means to show affection.'

Abruptly Stella stopped talking and started to gather her clothes, trying to make them look less disheveled than they were.

'You don't have to go,' Diana said.

'I should.'

'Will you call Gary at the Cape?'

'Not yet. You call him, tell him I'm fine, if that's what you think is best for him.'

Diana drove Stella into Norfolk to where she had left her car. On the way back home, running over what had been said that afternoon, Diana decided there had been nothing particularly unusual in it. A man and woman who had married young but had outgrown one another seemed pretty commonplace. Maybe there was another woman in Gary Herriman's life, but if there was she certainly didn't appear to hang around Langley.

Back in Norfolk, Stella took the opposite direction to Diana and headed back towards Langley. She was thinking more clearly about her marriage than for some time. Despite what she'd implied to Diana, she didn't think she felt any affection for Gary any longer. She sighed, the gap in her life smarting like an open wound.

She stopped at a red light and glanced incuriously at two motorcyclists who came up alongside. One of them leaned down and grinned at her through the window. She recognized one of the young men who had bought her drinks in the bar before Leandros arrived. He turned and spoke to his companion who waved a hand at her. When the light changed they rode, one on each side of her, for three blocks before forcing her to make a right and stop.

One of the young men opened her door and leaned in, grinning. 'Came back, did you?' he said.

'Please go away.'

'Hey, hear that? The lady said, would we please go away.'

The door at the passenger side opened and the other youth slid onto the seat.

'Get out,' Stella said.

'We've some unfinished business.' He took her arm and pulled her out of the car. She looked around desperately but the street was empty.

'You can't do anything to me here,' she said. 'Not in the middle of the afternoon.'

'That's right,' he said. He gestured to the building behind him. 'This is where we live, let's go and visit.'

He pulled her and she started to call out but the other youth's hand clamped over her mouth. They pressed close in on her, one in front, one behind. The heat of their bodies imparted their intentions more clearly than words. Within a few seconds they were inside the building, a crumbling tenement, Stella being half-carried, half-dragged up the stairs. Once in their room they began to rip at her clothing, then their own and despite her fear Stella felt a rich excitement spreading downwards from her stomach to her thighs.

'That's better, lady,' one of them said. 'Always knew you were hot for it.'

'Stop talking,' Stella said. 'Do it.'

They did as she ordered and first one, then the other, took her body and used it crudely without any tenderness. Later they took her together, entering her vagina and her mouth simultaneously. Stella was detached, as if watching a blue movie, and it even amused her that she outlasted them both. When the youths were too exhausted to do anything more to her she dressed and went downstairs, climbed into her car and drove the rest of the way home stopping only once to buy vodka at a liquor store.

She decided there was nothing to be gained by pretending to be anything other than what she had become.

WASHINGTON, D.C.

'What do you want us to do down there?'

Bobby Kennedy glared irritably at the speaker who sat, smoking unconcernedly, across the desk from him. 'I don't know, that's why you're going. Just take a look around, make sure they're keeping this thing secure.'

'If they're not, there isn't time to do much about it.'

'I don't expect you to tighten existing security, I just want to be ready for any future problems.' Kennedy leaned forward, dropping his voice slightly. 'By this time Monday we'll know whether or not we have the biggest publicity coup in history on our hands. If we have, then it doesn't matter how shaky security has been.'

'And if it comes out another way?'

'Then we need to be sure the wraps stay on.'

'Have you any reason to think they won't?'

Pushing his chair back from the desk Kennedy stood up to pace the room. He wasn't particularly worried over men like Magadini and Ziegler. Their loyalty and patriotism was unquestioned. All he would need do was assure them that the interests of national security would be served by keeping silent and they would clam up forever. No, the problem, if a problem arose, would come from one or another of the small-fry. He stopped pacing and sat on the edge of his desk. 'There may be some lower echelon people involved,' he told his visitor. 'Maybe some of those in on the secret have spoken out of turn. Maybe a wife, or a lover, has been told something. That's what you should look for. Do nothing now, just make a list of likely security risks. We can decide what to do later, when we know if anything is needed.'

The other man flicked ash into his cupped hand and stared up at Kennedy for a moment before speaking. 'Suppose we do find a security risk, and we need to close it off. Have you figured out yet how we're supposed to do it?'

Kennedy shook his head.

'Maybe you'd better start figuring,' the other man said.

Standing up, he reached over and carefully dropped the cigarette ash into a wastebasket. 'How will I know if it's a success or not?'

Kennedy grinned. 'If it's a success, the whole damn world will know. If everything goes quiet, you'll know we have a problem.'

His visitor nodded and crossed to the door where he hesitated, looking back at Kennedy, smoke trailing across his face from the cigarette hanging from his lips. 'Don't forget,' he said quietly. 'If it does go wrong and we have to close off a security risk there'll be no time to play around. We'll need to act fast. So you'd best make that decision on how you want it handling before Monday.'

As the door closed Kennedy returned to his chair and sat for some moments staring across the room. The man was right, a decision was needed but it wasn't one he relished making. Just one more reason to hope everything went according to plan.

Down below, in the street, Kennedy's visitor joined his companion in their brown Chevrolet. 'He means well,' he said, after he had relayed the substance of his meeting. 'Trouble is, he still doesn't understand the difference between names on a file and real live, unpredictable people.'

'I don't like it,' his companion said.

The other man lit a fresh cigarette from the butt of his last before gunning the motor and easing the Chevy away from the curb. 'Who does?' he asked. 'Anyway, look on the bright side. It'll be a whole lot warmer down in Florida than it is up here.'

1961
February 19 – February 23

CAPE CANAVERAL, Fla.

'See you guys later,' Wally Schirra said with a wave of his hand. He went up the aluminum ladder into the belly of the C-131 freighter that was to take him and the other astronauts to Edwards. Gus Grissom, Gary Herriman and Joe Ziegler responded to the wave, each with differing emotions.

As the freighter doors closed and the engines started up, Gary felt a strange loneliness come over him. For the first time the reality of the next few hours made themselves felt. It wasn't just another test launch; it was the real thing and he was going to be a part of it.

He glanced at Gus and Joe. Neither man looked especially happy. Troubling Joe was the knowledge that the good relationship he'd worked so hard to build up with the astronauts was ended. The next time he saw them they would know he'd deceived them, kept from them important information. They'd get over the anger and disappointment, he was sure of that. But he was equally certain they would never trust him quite as completely again.

Ziegler turned to walk back to the jeep. 'Come on, Gus, there's something I have to tell you.'

Grissom climbed into the jeep, thinking that whatever it was Ziegler had to say it would have a hard time compensating for the feeling of isolation from which he was starting to suffer. He glanced at Gary and conceded that he too appeared to be undergoing some kind of special treatment. All those extra hours on the FPT, the repeated tests and checks. Gus suddenly had the alarming thought that maybe they were about to be bounced off the program.

Although it was barely dusk, the perimeter lights were switched on and glowed faintly against the grey sky. Gus turned the jeep towards the huge bulk of the hangars housing the giant Atlas rocket. As they drew closer, the dark shapelessness of the hangars looming over them gave all three men an uncomfortable feeling of insignificance.

Gary turned to look back towards the ocean, trying to imagine what it would be like to be shot out over that rolling expanse of water accelerating to over 17,000 miles an hour. He'd probably never have a clear impression of it. Those first few minutes of the launch would be filled with activity, the kind of activity designed primarily to stop him thinking too much about what was happening all around

225

him. Later, when he was in orbit, it would be different, better. He would have time to look, to enjoy, and to think. Gingerly, he tried the thought that in a matter of hours all this would cease to be an academic exercise and would become reality. Surprisingly the notion didn't scare him too badly. All he felt was a satisfying surge of eager anticipation for the adventure.

Gus parked the jeep and the three men went inside the hangar. They stood for a moment watching the traction unit being coupled up to the base unit upon which the Atlas rocket was mounted.

Ziegler glanced around. There was a lot of activity but no one stood near them. 'Okay, Gus,' he said. 'No apologies for the secrecy. This isn't going to be just another test flight. This one will be manned.'

For an instant Grissom's stomach lurched with excitement. A manned launch. And Joe was telling him about it. That could only mean....but then a whole bundle of things dropped into place. The way Joe had been spending so much time with Gary; the extra hours' training the young astronaut had been putting in; the fact that, despite some recent gains, his own training had fallen behind since his injury; the realization that there was no way they could expect him to fly the mission at such short notice; above all the way Gary Herriman looked now. He wasn't surprised, disappointed, or even excited. He already knew.

'Gary,' Gus said. It wasn't a question, just a flat statement of fact.

'That's right,' Joe said. 'Sorry, Gus. If it's any consolation, you were number one choice but that damn shunt of yours put you back.'

Grissom nodded, then, forcing a grin onto his face, he turned to Gary. 'Congratulations. Anything you need, any help wanted, just holler.'

'Thanks, Gus. It'll be good to know you're down here rooting.'

'Okay, Gus,' Ziegler said. 'We've set up a special control unit over in the medical center. We'll go over there and on the way you can ask me any questions you have.'

'I've got one right now,' Grissom said. 'Why all the secrecy? I would've thought this was something we'd be shouting about.'

Ziegler glanced at Gary Herriman before answering. 'It's a long story, Gus.' He turned and with Grissom following he walked towards the doors, beginning to outline the events of the previous weeks.

Gary Herriman stood alone for some minutes watching the fevered but controlled activity around the base of the rocket. He tilted his head back and stared upwards to where the capsule would soon be mounted.

'Big bastard, isn't she?' a voice said.

He turned to see Specs had come up unnoticed 'Sure is.'

Ziegler had notified Specs about the forthcoming flight that afternoon and he had also briefed one of the doctors from the space medicine team. An ambitious young man, Willard Carmody had the necessary ability together with a driving ambition that told him this project was a surefire ticket out of a rut. Gus was the last of the team. Until the flight was under way and the President gave the okay that was it, no one else would be told.

'I've got a little problem on your space suit, Captain,' Specs said.

'Oh?' Herriman sounded worried.

Specs grinned. 'Nothing serious. Can you come over in about ten minutes.'

'Sure.'

'You remember where the storeroom is?'

'Of course.'

'That's good. Some of the guys don't always remember. Only a few never forget.'

Herriman shrugged. 'It's over behind the radio testing unit.'

'Okay, see you there. Ten minutes.'

Gary Herriman watched the little man walk away, then turned his attention back to the coupling up of the traction unit. The job was almost over, the men involved moved back and moments later the engines of the traction unit were started up and the hangar doors, more than 100 feet high, were opened. Slowly, almost imperceptibly, the crawler unit inched towards the doors. The first ponderous stage of the flight had begun.

Turning, Herriman walked across the floor of the huge hangar, letting his thoughts drift over the past weeks, months, years. It was difficult to believe that a career he'd never entirely appreciated was about to hit a unique high. He wondered what it would be like when it was all over. What difference would it make to his life? There'd be publicity – he wasn't sure he'd like that. From his youth in Northampton, Massachussetts, he'd always tried to keep out of his father's limelight. Now the townspeople would want him back so they could moon over him. And that would be the biggest joke. To a military family home was a succession of three-roomed boxes they called married quarters. By the time he was four, Northampton had become just a hazy memory to Herriman junior, one he'd never had any desire to relive. But he doubted the good people of that damp New England bailiwick would forget their favorite son the spaceman.

Maybe that was what had hurt Stella the most. It couldn't have been much of a life for a small-town girl: the constant moving, the regulation-issue housing, the ever-changing cast of friends, the lack of roots. He vowed to make another effort once the mission was over, take Stella off on a long vacation to visit again places and people out of a happier past.

An image of Stella came into his mind, beautiful, jolly, walking with him through the woods, searching for a place where she could paint and he could sit and watch her. He shook his head, aware of a dull ache behind his eyes. He'd better check with Carmody. It would be a hell of a note if he developed a cold at this late stage. Carmody would have something for him, a pill or one of his hypodermics.

He was halfway across the floor of the hangar when he remembered he was supposed to be going to see Specs about his space suit. What the hell was happening? He must be letting all the tension and excitement get to him. He didn't usually forget things. He changed direction, heading now for the storeroom. The headache could wait, the space suit was more important. It must be, otherwise Specs wouldn't have troubled him about it.

NORFOLK, Va.

The two men were eating hot dogs at a stand across the street from a bar where their quarry had been for the past two hours.

'I can't remember the last time I ate a real meal,' one of them complained.

His companion finished his hot dog and wiped his fingers on a paper napkin before tossing it into a waste bin. 'We didn't take this job in order to eat well,' he said.

'Why did we take it?'

'Is that a serious question?'

'I suppose not. But this rheumatism in my shoulder sometimes screams it's one helluva way to make a living.'

Lighting a smoke the other man glanced across the street. 'Finish up,' he said. 'Here she comes.'

Stella Herriman came out of the bar and stood for a moment on the sidewalk, squinting at the daylight after the darkness inside. Two young men came out and joined her, one of them wrapping an arm around her waist.

'Let's use your bike,' she said. 'I haven't been on a motor-cycle in years.'

The two men started up their machines and Stella climbed on behind one of them, her skirt riding high up over her thighs.

Across the street the two men climbed into a brown Chevy and prepared to follow.

'Some way for the wife of an astronaut to act,' the one who had been complaining said.

The other man shrugged. 'She's just a woman. None of them is perfect even if we like them to keep smiling for the cameras.'

'Maybe, maybe not. She shouldn't act this way though. Not now.'

His companion nodded as he eased the car into the traffic fifty yards behind the two bikes. 'Perhaps she doesn't know what her husband's about to do.'

'He'll have told her.'

'Maybe.'

'He must have done. Christ, I would've told my wife.'

'You're not married.'

'But if I was.'

The driver didn't pursue the argument. He was married and there were a million things he didn't tell his wife. And his wife wasn't a drunk who hung around bars and young motor-cyclists. As far as he knew, he corrected himself. Making assumptions wasn't what he was paid to do. He checked everything, not once but twice or more. Like the way he had checked most of the people who were in on the secret. Along with their closest friends and relatives. So far this was the only one who looked like she would create trouble. Of all people, it had to be the wife of the goddamn pilot. Keeping her mouth closed could be a toughie.

WASHINGTON, D.C.

'The countdown is proceeding without any hitches,' Bobby Kennedy said.

The President came around the desk to stand beside his brother. 'Maybe now's the time to make the announcement.'

'I thought we'd decided to wait until he was up there and everything was functioning correctly.'

'I know but there's no doubt we would have greater impact on public opinion at home if we announced it first. That way we show absolute confidence in our ability.'

'There was no lack of impact when the Soviets sent up Sputnik.'

The President nodded in agreement. 'You're right, of course, but the psychological value of doing everything in the open could be useful to us later on.'

'Well, the press release is ready. We can bring it forward easily enough.'

Jack Kennedy thought for a moment. 'I'm planning on talking to the astronaut, let me do that first, then we can talk with Magadini and von Braun.'

'When do you want to talk to Captain Herriman?'

'As soon as possible.'

'I'll call Ziegler, tell him to get Herriman onto a secure line.' Bobby Kennedy said as he reached for the telephone and dialled.

'Security is still good down there?' the President asked.

His brother hesitated an instant before replying. 'Yes.'

The President didn't miss the hesitation. 'If there's a problem the time to tell me is now.'

'Gary Herriman's wife.' Bobby said reluctantly.

'What about her.'

Bobby Kennedy succintly outlined what he'd learned from his men who had been checking security at Langley and the Cape.

'Who else knows about her?'

'I don't know.'

'Then find out,' the President said, his voice taking on a harder note. 'Ask Ziegler, and the psychiatrist, McNair. I want to know why the hell of all the astronauts we have they're sending up a guy who's wife is a lush, maybe worse.'

'Maybe no one knows.'

'Then they should, dammit.'

At that moment Joe Ziegler answered the telephone and Bobby Kennedy told him the President wanted to talk to Gary Herriman.

'How well do you know Herriman's wife?' he added.

'As well as any of the astronauts' wives.'

'Do you know she drinks?'

There was silence. 'We know she has a few problems,' Ziegler said cautiously.

'Then why pick Herriman, in heaven's name?'

'What his wife gets up to doesn't affect him.'

'That's debatable.' Bobby paused. 'Okay, it's too late to do anything about it now. Call the psychiatrist, Diana McNair, tell her to talk to Stella Herriman. Once this thing goes public every newspaperman in the country will be after her. She could make us all look like a horse's rear-end.'

'Okay,' Ziegler said. 'I'll call Diana as soon as I have Gary on a secure line. There is something you can do for Gary, he asked me a

230

while back if his father, General Herriman, could be told about the mission before the news is released. I told him I'd ask the President.'

'I'll do it,' Bobby said.

Five minutes later the President was connected with Gary Herriman. 'The mission you are about to undertake marks a great advance for technology and our nation, Captain, and a thrilling moment for mankind,' the President told him. 'Many dreams will be realized by this flight, it represents the dawn of an era when man's achievements will outstrip his imaginings.'

'Yes, Mr. President.'

'It is a new frontier you will be reaching out for and what you do tomorrow will point the way for others who will follow in years to come. Our thoughts are with you.' The President hesitated, throwing a quick glance at his brother. 'And with your family. I am arranging to have the news passed to your father as soon as you have lifted off.'

'Thank you, sir.'

'There is no one else you would like us to inform?'

'No, thank you, Mr. President. Just the General.'

A few moments later the connexion was broken and the President frowned, looking at Bobby. 'He didn't ask me to tell his wife. What do we deduce from that? That he knows she's a risk or that he's already told her?'

Bobby shook his head.

'Well, whatever has happened this time, let's make damn sure that when the next batch of astronauts is selected someone checks the wives out. This kind of complication we can do without.'

'How about Magadini and von Braun? Do you want to talk to them right away?'

The President thought for a moment. 'No, let's go as planned. We'll release it to the press as soon as the guy's in orbit.'

Bobby stood up to leave but the President held him back. 'What steps are you taking about the wife? Whatever happens tomorrow she could be...' The President didn't finish.

'She's under surveillance. There's a discreet clinic she can be taken to to dry out, if it seems like a good idea.' Bobby stood for a moment, eyes fixed directly on his brother's face. 'But don't worry, Mr. President. Tomorrow's going to be one of the good days.'

231

'Sixty-three minutes and counting.'
Ziegler closed the door of the small room at the rear of the medical block and carefully locked it behind him. He walked briskly through the deserted wing of the building to the only other occupied room. The entire wing had been set aside for their use under the cover that certain tests were being carried out which demanded isolation.

The story accounted for locks, guards on the outside, and the fact that not even senior personnel were allowed into the section. Ziegler unlocked another door and went inside. The three men in the room looked up, one smiling a greeting, the others expressionless.

'One hour,' Ziegler said.

'Okay, let's make a start,' Specs said to Herriman.

The astronaut stood up, still no expression coming onto his face. 'Okay,' he said. He followed Specs into the adjoining room leaving Ziegler and Grissom alone. With the technician's aid Herriman donned the silver-grey space suit. Specs helped lace up the high boots and then, as Herriman slipped on the green webbing back-pack straps, Specs moved to stand behind the astronaut.

'You can sit down,' he said.

With Herriman seated Specs leaned forward to make sure all life-support system connexions were unobstructed so that when the final link-up was made in the capsule there would be no last-minute hitch. Ziegler had already cut the available time down to an absolute minimum and there would be scant tolerance for any delay.

'Don't forget to check the fly-by-wire system when you're in the capsule,' Specs said. 'Try to remember everything, forget nothing.'

'Right.'

Specs leaned closer and, grinning widely, began to tell Herriman a long and involved joke.

From the other room Ziegler watched, only partly listening to Gus. After his initial disappointment Grissom had lent his full support to the mission and had been particularly valuable in his help to Herriman. The problem was, and that was what Grissom was now telling Ziegler, that Herriman didn't seem to either want or need any help.

'He's cool, damn near ice-cool.'

'That's what you're all supposed to be.'

'We all can be when it's needed but he makes even Al seem like he's about to burst into flames.'

Ziegler nodded detachedly. He studied Herriman's face and noted that the expression didn't alter even when Specs appeared to reach the end of what was probably another of his jokes and laughed aloud. 'Maybe he still doesn't think it's going to happen,' he told Grissom.

'He'd better start believing it. One hour from now, he'll be on his way.'

Ziegler nodded, reached for the telephone and dialled an internal number. He spoke briefly, then replaced the instrument and went through to the adjoining room. 'We're ready to move the crew out of the tower,' he said.

Herriman stood up. 'Okay, I'm all set.'

Ziegler hesitated. 'No problems?'

Herriman allowed a small smile to touch his mouth. 'You mean, do I want to call it off? It's a bit late for a change of heart, wouldn't you say?'

Ziegler nodded slowly. Being a volunteer didn't mean you had no obligations. Sometimes events had their own power-plants and a change of mind, after all the aspirations that had been built around Herriman, would have required more courage than the act of volunteering had needed in the first place.

'If you'd sooner wait, Gary, I'll back you all the way.'

Herriman shook his head deliberately. 'Let's get to it.'

Ziegler glanced at Specs. 'Okay, get the truck.'

Specs nodded and went out, closing and locking the outer door behind him.

Along the corridor in the special control room the communications expert, Eddie Danvers, had devised a system which was so simple, yet so effective that Ziegler already suspected he could have single-handedly cut Mission Control's budget by several million dollars.

The unit was, of course, concerned with much less comprehensive links with the spacecraft. All they needed here were voice-communication equipment, life-support system monitors, and the astronaut's sensor read-outs. The medical data had necessarily been severely restricted in scope although the essentials, pulse rate, blood pressure, breathing, were accommodated. Development of that side of the operation had been handled by Willard Carmody and he and Danvers were capable of coping with everything coming into the control room from the orbiting astronaut.

Although the short duration of the flight made it unnecessary, Ziegler had prepared some of the others to take over should anyone need a break. When Magadini and Diana arrived there would be seven of them there, crammed into the tiny room, although Magadini would spend most of his time over at Mission Control, where his presence would be expected. Nevertheless he would be in touch with Ziegler on one of the three telephones they'd had installed.

Ziegler looked up as the door opened and Specs came back in. 'Truck's ready,' the space suit technician said.

'Okay.' Ziegler looked at Garfield Herriman. 'Let's go,' he said.

Herriman started for the door, his movements ponderous under the bulk of the space suit.

'Need this?' Grissom asked. He reached out and picked up the astronaut's space helmet.

The four men went out, Ziegler bringing up the rear and locking doors as he went. Specs had backed up a panel-truck and the rear door was already open. Along one side was a bench and Herriman sat on it with Grissom, still holding the helmet, sitting next to him. Ziegler waited until Specs was inside, then closed the door and walked around to the cab.

Ten minutes later they were at the foot of the launch tower. This was the moment of greatest risk. There was no way he could prevent anyone at Mission Control watching through binoculars. Indeed the chances were good that someone would be doing precisely that. He was relying on the fact that at such range identification of individuals was remote. Their presence was covered by an exercise Ziegler and Magadini had devised. This was a method of rapid evacuation of the capsule in the event of a last-minute abort through explosion or fire risk. The expected method in such an emergency was to use the launch escape tower but it was costly and potentially dangerous. The method they were supposed to be testing was for egress through the swing-arm, which would be held in position longer than was usual after the close-out crew had departed.

The elevator carried the four men upwards swiftly and silently. None of them spoke.

At the top they moved into the swing-arm itself. 'Let's get things rolling,' Ziegler said. Grissom led the way towards the capsule with Herriman, moving more slowly, following. Specs brought up the rear but Ziegler stayed for a moment at the tower end of the swing-arm. He picked up a telephone and dialled an internal number.

Eddie Danvers answered. 'Yes?'

'We're ready to make the connexions. Stand by.'

'Okay.'

Ziegler waited until Herriman was being helped into the capsule. He saw Grissom turn and show an upturned thumb. 'Okay,' he said into the telephone, then replaced the instrument and hurried along the swing-arm to join the others at the capsule.

Herriman was wedged into the cramped space, lying flat on his back, every switch, every dial, every gauge, within inches of his hands and face.

'Cosy?' Ziegler asked Herriman.

'You won't get any argument when it's time to climb out.'

'Call in to insure you have voice contact.'

Herriman nodded and flicked a switch. Then he glanced at Ziegler and returned the switch to its original position. 'We forgot something,' he said.

'What?'

'I haven't got a call sign. We never gave this ship a name.'

'What do you want to call it?'

Herriman shrugged slightly, the movement almost imperceptible in the space suit. 'Anything will do. I have no preference.'

'Call it Stella,' Grissom suggested.

Herriman shook his head, a crease appearing between his eyes. 'No, not that.' He thought for a moment. 'There was something the President said to me on the phone. Something about a new frontier, wasn't it? Okay, let's call it that. Frontier.'

The astronaut flicked the intercom switch and called Ground Control. While he was doing that Ziegler stepped back, inclining his head to listen to the countdown coming over the loudspeakers situated at frequent intervals throughout the launch tower.

'Thirty-five minutes and counting,' the loudspeaker-borne voice declared.

Ziegler went back to the telephone and dialled Mission Control. 'Ziegler,' he said. 'We're still testing procedures out here. Any problems at your end?'

'Nothing, Colonel. Countdown proceeding.'

Ziegler said a silent prayer of thanks. That meant no one had picked up the voice contact between the capsule and the secret control room.

'You still there, Colonel?' Mission Control asked.

'Yes?'

'Jim Magadini wants to talk to you.'

There was a pause, then Jim came on the line. 'All okay, Joe?'

'Fine.'

'When are you coming back in?'

'What's the hurry?' Ziegler asked, irritated that Magadini should ask such a question particularly on an open line when clear communication between them was impossible.

'Everyone all right?' Magadini persisted, slightly stressing the first word to insure Ziegler knew he was talking about Herriman.

235

'No sweat, Jim. None at all.'

'Okay, Joe, I'll see you as soon as you get back.'

Ziegler replaced the telephone with a puzzled frown. It sounded as if Jim was letting the tension of the moment get to him. He went back to the capsule and saw that Specs was making a further check on the life support system connexions. 'How are we doing?'

'Like the instruction manual says...'

'Gary?'

'Sure.'

'Okay, we're closing you up.' Ziegler stepped back as Herriman flipped his helmet's visor forward and Specs began to close the hatch. He turned to Grissom who handed him a head set which was hooked into a closed circuit to allow communication with the astronaut to continue here at the launch pad. 'Right, Gary. We have about twenty-five minutes to liftoff. We'd better split before we start giving Mission Control some crazy ideas.'

'Right.'

'We'll be out of contact for ten minutes while we drive back. If anything needs doing talk to Danvers. If it's a real emergency he'll fake a hold on the countdown.'

'Okay, Joe.'

Ziegler hesitated as Grissom and Specs started along the passageway which ran through the swing-arm. 'Good luck, Captain,' he said. 'You may be going in secrecy but you'll be coming back to the most God Almighty headache a fanfare ever gave a man.'

Moments later Ziegler and the others were in the high-speed elevator taking them down to the solid security of the ground, a hundred feet beneath the capsule.

MOSCOW

The Colonel was feeling much happier as he walked into the Chairman's office, than he had on his last visit to the Kremlin. This time he had something important. The only thing he would need to be careful about was revealing to Khrushchev just how he'd done it. Cooperation with the CIA was not the kind of activity you talked about. Not if you wanted to keep your job.

With Kropotkin dead and Maisky vanished there had been no clues, no leads. The only possibility the Colonel could think of was that the Americans might know something and he decided to take a chance.

After they had gotten over their initial shock the CIA had been happy to cooperate. The death of Oscar Lennox had been unexpected, if the death of any secret agent could be so termed. He hadn't seemed important enough to warrant execution and Ross had begun to think Oscar had just been unfortunate enough to be in the wrong place at the wrong time.

As soon as the KGB Colonel began asking questions about Maisky and Kropotkin, two and two were put together with great speed and some accuracy.

Of course Ross had known Oscar was trailing Kropotkin but couldn't really believe that was a reason for killing him. Tails were easy enough to lose, particularly in Moscow where the police could be relied upon to remove any inquisitive foreigner from the scene for long enough to cool their enthusiasm for the chase.

When a KGB colonel asked questions about Maisky and Kropotkin, questions to which he should have had all the answers, Ross guessed that the right hand of the KGB didn't know what its left hand was doing. Ross was an old campaigner and while he regarded himself as a diplomat and no tool of the CIA, he sensed that Washington would approve any means he used to attain the desired end.

The KGB Colonel read the file Ross showed him and hoped his face didn't alter when he came to the passage about the woman Maisky had been with the night of Oscar Lennox's visit to the ballet. The name of Kropotkin's brother didn't mean anything to the Colonel but he checked anyway as soon as he left the American Embassy. The man knew nothing and had merely invited Helmut Groetchen to his daughter's wedding because Kropotkin asked him to do so.

With the woman, the Colonel had to tread carefully. As a senior KGB agent herself, she would know all the angles and might even have contacts that could hurt him despite his close links with the Chairman. He called at her apartment and led into the matter of the game she was playing with Maisky as casually as possible. He took a chance at one point, implying that he knew what was going on, and the woman opened up just enough to let a name slip. It was a man the Colonel knew, a lower echelon KGB officer who had a drink problem. Being a believer in the American maxim of quitting while he was ahead, the Colonel left soon afterwards. He had the alcoholic agent picked up and went to work with skill, enthusiasm, and a considerable amount of brute force. Time, he had decided, was of the essence.

He outlined his inquiries to the Chairman, summarized the results of the interrogation of the agent, and then sat back while Khrushchev mulled it over.

'What is your conclusion?' the Chairman asked eventually.

The Colonel looked inquisitively at Khrushchev. It seemed he was being treated as an equal which wouldn't do him any harm in the future. 'From what we got out of Kropotkin and the others it seems that the Americans were being fed information. Their agent, Oscar Lennox, picked something up by chance. Maisky took the opportunity to use Lennox, feeding him whatever he wanted Washington to hear. The object was to precipitate the Americans into making a manned spaceflight sooner than caution decreed. The rest of it, the explosive device Kropotkin designed, was a diversion. Maisky knew the Americans would find out about it, wanted them to do so in fact.' The Colonel smiled appreciatively. 'Maisky is clever. Very clever.'

'You think so?' Khrushchev's tone was icy.

'I don't approve,' the Colonel said hastily. 'But I recognize a first-class operation when I see one.'

'And the real plan. Will it work?'

'Maisky obviously thinks it will. In that case it would be folly for me to think otherwise.'

'Would you act on your opinion?'

'Yes.'

'Even if your life depended on it?' Khrushchev asked with a sly smile.

The Colonel swallowed. 'Yes.'

Khrushchev nodded. 'Very well, I will act on it too. As if my life depended on it.' The smile faded. 'We do not know when all this will take place.'

'No, but it will be soon.'

'There really is no doubt that this kind of operation will work?'

'None at all. The woman has done such things before. Not of this magnitude perhaps, but the principle was the same.'

'Very well. Return to your duties, Colonel. Keep a careful eye on your colleagues until it is over and we know just how many were with Maisky in this.' The Chairman smiled. 'There will be a lot of clearing up to do. Afterwards there should be room for promotion.'

The Colonel stood up and saluted. 'Thank you, Comrade Chairman,' he said.

After the KGB officer had left, Khrushchev sat for some minutes staring moodily at the wall opposite his desk. He didn't like the position into which he had been forced by Brezhnev. He had been made to look a fool and that was a score he would have to settle before long. In the meantime he had no choice but to inform

238

President Kennedy of his latest discoveries. There would be those who would see this as weakness but their short-sightedness made them less dangerous than Brezhnev who didn't number that among his failings.

Kennedy wouldn't like this particular note, especially coming so soon after the last one. And carrying much graver news too. Timing was important, the Americans had to be warned but there was no point in rushing things. He would send his carefully worded message through the usual channels. He had almost completed his first draft when a secretary brought in an urgent report from a high-altitude reconnaissance aircraft. Unusual activity had been observed on one of the Cape Canaveral launch pads. He read and re-read the experts' interpretation of the photographs. They had no doubts. The Americans were about to launch an Atlas rocket. It might be coincidence, just a routine test flight. On the other hand, it might not.

After some minutes Khrushchev concluded he couldn't take the risk. He would have to tell Kennedy and tell him immediately. Picking up a telephone he gave the necessary instructions. Emergencies like this precisely justified one of Khruschev's pet ideas: a "hot-line" phone link between the White House and the Kremlin. One day, maybe. But for now he'd have to be satisfied with an ordinary connexion.

CAPE CANAVERAL, Fla.

Alone in the capsule Gary Herriman felt completely relaxed. Everything around him seemed familiar, the long hours spent in the FPT were at last paying off. He moved his hands, letting his fingers brush lightly against switches, resting them on gauges already quivering and displaying information as the rocket beneath him came slowly to life. Soon, it would thunder and shake as it launched him upwards. Then the pipedream would become reality.

He closed his eyes and apart from slight pressure at the base of his spine he was barely conscious of body contact with the couch. He appeared to float, the way he had floated during weightlessness training in the C-131 transports.

'Frontier, this is Ground Control.'

Herriman's eyes opened. What was that? For a tiny moment of time he was completely disoriented. What was that voice saying? Frontier? Then he recognized Ziegler's voice and recollection flooded back.

'Hello, Ground Control. I read you.'

'Frontier, we have ten minutes to ignition and everything is go.'

'Roger.'

'Gary, everything okay up there?' The worried note in Ziegler's voice was lost in distortion.

'No problems.'

Ziegler's concern had stemmed from observation of the read-outs of Herriman's medical condition. His pulse rate had fallen and his breathing was shallow. 'He sounds all right,' he said to Willard Carmody.

'I can't really believe it but I think he fell asleep there for a few seconds.'

'Asleep? Now?'

'Well, that would account for it.'

'You should know but Jee-sus, that's taking relaxation a bit far,' Ziegler muttered with a grin. He glanced at Diana McNair who had arrived while they were at the Launch Tower. She didn't respond to his smile. 'Anything wrong?' he asked.

She shook her head. 'Nothing that won't keep until later,' Diana had been trying to contact Stella Herriman for the past couple of days. Joe's request, coming as it had as a direct instruction from the White House, had angered her. The assumption, implicit in the order, that Stella mattered only for the potential harm she could do the public image of the space program was the cause of her anger. Despite Diana's misgivings she had looked for Stella, knowing that, whatever the motives of the President and his brother, she could help the other woman. Unfortunately she hadn't been able to find her. But she had found her trail. Stella appeared to have abandoned herself to a life of booze and men without any attempt to be discreet.

So far, no one appeared to have recognized her but Diana knew it was only a matter of time. She had thought about calling Joe and asking for Gary's help but decided against it, knowing that Joe wouldn't let anything or anyone disturb the astronaut.

A metallic voice came from the loudspeakers. *'We are four minutes from ignition, everything is go.'*

The telephone rang and Diana answered it. It was one of the officials from Mission Control. She listened to him, then replaced the instrument and called out to Jim Magadini.

'What is it?'

'Mission Control wants you. There's an urgent telephone call for you, from Washington.'

'What do they want?'

'I don't know but they said it sounded important.'

240

Magadini turned to Joe Ziegler. 'Maybe I'd better go across there and take the call.'

'Okay, Jim.'

As Magadini went out of the door the loudspeaker rasped again. *Two minutes to ignition, everything is go.'*

Ziegler reached out to press the microphone switch so that he could speak to Gary Herriman.

In the spacecraft Gary had heard the two minute warning without any particular emotion. He still felt relaxed, was still experiencing a vaguely dreamlike state of euphoria. When Ziegler's voice cut in right after Mission Control he responded calmly.

'No sweat, Joe, it's a fine morning out here.'

The casual remark about the weather removed any uncertainty anyone might have been feeling. Gary Herriman was holding up to the pressures of the pre-launch excitement. He really seemed to be one of the true brotherhood of flying men, overcoming ground-based problems by the simple expedient of ignoring them. Such things were about to be left behind, figuratively as well as literally, when the rocket left the restraint of earth's gravity.

The loudspeaker crackled into life again. *'Third stage oxidizer tanks pressurized. T-minus one minute forty seconds.'*

Herriman turned his head slightly to look out of the narrow window at the sky which was already changing color as the sun began to lift far out over the ocean. A bank of lights on the instrument panel flickered on.

'Full internal power now on. All go.'

Gary suddenly thought about Stella. Not the woman of the past weeks and months but the Stella of years before when they had been joyous together. He remembered her as she had been on those days when they had walked in woods and along the banks of rivers, when she had painted and he had watched. He smiled remembering the way she had grimaced in concentration over some detail of the scene she was reproducing on canvas, one hand holding the brush, the other holding back her long dark hair as it threatened to fall onto the painting.

Gary moved abruptly, his body straining against the webbing straps holding him to the couch. What was he thinking about? Stella had never painted, never shown any interest in anything artistic. And her hair was blonde, not dark.

'Joe.'

Ziegler turned at the hard note in Carmody's voice. 'What is it?'

'Gary's pulse rate's gone up. Way up.'

Ziegler crossed the room in three strides. Carmody was right but

Joe wasn't too worried. The unnatural calm the astronaut had been displaying was being pushed aside as the moment forced its way in. It happened in combat, the instant a flyer stopped kidding himself that life was like the movies and admitted he really could get blown out of the sky. If it could happen in war there was no reason why it shouldn't happen here.

He flicked the microphone switch. 'This is Ground Control. Everything okay, Frontier?'

'Just dandy, Control.'

'Gas generator valves closed.'

'Looking good, Frontier. Small bump in pulse rate a moment ago. Something worrying you out there?'

'Just bored.'

'Guidance system on internal. We are go for ignition.'

'He's on his way,' Ziegler said quietly, more to himself than to the others.

Three miles away, gaunt against the lightening sky, the rocket pointed upwards. There was movement as the swing-arm pulled away.

'Nine seconds.'

At the base of the rocket, flames appeared as electrical contacts engaged and ignited the turbo-pump's exhaust gases. In rapid order the ignition sequence was pursued. Those first flames igniting other gases, then others, each stage of the process building up more and more power.

'Seven.'

Herriman was relaxed again, the dark-haired woman's face was familiar. He didn't know who she was but it was a familiar face. Friendly.

'Six.'

What was her name?

'Five.'

The roar of the engines echoed in his ears, the sound rolling across the three miles to Mission Control and the secret control room.

'Four.'

As heat built up in the concrete flame-trench the coolant water exploded into instant steam and dense white clouds billowed upwards to mingle with the flames.

'Three.'

Her name was there, close to his tongue.

'Two.'

'His pulse rate's up again, Joe.'

The thrust of the engines reached equalization with the millions of pounds dead weight of the giant rocket. All that kept it on earth were four hold-down arms.

'One.'

Her name?

Within an almost measureless moment of time the four arms released their hold and nothing remained to keep the rocket on earth. Yet, for an instant, it still did not move although the earth beneath it trembled. The last of the umbilicals fell away. The rocket began to inch upwards and tapered pins cast their dies so that nothing could now hold it back.

'We have liftoff.'

Ziegler closed his eyes. 'Good luck,' he whispered.

Herriman felt the pressure build up. It was just like the start of a run on the Big Wheel. Only this was better than the centrifuge because there wasn't the impression of being shot along a curving tunnel. This was different because he could see the sky. A sky which was changing in color as he rose, the sunrise accelerating from the east.

'We have a liftoff. Everything is go.'

The pressure against Herriman's chest built up and, just as that day on the centrifuge, a word, a name, was trying to force its way from his lips. It was the woman's name, the dark-haired woman with whom he had laughed and made love. The woman who had loved him as much as he had loved her. But he couldn't remember her name.

Then it came, forcing its way slowly into his consciousness from where it had lain buried for so many years. Her name was...

Softly, lovingly, he breathed her name aloud. 'Natalie.'

CAPE CANAVERAL, Fla.

'Who the hell is Natalie?'

'Are you sure that's what he said?' Gus Grissom asked.

'Sounded like that to me.'

'I heard him use the name once before,' Gus said. 'That day he was on the Big Wheel at Johnsville, when they really put the pressure on.'

'T-plus five minutes. Prepare to eject capsule.'

One hundred miles above the earth, Gary Herriman felt a jolt as the posigrade rockets blasted him free of the Atlas booster. The capsule began a gentle swing around until he could see the booster tumbling away earthwards.

'No problems up there, Gary?'

'Everything's fine.'

Ziegler turned to Grissom. 'You're sure?'

'Pretty damn sure.'

'Why didn't you say something earlier?'

'I didn't think it was important. To be honest, I thought the guy was having a fling with some floosie and I didn't think it was my job to rat on him.'

'Nothing to worry over I guess. I don't know who Natalie is but she must be important to him if he thinks about her when he's under pressure.' Ziegler really didn't think it was something to worry over. He'd heard hard-nosed fliers yell for their mothers when things got hot. Not weaklings but really hard men who looked as if they could tear the wings off an enemy aircraft with their bare hands.

He glanced at the doctor who was carefully monitoring the life-support systems. 'How does he look?' he asked Carmody.

'All calm again. I'd say he was enjoying the trip.'

Gary Herriman *was* enjoying himself but it wasn't the flight so much as the new train of thought that had begun at the moment of liftoff. He couldn't understand how he had managed to forget her. It seemed impossible. This woman, the only woman who had ever pierced his natural reserve to enter deeply into his heart and mind.

He could picture her clearly now, his mind free of restraint just as his body was free of the encumbrances of earth. Dark hair, a smile that mixed delight with joy at their relationship. He grinned. She had always said she couldn't understand how he managed without her around to guide him, to give aim and purpose to his life.

'His pulse rate's way down,' Carmody said. 'I think he's falling asleep again.'

Ziegler nodded. Beside him the telephone rang and he picked it up. It was Jim Magadini.

'Joe, I'm on my way across. Come outside and meet me.'

'Okay, Jim. Why...' He broke off as Magadini hung up. He frowned, then glanced across the room and caught Specs' attention. 'Call me if anything happens, I'll be outside.'

He met Jim Magadini in the corridor leading from the medical center's main building. Magadini looked drawn and worried.

'What's wrong?'

'That call from Washington. The President wanted us to hold the countdown.'

'Why?'

'I don't know. When I told him the rocket had already lifted-off he broke the connexion.'

244

'Maybe he's finally come around to our way of thinking and decided we should have waited.'

'Maybe.' Magadini sounded doubtful. 'How are things going?'

'Everything seems okay. No malfunctions and Gary, well, he seems to be keeping a tight asshole.'

Magadini didn't miss the hesitation. 'Are you sure about that?'

'I think so.'

Now it was Magadini's turn to hesitate. 'Look, Joe, I don't want to cause any panic but there might be a...a complication.'

'What *complication* ?'

'You remember the night someone took a shot at you?'

'I'm not likely to forget it.'

'Omar Rogerson noticed something in the surveillance report made by the agent watching Gary Herriman.'

'Noticed what?

'You said Gary hadn't seen anyone leaving the building as he came in.'

'That's right.'

'No, it isn't right. Remember, Rogerson had already assigned men to keep protective surveillance on the astronauts. Well, according to the man assigned to Gary, as he reached the building, someone came out. They spoke, not for long, just time enough for maybe a few words either way. Then Gary went on into the building, where he found you, and the other man left fast.'

'Why wasn't he stopped?'

'There was no reason to suspect anything. Rogerson's man hadn't heard any shots being fired. Anyway, that's not the point. What we need to...'

'Hold on, Jim,' Joe interrupted. 'That's crazy. Why should Gary lie?'

'I don't know.'

Ziegler stiffened as a thought came to him. 'When did you learn all this?'

Magadini's color darkened. 'Rogerson came to me a couple of days ago.'

'For Chrissake, Jim, why didn't you say something?'

'It's inconclusive. If I'd said anything, what would you have done?'

'Talked to Gary for one thing. Requested a hold for...Oh, that's it! You knew there was a good chance I would push for a postponement and this time the President would have taken notice.'

'Joe, what could you have told Washington? That we wanted an indefinite hold because we thought one of the astronauts might be involved in an attempt to kill the Astronaut Liaison Officer. What do you think the President would have said to that? Do you think he would've believed it? He'd figure we'd gone crazy.'

'Is that the reason you kept it to yourself? Because you were afraid of what the President might say?'

'No. Jesus, I don't know anymore. You know what the pressure's been like with appropriations due for review. With the whole damn space program in doubt, thousands of jobs on the line. We had to do what they wanted.'

'Even if it meant putting a man up there who might have...' Ziegler broke off. 'What the hell am I saying? Gary can't be involved. What possible reason could there be?'

'I don't know, Joe. None of it makes any sense to me.'

Specs appeared at the door. 'You'd better get in here, Colonel. Fast.'

Ziegler ran towards the control room with Jim Magadini hurrying after him.

Diana was leaning over Carmody's shoulder and looked up as Joe came into the room. 'Something's wrong up there. Gary's pulse rate's way up, so is his blood pressure, and his breathing is erratic.'

At that moment the loudspeaker carrying the voice of Mission Control echoed around the small room. *'We have a malfunction. Maintain tracking and report status.'*

'What's happening?' Joe asked.

'Can't tell,' Eddie Danvers said. 'We don't have the read-outs they have over in Mission Control.'

'Malfunction confirmed. The capsule's manual override control has engaged.'

'My God,' Ziegler breathed.

'What is it?' Magadini asked.

'It's Gary. He's taken manual control of the capsule. He's over-ridden Ground Control and switched in the fly-by-wire system.'

'You mean Mission Control knows he's up there?'

'I doubt it. They'll assume a malfunction. That's what it will look like to them.'

'What will they do?' Diana asked.

'Just sit there and pray, I guess. Once they see the capsule is performing normally they'll assume there's a glitch in the system.'

'His pulse rate's going off the fucking scale,' Carmody said.

'There has been an effective automaneuver,' the loudspeaker informed them. *'Flight plan has been affected.'*

'Now what?'

'There has been a course correction burn.'

Ziegler spun around to stare up at the closed-circuit tv screen. He

246

scanned the sequence displays which corresponded to the capsule's on-board instruments. 'Dear God,' he said softly. 'He's changed the direction of the capsule.' He took the microphone from Eddie Danvers and pressed the transmit switch. 'Ground Control to Frontier. Gary, this is Joe. Are you in trouble up there?'

No reply came from the capsule.

'Gary, answer me.'

Still no reply.

'Can he hear me?' Ziegler asked.

Eddie Danvers nodded his head. 'Pretty damn sure, yes.'

'Yes,' Willard Carmody agreed. 'I'd need more accurate equipment to swear my life away on it but there was a change in the sensor readings when you spoke to him.'

Ziegler turned to Diana. 'Any ideas?' he asked.

'Let me try,' she said.

As Diana began to speak to the astronaut, Joe Ziegler took Jim Magadini's arm and drew him across the room. 'Jim, we need to know what the correction burn means. Mission Control will be calculating the new trajectory. Maybe you'd better get over there.'

'Okay, but what good will it do to know?'

'We need to tell him how to put the capsule back on course. We can't just leave the guy until the damn thing falls out of the sky.'

'I'll call you as soon as I have anything.' Magadini hesitated. 'Maybe we should tell Mission Control what's really happening up there.'

'Not yet.'

'They're fumbling in the dark, Joe. As long as they think it's an instrument malfunction they'll be making all the wrong moves.'

'There aren't any right moves to make.'

'Maybe not but if they knew at least they'd be thinking constructively.'

'Okay, Jim. I accept we'll have to tell them sometime. Let's just hold back a little while longer.'

'Right. We'll see what happens in the next hour.'

Magadini turned to leave but Ziegler held him back. 'As soon as you have a couple of minutes, call the White House. Play it down but tell them the problem we have here and see if there's any link between this and the reason the President tried to put a hold on the launch.'

Magadini frowned. 'You think he might have known this was about to happen?'

'Right now, I don't know what to think.'

Diana McNair looked up as Joe Ziegler returned to her side. 'I'm not getting any response,' she told him.

'What was the last thing he said?'

'Specs talked to him.'

Ziegler went across the room to where the little man was intently watching the tv monitor. 'What was the last thing he said to you, Specs?' he asked.

'Just that the flight was smooth and he was enjoying it.'

'What did you say to him?'

Specs shrugged. 'Just that he was looking good from here and that we were all rooting for him.'

Diana, who had handed over to Gus Grissom, joined them. 'Joe, I've been thinking. This is just a guess but maybe the launch put a strain on him we didn't allow for. Maybe it's jolted him into some kind of mistrust of us all.'

'Guesswork?'

'Perhaps. But if there's anything to it it could be he won't respond to any of us.'

'Who then?'

'Stella?'

'What kind of moment is this for a cheap joke?' Ziegler snapped.

Diana shook her head at this uncharacteristic show of anger. 'It's better than just sitting here doing nothing.'

Ziegler looked doubtfully at her. 'Okay, I'll call Omar Rogerson and tell him to get Stella to a phone where we can patch her in; but I don't hold much hope.'

'Rogerson may have trouble finding her, but why not ask Gary anyway if he wants to talk to Stella? It might provoke a reaction.'

Ziegler went across to where Gus was talking over the microphone. 'Anything, Gus?'

'Not a damn thing.'

Ziegler pressed the switch. 'Gary, this is Joe again. We're figuring out a way to patch in a direct line so that Stella can talk to you. Okay with you?'

There was no answering voice from the loudspeakers.

'No reaction to that, Joe.' the doctor said.

Ziegler thought for a moment, then activated the microphone again. 'Gary, maybe you'd like to talk to Natalie. Tell me how to make contact with her and we'll patch her in.'

'That did it,' Carmody said. 'His pulse rate's up again. And his breathing's irregular.'

'Gary, who is Natalie? Where is she?'

From the loudspeakers came a scraping sound, then Herriman's voice, soft and distorted by static. 'Natalie. Where are you? Why did you..?' The last few words disappeared into a rustle of electrical sounds.

'Well, that got something,' Ziegler said. 'What we have to do is keep pressing him. Just what we'll achieve I can't pretend to know.' He glanced around the room. 'Look, Diana you and Gus both know him well. Take turns talking to him. A familiar voice in his ears all the time might keep him from doing anything else for the moment.'

'What are you going to do?'

'I'm calling Washington.'

'The White House?'

'Not the White House. The Pentagon. Maybe General Herriman's more a commanding officer than a father, but maybe that's what we need about now. Someone who'll holler at him, make him listen whether he likes or not.'

'I can try that,' Grissom said.

'No, Gus. He won't believe it from you.'

Grissom nodded. 'Okay, I'll keep talking to him, as one flying man to another.'

Ziegler nodded, he wasn't convinced it would work but he didn't argue. He placed an urgent call to the Pentagon using authority he probably didn't have. He checked the time. The capsule was already more than half way into its first orbit. In twenty minutes Gary Herriman would be coming in over the Pacific Ocean towards the western seaboard of America. His arrival should have heralded a triumph for American know-how but instead he was bringing with him uncertainty and, Joe admitted to himself, not a little fear.

For Gary Herriman the past few minutes had floated by as if they were happening not to him but to someone else. He was detached, a casual observer watching events, not participating in them. But it wasn't a man in a capsule, hurtling around the earth, he saw. Instead, it was a man sitting on the bank of a stream running through a wood. Water from the stream broke and splashed, droplets rising into the air where they glittered like stars in a night sky.

And there, a few feet away, sat Natalie, painting, occasionally speaking to him, her voice warm and soft. How could he have forgotten about her? Especially when the words she spoke most often, the last words she said to him when they parted, were that he would always remember her, never forget her. Always remember, never forget. He stirred uneasily. Those words were familiar, he'd heard them recently. Very recently. Since he had lifted off on this journey of recollection.

WASHINGTON, D.C.

General Herriman carefully locked his office door then returned to his desk and picked up the telephone. 'Colonel Ziegler, I'm as secure as I can be. Can't answer for the phone line but...'

'That's okay, General, we'll have to take that chance. Now, you understand everything I've told you?'

'Of course, Colonel. They may have taken away my dignity and replaced it with braid but they haven't gotten my brains yet.'

For the General, Ziegler's call had brought exhilaration and disbelief in almost equal proportions but he didn't question the information. He knew Ziegler's reputation, had even studied his service record. After his son's transfer to Project Mercury the General had taken steps to obtain files on everyone connected with the program. The exercise had no aim, it simply helped ease the frustration.

The records showed Ziegler to be a good man, one whose reliability had been proven in battle conditions. Ziegler wasn't a man to panic easily, of that the General was sure, but he must have gotten this thing wrong. If his son wasn't talking to Ground Control it wouldn't be his fault, just some damn piece of equipment acting up.

'Okay, General. What we're doing is patching you into the radio-link but don't worry over call signs. Just talk as if you were making a telephone call to him.'

'You want me to say anything in particular?'

'No, say what you like.'

Ziegler listened as the old soldier began speaking to Gary. After the first few words he could believe the comments he'd heard about the General's attitude towards his son. There was no warmth, no affection, just a senior officer, from another generation of military life, failing to communicate with a junior officer.

The General wasn't the only man in Washington who, at that moment, was focusing on Frontier. Since his telephone conversation with Chairman Khrushchev a constant stream of visitors had been calling on President Kennedy. Most were military advisers brought over from the Pentagon for briefing on events few could believe were really happening. The presence in the Oval Office of the President's brother only heightened their disbelief. It looked like another of the Attorney General's hypothetical exercises and, until the President's gravity penetrated even the most suspicious skulls, a bundle of hypothetical answers were trotted out.

The President's frustration was only aggravated when Jim

Magadini's call came through. He listened as he was given the revised trajectory, based on the course correcting burn Gary Herriman had made, then told Magadini the substance of the conversation he'd had with Chairman Khrushchev.

When the President had finished speaking, Jim Magadini replaced the telephone and hurried out of Mission Control. Whatever happened, they must get Gary back on his original course. The alternative didn't bear thinking about.

In the Ground Control unit the telephone link with General Herriman had broken. There had been no response and Joe Ziegler was trying desperately to think of some other angle. He told Specs to take over and start talking to the astronaut. 'Tell him some stupid joke, any damn thing. Just break through.'

Ziegler drew Gus Grissom and Diana across the room for a hasty conference to decide what, if anything, they could try next. No one had any ideas.

At the console Specs was speaking in a low voice, doing as Ziegler had instructed. He glanced quickly around the room. Willard Carmody was intent on the sensor read-outs, Eddie Danvers was tinkering with the tv monitor trying to sharpen the picture, and the others were out of earshot. Specs had taken a chance in speaking to the astronaut just after liftoff and now he had to take another.

'Hi, Captain,' he said softly. 'This is Specs. Remember me? I guess you can't forget me, can you? That's what everyone says, see Specs once and you never forget him. Always remember, never forget. Like that broad, Natalie. I reckon you'll always remember her, what she means to you, what she said to you. Always remember, never forget.'

Specs looked up to see Diana McNair had left the others and was close enough to have heard his last few words. There was an inquiring look on her face and Specs tried a grin and a shrug, as if saying, I'm trying, I'm trying. He went back to telling Herriman the joke he had begun a few moments earlier. He dare not risk pushing it any further. From here on he would sit it out. Now it was up to Maisky.

ZEPHYR SPRINGS, Fla.

The house was much the same as all the others in the quiet street on the north side of the small community. The only thing that looked any different was the large and complex radio antenna mounted on the garage roof. Inside the garage Maisky was sitting, listening thoughtfully to Specs talking to the astronaut. Reception was excellent, the radio communications expert who had set up the equipment had done his job well. It was unfortunate, but necessary, that he'd been obliged to instruct Specs to throw the man to the security people. No doubt the Americans would put him away for a long time but when he was released he would be well looked after.

Specs would be remembered too. His work had been beyond reproach. The risk he had taken in reinforcing Herriman's state of mind, by using trigger words and phrases, during the brief communications he'd had with the astronaut had been entirely justified. Maisky hoped it wouldn't result in Specs' true role being recognized. He could be of inestimable future use.

He checked the time. The capsule would now be completing the first orbit. That left two more orbits in which to effect the final moves. Less than three hours, but time enough.

He started a tape recorder, listened for a few moments, then made minor adjustments to sound levels before winding the tape back to the beginning.

Maisky sat for a moment, thinking about the few words he had just heard spoken. The woman had a pleasant voice, low and thrilling and much younger sounding than her real age. He smiled, thinking back to the night of their visit to the ballet and the little game they had played on Oscar Lennox. He wondered what she would be doing at this moment. Perhaps she would be sitting in her Moscow apartment, the radio tuned to the Voice of America unable to resist savoring the results of her handiwork.

He felt a rare pang of sentimentality and chose to hear her once again before playing the recording to Herriman. He turned the tape recorder on and brought life to her voice, soft and warm, loving and sensual.

'Hello, Gary,' she said. 'Remember. I asked you never to forget me. This is Natalie.'

CAPE CANAVERAL, Fla.

As Magadini came into the control room his expression was enough to alert Ziegler to the fact that however bad things looked at the moment, they were about to get worse.

'I've just talked with the President,' Magadini said. 'The reason he tried to put a hold on the launch was that Khrushchev told him the mission had been spiked.'

252

'Khrushchev?'

From his place at the console Specs turned at the name. The moment to make a getaway had passed. If they were onto him he wouldn't get far, probably not even off the Cape.

Magadini was continuing. 'When Gary was based in Germany, the Russians got at him. A woman agent, Natalie Voronova.'

'Natalie.'

'That's right.'

'You mean Gary's a Russian agent? I don't believe it.'

'No, not that. He's been conditioned, programmed.'

'Brainwashed?'

'To do what?' Diana asked quietly.

'First to make course corrections, then to respond to her orders and bring the capsule back to earth at a predetermined place.'

'In Russia? What good will that do them.'

Magadini shook his head, his face grey. 'No, not a soft-landing. He's to bring it down in a crash-landing on a densely-populated area. Probably a city.'

'Where?'

'Khrushchev didn't know but the course correction burn has moved the capsule into a more northerly orbit, somewhere over Central Europe. We're now trying to calculate a likely terminal zone, based on the expected duration of the flight.'

'Jesus,' Ziegler said quietly.

For a moment there was a silence in the control room, broken only by the hum of equipment and the sound of static on the loudspeakers still open to the orbiting astronaut.

The sudden interruption of the silence by the voice of Mission Control startled them. *New mid-course correction effected.*

Ziegler grabbed the telephone and thrust it into Magadini's hand. 'Get a new trajectory calculation fast,' he said. He picked up another telephone and dialled.

'Who are you calling?' Diana asked.

'We don't know what his new burn will do. Maybe he's back on the right trajectory for a safe splash-down in the Pacific. But if he isn't, then we still need someone to talk him back into obeying our instructions. We've all tried and failed. Now it's the President's turn.' His voice took on a bitter note. 'It's his responsibility, if it wasn't for him Gary wouldn't be up there.'

In the capsule Gary Herriman was relaxed and happy once more. Happier than at any time since he and Natalie had parted. If only he could see her face again, hear her voice. Then, almost as if he had willed it, he *did* hear her voice, softly rousing, alive and calm.

253

'Hello, Gary. Remember? I asked you never to forget me. This is Natalie.'

In the control room everyone had stopped what they were doing to stare at the loudspeakers as if they could see in them the face of the woman whose voice was filling the air.

'Do you remember, Gary? Those days we spent together in Villingen and what we talked about. How you said you would always remember me, never forget me. Now it's time for us to be together again. All you have to do is come to me. I will tell you what to do, how to reach me. Are you listening?'

'Natalie, where are you?'

'Listen to me, Gary, then come to me. I want you to do as I say, make the course corrections I will give you. Then we can be together again. Listen carefully now.'

'Jesus Christ,' Ziegler said. 'Can't we stop this?'

Danvers shook his head. 'No chance. Mission Control might be able to jam this waveband but I doubt they could set anything up in the time.'

'Can we talk to him at the same time?'

'We've been talking to him. It didn't help.'

'No, I mean use our transmission to swamp her voice.'

'We can try.'

Ziegler turned to Grissom. 'Gus, talk to him, tell him anything. Routine information, any damn thing at all, just keep talking.'

'Right.'

Ziegler realized he had the telephone in his hand and someone at the White House was trying to speak to him. He interrupted, demanding to speak to the President. Perhaps it was something in his voice, perhaps the President had ordered all calls from NASA to be connected without delay. Either way, within seconds Ziegler was talking to the President. Dispensing with greetings he rapidly outlined the situation.

'What do you want me to say, Colonel?' Kennedy asked.

'He won't listen to any of us, but there's a damn good chance he will listen to this woman. Try getting through to him, make him listen to you. Once he's doing that maybe we can feed him the information to put him back on the right trajectory.'

'Have you calculated where he'll come down?'

'Not yet. Anyway, he has time to make further burns.'

'Very well, Colonel, I'll talk to him.'

Ziegler turned to Danvers. 'Eddie?'

'Okay, Joe, he's patched in.'

Gary Herriman was irritable. Someone, it sounded like Gus, was talking over Natalie's voice. He couldn't hear her clearly, he was missing some words. Then Gus went off but Natalie stopped too. For a moment he was unsure what to do but suddenly another voice interrupted his thoughts. This voice was familiar, he'd heard it recently. It belonged to the President of the United States. It bewildered him. Why was the President talking to him? He was no one of importance, just an ordinary Air Force Captain.

'What you set out to do today, Gary, was to fulfill the great promise of this nation,' the President's voice rolled through the loudspeakers. 'Now that promise is marred but there is still time to correct that. You are an American officer and I call upon you, as a patriot, to return to your original course or give command back to Mission Control.'

'Jesus Christ, he sounds as if he's addressing a convention,' Ziegler said. He picked up the telephone breaking the connexion between the White House and the capsule. 'Mr. President we've tried everything except the one thing you can do. We don't want you to talk like a friend or a doctor or even a father. Command him! Talk to him like the President of the United States.'

There was silence on the telephone and Ziegler nodded to Danvers who made the connexion again. This time, when the President started speaking, his tone had changed. 'Captain Herriman, I am speaking to you as your Commander-in-Chief and as President of the United States. This is a clear and direct order. You will make the course correction which will be transmitted to you by Colonel Ziegler. Do you understand me?'

Ziegler turned to Carmody. 'Any change?'

'Pulse rate's going up. Blood pressure doesn't look very good.'

'Tell the President to repeat his last statement,' Ziegler snapped at Danvers.

There was a momentary pause before the President's voice began to repeat his command.

'Pulse rate going up,' Carmody reported.

'Again,' Ziegler said to Danvers.

Another voice came from the loudspeakers. 'This is Natalie. Do you remember, Gary? Those days we spent together and what we talked about...'

'Can we boost the President's voice?' Ziegler asked Danvers.

'I'll try.'

The voices mingled, one soft and sensuous, the other clipped and authoritative.

'...a clear and direct order. You will make...'

'...always remember me, never forget me...'

'...a course correction will be transmitted to you by Colonel Ziegler...'

'...make the course corrections I will give you...'

Ziegler spoke quickly to Danvers and the communications man started up a tape recorder, intent on putting the President's order on a continuous tape-loop.

'Joe.'

Ziegler turned to Diana who had crossed to stand near him, her voice pitched low.

'What?'

'Those words Natalie used. Always remember, never forget.'

'What about them?'

'Specs said the same thing.'

Ziegler stared at her for a moment then looked at the space suit technician who was standing watching the visual print-out. 'Are you sure?'

'Pretty certain, yes.'

Ziegler hesitated, trying to recall anything from recent events supporting Diana's implied suggestion that Specs was involved in this thing. Nothing came to mind but he decided not to take a chance. He told Diana to go out to the security guards and inform them that no one was to leave the building without his personal authority.

Then, before he could take any action to determine the truth of Specs' involvement, Magadini interrupted. 'Mission Control has the data for a course correction burn that will put him back on his original trajectory.'

Ziegler copied down the information, then checked with Danvers that the tape-loop was ready. 'Are we overcoming Natalie's message?' he asked.

'Can't say.'

Listening carefully, Ziegler identified the point where Natalie's message had reached. 'It's coming to the end. Before they have time to restart the tape we hit Herriman with this information.'

'Okay.'

'Joe.' It was Jim again, still holding the telephone. 'You have to get through to him, Joe, you have to.'

'I'm trying, goddamn it.'

'Joe. We know which city will be in direct line when he comes out of the third orbit.'

In the capsule Garfield Herriman was frowning in concentration. The confusion of two voices speaking at once had been troubling but at last the President's voice had stopped. Now it was just Natalie, her words softly insistent. Soon he would be with her. He looked again at the display which showed the target zone. He checked the time. Less than half an hour before they would be together again. Just minutes before he would hold her in his arms in Paris, the city of love.

ZEPHYR SPRINGS, Fla.

Maisky was irritated by the persistent attempts to over-power his transmission. He had hoped to avoid playing the tape of Natalie more than twice, now he had to play it again. That increased the risk of his signal being traced, always assuming the Americans had found time to carry out a trace.

As he rewound the tape he wondered if any attempt would be made to evacuate Paris. He guessed not. There wasn't enough time and he doubted if the authorities would take the risk of starting a panic which could be more lethal than the capsule itself when it finally smashed into the city.

The swathe the capsule would cut through the densely packed urban area would not be wide, probably less than a quarter-mile. It would be much longer than that, maybe as much as a mile. A small part of the city perhaps but size was not the point. Public outrage would overwhelm NASA. Project Mercury would be abandoned as would almost every aspect of America's space program. Missile construction would suffer, setting America far back in the arms race. NATO would be reduced to a squabbling, impotent group, each nation worried in case it would be next to suffer from American incompetence. America's standing throughout the world would fall to a level from which it would take generations to recover.

Maisky smiled a little sadly. It was a pity it had to be Paris, such a beautiful city. Even German occupation in World War II had been unable to damage what the Americans would soon destroy.

It would be a triumph. Once Khrushchev saw how he could use the catastrophe to his own ends he would realize just how clever they all had been. Poor old Kropotkin, for having the technical ability to prepare the data from which the events unfolding in space had been built; Brezhnev, for fastening onto the political implications in such a way that even Khrushchev would have to play along; and Natalie, for having had the skill to turn a piece of pure luck into the political coup of the century.

When she had met the young American Air Force officer, during a visit to the little town of Villingen, she had not been very interested. Then, when she discovered that he was easily directed, especially by a beautiful woman six or seven years his senior, she decided to string him along while she checked into his background. The discovery that his father was a three-star General, with a post at the Pentagon, had suddenly made Gary Herriman much more interesting than the dull, lowly flier she had first thought him to be. The conditioning – Natalie didn't like the term brainwashing – had been easy. Obviously Herriman had been accustomed to taking orders for years, probably long before he ever joined the Air Force. Additionally, he was a good subject for hypnosis and had an extremely low tolerance against drugs.

When Natalie had finished with him, T. Garfield Herriman, Captain, USAF, was an almost perfect sleeper. He could be activated at any time in the future should some occasion arise when he would be needed. Not that she had expected to use him as anything other than a route to his father. The news that he had been selected as a late recruit for Project Mercury had been an outrageous stroke of luck. One Natalie had not failed to manipulate when she was approached by the worried men at Baikonur.

Maisky smiled to himself, his earlier irritation passing. Even with Natalie and her group, and the unwitting presence of Gary Herriman in NASA, it had needed his talents to put everything together. He doubted Natalie could have gotten anywhere near this stage of success alone.

They had other people in NASA of course, all at relatively lowly levels, like Specs and the dispensible electronics technician from Titusville. Maisky had orchestrated all their activities just as he had arranged for the accident to Gus Grissom and the sabotaging of Bill Simons' aircraft.

The tape of Natalie's voice was almost rewound. He listened to the President, this time unopposed. He guessed they had it on a tape loop, something he should have thought of himself. Then another voice came on. This time it was Ziegler, giving instructions for a burn which would put the capsule back on its original trajectory. Damn him. Maisky leaned forward, willing the tape to rewind faster. At last it came off the spool, the loose end slapping noisily. He snatched the reel off, his haste beating his fingers. He slowed himself deliberately and soon had the tape ready for another run.

At that moment Ziegler's voice stopped. He checked his watch. He decided to wind on to the part of Natalie's message where she would give Gary Herriman his final instructions. The capsule would soon be completing its third and final orbit. It could prove vital to the success of the operation which message he heard last before re-entering earth's atmosphere and the capsule went out of contact.

Out of contact with Ziegler, or President Kennedy, or Natalie. Out of contact with anyone on earth.

WASHINGTON, D.C.

'All we can do is wait,' the President said.

The statement was incontestable. They had tried everything, even considered turning missiles onto the returning capsule. The reaction from the Chiefs of Staff had not been reassuring. Not only did they doubt an attempt would be successful, they were not even sure they could set up anything fast enough. That was a blow to the Executive Branch's opinion of the retaliatory capability of the nation's defense system, an opinion based upon assurances from those same Chiefs of Staff.

The question that had been asked many times in the last few minutes was, what will Khrushchev do? At first the answers had varied but now the consensus was hardening.

Khrushchev must be aware that if the capsule landed on Paris, with the resulting damage and loss of life, there would be an outcry. If any hint emerged, however tiny, of Russian involvement, there would be an overwhelming demand for retaliation. Such a demand would be unjustified, but that didn't mean it would be ruled out. Khrushchev must know that and would be preparing himself accordingly. Consequently, the President had been left without a soft option and so he did the only thing possible in the circumstances. He placed the nation's armed services on red alert.

Bobby Kennedy hadn't replied to his brother's remark. He knew there was nothing to do but wait and didn't need reminding of the fact.

'We've been led by the nose, right from the start,' the President said.

'It looks that way.'

'Everything, every damn piece of information, all the way from the CIA's first report from Moscow, has been fed to us.'

Bobby wasn't so sure but he didn't voice disagreement. He had a feeling the first encounter Oscar Lennox had with Maisky had been genuine but there was no point in quibbling. Practically everything else must have been designed to produce the impossible situation they now faced.

'We have to be sure the lid stays on this,' the President said.

'We can't conceal the fact that an American spacecraft will have crashed on Paris.'

'No, but we can insure no one knows there was a man in it.' 'What difference will that make?' Bobby asked.

'Back home we'll be facing serious criticism. We don't want the press getting onto the fact that we put a man up there against advice.'

'Some of NASA's people approved.'

'And some didn't. Add to that, we did it secretively which won't look good. So, let's take advantage of that secrecy. As far as the world is concerned, there was a malfunction of an inanimate piece of metal.'

Bobby nodded. He would like to place the blame on the Soviets but he knew that half the world wouldn't believe the story and the other half would demand a counter-strike. 'I'm beginning to wonder if Khrushchev's hand really is behind this,' he said.

Jack Kennedy shook his head. 'I don't think so. He'll try something, one of these days, but I don't think this is it. There are too many imponderables. He'll want something he can be sure of.'

'Okay, so we wrap it up tightly. Most of the people in the know are safe. Promotion and money can buy a lot of silence.'

'Money?'

'For the space program. Don't worry, I'm not about to bribe anyone.'

The President passed a hand over his face. 'Very well. Put it in hand, but be careful.'

Bobby strode out of the room, closing the door softly behind him. He wasn't worried about most of the men and women involved on the covert mission. As he'd already decided, men like Ziegler, Magadini, and Herriman's father could be relied on to know where their duty as Americans lay. Others, like Danvers and Carmody or any other lower echelon people could be promoted and all would benefit from an increased NASA budget. Stella Herriman and Diana McNair were potential problems. McNair's file showed she was strong-willed, not easily influenced. However, a bright spot, also detailed in the file, was her affair with Ziegler. That might well be the way to divert her from causing trouble.

Stella Herriman was a tricky one. So far his men had been unable to decide if she knew about the flight. She certainly wasn't behaving as if she knew. Still, the fact she was a drinker helped. There was no shortage of sanatoria into which difficult people could conveniently disappear. Forever, if necessary.

Then there was the astronaut himself. The Attorney General's stomach pitched as he caught himself hoping that, whatever happened, Herriman would not get out alive.

HOLMESTRAND, NORWAY

For Natalie the past few hours had been difficult and dangerous. The visit from the KGB Colonel had been alarming but not critical. She expected he would soon discover that too many people above him, in the KGB and in the Praesidium, knew what was going on and he would quietly drop his inquiries. She had been unprepared for the telephone call from a friend in the Kremlin telling her that someone had talked and that the KGB Colonel was answerable only to Khrushchev. Her informant had also told her that, instead of awaiting the outcome of the spaceflight, the Chairman had actually spoken to the American President on the phone. Apparently he had groveled and apologized and squirmed. By all accounts it had been a pathetic performance. One which should have shown his colleagues that he had to be replaced before their standing, in American eyes, was lowered to a dangerous level.

Unfortunately, Natalie couldn't afford to take the chance of waiting around until Brezhnev made a move. Like it or not, she had to accept that Khrushchev's crawling had placed her, and her associates, in a difficult position. They would have to keep out of the way, let things settle down, then regroup in whatever way seemed most appropriate to the post-spaceflight situation. Until then Moscow was not a good place to be. She had packed a bag and left her apartment within ten minutes of making her decision.

The trip to Norway had been circuitous and tiring but she was sure she was safe. The house, one she had used some years before, was pleasant and warm and the views across the mouth of Oslo Fjord were spectacular. The only drawback was that the place was unpalatably lonely. She would have to get word to Maisky. Perhaps he would come there, maybe she could join him in America. There would be much for her to do there. She might even find another well-placed American to conquer.

Crossing to the window she looked up into the sky. Somewhere up there the result of one of her most successful operations was orbiting the earth, ready to bring about human misery and political chaos. She left the window and poured herself a drink before turning on the radio and tuning it until she found a station broadcasting in a language she understood.

She had just settled herself in a chair, silently toasting her own achievement in the operation, when someone rapped on the door. She stood up and went to the door, drink in hand. Somehow, she wasn't surprised when she recognized the colonel from the KGB.

CAPE CANAVERAL, Fla.

'Joe, he's acting up again.'

Ziegler turned at Gus Grissom's low-voiced comment. The Mercury astronaut had taken over from Carmody while the doctor took a short break. A few minutes earlier Ziegler had taken Specs outside and told a surprised but obedient security guard to place the technician under arrest. There was no time to check out Diana's comments but he had decided against taking any further chances. With the end of the third and last of the scheduled orbits imminent he didn't want any distractions.

Grissom was right. Herriman's pulse rate was way up and for the first time there seemed to be some respiratory problem. Ziegler checked the clock and frowned. 'We should've lost him by now,' he said. 'What the hell is going on?'

In the Mercury capsule Garfield Herriman was confused and he was feeling decidedly unwell. He was nauseous and his head ached. Not just ached, it really hurt. The constant barrage of instructions, counter-instructions, questions, and more questions, was wearing him down.

He tried to recall precisely why he had taken manual control of the capsule. It hadn't been on the schedule. His instructions from Ziegler and Magadini had been crystal clear, he was to do nothing to give Mission Control the slightest hint he was up here. Then why had he done it? Specs, that was it. Specs had told him to take control and make a marginal course correction burn as soon as he was in orbit. Well, he'd done so and now everyone, Ziegler, Diana McNair, Gus, his father, even the President of the United States, was at him. Asking questions, giving orders. But not Natalie. She just wanted him to come to her. After all this time she had returned, and was so close he could almost feel her presence in the capsule. Natalie, who cared only about what was best for him. So why did the President want him to act against her wishes? The President didn't want him to go to Natalie. He wanted him to switch out manual control and go back on automatic. That way Mission Control would have the power to bring him back when and where they wanted. Which was just as it should be. He was under their command. He obeyed orders. So why was he going against their orders? Why was he arguing against orders from the Commander-in-Chief?

Suddenly he remembered Stella. Why was he thinking about another woman? Stella was his wife. Why should he be concerned at what some other woman wanted him to do? His hand hovered uncertainly over the control lever. Then Natalie's voice forced itself into his consciousness once more but this time, although the words were the same, the effect was different.

In a blindingly clear instant he knew that what Natalie wanted was wrong. It was against everything he had been brought up to respect and admire. It was against his father, his home, his wife, his country. Why did she want him to go against everything he loved? But he loved her. He shook his head angrily, trying to clear the confusion from his mind, closed his fingers over the control lever and...

'We've lost contact. He's re-entered the earth's atmosphere.'

Ziegler grabbed the telephone and snapped questions at Jim Magadini who had returned to Mission Control. He waited, tense, until Magadini came back with the answers.

'There was another course correction, just over a minute ago, when he should have been entering the atmosphere.'

'I guessed that. He was late going in. What did he do? Flatten the descent angle?'

'Some. But I don't think he got it right. He might have over-compensated.'

'You mean he's coming in too steep?'

'That's right.'

'What's his course?'

'The computer reckons the change would bring him down into the Atlantic Ocean, two hundred miles west of Ireland.'

'What in God's name is he doing?'

'I don't think even Gary knows the answer to that.'

At that moment Gary Herriman was observing his surroundings with almost detached calm. The color of the sky was particularly interesting. There was a yellowish tinge to the view through the narrow window, a yellow which, as he watched, darkened into glowing orange. He was suddenly aware that it was getting uncomfortably warm in the capsule. He checked the orange glow again but already it was brighter, more reddish in color. Slowly, pushing aside his detachment, the truth of what was happening penetrated his mind. The goddamn spacecraft was turning into a fire-ball. He shook his head, trying to figure out what had happened. The worst of the expected frictional heat should have been taken up

263

by the heat-shield but for that to happen the capsule's attitude had to be reversed. Only Mission Control had failed to effect the necessary maneuver.

Trust them to screw up when it really mattered. Then he shook his head again. What was he thinking about? He was on fly-by-wire. He had control, no one else. He could do any damn thing he wanted.

The red glow brightened. The heat was becoming intolerable. As he felt a violent shudder rake through the capsule he tightened his grip on the controls.

Down at the Cape there had been silence for several minutes and when the telephone rang the shrill sound startled everyone. It was Jim Magadini calling from Mission Control. 'We have no contact with the capsule. You?'

'No.'

'Maybe we should say a prayer.'

'I don't know how,' Ziegler said shortly and broke the connexion. He saw Diana watching him and held out a hand.

'When will we know?' she asked.

'Soon enough.'

'From those last readings I think he must be fighting a battle up there.'

Ziegler nodded. 'Maybe if I'd fought a battle down here none of this would've happened.'

'You can't blame yourself.'

'Can't I?'

She shook her head and took his hand. 'Poor Gary. All his life people have been giving him orders, telling him where to go, what to do, how to do it. Now, maybe for the first time, he's on his own.'

In the capsule Gary Herriman was struggling for breath. The temperature had risen several degrees higher than anything he'd experienced even in the severest test he'd undergone. And it was rising. He checked the instruments, his brain astonishingly clear. He knew what was happening, what he had done, and what had been done to him. He re-checked the course trajectory and the point of impact. The last correction he'd made had put him on course for Paris and Natalie. Now it was too late to make any more changes. Or was it?

He tightened his grip on the control lever. Maybe he could make a final correction despite the fact that the atmosphere was growing denser by the second. With an effort he turned his head to look through the aperture. The brilliance of the red glow was blinding. The capsule was burning up. Within seconds he would die, engulfed in a mass of molten metal.

His lips moved as he tried to speak but the g-force was too great. He could barely suck the hot air into his lungs. His grasp on the control lever slackened for an instant, then tightened again as he made one last, convulsive, effort to change the course of the capsule. He could feel very little now, except the burning, fearful, heat. Then, almost imperceptibly, he felt the g-force shift. He'd done it. He had corrected the course of the capsule for the last time.

With relief he saw the redness begin to fade into grey, then the grey turn to black. The sensation of burning passed. His feelings, as the glowing capsule tumbled out of the sky, were of contentment. He had reached a final frontier beyond which no one could pursue him. Once he crossed it, he would be alone and able to do as he wanted, not the way others chose to dictate. Then his life would be his own, not Stella's, not the General's, not his country's. Not even Natalie's.

As the interior of the capsule erupted into flames, a split second before disintegrating to spiral down into the Atlantic Ocean in a hundred smoking fragments, Gary Herriman knew peace.

NEWPORT NEWS, Va.

'Will you take the job?' Diana asked.

Ziegler turned from the window of her apartment to look at her for a moment before speaking. He knew the answer, he'd already made the decision. What worried him was her reaction to it. 'What about you?' he countered.

Diana smiled. 'You're not getting out of it that easy. You tell me first.'

He had been offered a job he didn't want to refuse, heading a special team of pilots testing new rocket-powered aircraft at Nellis. And not just leading from a desk. He would be flying as well, and that had been the clincher. The problem was Diana. She had also been offered a new job, a teaching post at UCLA. The money was good and the possibilities were endless. The only snag, something both knew but had so far avoided bringing into the open, was the coincidence. Two offers, of jobs they could hardly refuse, within a few hours drive of one another. It was too good to be true, unless someone had planned it that way.

Reluctantly Joe put his doubts into words. 'Are we being bought off?'

Diana shook her head slowly. 'No,' she said. She turned away, not wanting him to see her eyes at the moment of the lie. She knew that

265

a sense of duty to his uniform had made him a safe bet. She didn't have the same sense of duty. At least not to the nation or its administrators. But she did feel a sense of duty to Joe.

She looked up to see him watching her carefully. 'Take the job, Joe,' she said quietly. 'I'm taking the one at UCLA.'

He nodded. 'We'll be close.'

'Yes.'

'That will be good.'

'Yes,' she said again. She wasn't sure. Soon, maybe when they arrived on the West Coast, he would ask her to marry him. She would agree, happily, but starting a marriage with a major lie hanging between them went against everything she believed in.

'You're sure you won't miss all this?' she asked.

'Certain. Anyway, there's a good chance Deke will be grounded for a while. He'll do this job far better than I ever did.'

Diana went into the kitchen to make coffee. When she came back, Joe was looking through the window again.

'What's so interesting out there?' she asked.

'I was thinking about Gary.'

She stood beside him and slipped her arm through his. 'What do you think really happened up there?'

'I don't know. Maybe he tried following our instructions, maybe he tried to follow Natalie's. Maybe he just screwed up those final burns. Whichever it was, the end was the same.'

'If only he could have made a soft-landing in the Atlantic. We might have gotten someone to him in time.'

Ziegler shook his head. 'No, whether he planned it or not, he went the way any flyer would want. Given the alternative.'

'Which was?'

'Life in a gilded cage.' He turned away from the window and put his arms around Diana. 'I don't want to talk about it any more.'

'That's the worst thing you could do, let it fester.'

'Sounds like we're getting into some heavy professional advice, here.'

'I'm just a dumb old psychiatrist who's in love with her patient.' Her hand felt for his and she led him gently towards the sofa.

'All I know is, I don't want to talk about it...don't even want to *think* about it, if that's humanly possible, until I'm ready.'

'Gary won't go away, Joe, just because you and Jim and the people in Washington don't talk about him.'

Ziegler smiled for the first time, a brittle, crooked smile. 'For a super-bright college girl, you've sure got a lot to learn.'